WHITE LION
CHRONICLES

ATHERA'S
DAWN

BOOK
THREE

Other books by...

CHRISTOPHER HOPPER

The White Lion Chronicles (series)

Rise of the Dibor – Book I

The Lion Vrie – Book II

CHRISTOPHER HOPPER
&
WAYNE THOMAS BATSON

The Berinfell Prophecies (series)

Curse of the Spider King – Book I

Venom and Song – Book II

WWW.CHRISTOPHERHOPPER.COM

THE
WHITE LION
CHRONICLES
ATHERA'S
DAWN

CHRISTOPHER
HOPPER

SPEAR
HEAD

NEW YORK - BALTIMORE - SEATTLE

Cover design and layout by Christopher & Allan Miller for The Miller Brothers, and Christopher Hopper; The White Lion Chronicles logo by Jason J. Clement for jasonjclement.com
Interior layout and map illustration by Christopher Hopper; interior grunge background by Jason J. Clement for jasonjclement.com
Wax seal design by Hillary Hopper for hillaryhopper.com
Edited by Sue Kenney for kenneyediting.wordpress.com
Author Photo by Jennifer Hopper for jenniferhopperphoto.com

Published by christopherhopper.com in alliance with Spearhead Books
Visit spearheadbooks.com

Printed in the United States of America

First Edition: 2011

ISBN: 1467932671
ISBN-13: 978-1467932677

To Evangeline, Luik, Judah, and Levi.
May the sun always shine brightly on your faces.

"…making known to us the mystery of his will, according to his purpose, which he set forth in Christ as a plan for the fullness of time, to unite all things in him, things in heaven and things on earth."

~Ephesians 1:9-10

THE WHITE LION CHRONICLES
BOOK III
ATHERA'S DAWN

Dionian Essentials

Part One

Part Two

Part Three

Epilogue

Dionian Essentials

LANGUAGE GUIDE

All written text of the following account has been scripted in English but was derived solely from the common Dionian tongue and usage of the people of Dionia. Names have been kept as original as possible except where deemed necessary by the author to make them more conducive and suitable for the reader.

Certain words and phrases have been left in the original tongue, scripted using the Latin alphabet for English readers and roughly translated accordingly, either because a direct translation into English was impossible due to the expansive vocabulary utilized by the native people and the subsequent inadequacy and lack of words existing in the English vocabulary, including expressions and words used in the common vernacular; or because an older dialect, such as First Dionian was used, making literal translation near impossible, as the only translation can be derived and implied from felt and/or experienced emotions.

The translation of all Dionian linguistics is based upon the spoken word, rather than the written word (though still used in documentation), making the sound, diction, emphasis and oral and guttural technique used to pronounce each word and phrase absolutely imperative in proper communication. For this reason, should this work be translated into any other language, all people and place names unknown in the written English and resulting translation into the desired language, as well as translation of unknown singular and plural nouns and phrasing, should retain the auditory qualities as properly pronounced in English using the pronunciation guide in parentheses directly following each footnote. If a consonant or vowel does not exist in the translated language, an author's note must appear to properly define and explain the desired sound.

Written:	Pronounced:	Meaning:
roua	*R'ROO-uh*	"ways"

NOTE: Here the "R'R" is pronounced as a rolled "r".

| afe | *AYF-[eh]* | "one" or "one who" |

NOTE: In this case, the sound of the "e" at the end of the word does exist commonly in English and must be spoken with a quiet, fleeting exhaled breath. This is also for all people and place names ending in "e." Not a true syllable.

| Najrion | *NAH-sherEE-auhn* | character name |

NOTE: The letter "j" followed by "r" in a name is pronounced with a soft "j" sound.

NAME PRONUNCIATION GUIDE

Here are a few common titles and names in The White Lion Chronicles that – with practice – will help the authenticity of your journey in Dionia.

Name:	Pronounced:	Name:	Pronounced:
Athera	*uh-THEER-uh*	Morgui	*MORE-guy*
Dionia	*dee-OH-nee-yah*	Dairne-Reih	*DAYern-[eh]-RYE*
Luik	*LOO-ick*	Ciana	*see-EN-uh*
Hadrian	*HAY-dree-in*	Rourke	*ROORck*
Li-Saide	*lee-SAYED-[eh]*	Naffe	*NAYHFF-[eh]*
Jrio	*sherEEoh*	Ligeon	*LIH-jee-on*

Glossary Guide

The main spoken language of Dionia is appropriately named *Dionian,* or hereafter mentioned as *Modern Dionian. Modern Dionian* denotes the language utilized from the time period *after* the First Battle to the present. A reader will notice that in many definitions there is often one of two references made: *"First Dionian"* or *"an ancient Dionian word"* (hereafter mentioned as *Ancient Dionian*). *First Dionian,* or *The Old Tongue,* is traceable to the beginning of Creation, *before* the First Battle, and these words are most closely related to *Modern Dionian.* The syntax, emphasis, and pronunciation have remained relatively the same given its vast history, or with only minor discrepancies (enough to link it with a *First Dionian* reference). *Ancient Dionian,* however, is unique in its pronunciation *and* definition, as the root of each word is not necessarily tied to a modern equivalent or even *First Dionian* reference, meaning the origin of the word is simply unknown. Rather, such words have been adopted into *Modern Dionian*, though their history is in question.

Examples:

Boralee (*bohr-uh-LEE*): Ancient Dionian: *disciple;* unknown.

Frrene (*FREYN-[eh]*): Modern Dionian: *disciple;* First Dionian root.

BOOK I
GLOSSARY

Afe di empaxe li roua lonia ene froue napthixe bruna *(AYF-[eh] dee ehm-PACKS lee R'ROO-uh LON-ee-uh een froo nahp-THEECKS br'roona) First Dionian: literally translated, "One who holds the ways old and every spoken word," meant to mean, "A keeper of the old ways and all words spoken."*

Biea-Varos *(BEE-uh-var-OHCE): verb; forward command form of the ancient Dionian word most closely related to the modern word "courage"; to be of great fortitude, resilience and persuasion; devoid of fear.*

Boralee *(bohr-uh-LEE): noun; ancient Dionian name meaning disciple, exact origin not known.*

Courbouilli *(coor-BOO-ih-lee): noun; armor made of leather hardened through boiling in oil; noted for its light weight while still maintaining great strength and resilience to blows.*

C'symia *(sye-MEE-uh): First Dionian: intimate and most respectful form of "thank you."*

Dairne-Reih *(DAYern-[eh]-RYE): noun; closest literal translation is "fallen kings" or "fallen angels"; the army war host of Morgui comprised of the fallen angels of Athera or heaven.*

Dairneag *(DAYern-ee-AHG): noun; a singular demon of the fallen angelic host; a member of the Dairne-Reih.*

Dibor *(DYE-bohr): noun; First Dionian: literally meaning "guardians", "centurions", or "a sacred protectorate"; singular Dibor or a Dibor meaning one of the members of the Dibor or brotherhood; also to address as a brother.*

Difouna *(dee-FOO-nuh): verb; slang of the command form of "difounale," Dionian word most closely related to the verb "to go."*

Dyra *(DIEruh): noun; a rare and little-known composite material made from forged elements; created by the Tribes of Ot in Grandath.*

Gita *(GIH-tuh): noun; plural, Gitas; 1. an ancient Dionian word meaning "basket"; 2. one round of Rokla played to five points.*

Gvindollion *(GIH-ven-DOLLY-on): noun; an ancient Dionian word literally translated, "The Circle of Seven"; council gathering of Dionia's Seven Kings.*

Iyne Dain *(EYEn-[eh] DANE): noun; literally meaning "Heart Quest."*

Jhestafe-Na *(jehs-TAIF-eh-nuh): First Dionian: literally translated "Gathering Day."*

Kafe *(KAY-feh): noun; 1. an ancient Dionian word meaning "loss"; 2. the red ball in Rokla.*

KiJinNard *(KYEY-shjih-nard): noun; closest literal translation is "dead hound"; refers to the dogs that have been "taken" and joined with the ranks of the Dairne-Reih.*

Lion Vrie *(l'eye-uhn-VR'EYE): First Dionian: noun; most closely related to the word used for a knight or a warrior of nobility.*

Lytthlaroua *(L'EYEth-lah-ROO-uh): noun; Ancient Dionian; literally translated "ways of the heavenly," this name for the angelic host, or angels of Athera; singular: lythla (L'EYEth-lah); plural: lythlae (L'EYEth-lay).*

Mosfar *(MAWS-fahr): First Dionian: name given to the tribe of Dwarves at the beginning of creation; meaning "Creation Keeper" or "protector"; singular a Mosfar meaning one of the members of The Mosfar or brotherhood.*

Narin Haus *(NAR-in HO): noun; literally meaning "Narin High," or the upper half of Narin overlooking the Bay of Cidell; Narin Bas, or "Narin Low" refers to the lower, seaside, stilted portion of the city.*

Peshe *(PESH-[eh]): noun; a deed or act, or by inaction or abdication of responsibility, an allowance, of engaging in behavior or receiving the nature of a spirit directly opposed to the will of The Most High, His Righteousness, Truth and Light; anything that separates a creature from the presence of His Spirit; a grievous mistake or error with detrimental consequences spiritually and naturally. 2. verb; to engage in the action of said deed, act, mistake, or error. Most closely related to the Middle English word "sin" or the verb, "to sin."*

Riddosseldore *(rih-DOSS-elle-DOHR-[eh]): noun; one of the largest Dionian mammals, noted for the enormous horn on the forehead and long trunk above the mouth; most closely associated with an elephant and a rhinoceros.*

Rokla *(ROCK-lah): noun; 1. an ancient Dionian word meaning "two stones"; 2. one of the main sporting events played by the people of Dionia.*

Sacre Fina *(SAH-cray FEE-nuh): noun; Ancient Dionian for Last Rights or Sacred Rights, the final wishes of a Dionian King before being called to the Great Throne Room.*

Sif Gate *(SIPH-gate): noun; a portal for the translation of Dairne-Reih from one realm or location to another.*

Stri *(STR-EE): noun; plural, Stri; 1. an ancient Dionian word meaning "gain"; 2. the blue ball in Rokla; 3. term used to indicate a point.*

Syler *(SIGH-ler): noun; plural, sylers; name of a seven-stringed instrument played with the fingers and hands, upon which both beaten rhythm and melody can be issued at the same time.*

Varos *(var-OHCE): noun; an ancient Dionian word most closely related to the modern word "courage"; to be of great fortitude, resilience, and persuasion; devoid of fear.*

Vinfae *(vinn-FAY): noun; an ancient Dionian term used to designate the sword forged and used exclusively for the Dibor. Characteristics include its notable power when used in conjunction with the Tongues of the Dibor as well as its ability to differentiate between the Dairne-Reih and that of fallen man (or the* taken*).*

Xidaq *(KSYE-dack): verb; First Dionian; tense of the command form literally meaning to "attack showing [with] mercy."*

Book II
Glossary

Achlanieh *(AOCH-la-nee-eh): verb; Ancient Dionian; most closely related to the modern-day blessed, anointed, favored of the Most High, prosperous.*

Dia-splinttia *(dee-uh SPLEEN-thee-uh): verb command; First Dionian; to take one hundred paces in a specified direction.*

Erepht *(EH-reft): noun; First Dionian; right heading or bearing, to turn right in direction.*

Fedchulte *(FED-shult-eh): noun; Dionian, term used for what is commonly known as a catapult; plural: fedchults (FED-shultz).*

Fo'dettra *(pho-DEETH-ruh): noun; First Dionian; straight ahead in movement, direction, and/or bearing.*

Gkovin *(KOE-vihn): verb; Ancient Dionian; to slide or slip; plural; noun; a wooden board or various size used to sled down a steep plain; plural: gkovins (KOE-vihns).*

Heneff-tafle *(HEN-ehph TAHPH-leh): noun; First Dionian; literally meaning "wise wood"; a game of strategy played by the people of Tontha comprised of a square board with two armies of unequal strengths and differing objectives.*

Inussle *(en-US-leh): noun; Dionian; commonly related to the word season; the duration of a climate change; plural: inusslen (en-US-lehn).*

Kiiona le Ot *(Khee-ON-uh leh aught): First Dionian; literally translated "Come to Ot."*

Killnissi-noa *(kill-NEE-see-NO-uh): noun; Somahguardian dialect; literally meaning "mountain fire." Used to denote a volcano.*

Kynhe *(KINE-eh): noun; Dwarfish Tongue; most closely related to the modern word for winter, referring to the cold liyden following each summer.*

Leupheene *(loo-FEEN-eh): noun; most commonly related to the word for "sick" or "sickness," but such condition as is caused and directly associated with the increasingly prevalent manifestation of sin and resulting lack of strength and immunity in the body.*

Li-li *(LIE-LIE): noun; Somahguardian term used for a long slender boat carved of palm trees with either one or two additional hulls added for stability, attached by long struts; plural: li-lis (LIE-LIES).*

Liyde *(LIED-eh): noun; most commonly related to the word for "month," except the span of a year (summer) is divided into ten parts, not twelve; plural: liyden (LIE-din).*

Venxia *(phen-NECKS-ee-uh): noun; First Dionian; river or heavily-flowing stream.*

BOOK III
GLOSSARY

Diji-hi *(didge-EE-high): noun; singular and plural; modern Dionian for "flying water apparatus" (abbreviation "water flyers") consisting of a kite (diji) strung to a control bar, and a stand-on board (hi) designed to ride on top of the water when the rider was pulled by a sufficiently strong wind.*

Dylaithlok *(die-LAYTH-lock): noun; First Dionian; name given to taken birds of the air; most commonly raptors.*

Hasithe-morna *(ha-SITH-(eh) MOURN-uh): noun; First Dionian, literally translated "fever of death."*

Hewgog *(HUE-gawg): noun; First Dionian; a giant mutant Dairneag; a demon bred with the* taken *and various animals for size and immense power.*

Ieyth ne fora ou reenhe miyne *(ee-ETH Neh FOO-ruh oo REE-neh MEEN-eh): Language of the Mosfar; literally translated "from sky to soil bring covering guard."*

Porquill *(POOR-kwill): noun; a tactical maneuver in which long wooden spears are driven into the ground butt-first in rows, each series angled outward toward the advancing enemy.*

CHARACTER LIBRARY

Luik (meaning: *renowned warrior who gives light*): Dibor; Son of Lair, once Prince of Bensotha, now High King of Dionia, and King of Casterness; renowned for his mighty exploits among the Dibor; blond hair, grey-blue eyes.

Anorra (meaning: *one's good name and honor*): Daughter of Thorn, Princess of Ligeon. Skilled with the bow and on horseback, extremely cunning, agile, and a quick wit; long blonde hair, blue eyes.

Fane (meaning: *good-natured*): Mosfar; Son of Fadner, son of Dafe, son of Ad. Trained by Li-Saide in the ways of the Mosfar; red hair, freckled face, and of a thin stature.

Hadrian (meaning: *dark*): Son of Jadak, son of Jadain; went missing from his home in Bensotha; athletic with dark hair and deep, dark eyes.

Gorn (meaning: *faithful mountain*): Son of Jyne; origin unknown. Famed warrior of Dionia, teacher of the Dibor; deep black skin and piercing blue eyes, strong and muscular.

Li-Saide (meaning: *favored*): Mosfar; A dwarf of the Tribe of Li, aged counselor to the lineage of High Kings of Dionia, and Chief of the Tribes of Ot. Known for his large, baggy, multi-colored patchwork hat and quizzical bearded face.

Gyinan (meaning: *white hawk*): Highest centurion of Thorn's House and Anorra's teacher; slender, bald, with pointy features; narrow, pensive eyes; long jaw and tiny lips reminiscent of a bird.

Benigan (meaning: *kind, cheerful*): Dibor; Oldest son of King Purgos, Lord of Tontha; smaller than his twin brothers, though still a massive man; greater in speed and agility.

Boran (meaning: *victory*): Dibor; First of twin sons born to King Purgos, Lord of Tontha; black hair, like ebony; older twin of Brax, renowned for his immense strength, size, and climbing ability.

Brax (meaning: *exalted*): Dibor; Second of twin sons born to King Purgos, Lord of Tontha; dirty-blond hair; younger twin of Boran, renowned for his immense strength, size, and climbing ability.

Thad (meaning: *of good heart*): Dibor; Oldest son of King Thorn, Prince of Ligeon; looks the most like Anorra, long blond hair, same blue eyes.

Thero (meaning: *son of thunder*): Dibor; Second son of Thorn, Prince of Ligeon; large-built, red hair, wide face, resembling his father.

Anondo (meaning: *ready and eager for battle*): Dibor; Third son of Thorn, Prince of Ligeon; strongly built; fair hair and skin; toughest of all his brothers.

Jrio (meaning: *cunning*): Dibor; Oldest son of King Naronel, Lord of Trennesol; known for his keen ability for sailing and mastering all vessels powered by wind; dark short-cut hair, narrow eyes and dark face; reminiscent of a ferret.

Najrion (meaning: *son of man*): Dibor; Second son of King Naronel, Lord of Trennesol; slender, tall, and dark. Slain in the Somahguard Islands.

Naron (meaning: *honor*): Dibor; Third son of King Naronel, Lord of Trennesol; similar in looks to Najrion.

Rab (meaning: *bright fame*): Dibor; Youngest son of King Naronel, Lord of Trennesol; of a dark complexion and smaller frame; known for his constantly saving, and being saved by, Luik.

Cage (meaning: *valiant spear*): Dibor; Oldest son of King Daunt, Lord of Jerovah; known for his ability on horseback; long dark hair.

Daquin (meaning: *soldier of attainment*): Dibor; Second son of King Daunt, Lord of Jerovah; known for his ability on horseback; a large brute.

Quoin (meaning: *swift*): Dibor; Youngest son of King Daunt, Lord of Jerovah; known for his ability on horseback; smallest of the three.

Kinfen (meaning: *heroic*): Dibor; Oldest son of King Nenrick, Lord of The Somahguard Islands; largest of his brothers; adept at all maritime skills; dark skin like all those of the Island people.

Naffe (meaning: *bright*): Dibor; Second son of King Nenrick, Lord of The Somahguard Islands; dark complexion, broad face.

Fallon (meaning: *sea wolf*): Dibor; Third son of King Nenrick, Lord of The Somahguard Islands; dark complexion.

Fyfler (meaning: *reigning elder*): Dibor; Youngest son of King Nenrick, Lord of The Somahguard Islands; dark complexion and closely cut hair; wise and a good leader.

Fadlemir (meaning: *noble seafarer*): A native of Trennesol, Fadlemir was the Captain of King Ragnar's fleets, hailed as one of Dionia's most noted sailors. Dark complexion, tightly cropped dark hair.

Fedowah (meaning: *faithful, he who overcomes*): War horse of Tadellis found roaming Grandath; now belonging to Luik; a large dapple-gray with a pronounced head, muscular shoulders, and a speckled rear.

Cellese (meaning: *pleasant, in time of need*): Luik's dolphin at Kirstell.

Morgui (meaning: *beauty discarded*): A fallen lythla cast from the ranks of Athera; the enemy of Dionia and of the Most High.

Valdenil (meaning: *first among the fallen*): Son of the Dead; taken before the First Battle, made a prince under Morgui as he was the son of King Rill, son of King Ad; his first name was Velon; slain by Gorn in Bensotha during the Battle of Adriel.

Fonish (meaning: *noble and ready*): Adriel palace guard.

Pelidril (meaning: *origin, source of riches, wealth*): Team captain of Beneetha's Rokla team.

Analysia (meaning: *of high nobility, favor and grace*): Oldest daughter of Thorn, Anorra's older sister; noted for her refined manner much becoming of a queen; long blonde hair.

Lana (meaning: *fair and calm in still waters*): Youngest daughter of Thorn, Anorra's younger sister; curly blonde hair, sweet and jubilant personality; round face, always smiled, even when she cried.

Lair (meaning: *refuge*): King and Lord of Bensotha; father of Luik.

Pia (meaning: *faithful and duty-bound*): Lair's wife, Queen of Bensotha, mother of Luik; darker hair but a fair complexion.

Rourke (meaning: *storm of famous power*): Son of Lair, Luik's younger brother by fourteen summers; a squirrelly tuft of light brown hair, brown eyes, and a wide smile.

Ragnar (meaning: *strong counselor*): High King of Dionia, Lord of Casterness; dirty blond hair, wide cheekbones, deep-set green eyes beneath a firm brow.

Meera (meaning: *light*): Queen of Casterness, wife of Ragnar, mother of Ciana; fair skin, long blonde hair, delicate face.

Ciana (meaning: *The Most High has been gracious; has shown favor*): Daughter of Ragnar, Princess of Casterness. Born in Luik's fourteenth summer. Blonde hair, grey-blue eyes.

Thorn (meaning: *mighty hunter*): King of Ligeon, Lord of the Northerners; wavy reddish-blonde hair and a beard to match; neck was the size of an ox's and strong blue eyes set wide in his large face.

Purgos (meaning: *of great value*): King of Tontha, Lord of the Mountain People; hulking brute of a man; dark hair and eyes, broad shoulders, muscular; one of the longest-living elders of Dionia; fought in the First Battle.

Naronel (meaning: *mountain of the sea*): King of Trennesol, Lord of the North Sea; dark bearded chin, strong hands, black hair; an expert sailor and maritime explorer.

Daunt (meaning: *unwavering judge*): King of Jerovah, affectionately called "The Horse King"; master equestrian; black hair; tightly-knit body, long, sinewy, and strong.

Nenrick (meaning: *powerful ruler*): King of the Islands of Somahguard, Lord of the Islanders; a master of maritime navigation; dark skin, dark eyes.

CHARACTER QUICK REFERENCE GUIDE

The Eighteen Dibor

King Lair, Lord of Bensotha
Luik

King Thorn, Lord of Ligeon
Thad
Thero
Anondo
(Anorra)

King Purgos, Lord of Tontha
Benigan
Boran
Brax

King Naronel, Lord of Trennesol
Jrio
*Najrion
Naron
Rab

King Daunt, Lord of Jerovah
Cage
Daquin
Quoin

King Nenrick, Lord of Somahguard
Kinfen
Naffe
Fallon
Fyfler

*Slain in the Somahguard Islands

"A man dies a deeper death by living with what he knows
than dying with what he doesn't."

~The White Lion

"If He wishes me to die, then so I die."

~Luik, High King of Dionia

PART ONE

Chapter One

SOUL SEARCHING

Tendrils of smoke slithered around the giant trees like snakes, squeezing them toward an inescapable death. Leaves cringed in their upper folds, the bark below trying in vain to fend off the intruder. The air was stained with the unmistakable scent of fire, and no breeze was present to ease the foul air. Any light from above was swallowed whole in the hanging haze of smoke, the wooded scene now hardly negotiable.

A hooded figure emerged from between the tree trunks only to disappear back into the smoke which swirled over the ground. The man appeared again, the haze parting as the man strode into a small clearing and looked above. He was of lean build, draped in a green cloak, and carried a rowan staff.

"Great God of Athera, lead me now." His eyes burned in the smoke as he fought to draw a breath devoid of the foul air and regain his sense of direction. But neither was possible. "I am in need of your direction, as I ever have been."

His next breath burned worse than the previous, and he hardly thought his prayer had been heard, let alone answered. His eyes watered, and nostrils roared with pain. A deep cough issued up, and he doubled over, wiping the spittle from the corners of his mouth with his sleeve.

He knew that he must accomplish his task soon or else be included in the numbers of the silent massacre to come, his remains forever burned to ash. That, and the subject of his searching was surely on the brink of death as well, if not already dead. He was so close.

I can't fail now.

Too much was at stake. Luik had left Tontha days ago for Somahguard. With any help from the Mighty Father he would be returning to Mt. Dakka within the week. But somehow he doubted it. Anondo and his brothers had been sent to Ligeon; there was surely trouble brewing in the West. He could see it in the sky. And what of Gorn and Anorra in Mt. Dakka? Morgui would not be so brash as to march against the Mountain Stronghold! But somehow his heart told him differently. There was trouble stirring across the realm, and he knew it would be many days before he would see light again. If ever.

Resolved that he must again try the secret words, he gathered his strength and stood erect for a last time. Still, doubt filled his heart. He had already beckoned the covering protection earlier, but to no avail. He would not last much longer in the woods without it.

It was his only hope.

With staff held high, the vile fog seemed to sense the man's mounting power and surged around him ever thicker; clearly the smoke lived, set by a most wicked mind. But ignoring the violent pressure to take his last breath, the man shut his eyes and spoke the command skyward.

"*Ieyth ne fora ou reenhe miyne[1].*" He felt as if his words were sucked into the smoke-ridden atmosphere, unheard by the Spirit. Eyes watered, throat burned. All lay still. Even the swirling smoke seemed to await the next moment, wondering if the chant would avail its said purpose. The man stood motionless.

Silence filled the wood.

Suddenly a low tone—felt more then heard—filled the air. No sense of direction was betrayed to the listener. The hum gained in presence, and soon the man's cloak trembled with the volume. The smoke ebbed and looked for a place of retreat.

A slight smile took up into the space of the man's cheeks, and his eyes opened. He grasped his staff with both hands and then drove the end into the ground.

---

[1] **Ieyth ne fora ou reenhe miyne** (*ee-ETH Neh FOO-ruh oo REE-neh MEEN-eh*): *Language of the Mosfar; literally translated "from sky to soil bring covering guard."*

Crrrrack!

With the sound of a lightning bolt striking but an arm's breadth away, a wall of wavering light encircled the man. Within this protective layer it was as broad day, pure and bright. He drew in a fresh breath of air within the security of the shimmering bubble. The tongue of the Mosfar yet held strength despite the increasing presence of Morgui.

All is not lost.

He rubbed the sweat from his face and then pointed his staff forward, producing a shaft of light. It dispersed the thick smoke and cleared a path ahead. Wasting no time, the cloaked man was off at once, striding down the path with renewed resolve.

I must find him.

He passed row after row of the ancient trees, shadowed by the enormous sleeping giants he had so grown to love. He grieved inwardly for them, knowing their pending fate, one he could not delay. But they were unimportant now; the lives of the Sons and Daughters of Ad and Eva were on the brink of annihilation. And the one in particular he sought must be brought back alive. The High King's life depended upon it; *his* life depended upon it.

He walked more quickly now, the smoke growing denser in the particular direction he headed. And the extent of his sight grew shorter for it. The power of Creation was diminishing.

Hold out for me a little longer.

His eyes darted from left to right, searching the underbrush. He knew he must be getting close.

A dark shape clung to the base of a tree. His heart quickened.

Can it be?

He ran and began calling out, but the shape, now clearly that of a collapsed man, did not move in the slightest.

I am too late.

Still clinging to his staff, he knelt beside the crumpled heap and pulled the shoulder around. To his utter relief, the second man groaned and tried to raise his head, squinting against the foreign light.

"Rest easy, my friend. All is well."

Safe within the inclusive realm of the protective wall, the man smelled fresh air and gasped. Soot covered his mouth; his eyes were red and swollen. The air filled his lungs too quickly, and they purged themselves in a violent series of coughs. He doubled over in pain, blood and saliva oozing onto the forest floor.

"Your strength will return shortly, Jadak son of Jadain."

Jadak winced and resisted looking up.

"How—how did you know my name?" Jadak shook again, racked with deep coughing. Then a gentle hand rested upon his chest, and his body suddenly was at ease.

"Because I know your son."

Jadak's weary eyes widened.

Just then a massive tremor surged deep beneath them.

"Dionia is restless. Come, we must part with great haste."

Still holding his rowan staff, the cloaked man bent over and lifted Jadak into his arms much like one would carry a small child across the chest. He turned and walked back the way he had come, with Jadak resting in his arms.

The action seemed effortless. Jadak wondered inwardly at the man's strength, for he did not appear to be a man of great stature.

"As you might think, the strength is not mine," the man said.

"Ah—aye, I was wondering," Jadak replied. *Did I say something?*

"Aye, but be at rest, son of Jadain. You are safe, at least for now. Let me do the rest of the work."

"And if they should ask me who my rescuer is?"

"Fane, son of Fadner. I should think you know my father."

"Young Fane? Is it really you?"

"'Tis I indeed, in flesh and spirit."

Jadak was at a loss. With everything he had just been through, an ordeal that no one could imagine, suddenly now the Light of the Most High was showering upon him full and bright. Though in his darkest moment, he was not forgotten; though in his deepest lament, he was not forsaken.

"When I crawled up on the roots of that tree, I knew it would be my grave."

"Yet the High King had another plan for you."

"Aye, this is clear," Jadak said, his eyes building with tears. His body was spent and his spirit worn; he had been wounded deeply, and still his heart had trouble receiving the grace that carried him.

"Why is it you rescue me?" Jadak finally asked.

"Many reasons, I should think, don't you?"

Jadak did not offer any.

"Come now, Jadak," Fane said as he walked briskly through the wood. "Are you not as coveted by the Most High as any?"

Jadak hesitated.

"Well, put your doubts to rest. It should be evident."

"And with all the souls in need of saving at this dark hour, you would journey into the bowels of this wood for an old man?"

"The Mighty King wishes that none should perish."

"And still, I would ask you of the other reasons."

Another tremor surged through the ground, rustling the branches above. But Fane did not lose a step and continued through the forest. The smoke was increasing, and both men knew that the fires were drawing nearer.

"There is another reason."

"And a truthful man would share it despite the feelings he knows it would call up."

Fane eyed him knowingly.

"You see, young Fane, I know a man's thoughts, too, though not as certainly as you."

"Very well," Fane relented. "I need you to help stop a mouse from whispering in the lion's ear."

Fane walked on in silence as Jadak contemplated his riddle; he didn't need long.

"He is in Mt. Dakka?"

"Aye."

"And he's been given audience with the King?"

"The King is not there now, but they have held company together before his departure."

"And now?"

"I should think him in the council of the Dibor and any number of the royal families."

"The new *King*, the *Dibor*—you assume I know much, Fane," Jadak admitted.

"And am I wrong?"

Jadak shook his head. "Nay, you are right as ever." He took a deep breath, knowing what was to come. "Then let us stop this banter and allow you to use every breath for walking until I can do the same. We have much to do and a deceitful mouse to silence. But if I may ask you, how did you know I was not utterly lost? That I was not *taken*?"

"Because your son said you were forever lost."

Jadak paused in thought.

"I—I'm not sure I follow."

"Your son is a liar."

Chapter Two

FEDCHULTS

Brax climbed a broad, stone stair to the ramparts above. He had grown so accustomed to the constant din of battle that he could not sleep in the silence his palace chambers afforded him. He felt better used on the battle line than resting, and more often than not he preferred his sword to his pillow. There was, of course, another reason he could not sleep. Though he held it as a close secret, no one near to him doubted what it was.

He tapped a weary and bloodstained swordsman on the shoulder and relieved him of his duty for a well-earned respite. The man gratefully bowed in acknowledgment of the King of Tontha and wasted no time in retreating into the mighty stronghold of Mt. Dakka. Brax then turned and surveyed the scene outside the wall.

Ever since the battle had begun, the sky had grown increasingly gloomy, and now no one could remember the last time the sun had been seen. The Dairne-Reih covered every open spot of land and poured back down over the slopes, far out of sight. They covered the mountain face like a dark blanket of wrath, churning under a dark sky. The movement was very much like that of a wayward sea, undulating methodically, and then suddenly bursting forth with a spray of clattering weaponry hoisted skyward. The demons clicked and shrieked as they moved, each anticipating their ever-nearing turn of mounting the massive walls. Then a chance to spill blood.

Newly-constructed siege towers ambled up the mountain track and were pitted against the fortress. But each time they were pummeled by Mt. Dakka's defenses, doused with tar, and then set ablaze by the archer's arrows. Siege ladders rose up and slammed against the outer walls, ascended by any number of putrid demons hoping to surmount the ramparts and unleash their carnage. But the ladders were hacked down or pushed off. Any that remained allowed only a few Dairneags to leap onto the ramparts before meeting a numbing end, slashed to bits and tossed back over the wall like so much rubbage.

Brax walked down the line, encouraging his men and lending his hand in any number of duties. Buckets of tar were passed up from below to fill the cauldrons. Wood was continuously hoisted on lifts and stacked beside the heating fires. Additional lumber was carried up the towers that Luik had constructed, feeding fires in their peaks used for directing troops to the most needed points on the wall and alerting them to enemies.

Broken swords were discarded and replaced. Worn, shattered shields were constantly exchanged for new ones. And replenishing the ever-dwindling stockpiles of arrows was a thankless chore. Still others put their hands to the simple tasks of passing out water skins, a treasure that no man refused.

The occasional injured soldier was carried off the line and seamlessly replaced by two new ones. Other skilled men ran to tend the wounds of those in need, wrapping, cleansing, and cutting in order to preserve what might be saved. Prayers were offered up to the Great God, but rarely did they see them answered.

All in all, the battle seemed to fall into its own rhythm, as those who study warfare know. The ebb and flow of exchanges became patterned, almost predictable; it was the sudden, violent breaks of rhythm that inflicted the most damage and exacted the greatest toll.

A desperate command came ringing down from the nearest watchtower.

"Take cover!"

Brax turned and saw that the enemy had begun flinging the burning stones again with their fedchults. The bright balls of fire sailed elegantly against the dim sky, a long tail of flames and smoke trailing behind. Lulled by the gentle lob—a grand arch that stretched across the sky as any number of fiery orbs careened toward the city wall—soldiers held their breath in awe of the terrifying beauty that raced to meet them.

Whatever mesmerizing power befell the warriors in that moment, it was brought to a blistering end in the next as the devastating weight of the stones slammed into the granite underfoot. Men were rattled to their knees, many sent tumbling clear off the battlements to the courtyards and rooftops behind them.

But Brax seemed unaffected by the assault. He stood right where he was, almost oblivious to the violence bursting around him. A few thought it was because he had endured so many of these barrages over the last several days, and was now numb to their effects. But most knew differently. They had been there, too; they had seen it all.

"My King," said an orderly, "word comes from the eastern wall. It has been breached."

Brax was shaken from his stupor and looked at the warrior. "C'symia, soldier." He turned and addressed another man beside him. "Commander, we're going to need two ranks of men at that breach. Can you handle it?"

"Aye, my Lord. As it is ordered, so it is done."

"Good. And if a porquill[2] has not been erected already, prepare one as a first order."

The commander nodded and departed, three more officers following close behind him with a wave of his arm.

The incoming fireballs were relentless now, hammering away at the outer wall, searching for weaknesses in the superstructure. Brax was confident that this first breach would be contained, but he knew it was only a matter of time before the gaps in the wall outnumbered the men to guard them.

He walked along the platforms encouraging his warband while more fiery projectiles battered the walls. The warriors did not know whether their King was simply fearless or just numb, but he made his way without wincing or bothering to avoid anything.

A massive boulder exploded against a nearby section of the structure and sent molten debris ripping past the crenellations. Brax didn't seem to notice. He continued upright, pounding the shoulder plates of the

---

[2] **Porquill** (*POOR-kwill*): *noun; a tactical maneuver in which long wooden spears are driven into the ground butt-first in rows, each series angled outward toward the advancing enemy.*

warriors, continually exhorting them in battle.

. . .

"He is mad," one man said to another, crouched behind a fold in the wall.

"Nay, he is King, and he knows it," replied the other. "His time is not done until the Most High orders it."

"So that's why he flaunts his life before the enemy?"

The other man thought. "Well, maybe he is mad, as you say. So it is a mixture then, of both knowing his place in the Kingdom, and of careless abandonment to that position."

. . .

Brax continued down the line and looked up to the watchtowers. High above, the flagmen waved torches, each signal ordering men to different sides of the city, indicating where the enemy was gathering for renewed assault. Brax thanked Luik in his heart for such foresight. Then he noticed a strange command from the nearest watchtower in the south: *prepare the crossbows.*

He looked back to the battlefield, stepped to the rail, and peered between the crenulations. Lumbering up the mountain track from the south were enormous timber cages, pulled by legions of Dairneags heaving heavy cords over their shoulders. The boxes rode on massive axles, large wheels affixed to either side, squealing loudly as they moved.

Brax realized the squealing was not from the wheels. He squinted at the first of five cages that lumbered up the lane. He peered into the darkness between the rungs, searching for what lurked inside.

Something moved.

He gazed more intently.

Suddenly a giant, yellow, bird-like eye appeared, darted around, and then fixed itself on the King.

An ear-piercing screech split the air.

"What in Dionia is—"

As if summoned to answer his question, a Dairneag lowered an ax.

A cable snapped.

The lid flew open.

Chapter Three

INTO THE DARKNESS

Anorra's head throbbed mercilessly.

She could not hear herself think.

And if any thought did enter her mind, it was of the extreme pain that the rest of her body felt. She was turned over and over, as if rolling down a hill. Each revolution brought a new wave of agony, followed by sharp stabbing in her temples. And all the while her soul was consumed with pitch-blackness. No shadows to focus on, no horizon to tell up from down, only the commotion that pulled her further into an unknown abyss.

But more than this, if such a measure could be followed and then endured by even more torment, were the incomprehensible feelings that tore at her heart.

First abandonment.

Then utter loneliness.

Violation.

And then fear.

She tried to fend off the encroaching tentacles that laced themselves tightly around her bosom, but to no avail.

She panicked. She thrashed wildly, but it only brought about more of the same. The vines of hopelessness relented for but a moment. Then, when all was still again, they resumed their stranglehold. Wave after wave bombarded her, two elements working in tandem: pain softened the will, and the weakened will bowed to the devices of torment.

Whether within or without, her ears heard the sounds of clashing metal and bone. Strained breathing all around was either her own or a host of troubled creatures; so full was it in her head that she began weeping, gasping for air, and then choking on her tears. She felt herself gag, the first thing yet that she knew was her own. She felt a hand squeeze tightly around her neck. A pungent odor filled her head.

She was awake.

Blood and bile mixed in her mouth. Her stomach retched, the pain overwhelming. She felt the contents of her gut run down the side of her face.

Anorra was suddenly jerked around, the loud growling of beasts in her ears. She heard a bone snap in her chest.

O Most High!

It was then she had her first clear thought.

I'm alive.

In her mind's eye she saw herself standing on the ramparts of Mt. Dakka. Rage and sorrow consumed her. Her arm pulled the bowstring back, finger at the corner of her mouth.

The arrow was away.

It sped through the dust of war and found its mark in the forehead of a Dairneag about to lower a hammer on a fedchulte's trigger lever.

Another arrow had been drawn and was awaiting its order between her hands. She searched the ground below her.

And then a brilliant flash of light, and a ringing in her ears.

For a moment it dazzled her.

She was flying.

Then the sudden shock of pain—pain that grew and seemed to reach no end—stole the breath from her lungs and unsteadied her soul.

All was black.

Then the clicking.

I am lost, she realized.

The Dairne-Reih.

She came to her senses despite the afflictions of her body. A wide shoulder dug into her stomach, a broad arm pinned her legs together. Every step her captor took jounced her frame, and more pain seized her. But the agony helped clear the fog, and soon she was aware of being carried away.

Hot breath stung her face as a Dairneag hissed and clucked its tongue at her. Her captor marched on, deeper into the enemy fold. More battle-hungry demons, which had yet to see blood spilled, sneered at her passing. They clucked and gurgled, each drawing close for a smell of Dionian flesh. So close did the monsters get, that Anorra's hair got caught in the teeth of one Dairneag and yanked out as it turned away.

Before long, the foul fluids of the Dairne-Reih drenched her head and clothes. Such a spectacle was she that often her captor would spin around to drive off any Dairneag that seemed to get too close, or too interested.

More distressing than all this, however, was the fact that all was still dark. She could not make out shape nor shadow. If it was in fact night, she could not see a single star. And if overcast, she did not see a torch or fire pit. All was empty, her sight devoid of form.

Thinking something inhibited her vision, she reached a trembling hand to her face. Just the effort alone caused her great discomfort. Her fingers touched dried blood and torn flesh. A flash of pain ripped through her eye sockets and into the back of her head.

O Great God of Athera—

She couldn't even finish her own thought.

She was blind.

This distressing find caused her to weep once more, now quite sure that her end was near. Far from the safety of her people, and farther still from the arms of her love, she searched her spirit for any hope, even the faintest glimmer of rescue. But none presented itself.

She knew now her body was mortally wounded. She could feel the strength leaving her body with each passing moment. Her bones ached, and blood continued to fill her mouth. She could not fight her way out of this…she could not even stand if given the chance.

• • •

Anorra did not know how long she went along, slung on the shoulder of the demon that carried her. But when the crowds of Dairneags dwindled, and fewer sought a lick of her face, she became aware of the chill that scourged her damp form.

The noise of battle was far and distant now, more a memory than a reality. She heard her own shallow breaths surrounded by the deep breathing of her captor, her little body carried on the rise and fall of its chest.

Then the demon stopped.

She tensed.

For a moment nothing happened. But then she heard a low murmur, and a strange vibration of the air, a wave that moved her hair and clothing in rhythm. The hair on the back of her neck and arms stood up.

The Dairneag took two steps forward.

Her body felt as though it were immersed in water, but for a second. It was heavy, even cold around her. Her ears popped. She winced.

And then, all at once, it was over.

With the calm came new sensations, and a completely new environment.

The first thing she noticed was the heat that kissed her skin. At first it stung and sent a chill down her spine. But soon she welcomed the warmth, the dampness and cold dissipating rapidly. She pictured the sun, high in the sky at midday, soaking her skin with its radiant glow.

The image ebbed quickly, cast out of her mind by a foul smell. Charred rock and burnt sulfur stung her nostrils. And more, the putrid smell of burning flesh. The overpowering odor seemed to stain her skin.

And then there were the sounds.

Far off in the distance, echoing through a series of long, endless corridors, came the most unharmonious shrieks and moans she had ever heard. Full of immeasurable sorrow and grief, they pulled at her heart until she was again reminded of her own hopelessness and utter despair.

As her captor began walking again, the wails grew louder. The bitter smell brought tears to her havocked eyes and formed a lump in her throat. Her gut heaved, but there was nothing left to expel. This was a most horrid place.

Each jouncing step sent wave upon wave of pain through her battered body. She gave one desperate attempt at trying to free herself, but the scalding agony that resulted made it her last attempt. She thought she heard herself moan in defeat, but she couldn't be sure, for she noticed the shrieks and hollers mounting around her, the air filled with audible torment.

The space around her expanded, and Anorra sensed she was in a great cavernous hall. Upon entering the room she sensed those within it looking on at her, their resulting screams evidence of a new arrival. She felt completely exposed, put on display for all to see. She thought she heard chains snap taut, followed by the lashing of whips.

Flesh split.

More tormenting cries.

A fresh wave of fear washed over her.

I want to go home.

She felt her captor turn this way and that, making his way deeper into the large hall. Eventually he came to a stop and spoke words she did not understand.

There was a jingle of metal, and then a thick grinding, and the occasional squeal.

Something was being opened.

She felt the arm that pinned her legs lower, her body sagging down the chest of the Dairneag. Then a scaly hand grasped her neck, and almost instantly she was dangling from the demon's claw, limbs limp.

The monster growled at her and produced the strange clicking in the back of its throat. She knew it was glaring at her. She knew it wanted to devour her. Bile squeezed between the Dairneag's teeth as it licked its raw mouth hole.

A shout from something behind her captor stopped the bloodlust cold.

Anorra sensed another Dairneag.

They clicked and barked at one another. Then, as if nothing more than a scrap of meat, Anorra was tossed through the air, flung to the end of a small cell; she landed with a crash on a gravel floor. Her body convulsed from the grueling blow, shuddering on hot stones. Their sharp edges cut her face and hands. She tried to lift her head, but it was useless.

The gate slammed shut behind her, and the demons walked away.

She was alone with the wailing and shrieks of company she knew not.

I want to go home, she thought.

Most High, please take me home.

Chapter Four

A WARBAND DIVIDED

Anondo swung his Vinfae ferociously, too fixated on the battle at hand to allow the overwhelming odds and imminent end to discourage his blade. If he were going to die, he much preferred his end to be met valiantly, and as late as possible. If his heart were to engage with what his head knew, he would have neither the strength nor desire to press on a moment more.

The appearance of the enemy had been swift and sudden, a perfect tactical assault in his mind. They had swept down upon them from the road running north into Tontha, the one side from which no one had anticipated an attack.

The force with which the Dairne-Reih battered Anondo's men was much akin to that of a spear driving through and splitting a target in two. It was the simplest of all tactics, but remained one of the oldest and most effective.

The enemy war host had run into their camp largely unheralded. Those men at the head of the defending line had taken the brunt of the barrage, driven back and run over, their bodies beaten to a pulp in the stampede. Only a few had managed to keep their wits about them, Anondo being one of them.

Demons flew overhead, leaping off the backs of their cohorts, vying for prey as the spearpoint of their assault continued to bury itself deep into the throng of unsuspecting men.

"Watch your back!"

Anondo spun around, sword arcing in one hand, spear in the other, both aiming toward a Dairneag of no unusual size. The beast raised a horned fist, but the twin tips of Anondo's weapons sliced through the demon's gut, spilling out its innards. Suddenly the carcass pressed toward him in the crush, his body quickly enveloped by the creature's gash, covered in its blood and bile. He stumbled backwards, trying to move away from the momentum, knowing that if he were to fall it would mean his end. At the last second his back struck something solid, another man or beast perhaps, and his fall righted. To his relief, the carcass of the demon was suddenly flung skyward, being hoisted by another Dairneag behind, this one of considerably larger size.

Anondo jabbed without hesitation. His spear drove into the demon's loins, producing a deafening screech from the foe. Enraged, it swung a scaly hand full of horns, each bathed with glistening fluid. Anondo ducked but felt the burn of sharp daggers sweep across his shoulder blade, tearing into his flesh. The demon raised its arms high, double-fisted. Anondo followed his spear jab with another from his mighty Vinfae, slightly above the previous penetration. The Dairneag bellowed again and then slammed its hands down on Anondo's back with devastating power.

The crushing blow delivered to his spine sent Anondo to the ground in a gasping heap, his sword and spear still in the midsection of his attacker. The beast raised its arms again for the deathblow.

Anondo rolled over to watch. He saw his weapons dangling just above his head.

The double-fisted blow came.

But in the time it took for the demon to lower its arms, Anondo had retrieved the spear and righted it, pointing it straight up into the oncoming hands of his attacker.

The demon wailed, his hands now bound together, flailing, completely forgetting about his target. For the demon it was a tragic mistake; for Anondo, it was all the time he needed.

He rolled to his knees and shook his head, trying to shove off the pain that nearly immobilized his body. He took a deep breath and reached out for his Vinfae. The weapon withdrew easily from the wound, and Anondo shoved the blade directly upward, a third and final cut into the Dairneag's midsection. The injured beast moaned and then finally fell to one side. Anondo was quick now to regain his feet, knowing the battle was far from over.

He retrieved his spear.

Two more Dairneags closed from either side. One was temporarily sidetracked by one of Anondo's men, which allowed Anondo to take care of the second. He feinted a wide swing and then a follow-through jab for the demon. His own attack was countered and taken by the beast's bone-plated forearms, glancing off wildly. The Dairneag reached for Anondo's head with both hands, but the attempt was slow. Anondo ducked and sidestepped the monster, plunging the twin points of his weapons into its side. The Dairneag tried to spin to face Anondo, but the effort only furthered the wound and eventually sent the beast to the ground.

Sadly, the first Dairneag finished with Anondo's kinsman and then turned for him once more. Fresh blood stained the monster's hands and mouth. This particular foe was covered with small horns protruding from individual plates all over its body, a sort of spiked defensive armor. Anondo couldn't recall ever seeing anything quite like it. Despite his fatigue and injuries, he couldn't help but suspect that these Dairneags were somehow *stronger* that he had ever remembered. And now, seeing a new type of armor, he wondered if in fact his conjecture held any merit.

The beast glowered at him, uttering a growl from within its throat, a distinct indication of intent to converge. Anondo was in no condition to take his time and decided he must look for the swiftest means possible of felling this foe. The giant strode to within an arm's length of him and drove its spike-laden knuckles forward like a battering ram.

Anondo leaned out of the way.

But instead of pulling back its arms, the Dairneag swung them laterally, striking Anondo's shoulder. He stumbled sideways, but remained on his feet and turned to face his opponent.

The monster huffed in pride and swung again, a backhanded blow blocked by Anondo's spear shaft. It then drove its other fist forward as before, aiming once again for Anondo's comparatively smaller head.

This time Anondo would strike back. He ducked the blow, and as before, drove his spear at the Dairneag's loins. But the spear bounced off the protective plate and left nothing more than a scratch.

Not only that, but Anondo was too slow.

The Dairneag reached down and with one mighty hand pinned him at the waist. He felt a horn puncture his abdomen. But the burning was forgotten when the demon hoisted him off his feet and threw him into a mass of men and Dairne-Reih. His head slammed hard against a fellow warrior's helmet, and he felt the breaking of ribs from within his chest. His right arm went numb from searing pain, and it was all he could do to keep his vision from going black.

He squinted, desperately holding on to consciousness.

The spiked demon charged. Anondo was convinced he saw it smile, its wicked eyes gleaming from between plates over its face. He felt the rumble of its stride travel through the ground and pound in his head. His left hand still clutched his spear, but the shaft was broken and the spearhead gone, his Vinfae surely lost in the tumult when his right arm had broken. The vibration of the ground increased with each pounding step the Dairneag took toward him.

The demon pulled back its fists a last time, ready to drive them into Dionian flesh.

There was nothing he could do.

Chapter Five

BATTLE ON THE SHORE

The sky was filled with arrows, a sheet of translucent black, teetering and wavering as they came with death marking their end. Time stood still in that moment for Luik, reality slowing to a near standstill…

• • •

Everything seemed pitted against him, and him alone. The fact that his men would pay for what was intended solely for him grieved his heart deeply. Truth be told, he had known it was coming, just not like this. And not so soon. His dream had told him differently.

He felt single drops of rain beat his face. He sensed individual hairs on his head being assaulted by the violent wind. He watched as the enemy li-lis paddled ever closer toward the surf, their archers reaching for yet another shaft to nock. The salty spray of the waves showered his legs and soaked his torso. His body ached, his wounds throbbing with pain.

Luik looked westward to see the dark sky and the funnel-like cloud ripping through the sea toward him. To the north, a wide swath of smoke rose skyward.

And there on the mainland shore, a tiny figure, that of a small girl,

49

hand upraised in greeting.

Reality came racing back to life…

• • •

"Everyone take cover!" Jrio yelled.

But there was nowhere to hide.

While most of the men had made it safely above to Kirstell's protective highland, a great many still remained on the exposed rocks below. And the barren surface held only a few boulders behind which anyone could take cover. The men simply covered their heads with their hands and awaited the inevitable.

But Luik looked skyward, determined to meet his end head on. The Dibor resisted the urge to shield themselves and followed their High King's lead. Meanwhile Kinfen and the others up above watched in helpless horror as their kinsmen were about to meet their end below. There was nothing that they could do but look on.

Luik's eyes followed the track of the cloud of arrows as they reached the highest point of their arch and began their descent.

He wondered how his sword brothers fared in Ligeon, how the rest were doing in Mt. Dakka. And he wondered if Anorra was safe. So many thoughts went through his mind in that moment. But one left all others in the shadows…

The Great God has forsaken me.

He tracked the arrows, now a breath away from riddling his men full of holes, men who had been faithful to him to the last; men who had left their families for a death-errand; men who, too, had pledged their lives in great service of The White Lion but had been forgotten in their hour of need, just as he had.

But his mind was hindered from pursuing the thought further. What his eyes saw was too wondrous to permit it.

As the arrows raced toward them, the air just above became alive, lit up with bursts of fire, intense heat, and dazzling light. Luik winced and raised a hand. He forced himself to look on between the cracks of his fingers.

As each shaft crossed the same invisible line, the arrow met an utter end, burned entirely in the blink of an eye. Not even ash remained, the devouring was so complete. The cloud of arrows was swallowed whole in nearly the same instant, brilliant bursts of glory fire consuming each shaft with the sound of a thousand torch flames rushing through the air.

No one moved.

Luik was the first to say anything. "Did you see what I saw?"

Jrio, now examining a sky devoid of enemy arrows, closed his gaping mouth and faltered, eventually finding his voice.

"Aye—aye, that I did. I think."

The *taken,* who had previously readied their next shot, stood abated in their course, those paddling missing a stroke.

"*Forgive me, O Most High,*" Luik whispered to himself. Then, turning to those around him yelled, "Prepare a defense!"

Those who just moments before cowered in fear of their lives suddenly rose up and drew their swords, some from their belts, others reaching back into the li-lis that Fyfler had stowed among the rocks. The *taken* prepared for the assault and readied their weapons.

Just then one of the boats pulled away from the larger pack and headed for the mainland.

"Where do they think they're going?" Jrio piped up.

"Giving up so soon?" Rab taunted.

"Nay," Luik replied. "They are going after her." He pointed to the small shape on the far shore, the one he had seen earlier, thinking it but an apparition. It was then Luik realized who *she* was—

Fia.

Every muscle in Luik's body sprang to life. Whatever fatigue and injury his body had accumulated suddenly vanished.

"I'm going ashore. Stay here and defend the men."

"Are you mad, Luik?" Rab grabbed his arm.

"I'm going! They will kill her. Or worse." Luik pulled away from his grip and shoved a li-li into the surf.

"Not without me," Rab insisted and jumped in.

"And me," said Cage.

"I will not permit it!" Luik ordered.

But there was no convincing them otherwise. Luik looked into their hardened eyes, to the oncoming boats, to the winding funnel cloud to the west, to Fia on the mainland, and then relented.

"Very well. Jrio," he addressed him, "stay here and order the men.

As soon as the *taken* are dispersed, get the men topside."

"Aye." Jrio pounded his chest.

"We'll help hold the shoals, too," came Kinfen's voice from up above. He rode the lift down with ten of the strongest men, swords drawn. "Now go!"

Luik climbed in the boat, and Cage shoved off, hopping in a moment later. The three of them took up paddles and began rowing with all their might.

Luik's boat had a clear advantage over the other boat in that they had a much shorter and more direct route to cover in order to get to shore. The enemy boat needed to cover a longer, diagonal course. And though Luik's crew was outnumbered two to one, he figured his vessel would be lighter and make the distance more speedily.

"Pull!" Rab yelled. "Pull!"

But the enemy boat made good time, the extra men pulling more than their weight. In the time it took Luik's boat to halve the distance to the mainland, the enemy boat had turned slightly away from the mainland and veered toward them.

"They are going to ram us!" Cage hollered. They paddled despite the oncoming collision, hoping it was simply a vain attempt to get them to divert.

It wasn't.

• • •

Kinfen and Jrio ordered the strongest men to the front line and the rest to a second and third line among the rocks. The footing was wet and slippery, but they knew their only hope of staving off the invaders was to prevent them from landing their boats. Striking them while they waded through the waters would be their best bet.

They had correctly figured that whatever protective covering had shielded them from the arrows would not necessarily shield them from bodily forms approaching Kirstell. But saving them from the archers was blessing enough; the Dibor knew they could match the *taken* in hand-to-hand combat.

The enemy li-lis were nearly upon them now. Everything had happened so quickly. Jrio felt as if he hadn't even gotten all his men situated before the first boat emptied of its men, who then plunged their way toward the rocks. Kinfen could sense the men growing anxious.

"Hold the line!" Kinfen ordered. "Don't leave the rocks!"

Two men on either side of him couldn't restrain themselves and jumped into the shoals, wading out to meet the enemy, swords whirling.

"*Noooo!*" Jrio hollered, trying to grab for them, beckoning them to come back. But it was no use.

"Hold the line!" Kinfen restated.

The two wayward men strode out to their waists in water, screaming with all their might. They engaged the first wave of the enemy, one man's blade hacking into the shoulder of a *taken*. The second man blocked two slashes from another of the *taken* and then delivered a lethal blow on the head of his attacker. Many men on the rocks felt their hope soar and were almost compelled to join their brothers, but Kinfen held them back with a threat.

"*Leave the line and I will slay you myself!*"

Whether he meant it or not, it had the desired effect. Men who moments before were itching to leap into the waves suddenly thought better of it. The *taken* they could quite possibly handle; a Dibor they could not. That, and they saw the fate of their brothers unfolded before them…

The one man deflected a solid blow from an onrushing attacker but failed to see the second foe to his left. A blade bit deeply into his back, dropping him beneath the water before he could even take a breath. The two *taken* then plunged their swords repeatedly into the waves until a foamy red froth bid them stop. The second man also was soon overwhelmed and met a bitter end beneath the sea. What was moments before a seemingly valiant, albeit hasty, effort suddenly left an ominous sense of dread among those on shore.

"Hold the line!" Kinfen demanded once more.

The *taken* waded through the red cloud in the sea and headed for Kirstell as more of the men jumped from the boats. They came with swords forward and eyes fixed. They made no noise, at least none that could be heard over the raging wind and pelting rain. One step after the other, the *taken* surged forward, all now in the water, heading straight for the island.

"*Hold the line!*"

• • •

When Luik realized the wreck was imminent, he ordered Rab and Cage to drop their paddles and take up their weapons. The enemy boat careened toward them at amazing speed, so much so that Luik barely had time to grab his Vinfae before the two boats collided.

Crrrack!—Shooonk!

The *taken* fell forward on one another while Luik and the others were nearly knocked sideways out of their craft, swords and paddles flying. No sooner did Cage get his bearings than one of the *taken* had jumped on him and started hammering him with his fists, obviously having lost his sword in the collision. Cage grabbed his Vinfae with both hands and thrust it up under his arm to one side, sticking the man in the gut. The victim let out a gasp of air and groaned. Cage stood up and sent the man tumbling into sea.

A second and third man leapt into their boat, but Luik and Rab both anticipated the move. Rab grabbed one man by the wrists and used his momentum to throw the man right off the other side of the li-li. Then Rab shoved the li-li away with two *taken* remaining at the oars.

Luik was not so fortunate, and his attacker came at him down the length of the boat and pinned him at the bow. The man swung once with his sword, and then a second and third time. Luik jumped back until he had nowhere left to go. The man knew Luik was trapped and charged at him.

But he should have known: *a Dibor is never trapped.*

Luik knocked the man's sword skyward and then jabbed him in the stomach with his elbow. He doubled over, at which Luik lowered the hilt of his Vinfae on the back of the man's neck. He dropped to his knees, and Luik pushed him over the side.

Cage finished off one last attacker and then hollered out, "They are making for the shore!" The remaining two of the *taken* seemed bent on getting to shore and retrieving the girl.

"Row!" Luik yelled, searching in the bloody hull for a paddle. The three of them quickly began rowing again. Cage in the rear felt their progress being impeded and then noticed a hand clinging to the gunwale. One of the assailants still held on, trying desperately to get in. He lowered the paddle quickly, breaking the man's fingers, lost a moment later in a sea swell.

The enemy boat was two lengths in front of them now, enough of a lead that Luik feared for Fia. She remained on the strand, but was clearly shaken and was beginning to retreat.

"Aye, run, Fia!" Luik shouted, waving his hand between strokes. "*Run!*"

Whether she just understood the simple command, or she feared for her life, she turned and ran back along the dunes, and then up toward the grassy plains of Jerovah. This seemed to infuriate the *taken,* and they dug harder into the water with their paddles. Moments later they were in the surf and jumped out of their boat: *their first mistake.*

Because of their shallow draw, li-lis were able to be paddled right up onto the shore so no time was wasted meddling in the surf. It was just what Luik was hoping for. They closed to within one boat length.

When Luik's boat came ashore they were well onto the sand, the two *taken* men running just a few spans in front of them. The Dibor leapt out of their slowing vessel and gave chase.

The *taken's* second mistake was that they thought they could outrun Cage, a son of the mighty Horse King, a title he now wore himself. He had grown up riding and running alongside the horses of Jerovah, his legs as sure and as swift as any in Dionia. And the *taken* were no match for his effortless speed.

A moment later he was upon them both. The first he jabbed right through the back with his sword, the point coming clean out the other side of his stomach. He released his Vinfae and went for the other. The man looked over his shoulder with dread. Cage dove forward and knocked the man into the sand with a shoulder to his back. The man lost his sword and landed face first into a dune. He tried to rise, sputtering and coughing, but Cage quickly grabbed the man's head and ended his plight with a sharp twist to the side.

It was all over.

Luik and Rab ran up over the dune.

"Fia!"

• • •

The *taken* leapt upon Jrio and his men with staggering speed, colliding against the defenders like waves crashing on the rocks, catching them on their heels. Jrio knocked a *taken* man in the head with his hilt, causing him to tumble unconscious into the waves, and then slashed at a second attacker who was aiming for his knees. The blow severed the man's forearm and he, too, fell into the shallows, screaming as he went. But before he had time to reset himself, a third man, holding a spear, jabbed at Jrio's head. The Dibor was forced to step backward, the man stepping up onto the stone. The man jabbed again and Jrio avoided the blow a second time, and then a third.

Then the assailant paused.

Jrio's heart sank.

"O no—"

Seeing an unsuspecting warrior in the line to Jrio's left, the spearman jabbed and withdrew a lethal blow to the man's neck. He looked back at Jrio and smiled as the victim fell dead.

It was a thoughtless act.

Now Jrio was furious and lunged forward, stepping in aggressively. The *taken* man parried Jrio's thrust easily enough, and Jrio passed behind him.

It was a trick.

As soon as Jrio was past him, he flipped his grip on his sword, pulled his arm sharply downward past his hip, driving his Vinfae deep into the man's back. The spearman fell forward off the blade into a heap on the stone.

But the spearman was quickly replaced by another foe, this one even fiercer than the previous. Jrio took another step back. And then looked around.

The line was collapsing; he was being forced to retreat.

But he was not the only one.

Kinfen labored with a monstrous man, a full two heads taller than himself; the man carried a massive war hammer with a long shaft, swinging it deftly. Kinfen ducked the first dangerous arc, a move that meant the death of a warrior to his right, the hammer pummeling the man's head in an instant. The heavy weapon continued in its arc and then suddenly came back around for another blow, but Kinfen stepped away.

He saw an opportunity as the hammer flew past him, exposing the *taken* man's side. He jabbed hard. But the enormous brute didn't even seem to feel the point of Kinfen's Vinfae slip between his ribs. The hammer came around again, but this time Kinfen couldn't move away in time.

It felt like a boulder coming down on his shoulder, knocking him to the ground, bone splintering in his arm. He gasped for air. The man above him gave a laugh. As if bouncing off of Kinfen's body, the massive hammer went around the other way and circled in for a final blow. Kinfen propped himself up with his good arm and realized his sword was gone. The hammer came at his head.

Thwwwack!-Clanck!-Splash!

The hammer's shaft was hacked in two, the head skimming off over the rocks and into the water. The weapon's sudden loss of weight caused the man to lurch sideways and lose his footing. His hands went up and he fell, tumbling off the rock ledge, and slipped beneath the waves. Kinfen looked up and saw Fyfler.

"Get up, sword brother!" Fyfler yelled, pulling Kinfen to his feet, his arm blue and already dangerously swollen.

"My sword!" Kinfen glanced around.

"We'll find it later," said Fyfler as he turned to dispose of a frenzied attacker. He parried two swings, and then plunged his sword straight through the man's stomach and out the back.

Kinfen saw his Vinfae among the wet rocks and reached for it, now cradling his wounded arm. By the time he stood upright he noticed that the line had broken and the rocky scene was a tumult of violent clashing and blood. The *taken* were upon them in force.

He felt a peculiar feeling in his spirit, much like what he had felt in Ki-Dorne. All around him, men were fighting their kinsmen, running each other through with their blades, driving their spears into their stomachs while looking full into one another's eyes. It was gruesome.

Aren't these brothers? he thought. *Are these not of the same blood line as I?*

Kinfen was deeply grieved, a profound troubling that went far deeper than anything he could explain. But as much as these thoughts brewed within him, he found himself a part of it once again, not as a bystander who could judge and pass judgment upon, but as a player, a man who had no choice but to engage in combat, the very thing that he wished not to do. But it was that or lose his own life.

Strong hands wrapped around his neck. He strained to see who it was but could not get a glimpse, the hands squeezing sharply. He couldn't breathe. Suddenly, one of the hands came off his neck, only to pound his swollen shoulder. The sheer pain brought tears to his eyes. He thought he heard himself moan out loud but couldn't be sure. The hand rejoined the other around his neck and squeezed once more, this time even harder. Kinfen saw stars and knew he was only moments from losing consciousness.

But he still had his Vinfae.

In one fluid motion, Kinfen reached up and around and drew the blade across the back of the man's neck behind him. His aggressor screamed in his ear and released his grip. The Dibor gasped for air and then spun around.

It was the *taken man* with the war hammer! The man brought his hand down from his neck and stared at the blood in his hand. Then he looked up at Kinfen again, and then at Kinfen's wounded shoulder. He smiled.

The brute swung at Kinfen once, missed, but then landed a second blow on his shoulder. Kinfen felt his knees give out from the pain. He stumbled. He backed into a large boulder that kept him from going all the way down. He couldn't take another hit like that, at least not and stay afoot. The brute drew back his fist once more and let it fly.

But the blow missed and glanced off Kinfen's head. The giant held a look of great surprise and then fell right into Kinfen, sliding down his body in a heap.

Luik stood motionless behind the man, bloodied sword in hand.

"Not to my brother, he doesn't," Luik yelled above the battle clash.

"C'symia," Kinfen said weakly.

"Come, we need to get you out of here."

"Nay, I stay and fight," Kinfen resisted.

"Aye, I know you can, but not against that." Luik pointed west. The storm with the swerving cloud-tail was closer than it ever had been. "We need to get everyone up," he pointed to the lift. "Now!" Luik addressed his men. "To the lift! We're going up!"

The battle line, fragile as it was, soon began retreating, the men drawing back toward the lift. Fia already stood in the wooden apparatus with five men to defend her, although no enemy was near. A few more of the wounded men climbed aboard, and the thing lumbered up into the air, pulled from above. But the wind was strong and jounced the lift into the rock wall. The first time it hit, everyone was startled, but unaffected. The second time, however, a man fell and landed on the rocks below. Two men ran to him, but he was dead.

Kinfen put a hand to his mouth and yelled skyward, "Pull faster!"

Luik looked up toward Fia for some reassurance that she was all right. She looked down and held up her hand, waving timidly. He nodded and then turned back toward the battle.

The *taken* surrounded them, backing Luik and his men up to the lift area. But this was advantageous; the warband was now more compact and much easier to defend. For the first time, the wearied Dibor and their men held a slight advantage. Because the attacking *taken* had to spread out around the radius of the warband, their line was thin. An attacking foe would be met with a line three deep and had little chance of getting more than one chance to strike before he himself was struck down.

This, of course, caused the attack to slow until an amazing thing happened: a standoff was reached. Both lines stood still, the *taken* about three strides away. At first no one knew quite what to do. Both lines just stood there examining one another.

The Dibor and their warband were bloodied, soaking wet, and exhausted. It seemed like an eternity since they had last seen Mt. Dakka, and no one knew how long it would be until they saw it again. The wind whipped at them relentlessly, a cool chill now felt in the air. Kinfen ordered more men into the lift when it returned, and then sent it on its way.

The *taken* seemed unaffected by the wind and the rain. And none of them seemed to pay any notice to the encroaching storm. They stood there silently, steadily staring at the warband with hollow, eerie eyes. Their clothes were familiar, those of anyone in Dionia, and yet their expressions were sad, almost distraught.

Suddenly it dawned on Luik what they were doing.

"They are waiting us out," he said to Kinfen and Fyfler. "Once we send up enough men, they'll outnumber us."

"And slaughter us," Fyfler added.

"Aye," said Kinfen. "And I'm in no mood for that."

It was then Quoin ran back to Luik and said, "They're retrieving the bows from the boats!" Luik turned to regard Kinfen.

"Or they'll just slaughter us now while we stand here," Kinfen amended to Luik.

No one moved.

"We need help," Luik finally said. "But there seems to be a shortage of that lately." He looked around in thought. "Kinfen, keep the men moving up. Quoin, Fyfler, tell the line to rush the archers when they're ready to shoot. It's our only option."

Chapter Six

THE DYLAITHLOK

Up from the first cage flew a shadow, a barely discernable form that seemed to merge with the night sky. Brax followed it for as long as he could, and then it vanished against the blackness above.

"Ready the crossbows!" he ordered again, echoing the flagmen from above. "We need more torches!" He grabbed an orderly. "Bring more torches! I want these ramparts glowing!" The orderly nodded and was off.

Brax searched the sky above, eyes darting wildly.

Hands grabbed him. He spun around with a start.

It was Benigan. Boran was trailing just a little behind. Gorn approached from the opposite side.

"What was that?" Benigan asked, pointing into the dark sky.

Brax shook his head. "I haven't the faintest—"

"They are the Dylaithlok[3]," Gorn spoke up.

"And they would be?" Boran questioned, catching his breath.

"Ad named them himself," Gorn said. "Eagles, all from Tontha and

---

[3] **Dylaithlok** (*die-LAYTH-lock*): *noun; First Dionian; name given to taken birds of the air; most commonly raptors.*

Ligeon. But captured by Morgui and subjected to long torture, somehow growing much larger because of it."

"So they did not choose their fate?" Brax asked.

"O, I suppose they gave in at some point," Gorn replied distantly. "After the beatings and manipulations, I know few that would not succumb to bitter rage and endless fury."

"Like it was placed *upon* them," Benigan suggested.

"You could say." Gorn searched the sky and spoke more quickly. "Though I would think of it more as it was placed *within* them. Morgui poured evil into them. Once majestic brothers of the air, they have been wrongfully enslaved, their souls all but destroyed, hollow…*lost.*"

Suddenly a terrifying screech, the likes of which none of them had ever heard, ripped through the air. Those that heard it covered their ears and bent their heads. The sound permeated the air so strongly, it actually had a sense of weight to it. Brax yelled something at Boran and Benigan, but all they saw was a moving mouth. No sound.

The screech abated.

All the men stirred, each looking around in bewilderment.

"Get great-crossbows to the towers!" Brax ordered once more, this time clearly heard by all. Benigan and Boran were off a moment later, planning how to hoist the massive weapons to the turret tops.

"I'm with you, King of Tontha," Gorn reassured him.

"C'symia, my friend." Brax addressed the warriors on the ramparts. "Archers, ready your bows and empty your quivers on whatever comes from the night sky." A rustle of wood and leather stirred immediately. "It will be fast upon you from any direction. And above all, watch your brother lest he be—"

But even those words were better demonstrated than spoken. Another screech tore through the night air, and then a horrible black creature materialized above them. Talons yearning, wings outstretched, a massive bird flew just above the men's heads and raced along the wall.

Without warning, its talons dropped and closed around a swordsman, hoisting him effortlessly off the wall and then disappearing into the darkness once more, the poor soul wailing as he vanished out of sight.

Not a single arrow had been loosed.

Brax was indignant.

"Easy, my King," Gorn admonished him. "They will not fail again. Sometimes a man cannot react in measure until he understands what his enemy is capable of."

Brax remembered these words, nearly beaten into him while on Kirstell. How long ago was that now? He couldn't even remember anymore. He simply nodded, assuring himself, "They will not fail again."

Just as the men stood, eyes searching the skies, another deafening scream erupted from above. "There!" one man pointed.

The archers were quicker this time. Brax heard the distinct sound of a hundred bowstrings being drawn, arrows sliding along their counterparts. He turned and looked up, finally getting a good look at the approaching monster.

Spilling out of the blackness above was a sickly, dark creature with yellow eyes, each one bloodshot and furious. Its gnarled beak was cracked and faded but seemed to bear strange tooth-like fangs, mouth agape. Its body was fully feathered, just like a bird's, save that it was considerably larger and that it appeared deeply scarred—wounded almost—surely beaten. Many of the feathers grew in perverted angles from patches of scar tissue, old and leathery. Brax even caught the fire glow of torchlight gleaming off what he only could reckon were open sores.

"Now!" a commanding archer ordered.

From far away it looked like a cloud of black rain surging upward from the ramparts, illuminated briefly by firelight, and then disappearing into the night sky.

Brax watched as the deadly arrows found their mark, drilling into the crazed creature like the pitter-patter of hail on bare earth. A spray of fluid followed in the bird's wake, but the Dylaithlok did not stop.

A few men began to scream and cover their heads as they realized the monster was set on them. The bird stayed its course, talons flaring, but it had grown weak from the assault. Instead of pulling up from its dangerously steep angle of attack, the monster slammed hard into the ramparts, more than a few men instantly crushed under its weight.

The wounded creature tumbled forward and then flopped violently, claws tearing, wings beating. Its venomous beak clamped around a man's torso and tossed him about wildly. He screamed for help, but soon met his end, head beaten into the stone crenellations.

The fury did not last long, however. Another heartbeat and ten men were on it with swords and a battle-ax to the head. The putrid body shuddered, jerked a few moments longer, and then went limp. Everyone stared in disbelief.

Another screech went up from somewhere above. Brax turned again to count the cages. "Only four more," he reassured himself.

"*At least* four more," Gorn corrected.

Brax eyed him.

"There are five cages," Gorn continued, "with at least one each. Didn't you watch to see if more came out?"

Brax looked closer. Sure enough, each cage was definitely capable of holding more than one, judging from the Dylaithlok's actual size.

"But I did not say there are more than five," Gorn said again, "just that it was *possible*. You must always—"

"Consider the possibilities, I know. I know." Brax huffed and shook his head. "We'll kill them all, five or five tens. And you," he pointed at Gorn, "next time you battle in my region, leave the counting to me."

Gorn grinned, dropped his shield, and picked up a second sword. "The counting is all yours."

Brax turned and looked to the two closest towers, noticing that they each were already hoisting one of the massive crossbows up the side. His brothers had made quick work of arranging the weaponry and were soon well prepared for the next assault.

A screech signaled another attack.

"On your guard, men!" Brax ordered.

The archers drew their bowstrings and crouched again. More screeching bellowed from the blackness. Eyes searched the sky aimlessly, looking for any shifting shadow. All was still, with no sign of the monstrous bird. A third screech went out, drawn on and on as if it would never end. But this time it wasn't a bird that assailed them. On three different parts along the wall, while the men's attention had been drawn skyward, siege ladders and been silently mounted, and Dairne-Reih leapt onto the ramparts.

"Swords!" Brax hollered. But the Dairneags were swift, chewing up and down the line with relentless spite. Their clawed hands and horned extremities slashed, pummeling when they could not skewer, hammering when they failed to gouge.

"Take them out!" the King yelled, feeling helpless as ever.

The wall defenders met the attacking Dairne-Reih with great force, at least stopping their lateral advance. But no one could get to the siege ladders to knock them off the wall. More Dairneags spilled over the sides, now leaping off the ramparts and down into the city below.

The Dylaithloks had also timed their silent attack just right, this time devoid of a warning screech. While the men were busy fending off the new wave of Dairne-Reih, four birds swept in at the same time. Most of the victims never even knew what hit them, either tossed headlong over the wall, or hoisted skyward in the bone-breaking clutches of overgrown talons or razor-sharp beaks.

"Gorn," Brax said earnestly, "I'll take the wall, you follow those," pointing to the Dairneags that had escaped into the city.

"Brax—"

"I will not have another Adriel!" Brax erupted. His eyes were ablaze. "This is my city and I—"

"I understand," Gorn said, placing a hand on his shoulder. "As it is ordered, so it is done." He turned and summoned ten men, and then raced down the nearest stairwell.

Brax looked to the towers and noticed Benigan atop one, readying one of the massive crossbows, and Boran in the other doing the same. "They will be ready," he reassured himself. "They *must* be ready."

And with that he hoisted his mighty Vinfae and pushed through his men. When he finally neared the fray, the going became tougher, more confined. The din of battle just ahead was violent and loud.

"To me!" he yelled to those closest. "We make for the ladders!"

Just over the heads of those in front of him, he could see the mighty Dairne-Reih lunging and sweeping with massive arms. The crush was strong, and Brax fought just to keep himself from being pinned against the wall. Still he moved forward, inching along as more men followed behind him.

He could hear the grunts of those up ahead, taking the brunt of the attack, parrying with sword and shield, and the inevitable cry of a man meeting his end. A warrior was suddenly flung up and over the wall into the masses below.

Brax's gaze narrowed.

He was very close now. Only three more men lay between him and his enemy as he stealthily moved along the wall. He pressed on and was soon in the front. The nearest monster had not even seen him.

Brax slipped behind the beast, to encounter another just ahead.

But his deadly Vinfae went straight to work. Summoning up a deep roar clothed in the Tongues of the Dibor, Brax let out a violent phrase and then swung his sword in a wide arc around him.

Both the Dairneags in front and behind tensed in agony, the blade severing deep into the back of one and the chest of the other. As they fell, Brax continued the momentum of the swing and then lunged forward, driving his blade into a third just beyond.

"Forward!" Brax bellowed, his clothing laden with the blood of his enemies. He pressed forward with a host of energized warriors behind him.

From up above the four Dylaithloks dove dangerously fast, plunging toward the ramparts, mouths and talons agape. A few archers managed to let off their missiles, but few found their mark. The birds were simply too fast. Brax paused as he watched all four Dylaithlok in succession rip men off the wall just ahead of his position. Their beaks snapped for limbs, their claws managing two men at a time. And as fast as they had come, they were gone, soaring back up into the heights, having claimed their spoils.

Brax growled and bared his teeth.

Do not lose focus, he told himself. *Focus!*

He surged ahead. His fourth victim was a muscular demon, a ring of horns around each wrist and neck, all protruding outward. The beast swung once, and then twice. Brax ducked and then used the momentum of the third attack to drive the monster's own arm into its side, the horns snagging its ribcage. It shrieked and tried to pull its arm away, only causing more damage to the wound. The demon spun, desperately trying to dislodge its hand. But Brax drove his Vinfae downward, deep into the monster's flank.

Now two men had taken up position to his right and left, and together, three abreast, the charge surged forward. Their next foes betrayed their sense of fear and soon met their own fate at the point of the sword.

The onrushing Dairne-Reih had slowed and thought better of their attack. Brax and his men pushed them past the first ladder, dispatched any near the top of the structure, and shoved it away from the wall. Before long, Brax had cut down enough Dairne-Reih to where he could see his men battling on the other flank.

He swung high and low, feinting to draw a clumsy thrust from a demon, and then took advantage of the opening to execute the beast. Before long, he clasped forearms with the warriors further down the wall, and together they surged forward, eager to meet the remaining two ladders.

• • •

High above, Boran had readied his crossbow, the men working quickly at his orders. The massive wooden weapon had been hoisted from far below and pulled over the side, fixed to the turret using clamps, the hewn bow beam bolted onto the main body. The men furiously winched the beam's tips together to affix the braided cord, and then slowly released the winch just as Luik had cautioned them: if it was not done properly, the bow could cut a man in two.

Finally, the bow cord was ratcheted back into place and one of the thick dyra-tipped bolts was set into its cradle. The dwarves had given Luik a chest of the prized metal when he had first returned from Ot to Mt. Dakka. Not only was there enough dyra to make a number of bolts for the crossbows, he had ordered the rest to be used for arrows for the most skilled archers, including Anorra.

Boran bent over and looked along the bolt, aiming into the night sky by pivoting the heavy platform ever so slightly. He stood up and then looked far across the open air to his brother in the opposite tower. Benigan met his gaze and raised his hand. He, too, was ready.

And the Dylaithlok did not disappoint. As if summoned by the brothers' own wishes, a series of violent screeches came from the sky. The four had returned.

"There!" one of Boran's men pointed quickly.

Boran saw it: a grim winged shadow emerging just over the center of the city, racing toward the wall…

…it was closer to him than to Benigan.

It was his shot.

He bent low and aimed the bolt. If he missed, it meant striking the city below. And if it was ill-timed, it meant hurtling the dead bird into the men on the wall, assuming of course, that he killed it.

"Steady," he coached himself. "Stea—dy."

He watched as the demon bird sailed swiftly over the rooftops. It was coming in low.

"We're too high," one of the other men stated.

But Boran ignored him. He continued to sight in along the shaft and lead his target just a few degrees ahead.

"*Stea—dy.*"

Squeeze, don't pull, he reminded himself. And then—

Shoooooounk!

The crossbow lurched forward, and the bolt was away. Boran popped his head up, and the others looked on. The bolt raced through the air, aimed dead on. The Dylaithlok flew onward, unsuspecting.

With a jarring blow, the bolt ripped directly through the massive bird's neck. Flight arrested, the demonized predator tumbled in midair and careened for the wall.

Boran held his breath; the heap of feathered flesh slammed into the base of the wall just below the ramparts, and slumped harmlessly to the city street below.

The men around him let up a whoop of victory and slapped him on the back. He was grateful for their encouragement but knew the hunt was far from over. All the cheering ceased when more screeching came.

Boran and the others looked up, but too late to do anything. A Dylaithlok had closed on their position and perched precariously on the crossbow. It lowered its head and let out a deafening screech. Spittle and bits of human flesh littered the men. The warriors clasped their hands over their ears and fell to their knees.

One brave soul, a swordsman from Bensotha, drew his weapon and charged the foul creature. The Dylaithlok ceased its hideous whine and tracked the man as he flanked it. With the speed of a serpent, the creature lunged and caught the man's arm. The next image was a blur, the bird shaking the warrior and then wresting the man of his appendage, the better part of his body flung over the side. The Dylaithlok chomped on the limb twice and then swallowed it whole.

But that was the last thing it ever did.

Boran looked up just as a plume of blood burst into the air, a massive bolt protruding from the bird's chest. The beast teetered on its perch and then pitched over backward, plummeting to the ground far below.

Boran stood up slowly and then peered across to the opposite tower. Benigan stood waving his arm and, as far as Boran could tell, bearing a wide grin.

"You crazy fool," Boran said with a chuckle. The feat had saved their lives, but was one of the most foolish, yet most intrepid deeds imaginable. Boran wondered if he would have been capable of the same. "You crazy fool," he repeated.

Chapter Seven

MASSACRE IN THE MOUNTAINS

Thad and Thero looked to one another and then back again to the enemy horde that had surrounded them from above. The archers of Ligeon had dropped their bows and raised their hands in defeat, sword points now edging them ever closer to the cliffs that circled the clearing. The remaining warband below stood motionless clutching their weapons; the two brothers noticed the fear in them, yet the archers above were unwavering, uncannily calm although their deaths were imminent. Outnumbered and tactically bested, everyone waited for the enemy to make the first move, as they had none of their own.

A man screamed out.

Thad looked to see a figure streaking through the air and then landing in the rocky clearing not five paces beside him.

Thud!

The murdered man wore the amour of Ligeon, his body broken.

"O Most High, save them!" Thero beckoned skyward.

But there was no response.

It happened all too quickly for those watching. Despite the warband's sudden pleading with the enemy above, waving their hands and calling up for mercy, the *taken* and the demons alike paid not the slightest attention. They moved forward as one, poking and prodding with their horns and weapon points like herding swine, heckling the bowmen who themselves remained calm and noble to the last.

The archers had no choice but to be impaled or to jump over the cliff. A few managed to leap down to rocky outcroppings and ledges that, if not stopping their fall altogether, lessened their impact below.

However the majority fell to their deaths, but not without their brothers' valiant attempt to aid them.

The warband below ran to the cliff faces with their arms outstretched. It was feeble at best. But they could not endure such horror with indifference; they had to do something. They tried to catch their brothers, or at least break their falls with their own bodies.

One man looked upward just as an archer fell on top of his head. The impact shattered the warrior's neck and crumpled him to the ground in a heap. The archer survived the fall but broke both legs. Another man indeed caught his counterpart, but broke his arms and back in the process. And yet others missed altogether, arriving a breath too late to a pile of flesh and armor that had moments before been a kinsman.

The enemy above bathed in glory over the scene with clattering weapons and beating their chests. Whoops came from those overhead while tears streamed from those below.

When the deed was done, Thad and Thero rallied their men, wounded and whole, and charged to the far end of the clearing. They retreated through a narrow exit in the rock that emptied out into a trail leading further east. But their escape was quickly followed as the enemy filed in behind them. Those in the rear were hacked to the ground; men carrying one another were swiftly relieved of their duty and ability.

The warband continued to run, Thad and Thero all the while looking for any advantage offered them. The trail continued to descend, and the Great Forest grew closer with the fading daylight. But the way was rocky, and they knew their wounded would not last long.

Smoke from another fire rose just ahead, heralding yet another Sif Gate, and most likely more resistance. Thad looked to his brother.

"Whatever is in the next clearing, we run through it. We *must* make it to Grandath."

"Aye, but that's where the enemy is headed."

"But the forest will hide those who are sly enough. This mountain peak is far from my liking. We cannot stop."

"Agreed," Thero replied.

As the trail curved around to the right, the warband flooded into a new clearing like waters through a broken dam. The three Dairneags and small host of *taken* that awaited were instantly overwhelmed. Thad was the first into the clearing. He ran up behind the largest of the Dairneags and drove his Vinfae into the monster's flank, cutting a wide wound as he ran past with his blade.

Thero went to the other side where a fold of four *taken* stood talking amongst themselves. They had hardly the time to look up and notice the surge of onrushing men before Thero's blade swept low and amputated legs from two men, and wounded another two assailants with quick thrusts to their thighs. Even in his frenzied state, Thero did not have the heart to kill them, hoping beyond hope that sometime in the future they would yield once again to the power of the Most High. He knew it was pointless to wish for such a thing, but he would have betrayed his scruples to do otherwise.

The warband dispensed with the remaining Dairne-Reih with minimal resistance, skirted the large Sif Gate and fire pit, and proceeded out the far end of the clearing. They continued on, the enemy trailing on their heels, before the path took a steep dive toward a stream below. Past the stream they could see the edge of the Great Forest now getting very close. And then a sight they would not soon forget.

Why they had not noticed the raging fire earlier was beyond them, but it certainly explained why the sky was growing dim. The sinking sun was diminished in force not from its descent, as they had thought—for indeed a fair amount of daylight remained—but from an ever-expanding sheet of black smoke that blotted out its presence. And feeding that smoke was a fire that stretched wide along the forest's edge, eating its way into the heart of Dionia.

"Great God of Athera!" Thero exclaimed, slowing slightly in shock.

"We cannot stop, brother," Thad said as he pushed Thero forward. "We must make it to what remains of the wood."

But even as he said it, he noticed the mass gathering of Dairne-Reih and *taken* that ushered the fire inward. The enemy remained a good distance from the heat, but seemed to scour the charred wreckage with great intent, following the wake of its destruction with care. And so many of them!

"There must be ten legions of them," Thero uttered as he ran down the decline.

It was then that their current course of action seemed to make no sense whatsoever; with enemy behind and enemy before, their fate was sealed. There are certain moments in confrontation when things seem to go one's way, even that thoughts are ordered with great light and inspiration; there are other moments, however, when things seem to happen much too quickly, where a loss of control outruns reason. This was such a time.

They bounded down the slope and crossed the stream. The enemy closed behind them. As they neared what was previously the forest edge they noticed the permeating scent of the smoke and the blackened rubble beneath their feet. Burnt trees stood like black ghosts, their limbs fragile and lifeless; charred timber was strewn about everywhere; and rocks sat scorched from the intense heat, still hot to the touch.

Thad looked around quickly. "There," he said, pointing to a section of the forest that was particularly thick. The fire was having a difficult time catching there and preferred the drier, more spacious routes. The Dairne-Reih seemed less interested in that area, completely unaware of the small warband that was charging behind them presently. "If we punch a hole through there, we'll have a chance of making it deeper into Grandath."

Thero glanced at him in mid stride. "And then what? The wood is full of fire and smoke. We'll die by the flames!"

"Or die by the sword. Which would you like?"

"I'll take my chances with trying to find Ot again."

Thad nodded in agreement and pushed forward, the warband following in the rear. But it wasn't long before the enemy trailing behind alerted the enemy up ahead. Moments later a few Dairneags began closing in on the men from the flanks.

Thad yelled over his shoulder, "Fight them if you must, but make for the break in the fire at all costs!"

The warband ran more quickly now, picking through the burned forest matter and leaping over fallen trees. One demon drew near and swung at a cluster of running men. One unfortunate soldier could not avoid the Dairneag and took the blow square in his chest; the force picked him off his feet and knocked him backwards to the ground. The beast pummeled him with its clawed foot.

Still the men raced forward, fixed on the small patch of growth ahead.

They were very close now. Despite one or two incidents, they ran practically unnoticed between the Dairne-Reih, whose numbers increased as they neared the flames. The demons were so fixed on eyeing the devastation, almost as if they were looking for something, that they completely failed to notice the trespassers.

The men could feel the heat increasing; the fire was much larger than they had first reckoned. And it had a strange characteristic about it, one that made it seem hungry, unsatisfied unless it devoured its prize. It was ravenous.

Thero realized it first...

...this fire was *alive*.

"Almost there!" Thad yelled.

"This is really going to hurt, isn't it, brother?" Thero asked, now quite out of breath and tired from running. The forest edge was just ahead about ten paces.

"Hurt is a relative term, Thero. Just take a deep breath."

"No problem there."

"Good. It's probably your last."

It was then that Thad gazed into the fire and the woods and thought he saw something extremely out of the ordinary...

...he thought he saw the flames *grin* at him. He realized that maybe this was not the best plan after all.

Chapter Eight

ROUTED TO THE WEST

The shaking of the ground beneath Anondo's back had not been from the spiked demon closing upon him, but from a massive Hewgog[4] even farther off, the likes of which no man had ever seen. In the moments just before the would-be deathblow, the Hewgog closed on Anondo's position, bloodthirsty for the King he was commanded to vanquish. The spiked demon was poised to strike when suddenly a massive arm threw him aside like a scythe discarding a head of wheat. The Dairneag flew to one side, colliding in a tumult of men and beasts, and there, left towering over Anondo, was a most horrific terror.

Standing nearly six men tall, the Hewgog were a disturbing race of Dairneag who had been bred with select animals and even the *taken*, a perverted invention of Morgui himself. Grossly obese yet immeasurably strong, their skin was pockmarked and warty, a sort of dim blue hue, and their shoulders were hunched over with long arms that could touch the ground. Their hands and feet were very much like that of a man's, save that they were proportionally far too large for their body. Both eyes and nose were bulbous and constantly leaked yellow mucus over a ghastly, foul

---

[4] **Hewgog** (*HUE-gawg*): *noun; First Dionian; a giant mutant Dairneag; a demon bred with the* taken *and various animals for size and immense power.*

mouth of missing teeth. A shabby tunic covered the ogre's midsection, and a metal collar bound its neck. Apart from being unpleasant creatures in appearance, Hewgogs were given over to extreme fits of rage that extended well beyond their own reasoning, and were therefore rather difficult to control after their orders were completed.

Anondo gazed up and forgot all about his injuries.

Move!

He rolled to the side just as a hammer-fisted blow shook the ground where he lay. The Hewgog delivered another blow, and he rolled away again. Now infuriated, the giant strode forward and stomped down; still Anondo evaded the crushing step and then gained his feet. He ran between the Hewgog's legs and turned to face the monster's backside, hoping to buy some time.

"Think, Anondo!" he cried aloud, feverishly taking stock of his surroundings. One advantage of the beast's presence was the complete lack of other Dairneags in the direct vicinity; the Hewgog's completely unpredictable behavior deterred not only men, but also their lesser brothers.

The Hewgog turned and faced Anondo. His time to think was up. All Anondo's men were otherwise occupied with their own melees. He had to do this himself.

The ogre moved forward again, this time drawing a hand to its opposite shoulder and delivering a backhanded sweep of its arm. Anondo fell to the ground prostrate as the dangerous arc brushed over his back, rolling him over a number of times. But he remained unscathed.

The monster growled in its throat and then let out a gurgled yelp of frustration. It shook its head and then reached out an open hand to grab him. Anondo gained his feet once more and avoided the Hewgog's clutches with a quick sidestep. But the maddened creature responded by making a fist and knocking Anondo to the ground. The same fist rose high into the air and descended.

In that flash of an instant, Anondo knew he was finished. He closed his eyes.

Then he heard a strange, bloodcurdling howl that made the hairs on the back of his neck stand up.

Everything around him stopped. The battle clash quickly faded, and all was still.

Anondo opened his eyes to see the Hewgog's fist an arm's length above his body, hovering in mid-air. But more fascinating was the look of pure fear that consumed the monster's odious face. The once menacing and dour expression was all at once turned to a strange, panic-stricken look of great concern.

The Hewgog stood erect and looked around. Anondo propped himself up, surprised at his good fortune, but equally aware of another unknown terror, one that made even his current adversary retreat.

Just then the howl came again, but this time much closer.

Anondo noticed the Dairne-Reih lowering their arms and looking to one another, disengaging from their opponents. The men of Ligeon and Tontha took this as a divine turning point and wasted no time in exploiting the opportunity.

But it was far from divine.

The few warriors that remained turned on their stunned enemies with swift retribution, many slaying their foes right where they stood. The men began shouting as they hacked the limbs from the fearful Dairneags, the monsters stumbling backwards in unrest. A few of the beasts even began fleeing as if looking for a place to hide. Anondo noticed their panic-stricken eyes darting from place to place. Even the Hewgog towering above him looked this way and that, backing away from him.

The next time Anondo heard it, the howl had multiplied tenfold, and then twice as much again, to the point that the air was filled with a constant rant of noise. It was as deafening as it was disorienting, and soon the men were drawn away from their attack, their foes outrunning them. The Hewgog turned and headed toward the mountain pass, looking to climb up the nearest cliff as a child might amble up a small hill. The Dairne-Reih were in full retreat, pushing past one another, completely oblivious of the warband.

In the commotion, Anondo looked for his standard. Fortunately the flag of Ligeon remained standing, despite their overwhelming losses. He ran to where a large band of warriors still defended the colors of his realm and shouted to his herald.

"Blow the horn! Summon the warband back!"

Anondo addressed one of his Captains, yelling above the howling. "Gather whatever horses remain among us. The mountain pass to Mt. Dakka is blocked and surely flowing with enemy reinforcements. If we are to ever see her ramparts and our people again, we must make for Narin at once."

"But King, we have them—"

"No contest, Fadlemir. Morgui sets upon us with an evil I do not know. He means to give chase. Now go!"

Anondo then turned to fetch a horse; those that remained alive had scattered and were running in circles. As Fadlemir and the other worked to call them back, the animals darted this way and that, greatly shaken by the ominous noise that permeated the air. They whinnied and shied away from their Lords, resisting capture.

Anondo managed to grab the reins of one passing by, calmed the creature as best he could, and then swung into the saddle. The stallion shivered incessantly and became increasingly restless on his feet, the howling growing by the moment.

"Mount your rides!" Anondo shouted.

The men were not mounting fast enough. He kicked his horse and rode to one side, trying to corral an overly-frightened brood of mares. A number of men raised their hands trying to prevent their escape. With Anondo's help they were able to secure a good number of seats for the men, but many of the animals shot past their pleadings and deserted the scene.

"We must leave now, Captain!" Anondo finally shouted to Fadlemir, satisfied that all his men had a mount, or at least shared one. He was utterly shocked to see how many under his command had actually fallen. With the Dairne-Reih cleared out, and with the improved observation from his height on horseback, the toll taken on his kinsmen was paralyzing: not more than five ranks of his original ten remained, a loss of over five hundred men.

"To Narin!" shouted Fadlemir.

"Hey'a!" Anondo cried, kicking his horse hard. The animal bolted forward and was away.

• • •

The mass of cavalry ebbed and flowed like a flock of birds, racing across the valleys of eastern Ligeon with marvelous speed. Moved by the sheer desire to flee, the horses were relentless in their haste, rising over the crests of gentle hills with breakneck speed, only to descend the other side with even greater momentum. They leapt across streams and weaved effortlessly through glades of trees, one moment striding through tall grass, the next ripping through glens adorned with thick ferns.

The howling faded, and then eventually stopped altogether. For a while Anondo and the rest of his warband thought the chase had been abandoned.

But the horses knew better. Despite their riders' pleas to slow, the horses remained vigilant, pushing themselves relentlessly. Sweat foamed on their flanks, and their breathing was labored.

Anondo knew it took five days to reach Narin from where they were; yet at this rate they would make it in three. But there was no possible way the horses could maintain such a demanding pace; they would be dead from exhaustion by nightfall.

"We must make them slow," Anondo eventually said to Fadlemir riding beside him. "They cannot endure this forever."

"Try making them," replied the Captain. Fadlemir had long been in the service of the Kings of Dionia. Originally from Trennesol, he had spent the last several summers in Casterness, serving King Ragnar in Adriel and tending to his ships. Like most of the sailors of the East, he was lean, yet incredibly strong, a toughness that came from long voyages at sea. His close-cropped black hair and dark-set eyes gave him an air of great authority, and he had proved his skill at arms throughout the battle for Adriel. Fadlemir was solid, faithful to the end, and true as the rising sun.

"Then they know we are still hunted." Anondo paused. "For their innate perception I am grateful. We must face our foe and be done with this."

"What are your orders?"

Anondo rode the undulating animal beneath him in earnest, his mind racing nearly as fast. It would have helped to know what was hunting them, its characteristics, and the speed at which it pursued. He knew it was fearsome enough to deter its own kin, and it had to be fast; the lengths to which the Dairne-Reih went to avoid it in the open were swift and unmistakable.

He then began thinking about the realm they traveled through: Ligeon, home to his family for generations. There had to be some asset he could use to their advantage. But what?

Suddenly he had it.

"I have an idea. But it's a long shot."

Fadlemir eyed him suspiciously. "If we don't do something soon, we'll be walking the rest of the way to Narin."

"Agreed. But it requires the horses to keep on longer than I'd prefer. There is a tributary of the Hefkiln River, the Goban, which flows from the north about two days' ride from here. But that's at a moderate pace at best. At this rate, I shan't think we'd arrive later than sun-down."

"That is a great deal to demand of our mounts," Fadlemir admitted.

"As I said, it's a long shot."

"Why the river?"

"There is a large dam which serves a mill, but also makes a shallow ford, the only one in either direction for many lengths."

"If we can cross to the other side," Fadlemir jumped in, "we can loose the waters and cut off our enemy."

"Or at least gain some precious time."

"It is risky, my liege. Risky. But plausible."

"Good, then," Anondo resolved, urging his horse even faster. "We make for Holden's Mill by nightfall!"

• • •

The horses were near exhaustion by the time the sun touched the horizon to their backs. Blood was caked around their nostrils, and their hoofs bled from the extended trauma. Yet it did not take much to prod them onward even after so many hours of riding; they knew that their enemy was close behind, and they'd rather perish than live knowing they'd let their masters down.

Anondo was about to call off the whole idea when suddenly he recognized where they were.

"The Goban is just ahead!" he declared urgently.

The path entered a small wood, meandering through clumps of pines and oaks, before emerging onto a generous riverbank that overlooked an even wider river. The shadows stretched long over the waters; but despite the fading light, Anondo was pleased to see the large dam to his right, five times the height of a man. It was just as he had remembered, though definitely aged. There on the far shore was the old mill, wheels still turning gently in the upper channels. The dam itself was constructed using layers of massive timbers bound together and filled with a combination of dried clay, lime, and sand. But the change in seasons had taken its toll; the structure showed definite signs of fatigue.

"Across with you!" Anondo allowed his men to pass by as he turned and rode up to the wall. All throughout, the King could see small fractures in both wood and bond that inevitably had grown large enough for water to seep through. It was just as he had hoped; for indeed he had not been entirely sure how he'd bring down such a monstrous creation, one designed to last for generations by its makers. "Fadlemir, to me," Anondo called to his Captain. The man drew near, and Anondo spoke, eyes examining the wall. "A dam does not need to be brought down in whole," he uttered.

"But only in part," Fadlemir finished. "Create a small hole, and the water behind will do the rest."

"I need two tens of men and any polearms you can find," Anondo turned to his Captain. Fadlemir set to his task while Anondo dismounted and inspected the dam even closer. He let his fingers search the trickling waters until he found a large enough gap and then turned to the men coming toward him.

"Here," he gestured. "Hand me a spear."

A warrior passed him a sturdy shaft and the King inserted it into the largest opening he could find, leaving it protruding from the wall on its own. He then looked back. About half the men had successfully forded the river to the other side.

"Another!" Anondo thrust out his hand.

He used the spear point to pick away at the hairline crack. He jammed it into the hole he'd created, but it didn't hold. Frustrated, he dug more until the stave remained in place. Satisfied the effort was worthwhile, he ordered the other men to follow his lead. They quickly set about gouging holes in the most promising leaks and then jarring the dam with the polearms.

As more of the men forded the riverbed, Anondo prepared to unburden the dam.

"When the men are across, pull down on the shafts like so." The King demonstrated with the first pole he had set, grabbing it with both hands and hoisting himself up on its end so it levered the timbers in front of him. The result was a muffled groan of the ancient timbers, followed by a crack and a sudden increase in the trickle. It was hardly the dramatic effect Anondo had hoped for, but then again it was only the first spear, and this a mightily imposing dam.

He looked over his shoulder once more.

There remained but another five tens of men yet to cross.

"*Almost*," Anondo said to Fadlemir. "Men, make you ready."

And then came the howls.

Anondo watched Fadlemir's face drain of its color. The other men turned to regard their King. The horses crossing the ford stopped, ears perked.

No one moved.

The methodic sound of flowing water was interrupted by the long, drawn-out howls of their pursuers.

A horse whinnied and took off for the far bank, its weary rider tumbling off its back and splashing into the water. Startled, a good many of the other horses darted for the shore and tore up the bank into the waiting woods. The men tried to control their steeds, to no avail. Men were knocked off, jostled left and right, and tripped up in an attempt to help one another. Those safely on the opposite bank shouted to one another trying to bring order. Within moments the scene in the riverbed was one of total chaos.

"Get out of here!" Anondo screamed, waving his hands. Time was suddenly a precious commodity, one they couldn't afford to waste.

Fadlemir raised his arms at one riderless stallion and coaxed him toward the far bank. When the beast did not heed him, Fadlemir splashed water at it. "Get! Get!" The horse spun around and charged up the hill.

When the last of the men were up the bank, Anondo turned to those standing with him and indicated the dam. "Now!"

The men grabbed the spear shafts and worked them violently. Pushing, pulling, prodding—the warriors stood against the wall trying desperately to work the timbers loose. They found themselves working in twilight, stars slowly emerging from their late afternoon courses. It hadn't yet dawned on any of the warriors what might happen should the dam burst with them in front of it; they all just assumed they'd get it started and then run away.

The structure creaked and groaned.

"Put your backs into it, men!" ordered Fadlemir. While a certain amount of success was achieved, increasing the water flow through the cracks, their efforts seemed far from producing the desired effect.

"Harder!" urged Anondo.

Just then another howl went up as before. Much nearer.

"They're coming," Anondo said.

"Who is?" asked one of the warriors.

"Shut up and work!" Fadlemir ordered him.

Anondo pried with all his might, forcing his weakened and battle-beaten body to work beyond its means. But in the end their efforts were unproductive, save for a few more trickles developing.

"It is no use," said Anondo at last.

More howls joined the first, growing louder by the moment. The men glanced to the eastern sky.

"You are giving up, my King?" Fadlemir inquired, still working a polearm.

"It is a faulty idea," the King admitted.

"Nay!" came a voice from the far bank. Anondo and the others turned to see a large retinue of their men wading into the waters with polearms. "It is a sound idea, just undermanned," called one of Anondo's horse herders named Colvin.

"Make room, make room!" ordered Fadlemir. The new workers lined up against the dam on either side of Anondo's position and proceeded to jam their weapons into the wall.

Now the howling came from the wooded glades the warband had passed through just before the river.

"Heave!" shouted Fadlemir.

"As one," cried Anondo. "*Heave!*" The shafts strained against the massive timbers, and then...

Pop!

The loud burst echoed down the riverbed.

"It's working!" exclaimed one of the men.

"Again," Anondo ordered, "*heave!*" The throng of brothers worked their polearms as one, a single unit of brute force against the massive wall.

Pop-craaaack!

This time the damage was evident: a small fissure about the breadth of a man's hand opened near the middle of the dam. Water shot out so forcefully it knocked three men off their feet.

"*One more time!*" Anondo hollered. He knew they had to make this one count. The dam creaked even as the men readied for the final jounce.

Anondo grasped two spears and was about to give the command when he heard a low growl from behind him.

He held his breath and slowly looked over his shoulder.

There, standing in the middle of the river, was a single massive *hound*, about four times the size of a normal dog. Its snarling mouth was dripping with foam, its fur matted with sweat. And with one look in the creature's demonic red eyes, Anondo knew what had been chasing them: the feared KiJinNard Hounds. *Hounds of the dead.*

"*Bring it down!*" Anondo cried. He grasped two spears and pulled with all his might, so hard in fact, that the shaft in his right hand split in two. "*Pull!*" The timbers groaned ominously…

…and at last, the dam began to break apart.

The fissure split wide and spewed debris everywhere. Half the men were washed downstream in a heap. Anondo stood aside and watched helplessly as one of the men was tossed about and collided with the *hound's* legs. The beast had been watching; it opened its jaws and closed them around the man's torso, nearly splitting his body in two. The warrior screamed out in terror. But his cry was cut short, never to be heard again.

"To the forest!" Anondo commanded.

He drew his Vinfae, ducked under the focused torrent of water, and then charged for the wood, his men following behind him. The *hound* watched this curiously.

Anondo stopped on the bank and let his men pass by, and then he turned to look downstream where those caught in the current now gained their feet. Likewise, the *hound* followed the King's gaze and spotted the warriors splashing through the shallows.

"Get up! Get to the wood!" he waved his arm, looking from beast to warriors in a frantic rhythm. "Move!" But the floundering men must have proven to be more appealing prey than Anondo's men upriver, for in a moment the *hound* turned and bounded toward the men, jaws gaping.

Anondo made to cry out but noticed a new presence in the flooding river. There on the bank was a host of glowing red eyes peering across at him. And in the darkness he could hear growling. He instinctively counted the sets of eyes, but more pairs filled in from behind, making it impossible to number. It was an entire pack.

He felt a hand grab his arm.

"My King! Make haste!" Fadlemir yelled, yanking him up the far bank.

Anondo looked despondently downstream; the men were gone and the *hound* thrashed in the blood-red waters. He glanced up at Fadlemir and then noticed his ranks of men and horses filling the wood beyond, all of them ready with swords drawn and faces like flint.

From somewhere among the *hounds* amassing behind him, Anondo heard a deep, dark groan from the dam. The *hounds* noticed it, too, their eyes shifting from Anondo to the structure and back again.

"The dam is about to give way," Fadlemir uttered quietly, as if the sound of his words would somehow prevent the fortunate event from happening.

The *hounds* knew it, too.

"They're going to cross," Anondo stated flatly.

As if they heard him, the entire pack leapt from the riverbank and plunged into the deepening water.

Anondo looked to the dam, hand squeezing his sword handle. "It didn't work."

Chapter Nine

KIRSTELL'S REFUGE

Luik ran back to help Kinfen load more men in the lift while Fyfler and Quoin spread the word down the line: "When they reach for their arrows, charge!" Thunder clapped overhead and the sky lit up as broad daylight. Luik glanced west and caught a glimpse of the funnel cloud spinning ever closer.

"Don't worry, my Lord," Kinfen said as he sent the lift on its way, "we'll make it."

Luik appreciated his friend's optimism, but between the storm closing in and the enemy waiting to strike, their situation was beyond hope.

The advancing *taken* had passed out the bows and focused their attention on the receding numbers of the warband. Luik felt a sickening knot form in his stomach. He looked up to the headland above. Faces looked down upon them, all shouting at them and urging them to go faster. Fia's small face stood out among the others, her small voice of encouragement lost in the tumult.

Luik heard Cage's voice give the command, *"Varos!"*

Luik spun to watch his men charge into the waiting line of the *taken*, their adversaries' hands reaching back for their arrows. The warband closed the distance across the slick rock. Kinfen left his position at the lift and ran after his brothers, sword high. Luik did the same.

The *taken* nocked their shafts.

The Dibor charged, bounding forward.

Eyes squinted.

Legs pumped.

Arrowheads glinted.

Swords gleamed.

And the distance lessened.

Then a strange sight: feathered shafts suddenly appeared in the heads and shoulders of the enemy, raining down from somewhere above. The arrows protruded like quills, routed deep into the unprotected flesh of the *taken*. The sharp sound of bones splitting went up everywhere; air escaped through open mouths and chests filled with breath.

A few of the *taken* had managed to draw back their bowstrings, haphazardly sending their arrows into the onrushing warriors. Five of Dionia's men tumbled forward in midstride. Three were struck in their extremities, while two others were driven through the face and heart. The rest of the warband fell upon the wounded archers and ended their plight.

It was over in a matter of moments.

Wherever the defense had come from, it made short work of the *taken*, and whoever among them remained alive was swiftly finished off with the sword. Luik surveyed the scene, and then slowly turned in wonder and gazed up the cliff face—past the cluster of boulders, up past the rocky outcroppings—and then fixed his eyes on a spectacle he had never seen before.

There along the cliff top, standing as a noble race of ancient guardians, were warriors dressed in robes of red and purple with armor of gold. They held a longbow in one hand and an elliptical golden shield on the same forearm. Their gleaming open-faced helmets were mounted with wings, looking as if they would fly away at any moment, while a single stem covered the nose.

"Who in Athera's great name are they?" Cage muttered. The rain beat on his head, wind whipping his hair.

Luik looked to the storm in the west. "Come, there is no time. To the headland!" Luik and the other Dibor gathered the remaining men and loaded a group in the lift. With so many hands at work above, the wooden carriage flew up the cliff-side, returning only moments later for the next load. Six trips were made before Luik and a handful of others stood alone on the rocky beach.

The funnel cloud was only a short distance offshore. The ominous black snake twisted wildly and sucked water up from the surface of the sea only to spew it back out again somewhere far above. The raging winds increased, and soon no one could hear above the roar but for a shout in the ear.

Luik looked up as the lift returned; he saw Kinfen and the others yelling from above but their voices were drowned out in the storm. He looked back at the funnel.

"My liege, it's time to go!" Fyfler cupped a hand to the King's ear.

Luik glanced around and made certain they were the last ones on the rocks. He nodded and stepped into the lift. Cage, Rab, Fyfler, Quoin and the rest jumped on board and then gave a wave skyward. The wooden crate lurched and shot up. As the group soared over the shore, they surveyed the bodies of their brothers and the *taken*; it was a gory scene Luik wished never to remember.

The lift swayed in the driving winds, braided cords groaning under the stress. Suddenly the lift slammed with a shudder against the rock wall. The Dibor fell to the floor and reached for the railing. But Rab was not so fortunate. He flipped over the beam, flying free of the lift's protection.

There, in midair, time stood still.

He looked down to the mass of rocks and arrow-riddled bodies below.

His body took speed…

"*Hey'a!*"

A hand grabbed his wrist and he jerked to a halt. Rab swung freely, legs dangling over the height. He looked up.

It was Luik.

Rab smiled knowingly; they both had lost track of how many times they had saved one another, and this only furthered the score. Luik smiled back and then hauled him up with the others. The lift then continued its rapid ascent.

Luik heard shouting.

"*Faster! Faster!*"

It was Kinfen driving the men relentlessly from above. The lift was nearing the headland. The pulleys squealed as the ropes whistled through their blocks.

From this height Luik also noticed the speed of the encroaching storm; it was not only deadly, but dangerously swift.

"It's driven by Morgui himself," Fyfler shouted.

"Nay," Luik disagreed, "I think it is Creation's making."

Fyfler turned to him, curious.

Just then the lift jounced into the blocks above and the ride came to a sudden halt. Luik stepped out and onto the path, now a muddy rut. He looked about and saw the faces of his warband, each clinging to the ropes. And there, littered throughout the trees standing along the cliff's edge, the mysterious robed bowmen.

Everyone was looking at Luik. The rain and wind tore through the woods, leaves and branches flying everywhere. *What a strange scene*, Luik thought.

Fia walked forward and took his hand.

We must move, her eyes implied.

"To the Central Hall!" Luik raised Fia to his back, and then strode down the pathway and took off running. It had been nearly three summers since he had last seen Kirtsell, but his feet took to the trail as if he had never left. Fia clung tightly, arms wrapped around his neck, as Luik emerged from the wood and into the large field that he'd often trained in, bounding over rocks and following the sweeping curves of the shallow hills.

Luik cast a quick glance behind him; his men followed, the new bowmen farthest back. Eyes returning to the trail, he looked skyward. Luik had hardly noticed how black the sky had become. Suddenly the field around him lit up as if in broad daylight.

Boooom!

A shaft of razor-edged light careened down from the storm and struck a patch of forest in front of them. The men faltered. Luik turned around.

"Press on!" he waved. "*Press on!*"

They looked past him in dread as flames burst from the wooded canopy beyond.

"We're not going in there, are we?" Fia yelled in his ear.

"Aye, Fia. But the flames will not last."

Luik moved more hesitantly, now trotting down the path. But his view of the nearing funnel sent him running once again. He watched as the wind whipped up the flames in the treetops. They twisted wildly, but with nothing dry to burn, the orange glow soon died, never to reappear.

Luik could see the path enter the woods up ahead. The brush to the sides grew thicker as they neared. Moments later they were bounding along a dark trail, weaving between tree trunks on a well-worn track. He knew every branch here, every fold and turn. All was exactly as he had last seen it. Even in such a moment of crisis, this unchanging wood was a place of great comfort. He had always dreamed of coming back here, yet he had secretly held to the probability that it might never happen, that this place of his boyhood dreams would remain just that—*a dream.*

Kirstell was all he had known for four summers of his life, four summers that had changed him forever. It was here he had become a warrior, consumed by Gorn's teachings; it was here he had made friends more true than any others he would ever know; and it was here he had touched realms of the Most High he had never known existed.

It was also here that he had learned his life was no longer his own.

"Give everything. Endure anything," Gorn had once said while walking with them on this very path. "Your life is not your own, but you must make certain there is something in it worth giving. And then just how much will you endure to see that is indeed given?" Gorn had turned to him. "What will it cost you, Luik son of Lair?"

Luik's feet thumped dully along the beaten trail. Fia's breathing was quick in his ear. She was nervous. The men followed him deeper into the wood.

What will it cost you, Luik?

The mounting winds were tossing leaves and small branches. Debris from the forest floor smattered his wet clothing. The funnel was very near.

"We're almost there!" Luik yelled over his shoulder.

The trail began to widen as it rounded the final few turns. Luik followed the ground with his eyes, convinced at one point he could see footprints that were his own, made there long ago.

The path ebbed slowly around a large oak and then spilled them out into a large square, covered above by a thick canopy of green. Leaves and vines interlaced, all bound by groaning limbs. Great lettings of flowers and greenery swung violently, their sweet fragrance washed out by the tormenting winds.

In the center of the square was the firepit, each rock just as Luik remembered. And remember them he did. How many nights had he sat around that pit with his fellow Boralee? How many times had he studied the rocks as they took on the warm orange glow of the dancing flames?

Luik slowed and then looked to the Great Hall. The massive trees that formed the outline of the structure were as secure as ever. More like trees one would find in Grandath, they grew tightly packed in a perfect rectangle, their girth nearly touching even at the height where the thatched roof had been constructed. Between the trunks, timbers and stone had been used to make walls, as well as the wide steps that lead to the entrance.

"She still stands," Jrio exclaimed.

"Of course she does," Rab punched him in the arm. "Did you suspect otherwise?"

"Come," Luik ordered, "everyone inside."

Fia slipped to the ground and was the first to bound up the steps. Those wounded or too weak to walk were carried in next, followed by the rest of the fighting men.

Cage stopped by Luik and then looked up through the cracks in the foliage and said, "This monster will sift Kirstell like wheat, I fear."

"Unless there is still more to this home of ours than we know of."

When the last of the warband were inside, the mysterious archers filled the square, and one approached Luik, standing amongst the Dibor.

"Hey'a, King Luik, Lord of Dionia." The man's voice was regal and alive, clearly audible above the maelstrom.

"Hey'a—" Luik was suddenly taken aback. *He knew this man.* "Hey'a servant of the Most High," was all Luik could think of. The man was notably older than most, yet still retained a youthful glow about him. Despite the dim light that filtered through the canopy, Luik could tell the man's face was worn and had seen many days in the sun...*and* the darkness. But Luik could not place him.

"The storm is upon us. May I suggest a secret place of hiding within the Great Hall?" Considering the fact that Luik had never actually *been* in Kirstell's Great Hall before—one of the only places on the island that could be said of—he was more than willing to comply.

"Lead the way." Luik gestured with his hand. The bowman strode forward, robe flowing, followed by the Dibor, and then the rest of the mysterious warriors. Up the staircase and into the Great Hall they went, a moment later consumed by darkness.

Chapter Ten

ESCAPE FROM NARIN

The first hound leapt upon Anondo while he was still looking at the breach in the dam. It knocked him to his back with one paw while its jaws spread wide, aiming for his neck. Anondo could not roll free of the beast's weight, but bent his head to one side, avoiding the razor-sharp teeth. Anondo hacked at the *hound* with his Vinfae, knocking it off balance and burying its muzzle in the dirt. A severed limb gave way, and the animal toppled over.

The King rolled to his stomach and on his feet a heartbeat later. He turned and looked on as the rest of the red-eyed *hounds* bounded through the river water, splashing everywhere as they engaged his men.

We will be slain here, he thought. *Slain to a man.* But his thoughts were interrupted by a deafening sound.

Crrrrrrrrrack! Whoooosh!

In the blink of an eye, the dam gave way, and the entire riverbed was consumed by a deluge of white water. One moment the *hounds* were rushing toward Anondo, the next they were swept away by a torrent plunging down from above. The roar of the flood took everyone by surprise, even the remaining *hounds*. They turned around to watch as their brethren disappeared in an instant. It was all the time the warband needed to dispatch the rest and send them either into the raging river or back to Haides itself.

The men gathered around Anondo and looked on. The light continued to fade around them, the night quickly arriving.

"We should be able to make Narin in three days," Fadlemir said.

Anondo did not reply right away. His eyes were busy searching the far shore. Though the strand and the woods beyond seemed empty, his intuition told him otherwise. The waters rushed by them, churning forcefully.

"My liege?" Fadlemir spoke up after a time.

"Aye," Anondo said distantly. "Three days."

"What is it?" Fadlemir asked, hesitating.

Anondo pulled his eyes from the river and looked at his captain, "It is nothing, Fadlemir." He turned to the woods. "Make camp and let the men rest. They deserve it."

As Fadlemir turned to give the orders Anondo glanced back over his shoulder. He searched the woods across the river one more time. He thought he saw something move in the shadows, a glimmer of red. He waited a moment longer, but decided it was only his imagination and rejoined his men.

• • •

When they awoke the next morning, the warband was grateful for the rest, albeit a short one. They retrieved the frightened horses from the wood, and watered them before setting out again, weaving onward through the forest for half the morning before spilling onto a broad plain. The sunlight warmed their bodies, and the horses took to running.

The warriors rode easily, well contented they were not being pursued. In the three days that followed, each man wrestled with the previous days' events. They had gone from a confident defense in Tontha, with a solid plan in place, to retreating. Their numbers were immensely reduced, those that survived just happy to be alive.

Anondo wrestled not only with the fate of his men, but of his brothers, Thad and Thero. He had sent them on what he was now sure was a fool's errand. He scolded himself for being so hasty in wanting to spy out the enemy; had they stayed with him, perhaps the warband could have made their stand at the border. Perhaps everything could have been very different. Perhaps…

Regret plagued him night and day. When the warband made camp on the plain for the night, he looked up at the stars and tried to imagine Dionia before all this, before Morgui had attacked and changed everything. Before Adriel had fallen, before he and the others had been sent to Kirstell, what was it like?

Remember.

He searched the stars above and tried to remember a time when he saw these same beautiful lights, from his home, perhaps, or during Jhestafe-Na when he would travel with all his brothers and sisters down into Bensotha for the feasts. Perhaps after a long day of playing rokla he had lain back in the grass and marveled at the luminous sky.

Remember.

But he couldn't.

The task was too hard. The good memories were too far away. All he saw was a sword, swinging and drawing blood…swinging and drawing blood, the blood of his enemies, and the blood of his brothers. He wondered if he had had any good memories at all. His mind wandered to and fro, but in the end, his extreme fatigue won and he trailed off to sleep.

• • •

When Anondo woke on the third day, the dawn had come all too soon for him and the others. But the thought of reaching Narin, now so near, urged him onward. They mounted the horses and made for his home with haste.

Fadlemir rode alongside the King, and asked, "What would you have us do upon our arrival?"

"If the Great God smiles on us, my father's ships should still be moored in the south of the bay. Their rigging was built to hold fast through any storm, even those of the inusslen. Had I only thought to use them when last we fled north together.

"We'll ride through Narin Haut, cross the Hefkiln, and then make our way along the southern coast. We'll release the horses and gather the tenders. Once all the men are aboard, we'll cast off and make for Tontha's northern shores. Our passage back to Mt. Dakka should be unhindered."

Fadlemir inclined his head and rode on in silence. By midday the Great Hall of Narin came into view, and with it, Anondo's memory of the gruesome scene it held within.

"Perhaps we should gather food from the storehouses of the palace?" Fadlemir suggested.

"Nay, there is nothing for us there," Anondo replied.

"But, sire—"

"Fadlemir, it is not for you to ask again."

"My apologies, my Lord."

The warband entered the upper city through the main gate on a broad lane that eventually wove its way to the lower city below. But they soon turned south onto another wide avenue that arrived at a massive bridge.

As the horse hoofs clopped onto the thick wooden planks of the structure, Fadlemir peered over the side rail. To his left he surveyed a waterfall that plunged far below them into a wide pool of boulders and blue-green water. To his right, the river slowly crept into the waiting bay, and from there, the Faladrial Ocean glimmered under the high sun like a blue field littered with diamonds.

They reached the other side and continued south along the edge of the bay as the trail sloped down to the water. The men all saw the royal ships of Ligeon moored in a shallow creek, and just along the shore, ten or more small tenders, boats built to carry men and supplies to the larger vessels.

The flagships of Ligeon were themselves quite a sight to behold. The three masts of each stretched high into the sky, sails furled. The sleek lines of their bows rose from the water, graceful as a swan's chest, giving way to the elegant prow that arched in and then out, like a neck, and terminated in a carved bird's head. Giant wings on the port and starboard sides, made of wooden frames covered with canvas, spread out over the glistening waters as if ready to take flight. The stern tapered off, mounted with a span of canvas that looked like tail feathers.

Anondo's many fond memories aboard these ships pushed aside his depression, remembering travels along the coast both north and south with his father and brothers. Whether traveling with royal delegations on the King's business, or simply for a pleasure cruise, the sea was always a welcome place to Anondo, and the ships his home. They took him to distant lands by day, and then flew him home to his mother's arms by night.

And it was at the helm with his father that Anondo had learned to command the magnificent vessels, discovering the ways of the sea, and the orders that made the ship adhere to them. A seaman did not rule the sea; far from it. But rather he was carried by it, going wherever she desired. Surely she could be ruled for brief seasons and times, coaxed into the brilliant dance of a voyage by the sailors who manned the lines and tiller. But in the end it was *she* that decided the course. And if all listened to the masterful voice of the Mighty Creator, the dance was harmonious and rewarding. Anondo had never known a day at sea that was not a jewel, a very gift from the Father of Lights.

The warband neared the tenders and dismounted. Anondo was in the midst of ordering his men into the boats when a long, woeful howl cut through the air.

Everyone froze.

Anondo muttered to himself, "For all the riches in Athera—there *were* more." He looked to Fadlemir. "The *hounds* have followed us."

"But I thought—"

"Aye, so did we all," Anondo said. "They needn't find a way across the Hefkiln; they simply waited for us to cross. Quickly now, to the tenders. We'll need at least five trips the way I count it. We'll take the three fastest ships in the fleet." He indicated the three and then assigned his most sea-savvy captains to each.

"You heard him!" Fadlemir burst out. "Start rowing, and make haste! The last of you will have the flesh of your backsides bleeding by nightfall." The men leapt to work, needing little encouragement, shoving the boats off the quay and taking up the oars. When the first tenders reached the ships, the men ascended the mooring lines and dropped the ladders. As soon as the tenders were emptied, save for two men, they returned to the shore for the next load.

"Fadlemir, assign two scouts to the ridgeline there and there," the King pointed. "I figure we have three trips before they are on us."

"Hey'a," said the Captain, and was off.

Anondo turned and helped the tenders come ashore. The next round of men leapt into the shallow wooden boats, and again the King helped shove them off.

He looked out at the ships. The captains were already making ready to sail. Men were scaling the ratlines, unlashing the sails as fast as they could. When the tenders arrived, lifts were lowered to speed the hauling of supplies, what few they had left. When the last man was on the ladder climbing upward, the tenders shoved off and returned.

Another howl filled the air, this time closer.

"Row faster!" Fadlemir ordered from the strand. "Come on men, *faster! Biea varos!*"

Anondo turned to see the scouts finally reach their positions. He looked back to the men on the shore. By the time the third wave was off to the ships, Anondo looked back to the scouts. No longer in their positions, the two men were running down the slope, hands waving.

"Great God—" Anondo whispered, Fadlemir noticing the King's consternation. A *hound* appeared over the headland and raced down the hill after the scouts. Anondo urged them on under his breath. "*Come on.*"

"They're not going to make it," Fadlemir admitted.

"Do we have a bow?"

"Nay, my liege."

The first *hound* was joined by a second, both but ten strides behind the fleeing men. Turning to address those behind him, Anondo gave the order to draw swords and form lines. "Rid yourself of all armor as well."

One man broke the line and ran forward.

"We must help them!" he yelled wildly.

"You will get back in line," Fadlemir ordered.

But the man ran forward past his Captain and his King.

"Get back in line, warrior!" Fadlemir commanded.

Anondo put a hand on his shoulder.

"Fall back, Fadlemir," he spoke softly. "We join the line and wait for the tenders to arrive. When they shove off, we swim for it."

"My Lord?"

"We don't have time for another load after this. We'll have to swim, or die trying."

"But there may be only three or four more. We can take them."

"Nay, Fadlemir. We can't."

As if prompted by his words, over two tens of *hounds* appeared over the horizon and eyed their prey on the quay far below.

"Great God of Athera," Fadlemir muttered.

The leading two *hounds* caught up with and devoured the scouts, followed by the single warrior who ran headlong to his death.

"Fool," said Fadlemir.

"A valiant fool," added the King.

Fadlemir marveled at Anondo's ease under pressure. The King turned this way and that, taking in each element of their surroundings, making decisions and then revising them all in a matter of moments. Upon joining the line himself, Anondo ordered the ranks to fall back, standing in water up to their knees. He addressed his men. "For those that can, get in the tenders when they return. They rest of us will swim for it."

The *hounds* were racing toward the shore with immense speed. They pounded the ground, clumps of dirt and grass flung high into the air. The hackles on their backs were raised and drool swung from their chops. They snarled, chomping at the air. Anondo thought they could take a good number of them out before turning to swim.

But then another host of KiJinNard Hounds emerged over the headland, more than Anondo or Fadlemir could count. There was an audible gasp among the men, a sound drowned out by the pack's doleful wail as they crested the hill.

"Swim for it!" Anondo ordered.

The remaining three hundred warriors turned and sheathed their swords. They high-stepped through the deepening water before plunging in headfirst, reaching long for each stroke. A few of the men had tragically forgotten to discard their breastplates or hauberks, the heavy plate and chain mail armor dragging them under.

Anondo rolled over for a glance at their enemy.

The first wave of *hounds* was on the shore; two more strides and they'd be in the water. Anondo gained another stroke before he heard splashing behind him, and then the snapping of bones.

He looked again to see one of his men dangling by the leg from the mouth of an infuriated *hound*. The man screamed as the beast shook him wildly and then tossed him.

Two other hounds busied themselves with a cluster of men, pounding them into the water. The massive dogs' heads plunged below the surface, churning up red foam in the surf.

Unable to reach any more of the fleeing warriors on the strand, the *hounds* waded out and began swimming toward the ships.

Anondo yelled between breaths, encouraging his men not to lessen their pace. They had to reach the ships.

Suddenly Anondo caught site of the tenders up ahead. They were returning! But instead of two men, there were at least four in each, two to row and the others carrying long spears and curved polearms. They went to the rear, to those having the most trouble, and picked them up. The closing *hounds* saw this and became even more aggravated.

But the spearmen were ready.

An oarsman reached out for a struggling warrior. The two clasped hands. Just as the warrior was climbing aboard, he heard the snarl of an enemy dog. He pulled his legs up and jumped into the boat, slamming his head on the opposite gunwale. But the action saved his life, as well as his legs. Instead, the *hound* received a mouthful of iron as the blade of a spear shot to the back of its throat. It yelped and thrashed about, eventually sinking below the surface with the spear lodged in its neck.

The tenders went about saving all they could, and successfully fending off the *hounds*, as the dogs were no match for the spears, given their disadvantage in the impeding water.

By the time the tenders were returning to the ships, the next wave of the KiJinNard was entering the waves.

Halfway there, Anondo encouraged himself. His arms and legs were growing tired. The fatigue of the last five days had taken its toll. He rolled onto his back, hoping for an easier swim. He watched as the *hounds* filled the shore, wading into the surf, line upon line. *There are so many.*

He rolled back onto his chest. The tenders had given up their cargo and were coming back for another load. The advantage this time was that they need not travel out so far; the men were in deeper water.

Behind him, the snarling heads of the *hounds* bobbed above the surface, the rest of their ugly forms hidden by the water. It looked so strange to him, almost humorous, seeing all these heads making for him and his men. But the death in their eyes reminded him this was no game. And the *hounds* were good swimmers, too. They were closing the gap more quickly than Anondo had hoped.

The tenders went through the bulk of the men and began picking up those in the rear again. There was enough distance between them that the spearmen laid down their weapons to help load the boats. Anondo looked on.

He noticed that many of the heads had disappeared.

Strange…

More and more men were hauled in. No one seemed to notice the *hounds* disappearing.

Then it happened.

Two men were lifting a warrior out of the water, each grabbing a hand. Anondo could see the warrior's face. His eyes widened in terror as a massive mouth came up from underneath him, consuming his legs, foot to knee. The massive jaws closed on him and then retreated into the water, man in tow.

The action was so fast that the two rescuers didn't have time to let go and were likewise pulled overboard. The boat rocked wildly and the remaining men shouted orders, some reaching for those now in the waves, while others picked up weapons to fend off any more *hounds*.

Three more beasts burst from the depths and chomped at the men in the water. A spear flew, teeth gleamed, shouting, and then the unthinkable…

Two *hounds* appeared on the opposite side of the tender, paws reaching overboard, and then flipped the craft. About eight men in all went tumbling into the waves.

There was nothing that could be done.

The boat was ripped apart in a matter of moments, and all that remained were bits and pieces of men and wood littering the sea.

Some of the tenders watched what happened and backed off from their objective, while others were not so lucky and succumbed to the same grievous fate.

All along the rear of the pack Anondo heard short cries for help—and then nothing. The pleas disappeared almost as fast as they had been issued.

He looked back once more.

His men were being plucked from the surface like mayflies sucked down by trout. One moment they were swimming strong, the next, pulled under in a short but violent burst of carnage.

They are faster beneath the waves, Anondo concluded.

But they could not hold their breath forever. A part of them was still mortal, as they were once Dionian flesh and blood.

"Wait for them to surface!" Anondo ordered those in the tenders. "You'll get your chance!"

All around the men heard the order. They stood poised and ready, spears aloft. For a moment, nothing was heard but the men swimming desperately through the water. Anondo could tell they were slowing, fatigue setting in.

"Wait for it!" Anondo bolstered their faith.

The spearmen searched the waves, eyes moving to and fro.

"Wait for it!"

And then a head popped up from the surface, no man in sight. The *hound* took a deep breath. But that's all it took.

A sharp polearm blade drove down into its muzzle, pinning its mouth shut. The beast thrashed, the shaft snapping in two against the side of the boat. But the blade remained fixed. The next breath was all water for the *hound*, and it drowned almost at once.

The spearmen had their choice as a great many surfaced all about the same time. Many of the *hounds* had fixed on a warrior in mid-stroke, but many had not and were simply in need of air.

This round certainly belonged to the warband as they slew over five tens of the *hounds* in the waters. When the slaughter was finished, the tenders plucked up the survivors.

Anondo reached hard for each stroke. The ships were very close. But so was the enemy.

Just then he felt something clip his foot.

His heart stopped.

He glanced over his shoulder to see a large *hound* matching him stroke for stroke. Its head ducked beneath the water and tried to bite his foot, barely missing.

Every muscle in Anondo sprung to life, and he made a mad dash for the rope ladder, not more than ten and five strokes away. The *hound* chomped again, this time managing to clamp onto the King's ankle.

Anondo yelled out in agony, writhing in pain, losing momentum. His leg burned.

The weight of the clinging beast began pulling him under. He splashed, just trying to keep his head above water.

Kerrrfloooom!

101

All at once there was a massive explosion of water behind him.

The force threw him forward, his body tumbling about under the surface. Bubbles everywhere, the first thing he noticed was that his foot was free. He looked for daylight, the surface. Getting his bearings, he shot upward and then burst into the air. He gasped for breath. Someone was shouting.

"My King, over here!"

He looked about. Fadlemir clung to the ladder, hand outstretched. "You can make it!"

Anondo shook his head and began swimming the final few lengths. He reached out a hand, and Fadlemir grabbed his forearm.

"C'symia," Anondo said, out of breath. Fadlemir clung to the side of the ladder and allowed the King to pass before him. They both climbed up quickly. Anondo landed on the deck and looked around, spying the source of his aggressor's defeat; temporarily mounted to the gunwales were massive crossbows, smaller versions of the ones Luik had ordered for Mt. Dakka. Simpler, and older in design, Anondo realized they must have been constructed by his father, long ago. But he had never seen them.

Three men worked each of them, two operating the double action winch that pulled the line back, while a third loaded the large bolt.

They aimed, and then let the bolt fly.

The result was a huge plume of water that shot into the air.

"I didn't think you would object," said one of the captains, coming to the King's side. "We found them below decks while loading the supplies."

"Object? Nay," he said in a half smile, "be about your work." Anondo slumped forward and reached for his ankle. He groaned, falling into Fadlemir's arms. The others noticed the open wound and the blood pooling on the planks.

"Let's get you below," said Fadlemir.

"But the men—"

"Are fine now, thanks to your father's invention."

The crossbows continued to pick off the *hounds* until the bloodthirsty creatures realized it meant death to advance any farther than they had. They eventually relented and paddled back to the shore. The warband cheered and hauled the rest of the warriors up into the ships.

Fadlemir gave the order to release the mooring lines and set sail.

"At the mouth of the bay, we head north," he continued.

"But Captain, sir," said the helmsman. "What about that?" He pointed cautiously to the sky ahead.

Fadlemir followed his finger.

Rolling in from the northwest were black clouds that flashed with spectacular light.

Chapter Eleven

CHASED BY FIRE

Thad and Thero burst through the burning forest edge, fire licking their flesh. Brittle branches snapped underfoot, charred by the roaring flames. Cinders were flung into the air all about them, landing in their hair, smoldering against their skin. Less than two tens of men followed the twins into the wood. They had lost more than half of the warriors in the mountain pass, and a few more had been picked off in their rush to Grandath. But now, charging through the smoke-filled woods of the Great Forest, Thad had thought better of his plan and was quite sure he had sealed the fate of his remaining few warriors.

"I can't see anything," cried one of his men from behind.

"This way," Thad yelled. "Stay with me!"

Once past the forest edge the woods were filled with a deathly grey smoke. It was so thick that seeing was nearly impossible and breathing even more so, the air sucked right out of their lungs, eyes burning as if aflame.

Men fought for each breath, choking as they went. Thad and Thero both continued to shout, trying to keep the men assembled, but they knew it would not be long before they were scattered among the trees, lost forever in the suffocating world they had entered.

This had been a mistake.

Thero, desperate for air, gasped hard, covering his mouth with the upper fold of his mantle. But all he took in was a chestful of burning smoke that set him gagging. He doubled over, and his stomach spent itself in one spasm after another. He eyes watered, and no matter how hard he shut them, the stinging only continued.

Thad tripped over a log, suffering from the same condition as his brother. He rolled on the ground, holding a twisted ankle.

We were wrong to come here, he scolded himself. *I was wrong.*

He heard his men fumbling through the wood, running into trees and coughing hysterically. To come so far and be killed by so little; it was a depressing affair.

Thad rolled to his side and opened his eyes. He caught sight of Thero's legs; his brother was recklessly stumbling through a thicket of withering ferns.

And then Thad realized it…

"I can see!" he blurted out.

From down on the forest floor, he could see. Granted, not much, but enough. The smoke was considerably thinner, and breathing even bearable.

"Down! Get down!" he ordered. He saw Thero spin toward the sound of his voice. "Thero, lie down!"

Thero dropped to his knees, a hacking cough forcing blood into his hands.

"Lie down, man!"

Thero eventually fell on his face, more out of defeat than will. He lay there for a moment hidden among the ferns, his lungs expelling the death bound up within them.

Soon his coughing stopped.

Thad watched for movement.

Thero didn't stir.

"Thero?" Anxiety gripped Thad's heart. *"Thero!"*

Thad rolled onto his belly and began frantically pulling his way along the forest floor. It smelled of must and damp leaves, but it was a welcomed smell compared to the smoke just above him. He dug his elbows into the soft terrain and pushed forward with his knees.

"Thero!" he yelled again.

Still nothing.

He pulled himself over a log and then tumbled down into the glade of ferns. Foliage inhibited his vision, but he beat it aside, long willowy leaves slapping him in the face. He pulled at the roots, drawing his body farther into the undergrowth.

Searching wildly, he stole glances through the breaks in the plants, hoping to catch sight of Thero's clothing, a glint of his armor perhaps.

"Thero! Can you hear me?"

Suddenly Thad heard a soft moan.

He looked to his left. "Thero!"

Thad pushed himself up and ran the short distance to where his brother lay. He then sank back down into the protection of the lower air. He shook Thero's forearm.

"Thero, speak to me, man!"

"I can't," mumbled Thero. "And let go of my arm."

"Gladly." Thad rolled onto his back and cupped his hands to his mouth, hoping his next words would be heard by any of his men in earshot. "Warriors of Dionia! To your bellies! Get down and breathe easy!"

He repeated the words and then waited. He heard men coughing all through the forest, some deathly so. After a short wait the coughing lessened, and soon only the roaring fire could be heard in the distance.

He waited there with his brother as Thero collected himself. The two conversed briefly until Thad noticed movement nearby.

"Someone's coming," Thero stated.

"Aye," Thad propped himself up and looked over the ferns. "Who goes there?"

"'Tis I, Blandon," said a warrior. He worked his way among the ferns to where the twins were.

"Breathing easy?" Thad asked.

"Easier," Blandon replied with a grin, "but I would much prefer the sea breezes of Narin to this." He coughed once again.

"As would I, sword brother," Thad replied. "Blandon, gather whom you can. Meet us here. Quickly now, we haven't much time to waste."

Thad bade his brother stay put and made to move. But the sharp pain in his ankle sent him to the ground.

"What is it?" Thero inquired.

"My ankle," he said, reaching for it.

"You stay here," Thero ordered. "I'll rally who's left of the warband."

Without any objection, Thero was away, pushing through the ferns on his hands and knees. Thad began shouting, giving Blandon and Thero, and any of the other men listening, a point to come to.

"Follow my voice! This way! This way!"

Slowly, he heard men rustling through the underbrush, crawling on their bellies toward him. Within a few moments, he was joined in the glade by no more than nine of his warband.

Thad continued to cry out until finally Thero and Blandon returned. Blandon had one man with him, Thero none.

"Any more?" Thad looked at them forlorn.

"Nay," Blandon shook his head. Thero likewise.

"But that's—"

"I found four who had succumbed to the smoke," Thero said gravely.

"And I, two more," added Blandon.

"Six men," Thad muttered. A hand grabbed his forearm.

"Brother, we must move, as you said."

"Aye, Thero, right you are."

"Which way?" asked Blandon.

"There," Thad pointed. "The smoke files away from the flames, to the east. To me. And stay low!"

The warband waited as Thad and Thero passed, and then followed them, digging their elbows into the soft forest floor and pulling themselves onward. Now only ten and two strong, they moved quickly over logs and between trunks. The smoke swirled overhead, leading them away from the source and deeper into the Central Forest.

As the men spent themselves on the strenuous effort, they soon noticed that the smoke was not dissipating as quickly as they had hoped. In fact, the ceiling above them was moving lower and lower overhead. The air was also growing hotter.

"We are indeed moving away from the flames?" Thero questioned his brother.

"Quite. Yet one would presume otherwise."

"Aye," Thero looked behind them.

He paused.

"Tell me, Thad." Thero tried to catch his breath, sweat streaming down his face. "What do you see there in the distance?"

Thero indicated a strange orange glow in the midst of the smoke far behind them.

"The flames are advancing," Blandon spoke up. "But so quickly?"

"Aye," Thad said. "We are being *followed*."

"Followed?" Thero looked at him, and then back at the glow. "By the Dairne-Reih?"

"Eventually. But first by the *fire*."

"I don't understand," said Blandon.

"It *lives*," answered Thad. "I saw it just before we entered the wood. It has a *soul*."

"But that's—"

"Impossible?" Thad cut Blandon off. "Man, what have you seen in these last days that has not been impossible? I tell you, if we do not outwit this devil, it will consume us whole and be all the more pleased for having done so. It *lives*, and it lives to kill us."

"And your plan?" Thero inquired.

"Run while we can, then rest to breathe down here."

"Serious?" asked Blandon.

"Aye," said Thero. "It's the only way."

And so it was that the men began the grueling exercise of standing and running blindly through the woods; when their breath was nearly gone and their legs could carry them no further, they knelt down and then laid prostrate, sucking air in and wiping the tears from their eyes.

This was most taxing on Thad. His ankle burned incessantly, but he reminded himself it was nothing like the scorching heat he would endure if he were too slow.

"Faster, men!" Thad would yell as they raced through the smoke. When he felt the team slowing, he'd encourage them again and again until the pace resumed to what he felt a necessary speed.

Suddenly he tripped and crashed to the ground. Thad didn't realize he was himself screaming in pain, but Thero tried his best to soothe him.

"Easy there, brother," he said, examining his leg. The twisted ankle had caused another injury: this time, a fracture in the lower leg. White bone punctured the skin, both smeared in fresh blood. Thero looked back toward the glow in the smoke. It seemed as though they had not made any progress at all.

It was gaining on them.

"It's just my ankle," Thad finally spoke up. "I'll manage."

"Be that as it may," Thero covered, "I think it best that we carry you the rest of the way."

"Nonsense." Thad made to stand up.

His leg buckled. A wave of pain shook his body from head to toe. He stumbled back to the ground and looked down at his misshapen limb.

"O Most High," Thad quivered. He looked up to Thero. "It's bad, isn't it, brother?"

It was the first time Thero ever remembered seeing his brother afraid.

"Don't be fearful, now. There's nothing to dread. The Great God is with you." Thero looked into his twin's eyes. "I'll carry you."

Blandon and the others assisted in bracing Thero as he lifted Thad from the ground. He stood cradling him in his arms and then moved forward. He made only a few steps before needing to kneel and catch his breath. But the effort just to lower Thad was overwhelming.

"I'll take him next," said Blandon. He moved to where Thad lay and said, "Here, grab my neck."

Thad wrapped his arms around Blandon's neck and was lifted into the air, dangling from his back. They made it a good number of paces before Blandon knelt down. He took another breath and then stood, moving forward another few strides. Twice more they made headway and then collapsed in a heap.

"Let me help," said another man. He stepped in and bore Thad likewise. He made a go of it three times before passing Thad off to yet another of the warband.

But the tedious process was very slow.

Thero looked back. The flames were advancing. The smoke was heavier, and the air along the ground was growing foul.

"We're not moving fast enough," Thero said to Blandon, both taking a knee.

"I'm slowing everyone down," Thad said, hanging from a man's back.

Thero looked to Blandon in pregnant silence.

"I know it's true," snapped Thad. "You need not lie to me." Thad looked to his brother. "Thero, have them put me down." He coughed.

Thero did not move.

"You there," Thad spoke to the man who carried him. "Release me."

"As you will," replied the warrior. He knelt and eased Thad to the ground. Thad winced at the pain it produced in his leg.

All the men lay prostrate in the undergrowth.

"All of you," Thad spoke loudly, "listen to me now. I am under orders of the King of Ligeon, and the High King of Dionia. You are under my command. To disobey me is to defy the High King Himself. If you take me any farther, you will perish. This evil can be outrun, and with any help from the Tribes of Ot, you will be found safe in the Secret City by nightfall. Each of you…"

Thero lost track of Thad's words. It was in that instant that he realized what he had to do. He turned and looked back to the glow in the distance, now so close he could hear the roar and see the flames. It loomed toward them as they lay in the leaves. Thero felt it drawing him, asking for his soul.

But he would not give in.

Thad's words came rushing back…

"…for Dionia, and for your King!"

Thero stood and walked to Thad. He then knelt and cradled his brother in his arms. Thad made to object, but Thero stood, and the smoke stole any breath Thad had.

"Onward!" Thero cried.

The men responded quickly and rose to their feet, but their hearts were far from their orders. They understood the situation all too well. Help, and they forfeited their lives, for their aid would not be enough for Thad or themselves; run, and they might live to fight another day.

"Do not stop for anything, save the Dwarves of this realm!" Thero added. "Do not stop for friend or foe." He looked to Blandon, tears washing lines down his blackened face. "You must survive and give an account to the High King! He is the best of us all! *Varos!*"

Thad squinted through the smoke, his eyes watering. He looked up to Thero's face, smeared with black soot. "What are you doing?" he asked quietly.

"Going with you, what else?" Thero replied. He began walking forward, his brother grasped in his arms. "*For Dionia! With haste!*"

With that the men took off running. Their feet trampled the forest floor, branches snapping, bushes shaking. They raced through the woods as fast as their feet would carry them. And when their lungs burned for their next breath, they stooped to suck in air, off again a moment later.

Thero strained his legs, pushing himself for the next step. Exhausted, he sank to the ground in a heap, Thad crashing in front of him.

"Leave me," Thad moaned. "You can outrun this. You are strong."

"And live knowing I left you, my brother?" Thero shook his head. "Then I would not be a true Son of Dionia, much less a Dibor. And likewise, do not call me your brother."

Thero looked back; the rage of the fire was upon them. He felt the heat burning his face. He summoned all his strength and reached for Thad, taking him up once more.

They made it only a few paces before Thero collapsed again.

The rest of the warband was nowhere to be seen.

"God's speed," Thero prayed over them, reaching a feeble hand forward. He looked over at Thad. Both their eyes were swollen and bleeding. They were beyond tears, and their lungs past trying to expel the dangerous air. Thero's arms and legs burned, yet he willed himself to make one more go of it.

"Shall we, my brother?" Thad asked, looking over at him, their bodies sprawled in the dirt. The air was fervent.

"We shall, Dibor," Thero replied and pressed himself up again. "We shall until we can no more."

The fire was just behind them now, racing forward without discretion. Thero shuffled to his broken brother and scooped him up. He kissed him on the forehead and made to stand. Everything in him resisted the action. But he cried out and willed his legs to straighten.

When he gained his feet, the two brothers strode forward like the warriors they were, and in the twinkling of an eye, they were taken home as the heroes they would always be.

Chapter Twelve

EYE OF THE STORM

Dim light hung in the doorway, soaking the Great Hall's wooden floor with a muted wash of green. The tree limbs outside were swaying well beyond their liking, a sound like sitting inside a waterfall. Though now well within the massive fort, the sense of vulnerability had not diminished. The storm that drew ever nearer would not spare even the strongest of trees. But somehow the stoic leader of the mysterious archers was one step ahead of all this.

"We must go deeper," he addressed Luik.

"Deeper?"

"Aye. There is a great deal you do not know," the man swept his hand through the air.

"Clearly. Lead on," Luik replied.

The warrior turned and walked deeper into the hall, soon swallowed by the darkness. Luik snapped his fingers, and at once Jrio, Cage, and the other Dibor were watching his every action. "We move at once. Bring the wounded."

The space was soon a flurry of activity, though the only sounds were the rustling of clothing and the moans of the injured. Luik strode forward after the leader, leaving the light of the doorway behind. He sensed a line forming after him, the mass of men following eagerly, none wishing to take the brunt, or any part, of the storm. A little hand slipped into his. "There is nothing to be scared of, little one," Luik said.

"I know," Fia replied, her tone less than convinced.

Just ahead a voice came in the darkness, "Watch your step."

Luik slowed. He waited for his eyes to adjust to the black around them. Slowly, he made out an even darker space before and below.

"Step down," said the man.

Luik turned around and spoke to Jrio, "Tell those behind to watch their step. We're going down." It obviously would have been easier to have a torch, but urgency did not permit it. Wherever the leader was taking them, Luik trusted that the man knew best. And frankly, he didn't have time for anything else. It only made sense: the farther away from the storm, the better; and in this case, *away* meant *deeper*.

Luik led Fia slowly down the first three steps until they could both be sure of the spacing. After that the going was swifter, albeit consumed in utter blackness. Now, not even a hand on one's nose was distinguishable. They continued down the subterranean staircase with the sound of numerous pairs of thumping feet behind them. Then the voice again:

"Turn here."

Luik searched forward with his toes. The last step did not give way to another but went on level. A landing. His left shoulder butted against a wall.

"This way." Fia pulled him to the right. They turned the corner and started down the next flight of stairs, only these were of a different material than the first. Stone.

By the time they reached yet another turnaround, it was apparent they were well below the island's surface. The air had cooled significantly and was full of the rich, damp aromas of the ground. All that could be heard was the patting of feet against the cold stone steps and the dripping of water somewhere farther down.

They came upon still another turnaround, continuing their subsurface plunge away from the tempest above. *Surely the storm is upon Kirstell by now*, Luik thought. Yet they moved in utter stillness.

After the fourth set of stairs, Luik and the others noticed the softest implication of light ahead, though barely a hint. He almost dismissed the notion, thinking his eyes were being too hopeful. But toward the end of the staircase he was sure it was light, albeit remote.

They rounded a final turn and entered into a large hall dimly lit from somewhere in the rear. The space's height and depth were hard to discern, but from what Luik could tell, the hall was an enormous storage room. It was filled with clay vessels great and small. Wooden crates covered in skins lined the immediate walls, and weaponry of various kinds was stacked in neat piles. The air was still cool, but took on the faint aroma of wine and fermented mead. Large wooden vats stood like bulbous, sleeping animals to one side, containers he was sure held the precious liquids he smelled.

The source of the murky light came from a small doorway halfway down the hall to one side. The low arched passageway was seemingly indistinguishable, save that a faint light emanated from it. Luik felt compelled to explore more, but the voice of the lead archer broke the silence.

"Rest here," he said loudly. His words bounced around the hall, echoing at length in the abyss. There was a slight pause, and then a percussive blow followed by a bright light bursting forth. Everyone raised a hand to shield their eyes. Squinting hard, they peered at the torch the man now held aloft.

The warband looked around and at once made themselves comfortable amidst the items. Furs and skins were collected to make litters for those wounded. Others propped the weary on the crates and examined wounds by firelight as more torches were gathered and lit. Others found buckets and jars, filling them with wine and mead from the massive vats. The drink was happily passed among the men, and soon the mood had become immeasurably more tolerable. Those who moments before were considering their imminent doom were now caught up in the unexpected boon all about them.

Discussion commenced, and nothing seemed so profound as what good fortune had brought them to find such a trove of respite and retreat. Each man agreed with the others; some even let out a chuckle or grunt of laughter, but nothing too genial, as that would have been inappropriate given their losses. A merry sobriety was the best way to put it, the necessity of recognizing grievous circumstances while savoring the good fortune of the present, trusting it would give way to an even better end.

Would a better end be found? No one could be sure. But without hope, a man is simply a dried leaf; he retains the shape and form of what he once was, but one gust of wind—one ill-cast strike—and he is shattered into oblivion, the brittle fragments of his soul impossible to piece back together.

Luik helped a few men around him get more comfortable, and then offered them some drink. He situated Fia in amongst a stack of furs in a crate, kissing her lightly on the head. He marveled at her resourcefulness. At her dedication to him. At how this little one had traversed a dangerous land that had consumed far stronger men just to make sure "he was safe and sound."

"I followed you for a long time," she offered up, fighting the pull to sleep. "All the way down the coast. I know I wasn't supposed to. Please don't tell." She yawned. "But I asked the Most High to be with me. And He was. Even gave me that horse to follow you along to Kirstell." Drawn in by the warmth of the hides, she made herself comfortable and soon was fast sleep. Content to see her drawn helplessly into her dreams, Luik pulled himself together and made to slip away, the curious doorway beckoning him mercilessly. He glanced around and, seeing he wasn't drawing any attention, made for the doorway.

"Come. Sit beside me," the lead archer said just to his left. Luik turned toward the voice. It was more than a simple suggestion. Luik stared back down at the doorway, and then at the warrior again. The man sat on a large fur, the torch propped up beside him against a wooden shelf. Luik looked once more at the doorway. "It can wait," the warrior said to Luik.

Luik was slightly embarrassed that his intentions were so obvious, as if his mother were chiding him for misbehavior, albeit innocent. The warrior patted the fur beside him. Luik walked over and sat down.

"I can't thank you enough for your help, Sir—" Luik cut off, hoping the man would fill in the blank of his name.

"It is my duty, my King," he replied, placing his fist against his chest and inclining his head.

Luik felt outmatched, but couldn't tell if it was purposeful, or a product of genuine humility. This man was respectful, even honoring, yet gave nothing more than he was directly asked for. *A true servant.*

"Where do you come from, my friend?" Luik inquired, not wanting to rush the conversation, nor solicit information in undue time; this man was surely aged enough to expect such behavior as inappropriate. The true art of conversation is not in what is accomplished, but in how it is said.

"I believe it is the same as you, my Lord," he said with the faintest hint of a grin. "The greatest realm of Dionia."

"Bensotha then, is it?"

"Aye, my Lord."

"The greatest of the realms," Luik bowed his head slightly. Even the mention of her name took him somewhere else, back to the land of his youth, back to the memories that he dared not invite into this present world lest they too be trampled.

"Pardon me for asking," Luik said, "but I feel as I know you, Sir—"

"To my knowledge we have never met," replied the warrior. "Although I have been waiting for this day for some time." He reached up and took his helmet off, placing it beside him on the fur.

Luik looked on in wonder, though still not able to place a name with this face.

So long ago, Luik thought. *I've seen you before, as if in a dream.*

The man's weathered face was tan and healthy. Though his dark hair was showing signs of grey, his green eyes were still those of a young man, full of life and zeal for the days to come. He was not overly tall, but certainly bore the build of an ox, broad and heavy. And when he smiled, it was as if all those in his presence were taken back in time, to a world far removed from evil, a place that knew not the name Morgui.

"Perhaps you were a friend of my father's then?"

But if we've never met, why would that matter? Luik was striving for anything. He was getting closer. He could feel it.

"I am a friend to all Dionians, my King, your father one of them."

"Ah, I see," Luik said grandly. But it helped him not in the least; he was no closer than he was before.

"Allow me to help you," said the man, sensing Luik's mounting frustration.

Luik replied with a courteous smile. Truth be told, he was dying to know.

"Perhaps it feels like you *know* me because you have been told *about* me."

"About you?" Luik was puzzled. "A story then?"

"More than a story, I would imagine. More like a glimpse of history."

The man then removed his cloak and pulled off his mantle.

Beneath that, he grasped the bottom of his chain maille shirt and that of the hauberk, and lifted them up to reveal his chest. His muscles were still full and strong despite his obvious age.

But that is not what caught Luik's eye.

There in the center of his ribcage, just between his pectorals, was a pattern of emaciated scars, eight holes to be exact. Eight finger-sized wounds, four each side of center, forming two vertical lines. They had healed over with the typical rankled flesh of a scar and had become a symbol, one Luik was supposed to know.

Gorn. Smoke. The fire.

The memories came flooding back.

The circle of boralees. The story…

…remember the story.

He saw images, the images he had seen in the flames. They raced toward him, passing through his mind's eye as fresh as they were the night he had first experienced them.

Friends on the hilltop. The starlit sky. A voice in the woods.

He could feel the tension in his chest.

Velon. And then Grinddr. Velon pierced him in the chest with his fingertips.

Grinddr?

"But I thought—"

"Thought I was dead, did you? You mean to tell me old Gorn never told you my story?"

"I—"

"Well then, I'll have to make up for his inabilities. You know how he can be," nudging Luik in the side.

Grinddr, who just moments before appeared to be the epitome of a close-lipped, hard-line soldier, was suddenly beaming and ready for a good yarn. Luik was still having trouble piecing it all together, while Grinddr was already bounding headlong down the trail of retelling his past. This was Grinddr…*the* Grinddr in the flesh!

"Of course he wouldn't have said anything to you, now would he," Grinddr concluded for himself, "as that would have jeopardized everything. Ah, Gorn, you're a smart one. But seriously, knowledge must be certain to keep its companions close, and those numbered small. Who knows who could be listening? Even now! I risk it just retelling it to you, but to you I must. If I cannot disclose these things in the presence of the

High King, whom can I trust? Surely that would be a dark day when not even Dionia's King can be sought out to bear a secret."

"Surely," Luik agreed, trying to keep up.

"Ah, but look at us, talking in the open."

"But we are among—"

"Among friends?" Grinddr drew close and lowered his voice. "Are you *sure*?" He drew out the last word. Luik regarded him with a blank stare. "Come then. You want to know where the doorway leads, so I will show you."

"Am I that obvious?"

"In a word? Aye."

Luik forced his aching body to stand. "You sound just like a friend of mine, a certain dwarf. And if I didn't know better—"

"You'd say I was friends with him, too?" Grinddr stood and began walking. "I am."

"But—"

"Come, my King. There is much to discuss."

Resigned to the fact that he wasn't going to get anywhere with this fellow until the man thought it was time, Luik fell into step beside Grinddr as they walked inconspicuously toward the doorway. And that not as reluctantly as his outward manner showed, for inwardly Luik was as eager as a little boy to know what lay beyond.

Grinddr paused here and there, examining the contents of a crate, or sampling the mixtures of one of the capped jars. He'd cast a quick glance behind them. Satisfied no one was taking any notice of their advance, he moved on, Luik following.

Soon they were adjacent to the doorway, a pale, blue-green glow spilling from the archway. Grinddr looked behind them and then banked through the opening and into a long, low-ceilinged tunnel.

All at once Luik felt the hair on the back of his neck stand up. He knew this place, bathed in a cool, shimmering hue. All along the walls were markings, scripted in the dwarfish tongue.

The Tribes of Ot.

The further along they went, the more the light began to dance along the floor and ceiling until finally they emerged into a room. And there, just as Luik suspected, was a standing pool of water, glowing like all the others before.

"The Sea Cave," Luik murmured to himself.

"So I've heard it called," Grinddr added. "A childish name, I must admit, but one that has stuck ever since they said you four termed it such."

"We four?" Luik was surprised.

"Aye. There are no secrets among those who live in secret."

"So I'm discovering," Luik said.

"Ah, come now. I see I am flustering the High King, something for which I would not like to be remembered." He moved along the perimeter of the room and glanced at the ancient runes carved along the ceiling and walls.

"I indeed suffered a mortal wound when Velon struck me. But had he not first been my nearest friend, kinsman of my kinsmen, I would not have endured such a blow to begin with. For I knew in him was good. I knew, as he knew, that only good was in the land, just as the Most High had fashioned it. And I could not believe, nor would have ever figured, that such a deception had entered our midst, let alone entered him.

"But I was wrong. For when he confronted me, Velon was far from himself. He was in fact another. He was *Valdenil*. He had given in. Granted, he was not born evil. The Great God makes no mistakes. But he *chose* evil. There is a difference, you know. Never confuse them, my Liege."

Luik nodded.

"But if there was one thing lacking in that time, it was evil, believe it or not. As Valdenil fled that day, apparently terrified of the rising sun in the West, my remaining friends set upon me with their love, willing that I should not die, but live. The presence of the Most High was soon upon me once more, and I was whole. But I was left with the scars, I think as a reminder more than anything else." He paused and walked to another part of the room.

"I was soon taken into the High King's service, not because of any great merit, but because I had been there, from the beginning. I had seen *evil* with my own two eyes, staring it in the face. It had come against me, and I had won. *The Most High* had won in me, is how I like to put it.

"So advisor I became, serving in the court of the King. During the First Battle, I was appointed a captain in the newly formed Lion Vrie, leading many men into battle. And they followed me without question. Any success I have is because of them, though they always said it was because of me." Grinddr stopped for a brief moment, and Luik watched as his eyes grew distant. "People often think scars give us power that we ourselves know is not there. Scars merely remind us of where we've come from; that really, had it not been for the healing power of the One, we would be nothing. They thought I was *something* because I had seen the enemy; evil had breathed on me. But I was only *something* because the Most High had touched me.

"In any case, we won, and drove Morgui out of our midst. At least for a time."

"You have *seen* Morgui then?" Luik asked.

"Aye, my King. That I have."

"And what does—"

"What he looks like you will discover soon enough," Grinddr trailed off. "Soon enough, I fear." His words took on a melancholy air. "Soon enough."

Luik picked up the conversation, asking, "So if you are in service to the Kings, how come I have never met you before?"

"Ah, a worthy question indeed. After the First Battle, I found myself in the court of the Kings for summer after summer, granted lands in Bensotha, and any other of the realms I wanted for that matter. I took no other, of course, for what was the need?" Luik smiled in affirmation. "Bensotha alone held my love. I never married, and thus had no children. But I was married to the land, you might say, bound to her success and freedom as if bound to my own body."

"You sound like a King," Luik smiled.

"Oh, I might say I do. Now look at me, babbling on here. Forgive me, Sire."

Luik waved his hand dismissively. He found himself growing very fond of Grinddr and could see why he had been in the service of each of Dionia's Lords. While he retained all the qualities of a warrior, both physical and mental, qualities that he had displayed just moments before on the shore above, Grinddr also revealed a childlike glee, a wonder for life and a love for living it. He was a simple man, really, yet one who had surely seen much conflict and endured many a loss. How he was able to maintain such a jovial demeanor, thinking of himself no more than he ought while amidst such hardship, gave Luik great confidence. "Please, do go on, Grinddr."

"Where was I, then?"

"In service of the Kings."

"Ah, yes. Your father, King Ragnar, called me aside one day. He said he had a special errand for me of the utmost importance...that the future of all Dionia rested upon what he was about to do. He knew something was coming. He could *feel* it." Grinddr moved along the pool's edge, looking deep into the waters. "He said that I was to be entrusted with an island, and that I was to guard it with my life. Upon it the last hope of Dionia would be trained, taken as youths and released as the most elite warriors Dionia had ever seen." Grinddr looked up into Luik's face. "And one of those warriors would be his son."

"Kirstell," Luik whispered.

"Aye. The Dibor. Though this was long before you were born, good King. Your father had much foresight given him by the Most High. He shall be forever remembered for it."

"So Kirstell's protection was—was *you* then?"

"I was given one hundred warriors, each trained as a Lion Vrie, but given a new title. We were named *The Immortals* and granted abilities far beyond our understanding. The men you see with me have been truer than any other, each taking a vow of secrecy, never to be seen again in the light of day by anyone other than their own warband. They have devoted the last four tens of summers to Kirstell's defense, waiting for the Dibor to come. And even after your departure, we were ordered to stay. I can't say it has been an easy task; things were certainly more exciting when you all were around." A smile crept onto Grinddr's face. "At least you gave us something to watch—and something to fight for."

"Fight for?" Luik interrupted.

"You mean to say, you really think your time passed without incident from the enemy? That the conflict on the beach when you first arrived was the only attempt on your lives during those four summers? Who do you think kept you from drowning beneath the waves?"

Luik did not dare to reply.

"O no, my King. If you only knew. We were kept quite busy. And happy for it, too. It was the most activity we had seen since, well, since the First Battle. As much as Ragnar could sense what was to come from the enemy, Morgui also sensed something forming against him. And try to stop it he most certainly did!"

"So you and your men were our *covering of protection*, as Gorn told us."

"Aye, that we were. Able to move in and out of light and darkness, and even time to a degree. Not a single Dairneag touched Kirstell's shore for four summers." He bowed slightly.

"C'symia," Luik offered, though he knew he would never know the full extent of The Immortals' works. "What about how the arrows burned up on the shore back there?"

"Simply part of *our new abilities* I mentioned before, nothing more."

"Ah, I see," Luik said for effect, though he hadn't the faintest idea.

"So, my King, as you can see, I have been in the service of every King of Dionia, and now to you, my Lord."

"I still don't understand. Why did you remain on the island even after we had departed?"

"Those were my orders. Though, in truth, we all suspected that you would one day return and would have need of us again."

"As *you* can see," Luik said, "I am forever indebted to you for saving us earlier."

"There is no debt owed, King Luik. It was demanded of us."

"And so you are still bound to remain here?"

"Unless the High King orders us otherwise," Grinddr offered up hopefully.

"I can think of a few orders of my own," Luik smiled. "Now, assuming the storm above passes over, if it has not already done so, we must get back to Mt. Dakka at once."

"Agreed."

"It would appear to me that the easiest way would be to take our men back though this portal into Ot, and then on into—"

"I'm afraid that's impossible, my King," Grinddr put in.

"How so?"

"Li-Saide—you know him well—has broken all the links."

"Links? What do you mean?"

"If you were to jump into this pool, seawater is all you would find."

"I don't understand," Luik said.

"The dwarves have much reason to believe that there is a traitor in our midst. They believe someone has compromised the knowledge of the portals, your Sea Caves, if you will."

"They fear for Ot's safety," Luik surmised.

"And for the scrolls of our people," Grinddr added.

"So Li-Saide has rendered the portals useless from Ot's side?"

"Precisely."

"I assume you have seen the fire burning in Grandath then?" Luik asked.

"Aye. Morgui is searching for the doorway into the Secret City."

"Then we've got to stop them. We need to get to Mt. Dakka right away. From there, we'll rally our forces and request Li-Saide to re-open the portal connecting Mt. Dakka to Ot. It would allow us to defend Ot from the inside out. Tactically, Morgui can only enter from one small entrance. As long as we can hold out, we can defend Ot to the last Dairneag."

"Agreed. Just give me the order, High King," Grinddr bowed low.

"Servant of the Most High, you are hereby freed from the Isle of Kirstell. See to the men; make sure they rest. We leave for Mt. Dakka at dawn."

Grinddr looked up into his new King's eyes, hope burning afresh. "So it is ordered, so it will be done."

Chapter Thirteen

SEA HUNTER

By the time the three ships escaped from Narin Bay, it was clear to all that their being pursued was far from over. A dark storm brewed in the west and now Fadlemir and the others were sure it was advancing...

...toward them.

Fadlemir gave the orders to come about on a broad reach to the north. They couldn't have asked for better wind. The two other ships followed in kind and soon after released the extent of their sails from all three masts. The winches worked, extending the massive wings to the port and starboard sides, finishing each vessel's bird-like visage. With the course set, the order was given to trim sail, and all at once, the flagships of Ligeon surged forward.

Their bows plied the waters like swords, winnowing one glistening side from the other. The hull slipped through the water effortlessly and left a seamless wake behind. As each ship heeled over, the leeward wing cut the water on the far side and helped to stabilize the ship. The windward wing was trimmed even further to force air around the mainsails, adding precious speed to their route.

"Captain," one of the deckhands shouted. Fadlemir made his way to the bow and looked over, peering down at the leaping dolphins that now accompanied them.

"A sign of blessing," he called to those around him. They smiled for the first time that day, happy for the company and for the favorable winds.

"Goodrin," Fadlemir turned to his second-in-command, "you have the helm." The man nodded in acknowledgment as Fadlemir moved back to mid-decks and slipped below. He entered into the storage rooms, laden with huge casks of water, wine, and mead. Other barrels contained grain and flour, and beside them instruments for cooking. Stockpiles of wood for fires were bundled tightly together, and metal prongs and skewers for spits stacked to one side. Row upon row of weapons lined an adjacent wall. Swords hung from brackets, dangling like gleaming teeth; spears were lashed together in manageable clusters, easily hoisted over a shoulder and hauled above decks; and various forms of shielding, designed specifically for battle at sea, were stacked neatly in one corner.

Fadlemir continued through the barracks, the musty smell of human dwelling and old bedding filling the air. More than a few of the injured men already slept soundly in their swinging cots, wrapped up like butterflies in cocoons swinging back and forth in a lazy summer breeze. The light was dim here, the sounds a mixture of creaking wood and chains combined with the steady lapping of water against the hull. Beyond that, the dull snores of the dreaming crew.

He passed into the ship's lounge, a large room reserved mostly for royalty, decked out in lush carpets, lavish furniture, and grand paintings and carvings depicting the realm of Ligeon. Passing through the lounge, Fadlemir ducked under a low door and emerged into the King's Quarters, an even grander room than the previous with a massive four-poster bed taking prominence. Three attendants hovered over King Anondo's leg like pigeons on a handful of seed.

The men spoke in hushed tones. Fadlemir stepped aside as a fourth attendant brought in a bucket of fresh water then excused himself. Fadelmir then moved to where the King lie. The men used fresh cloth, dipped it in the water, and cleansed the wound again. The sheets were stained red and soaked in water and blood.

Anondo groaned.

Fadlemir drew closer and noticed that it was not just Anondo's foot that bore the brunt of the damage, but his whole body was wracked with bruises and lacerations. Blood and dirt were caked like clay on his skin, now riddled with black and blue splotches. His tunic was matted and torn, his leather armor severed as well as the flesh beneath. But it was his lower leg they seemed most intent on.

"He's losing too much blood," one of the men said, now aware of Fadlemir's presence. "We can't make it stop." The man removed one of the cloths for Fadlemir to see. The flesh was chewed right off the bone around the ankle, a foot dangling loosely.

Anondo moaned from the pain, too fatigued to do anything more about it. He lay nearly motionless, slipping in and out of consciousness.

"Cut off his foot," Fadlemir said flatly.

The three attendants stared at the Captain.

"Leave it, and the flesh will rot, eventually tainting his blood. Then he'll lose his leg. From there, it may kill him. Act now, cleanse and seal what is left, and he'll keep his leg and his life." Fadlemir spoke forcefully. "Those are my orders." He withdrew his own sword and handed it to the nearest attendant. But the man just stared at him. "Fine." He pushed him out of the way and placed a piece of wood beneath Anondo's ankle. The King groaned. "I am sorry, my Liege. I sacrifice the little to gain the greater. I know you will understand in time. Forgive me."

Fadlemir grasped his sword with both hands and raised it high above his head.

Crack!

With a swift swing, the blade severed the bone, the dead limb falling to the side.

Anondo cried out and rolled slightly, aimlessly grabbing his thigh. Tears poured from his eyes.

Fadlemir pressed clean cloth against the gaping wound and then addressed the attendants. "The consequences are on my head. Wash the wound. You there," he faced the man who had brought the water, "heat an iron, or a sword, anything you can find in the ship's fires until it glows red, and bring it straight away. Go!" He turned back to the others. "When the wound is thoroughly cleansed, burn it shut and bandage it. Make sure he drinks and gets his rest."

But they all stood there, stone still.

"Get him some wine, man!" Fadlemir yanked one of the men forward and shoved him out the door. The other two snapped to attention and started to wash the fresh opening. Satisfied with his orders, Fadlemir left them to their work and returned topside.

The first thing his eyes looked to was the following storm to the west. The sky had darkened considerably save for the consistent flashes of light emanating from within. It took on a sickening blue-green hue that Fadlemir thought quite unusual. He moved back to the helmsman.

"Captain, I daresay it seems to be moving," said Goodrin.

"I know," Fadlemir acknowledged. "It's following us."

"Aye, though I wasn't going to say it."

"That's because it *sees*."

Goodrin hesitated. "*Sees?*"

"It lives, if that can be said, prompted by the hand of Morgui to consume us."

"Is that all?" Goodrin tried to lighten the mood.

Fadlemir only entertained a brief smile. He looked up to the sails and searched for any luffs, but his eyes saw nothing. "We're getting everything we can out of her?" he asked Goodrin.

"Aye, that and a little more."

"As I thought." The two other ships were right on their heels. "One advantage of the storm is the strong wind. At this rate we could make an eastern passage into Tontha in four days, maybe three."

"An unexpected boon indeed," Goodrin agreed.

"Press her, Goodrin," Fadlemir encouraged him. "Press her hard and fast. Let me know when you are tired." Goodrin nodded, and Fadlemir left him to work the deck with the others.

• • •

It had been a full day, reaching fast across the Faladrial Ocean. The wind continued to buffet the soul of each vessel as they careened northeast toward Tontha. The ancient wood groaned under the constant barrage, the storm berating every piece of canvas hoisted into the sky. And despite their efforts, the men could not seem to pull away from the foreboding black that pursued them.

A deckhand roused Fadlemir.

The Captain stood and ran a hand over his face, and then through his hair. He looked around. A few other men took their shifts of fitful rest beside him, hidden below decks from the brunt of the wind, but not from the sound. It howled, beating against the hull and running through the shrouds with terror. How he had gotten any rest was hard to say, but his fatigue had certainly bested the blowing without.

Fadlemir glanced at the man who woke him. "How is she?"

"All secure and trimmed hard. The men are rotating as ordered."

"And you?"

"Me?" The deckhand was not used to being asked how *he* fared. "I'm well, my Captain."

"Good, get some rest. Take my place, would you?"

"But, sir—"

"Take my place. You look like you could use it."

"Aye," he obeyed. "C'symia."

Fadlemir left the man and walked back through the ship to the King's Quarters. He peered into the great room. Anondo lay sleeping in the bed, now covered in heavy blankets. Fadlemir pressed the door open further and walked in. The attendant stood promptly and waited for Fadlemir's orders.

"How does he fare?" the Captain asked.

"The *hasithe-morna*[5] persists," the attendant replied.

Fadlemir walked quietly beside the bed and touched the King's forehead. He lay shaking, his skin hot to the touch and growing hotter. His hair was damp and his skin wet with perspiration. The Captain then reached down and lifted off the covers.

"We need to keep him cool," he instructed. "Until this breaks again. Then cover him back up as I told you before."

The man nodded.

Fadlemir removed some of the bandage to view the wound. It was red and swollen, leaking yellow and white fluid.

"When was the last time you cleaned this?"

"I don't remember, Captain. Perhaps two hours ago?"

The attendant asked it more like a question than a statement. Fadlemir was beginning to show signs of frustration. The emotions came upon him suddenly, so fast in fact, that he did not even notice his own propensity to bend toward them. Granted, it was not all this man's fault, for indeed the extreme circumstances in which each man found himself

---

[5] **Hasithe-morna** (*ha-SITH-(eh) MOURN-uh*): *noun; First Dionian, literally translated "fever of death."*

were reason enough for dire concern, but since this attendant was the unfortunate soul closest to Fadlemir, he got the brunt of it.

"You don't *remember?*" Fadlemir covered the wound back up and turned slowly. "You don't remember how long ago you attended the injuries of your *King?*"

"But, Captain—"

"Hold your tongue," Fadlemir spat. "What you have is no small duty. If I ask one of my men, 'When was the last time you watered your horse?' he replies, 'Just a moment after we finished dinner.' If I ask a soldier, 'When was the last time you sharpened your blade?' he says, 'Three days hence.' How much more when I ask *you* about the wellbeing of your *King!*"

"I'm sorry, my—"

"Indeed!" Fadlemir marched to the door. "See that it's cleaned immediately. I shall not need to remind you again."

"Aye, sir," the attendant uttered.

Fadlemir walked out and closed the door firmly. He made it about three steps into the lounge before his words caught up with him, and everything else he was feeling, for that matter. It was as if a wave washed him off his feet.

He suddenly saw the finality of each issue flood his soul, and his own hands helpless to keep it all together, like tapestries unraveling from high in the sky. He saw himself running to and fro, trying desperately to pick up the threads and keep them from pulling away from the images they so masterfully portrayed. He reached out to steady himself, grabbing the back of a high-backed chair.

Ligeon, the beautiful country that had once been a gleaming jewel of Dionia, was now fading into oblivion, ransacked by more Dairne-Reih then he could ever count; his men, hewn to less than half of what he had left Mt. Dakka with, were beaten down and desperate for hope; and his beloved King, once valiant and strong, was now a crippled mass of trembling flesh, and that at his own hand. He knew his words to the attendant had been severe. He would apologize later.

The storm that threatened to destroy them all now seemed almost an afterthought to him, his head swimming in doubt and inadequacy. But oddly, it was the one thing that brought him back to reality. It was the one thing he could try and match wits with.

He shook the encounter with the attendant from his head and took a deep breath.

"Who I am under pressure is who I really am," he muttered to himself. "You must help me, Most High." He rubbed his face and then moved back through the barracks and then into the storage room.

He looked around.

A wave of inspiration struck.

He mounted the stairs and emerged above. The strong wind dispersed any lingering feelings of dread. He moved aft and looked toward the encroaching storm. It was then his eye caught something he had never seen the likes of.

"What in the name of the Great God is that?" he asked Goodrin, staring at a strange, snake-like tail that danced between sky and sea.

"It appeared at dawn," Goodrin confessed. "Started like a vapor. Before long it grew, spinning wildly."

"It does not bode well."

Goodrin nodded. "And we're not making any headway."

"Have you gotten any sleep, Goodrin?" Fadlemir inquired, brushing off the previous comment.

"Enough," said the helmsman.

"Hardly so, I think." Fadlemir cast him a wry eye, and then addressed the storm. "It's gaining. So we must be faster."

"But how?"

"Lighten our load. Everything we don't need goes over."

"Sir?"

"If we raise her out of the water, even a span, we gain time. And we must make landfall with time to spare; this beast will take us at sea, or on land. The coastal mountains are our only hope. But we need time to secure their protection."

"As you say, Captain."

"I have the helm," Fadlemir said. Goodrin moved forward and began giving orders. His voice rang out amidst the howling wind, bellowing and barking to the men.

Before long the crew had hauled everything they could from below decks, from grain sacks to wine vats, from the barrels of flour to shielding, plopping everything amidships. A second crew of men, those topside, heaved the precious but now lethal items overboard, to be swallowed quickly by the following sea. The large crossbows were dismantled and pushed over, even the ship's anchor was cut loose and dropped with a massive splash; the only option from here on would be to beach the ships. The two vessels behind followed Fadlemir's lead. The men even brought up the weaponry and prepared to heave them over.

"Not those," Fadlemir ordered. "Everything but those. We keep the weapons." The crew nodded and took some small pleasure in his words. That the Captain would allow them to maintain their own sense of security was mildly comforting. They stowed the swords and spears again, but everything else went.

A short time later, after a significant load had been unburdened from the ship, Goodrin returned to the helm and peered over the side. The ship was indeed riding higher, perhaps even higher than Fadlemir had guessed she would.

But he waited for the report.

"We're higher—and faster," Goodrin smiled.

"Aye," Fadlemir said, looking up to the sails. "Ease out the mainsail," he ordered. "She's sheeted in too tight. And trim the foresails; we need to squeeze every drop out of her."

"Aye, Captain," Goodrin replied and was off.

Even the slight adjustments propelled them a bit more. And that was all Fadlemir was hoping for: *a bit more.*

For the first time that day, the fleet began pulling away from their dark pursuer. The wind maintained every thread of its strength, yet the storm was left trailing behind.

But not by much.

By the dawn of the second day, Fadlemir and Goodrin were able to make out certain landmarks along the shore to the east. Goodrin pressed the corners of the thick parchment map against the bulkhead and pinned them down with daggers. The dwarves of Ot had drawn the ancient scroll long ago. It bore the High King's seal and the insignias of the Lords of Ligeon.

"We'll make our landing there," Fadlemir tapped a sharp curve that followed inland easterly and then jutted due north, just over the border into Tontha. "We'll take cover in the lower foothills and weather the assault. When it's over, we'll move east and make for Mt. Dakka. Four days, I presume, six at the most."

The swirling funnel-like anomaly that followed grew with the passage of time, not only in size and power, but in sound. The demonic hunter issued forth an odd whistle, harmonic, but far from melodious.

Its rage was clear, its result certain. Judging from the way it sucked up the ocean and spewed it out from high above, Fadlemir knew that there would be no surviving an encounter with the beast.

As dusk hastened to a sky already dark with cloud, Goodrin had a hard time navigating the waters leading ashore. He used the rising mountains as guides, but they could not tell him what lay in the shallows ahead. He picked his course carefully, but knew most of it was guesswork. He read the surface of the water, discerning between wind ripples and rocky shoals. But it was terribly hard to see. Only the occasional flashes of light from behind gave any relief to his failing perspective.

Lookouts on the bow and in the rigging shouted back to him, indicating variations in color and texture of the water. But with the fading light, not even they could be sure of their readings. The waves were heavy but not unbearable. A slight rain was starting to fall.

Fadlemir was among those forward, leaning out on the bowsprit, a single line in his hand. He peered hard into the waves, focused on depth alone. The ocean floor rose in and out of his vision, vibrant and colorful one moment, and then dipping away into dark oblivion the next.

"*Rocks off the starboard bow!*" a lookout above shouted, hands waving. Goodrin threw the wheel hard to port and the boat lurched, turning in an ungainly motion. Men everywhere fell to the deck, tumbling against the bulkhead and slamming into the masts. The two other boats followed closely behind and matched Goodrin's maneuver.

The rain came on stronger and made the deck increasingly slippery. Fadlemir knew the storm would not give them any quarter. A flash of light filled the low sky, followed by a terrifying crack that ripped through the air. The eerie voice of their pursuer was growing. "I hear you. I hear you," Fadlemir spoke intimately to the encroaching monster, looming high over the water. "But by the name of the Creator God, you will not take us." He stared into the sea, studying the bottom that passed quickly underneath. Suddenly, he noticed a strange tendency in the sand, and instinct told him to act.

"*Hard to starboard!*" he yelled back over his shoulder.

As if his voice commanded the very life of the boat, the ship listed to port but then surged to starboard. Men moved across the deck once more, but fewer of them fell, ready this time for the sudden shift. Fadlemir glanced back into the waves and watched as the bottom raced toward the surface, the shallows coming on quickly. He was sure they would run aground. He held his breath as the massive ship slid speedily over the sandy bottom, the keel surely not more than an arm's length from getting buried. Then the sandy bottom dropped away. He glanced back at Goodrin and smiled. *"That was close,"* he yelled.

Shrooomph!

All at once the ship pitched forward, the bow digging deep into the ocean floor. The deckhands flew forward, toppling over anything in front of them. Those in the rigging clenched the lines as their bodies extended out over the water, footing lost on the slippery booms and ratlines. Heads cracked on solid hardwood, ribs snapped against iron fixtures. Bodies slid down the deck, careening toward the bow with all the speed the ship had held. A few of them cried out as they pitched overboard, some falling perilously from high above.

Then the second ship slammed into the first, burying its prow deep into her stern. The bowsprit burrowed through the transom and gouged the aft deck. Goodrin felt the planks beneath him bulge, and all at once he was hoisted into the air as the entire aft section of the ship was pushed aloft. Wood splintered, chains and lines snapped, and men hollered in the chaos. More men tumbled into the sea, and sailors from the second boat flew onto the first, thrown like flightless birds against the rigging.

The third ship turned hard to port, but caught the second vessel amidships, pulling it sideways. The second ship tore away from the first, ripping off the aft quarter of the boat and opening a gaping hole in the stern.

Fadlemir was barely holding on, his whole body dangling over the water from a single line now snagged around the forestay. Suddenly the line went limp and he looked up…

…the mast had given way and was falling toward him.

He kicked his legs and let go of the line, trying to put some distance between himself and the ruined ship. At the same moment, the mast raced down and slammed into the foredeck, breaking in two and shattering the deck planks. Fadlemir was swallowed in the waves and covered his head. Debris fell all about him, yet he remained still in his undersea protection.

His world went from one of total chaos, strewn with the shouts of men and the tearing of wood, to the underworld churning of bubbled blue. The sea swallowed the terror above like a whale swallowing a school of fish. Now only muffled sounds and bubbling gurgles journeyed through the depths, separating him from the catastrophic events above.

Fadlemir opened his eyes. He could not tell which way was up. His eyes darted quickly in the dim underworld, searching for clues. But then his eyes caught something unusual: light under the water.

There, to one side, he made out the submerged windows of the King's Quarters near the bow. A number of lanterns burned brightly behind the glass. Fadlemir righted himself and then swam over, peering through the portholes. King Anondo had tumbled helplessly onto the floor, the room disheveled. But then he noticed one lantern burning a little too brightly. Only, it wasn't a lantern after all.

The room's massive rug was on fire.

Fadlemir struggled to the surface and took a gasping breath. He searched for a line, a chain, anything to get back topside. His eyes darted along the hull. He swam the length of the starboard side and took hold of some rigging, now dangling haphazardly in the churning sea. One hand over the other, Fadlemir fought with the ropes, banging against the side of the hull. The work was tiresome and he felt his muscles burning. His feet slipped and were caught more than once, twisted instantly in the swollen knot-work. But he was still able to pull free and managed to climb higher on his ladder.

Soon he was topside and tumbled onto the deck. All around men lay groaning, doing their best to stand, pulling themselves up on anything their hands could reach. Blood mixed with the salty waters and flowed between the boards. More than one of his men lay unconscious, tossed helplessly by whatever wave managed its way over the rails.

The sea was getting worse, and the boat lurched in urgent rhythm. Fadlemir struggled to keep his balance against the buffeting waves, picking his way slowly through the wreckage to the doors below. But he could go no further. The main mast lay straight across the entry, never to be moved again, except by the elements themselves.

Frustrated, and with time running out, Fadlemir spun around and looked for another access point below. But there were none. The twisting monster was much closer and all points leading belowdecks were blocked. He knew there was only one way to rescue his King. Suddenly a familiar voice sounded behind him. It was Goodrin.

Fadlemir rushed aft, bounding over sail and boom, only to find his friend pinned down by wreckage from the following ship. His legs were nearly severed, blood flowing steadily from his mouth. Fadlemir choked on his own tears, now face to face with the terror that was stalking them all. Goodrin tried to speak again.

"Hush now," Fadlemir pleaded, dropping to his knees.

"I'm so sorry," Goodrin uttered. Then he coughed a fine spray of red mixing with the rain.

"Come now, it was a fine bit of sailing," said the Captain.

"I'm sorry," said Goodrin again, growing delirious.

"I need you to stay here and man the helm," Fadlemir instructed, handing him a chunk of the wheel that had broken off. The battered helmsman grasped the wood tightly.

"I can do that," he replied, his voice weakening.

"Steady as she goes."

"Steady as she goes," Goodrin replied.

He would never speak again. His eyes lost their life, peering skyward. Fadlemir closed them and quickly got up.

What moments before had appeared to be a clean break to the shore had become a tumult of destruction. It had happened so fast. And lives were fading without hesitation. Any that survived now splashed in the waves, either struggling to get back aboard or making an effort to swim ashore, beating the storm. Only a few valiant souls remained behind, all occupied with injured sailors. Smoke was rising from the bow. Fadlemir had to save the King himself.

He bounded back through the broken booms and sails, and swung over the bridge rail. He tried to pick his way down the tousled rigging toward the churning sea, but his grip slipped, feet sliding into the knots. He felt a moment of panic as he toppled over backward into the water, now upside down. And his feet were stuck.

He sucked in a mouthful of water then lifted his head and chest out of the waves. He tried to wrestle his foot free, but it was twisted. He clenched his teeth and reached for the rigging, pulling himself fully out of the water. Soon he was high enough above his feet that he freed himself, and then finished his descent.

Once in the sea he swam forward and dove. His eyes quickly found the windows, now aglow with light. One look and he knew the fire had spread. Anondo still lay on the floor, unconscious. Fadlemir knew whatever he did next must be swift. He would have precious little time, and only one chance.

Pulling his knees up to his chest, Fadlemir positioned himself in front of the windows and then uncoiled himself, striking the glass. It did not take much as the massive pressure of the water already weighed heavily on the thin partition.

Fadlemir was sucked into the hull. He tumbled onto the floor, driven down by the gushing water, something sharp slicing his forearm, and then his thigh. Glass shards. He knew it would be pointless to contend against the raging force, so he let himself be swirled about, taking but one breath in the midst of the tumult. Soon the room would fill with water, and it would be easier to maneuver.

Now that Anondo being burned to death was no longer a worry, Fadlemir knew he had to keep him from drowning. The King's limp body emerged face down in the churning froth. Fadlemir fought against the current. He reached out and caught hold of Anondo's dangling arm, drawing him near. With his other hand, he flipped the King over and searched his face for life.

The room was nearly full. They needed to make their escape. With Anondo almost pinned against the ceiling, Fadlemir took a deep breath and dove, dragging Anondo with him. The work was difficult. Fadlemir felt fatigue fight him from the beginning. He kicked with all his might, one arm wrapped around the King's neck, the other beating the water frantically. He reached out, pulling hard for every stroke. He passed through the window and then pulled Anondo through behind him. Once clear, Fadlemir kicked furiously toward the surface, bursting into the air, lungs aflame.

The rain was pouring down now, the seas alive and wild. Fadlemir's first breath was followed by a quick second, full of seawater. He held the King close, hoping he was breathing. Waves crashed over them, threatening to cast them back down into the depths, back into the darkness.

Fadlemir felt something strike his head. Small specks of light filled his vision, followed by a sudden pull to sleep.

But he could not—he would not give in.

Blood trickled into his eye. He was alert once more.

He turned and spied what had struck him: a large plank from the ship's hull tossed about in the waves. With his free hand, Fadlemir reached out and drew the board toward them. It was all he could do to heave the

King onto the plank, positioning him so as not to capsize it. He wiped more blood from his eye and choked on another mouthful of water. He then searched for the mountains, but the rain blurred his sight.

Fadlemir glanced over his shoulder and looked which way the ship faced; they had been heading straight for shore. He turned the board to face the same direction, holding it high in the water and propelling it with his legs. Then he worked his legs for all he was worth.

The board started forward, reluctantly at first, Fadlemir kicking it up a wave. Once he crested the top, they surged down the backside with increased momentum. But any pleasure was lost as he beat hard against the next swell.

The Captain's legs felt like lead, muscles burning from fatigue. *Rest just for a moment*, he thought. *Just to catch your breath.*

"Nay!" he roared, shouting against the waves and the rain. "I will go on!"

But the declaration did nothing to ease his pain. His head swooned and his shoulders throbbed. He cast a brief look over his shoulder; the sight of the swirling hunter behind him pushed him onward. It wouldn't be long before the ravenous beast ate the ships. He had to keep going.

Suddenly, as they crested a swell, Fadlemir caught site of a wide white strand separating the sea from mountains that faded into a lowering sky. "Almost there, my King," he said, not sure if Anondo could hear him.

The furious wind bit hard at the two men, whipping water in every direction, turning the ocean's surface into a belated lament for a long forgotten respite. Fadlemir pushed onward, compelling his legs to kick harder than ever. He gulped down more than one mouthful, choking, vomiting, and then gasping for air. His arms began to shake, hands barely clutching the plank, shoulders knotted and spent.

His right foot struck bottom.

Fadlemir looked up. They were riding the surf into the shore. His left foot nestled into the sand, and in the next moment, he made to stand. But his weary legs buckled and the Captain stumbled, shoved forward over the plank by an incoming wave. He flipped off the side, Anondo spilling into the froth with him.

Another wave slammed into him, throwing him around with the churning sea. His shoulder struck hard against the bottom and his shirt filled with the abrasive sand. He drank sand and salt, his eyes stinging with pain.

Once the waves were through with him, Fadlemir sat up in the shallows and fought for clean air. He squinted, searching for Anondo. The King lie face down a short distance away, his limbs dragging on the sandy bottom.

Fadlemir climbed to his feet, stumbled once more, and clumsily splashed his way to Anondo's side. He bent over and hoisted him out of the water, and then dragged him by the arms to the beach. A new wave roared forward and then crashed onto the shore, driving up the beach and pushing Anondo up even further. Fadlemir fell backwards, struggling to keep moving. He was so tired. He had to rest.

But still something within him told him to carry on. He had to get the King to safety; it was his greatest objective, and he would not fail.

Fadlemir pushed himself off his elbows and rolled onto his knees. Anondo floated on a thin film of retreating water. Fadlemir grabbed him as the water receded, and then stood. This time, he bent over and agonizingly hoisted the King's limp body onto his shoulder, willing his knees straight. He turned and began walking up the beach, feet sinking deep with each step under the weight. There were no other footprints, just his. That no one else had made it to shore saddened him.

Until that moment, Fadlemir had almost forgotten about the tempest racing after them. But when a violent cacophony of noise went up from behind him, he knew it had reached the ships. He spun to see the whirling beast devour the three vessels, swallowing them completely out of sight. But not for long. Within moments he saw the boats lift out of the sea, held aloft magically, and thrown around within the whirling tail. In the next instant, they shattered, pulled apart into countless fragments.

Fadlemir looked on in disbelief. He couldn't move. The destruction was so complete, so swift.

Schunnnk!

He looked to the ground beside him and saw a large shard of wood impaled in the sand. Fadlemir stared at it, his mind working; it looked to be a splintered section of mast. He looked back up and then studied the space surrounding the funnel; it was swirling with debris from the boats, spewing out like bones of devoured prey.

Fadlemir caught something out of the corner of his eye.

He turned. A huge object was flying right at him. Fadlemir dropped to his knees and ducked. The bulbous anchor housing—complete with trailing chain—whizzed overhead and tumbled, sand spraying everywhere. But the chain did not clear the two men before snapping back into Fadlemir's side. The blow also struck Anondo's back, and for the first time, Fadlemir thought he felt him respond.

Despite two broken ribs, the Captain was again aware that they needed to get off the beach. He stood and started forward. He had not taken three steps before another splinter from the ships slashed across their path, plunging into the beach. Then another object landed with a solid *thud* behind them.

Fadlemir began running. He could not feel his legs.

The strand was soon a deadly tumult, shrapnel flying everywhere. He neared the first signs of foliage. Already battered by the wind, the scraggly trees and shrubs were assaulted by a barrage of lethal projectiles.

Thwip!—Thwack!—Shwip!

Wooden shrapnel tore through the leaves, limbs severed and dropping to the ground, tree trunks blasted and torn from their rooting. Still Fadlemir drove hard through the underbrush, bounding over the dunes and dodging trees. He felt a few small fragments bite his flesh, certain he had been struck, but he did not lessen his pace.

A giant explosion of sand and wood erupted a few strides in front of him…

…a ship's entire bow crashed to the ground. Fadlemir stumbled, but regained his balance and moved around the mass. This *thing* seemed to be *aiming* for him.

Still Fadlemir surged forward, now putting great distance between them and the beach. The storm gave up a deafening shriek, as if screaming in defiance. But Fadlemir ignored the tirade. Even the onslaught of rain didn't seem to bother him. He was completely focused on what lay ahead: a strange opening in the side of a rock face…

…just big enough for a man.

With a sudden burst of renewed energy, Fadlemir pressed each stride a little farther. He heard another large object fall hard behind him, but he didn't even turn to look. His eyes were fixed on the opening.

Push yourself.

His lungs burned. Breathing was strenuous.

Almost there…

Suddenly three spears materialized, impaling the ground in quick succession. The Captain slowed out of wonder. Just then a few more appeared. And then a sword.

It cannot be—

But it was. The beast was *alive*. It *knew*.

A blade sliced Fadlemir's calf. His leg buckled. He and Anondo spilled to the ground in a heap. The Captain rolled in agony. He grabbed his leg and tried to examine the wound; it was deep, the muscle severed from the tendon, now balled up behind his knee.

He looked up.

The cave was only a few strides ahead.

Fadlemir clenched his teeth and elbowed his way through the sand-rooted brush.

"You will not take my King," he growled in defiance. "Not this time."

With one arm hooked under Anondo's shoulder, Fadlemir got on all fours, favoring his good leg, and began dragging his Lord forward.

The storm bellowed again, unleashing another barrage of shrapnel at the pair.

Fadlemir reached the small, chest-height opening, big enough for only one man to fit through at a time. The hole had been uncovered by the torturous winds, blowing aside plants and vines that had long since hidden it. The massive amount of rubble surrounding it suggested that the cave was much larger than the small gap appeared.

Fadlemir stood, favoring his good leg, and picked up Anondo. He leaned him against the rubble, and then hoisted him from the waist, shoving his head and shoulders into the hole. He grunted, trying to overcome the pain in his leg, doing his best to keep his balance. He repositioned his hands, but before he could push, the body moved forward. In the same moment, Fadlemir's body was drilled through with countless shards of wood and metal, pinning him against the rocks. All he could do was look his last into the hole as two small sets of hands pulled Anondo from within.

PART TWO

Chapter Fourteen

AT TABLE WITH THE ENEMY

Anorra had finally fallen asleep, though anyone would forgive her for not terming it such. The quasi-rest she took was brief and far from replenishing. The hot rocks slowly seared her exposed skin and smoldered what clothing remained. The heat dried many of her cuts, while others blistered and ran. But her exhaustion was so overwhelming that her body took advantage of whatever quarter was given. The simple torment of being held perpetually between waking and sleeping racked her spirit mercilessly.

The environment surrounding her took rather than gave, a disturbing attribute well known by its inhabitants. It held no care for its victims, solely bent on self-gain. And after stealing away the virtues of a prisoner, it went further, demanding interest on its own usury, willing away all fortitude so completely that only a hole remained, a vacuum of inescapable despair.

Anorra's body, broken and bruised, lay like a trampled flower discarded into a dark corner and left to die. Truly her thoughts were on death, wishing it to carry her away into the Royal Throne Room. But so far removed from civilization was she, from life, from her people, that she feared not even the Mighty Hand could rescue her, wherever she was.

The shrieks never seemed to ebb. A constant cacophony of mayhem, calls of despair, laced around her head, stifling the light of her heart. Even while pushing toward a sleep-bent daze, the horror of tormented souls pulled on her sense of compassion, and then crossed the line to personal terror.

Out of the blackness she heard footsteps. Someone was coming. The screaming escalated. Another monster most likely: a demon to devour her, to strip her of her dignity and ingest what pitiful form remained.

A jingle of metal, and the sharp clink of a lock.

"What intruder has cast thy lily upon the rocks and left her to die?"

The words were so out of place. So foreign. Spoken by a voice… so soothing. Even royal.

"He that hath done this will never deny that, when he hath done this to you, he hath done this to me also."

The voice was strong and handsome, full and overwhelming. She heard footsteps draw closer. She tried to lift her head.

"Rest my lily, white and fair. Rest easy in my arms now."

He picked her up gently. Her body relaxed. And suddenly she was free of pain. But rather than brighten to the relief, she dove into a deep and much needed sleep.

• • •

"How do you feel?"

Anorra heard the words as if tethered by a long silk ribbon to her consciousness. While the darkness was sweet, his voice was sweeter. She blinked, wide-eyed, allowing the dim light of the room to pierce her eyes.

"I—I can see."

"Of course you can," he replied.

Anorra was lying across a wide, cushioned chair. Her head was propped up with pillows, and a soft blanket covered her legs. She looked down and noticed she was clothed in a shimmering white dress, gilded in gold. Soft light came from countless candles, peeking out from behind red drapes and perched upon black wrought-iron fixtures.

She suddenly felt exposed at having been dressed unawares. *Who touched me? Who* saw *me?* Unless she had dressed herself. *Did I?*

"Come, my lily fair. You must be famished. Dine with me."

Anorra turned toward the voice. A gorgeous man sat at a table decked with a red satin tablecloth and candles. An empty chair was half-turned toward her. She gazed into his eyes. They were warm and alluring. His face was strong and masculine, skin glistening in the candlelight. He was wrapped in a gently flowing mantle, and Anorra could tell this was a powerful man.

And then there were the sudden emotions that stirred within her. Something leapt in her belly, a fluttering that caught her breath. She looked straight into his eyes and felt her face warm under his gaze. He was so… *beautiful*.

"Need I request your presence again?" he inquired. "I will if need be."

Anorra felt herself rise from the blankets and walk steadily to the chair opposite him. It was almost as if she moved without thought.

But who was this man? She was not in the habit of dining with strangers. The action felt awkward, but looking at him, there was something she wanted.

Something she longed for.

He rose from his seat and put a hand on her chair as she gently lowered herself. His hands and arms were strong. This man's commanding presence was inspiring, to say the least, and Anorra found herself trying not to stare. She inclined her head in thanks.

A man appeared from the far end of the room, entering through a narrow door. He was dressed in a blue tunic, and his skin was deeply flavored by the sun. He moved swiftly, carrying a large silver platter. He stood over Anorra and produced two golden goblets, a jar of wine, and a board of warm breads.

Just as he turned, a second man appeared, much the same but dressed in a purple tunic. He lowered a platter of steaming meats, no two alike. He also produced two small bowls of dipping broth, spices swirling on the surface.

A third and final man brought a large platter, this one mounded so high with fruit Anorra thought it would topple over at any moment. But he deftly lowered the tray onto a smaller table beside them and disappeared back through the door.

Anorra was overwhelmed by the smells, her stomach churning wildly. She felt her mouth moisten, eyes taking in all that was before her.

And suddenly she realized how incredibly hungry she was. Famished even.

Without hesitating, she reached forward, grabbed a piece of bread, and ripped off a chunk in her mouth. The flavor was delicious, arguably the best bread she had ever tasted. She swallowed quickly and took a mouthful of the wine, the rich drink racing down her throat.

A thinly sliced piece of meat lay just in front of her, calling to her. She snatched it up to her mouth, but not before plunging it into the small bowl, drenching it in warm spices. The taste was so overwhelming she found herself rolling her eyes. Delicious!

Not able to control herself, Anorra reached for the fruit platter. The whole thing had been masterfully constructed, each piece of fruit hand-cut, prepared just for her taking. Flowering pears cascaded down split pineapples that lay upon mounds of berries. She didn't know where to start.

"Here, let me help you."

She had nearly forgotten about him. Anorra looked up and suddenly felt embarrassed, having eaten so ravenously. But he didn't seem to mind in the least, his eyes twinkling. He reached over and selected a piece of apple, covered in a bit of the berry juice, and offered it to her mouth. She leaned forward, staring into his captivating face, and took the fruit.

She closed her eyes and savored it. It was as if she hadn't eaten in days.

How long had it been?

Her eyes popped open.

She froze. She...

...couldn't remember.

Her host smiled at her and reached for another piece of fruit.

"Wait, I—" She hesitated, but didn't know why.

"Yes?" He brought a piece of banana to her lips and she took it without thinking. "Is everything to your liking?"

"Of course. It's...*perfect.*"

"Good," he smiled. Anorra looked into his face and suddenly felt warm, and not from the wine. He was too beautiful even to look at. Her skin prickled, and she tried to hide her giddiness.

"Have some more," he suggested.

But Anorra shook her head. "Who are you?"

"The Prince," he replied without hesitation. His words were

confident and reassuring, as if anyone should have known this fact, but he took pity on Anorra and indulged her. Anorra simply nodded and took another sip from her cup.

She tried to search back through her memories. *Why am I here? Where was I before this?* But her head was thick, and she couldn't place anything.

She remained ever hungry and ate more, the Prince never taking a bite. He seemed utterly content to watch her, taking great joy in her delight. The food was delectable, each morsel better than the first.

Finally, not knowing how much time had passed, Anorra dabbed her mouth with the fine linen napkin, and pressed herself back from the table a little. The Prince rose and gestured toward a grand stone fireplace. Wood crackled in the pit, giving off a fragrant smell of cherry wood.

Is it inussle already? But why else would there be a fire?

He touched her elbow as they moved toward the heat. She felt a flash from his fingertips, and her heart raced.

Large animal skins lay all about the black marble floor, as did oversized pillows of various colors. Everything looked soft and inviting. She couldn't imagine a more perfect scene. She knelt beside two pillows and then lay back. Her hands nervously smoothed her dress and she noticed once again how beautiful the gown was. But she never remembered seeing it before.

"So you haven't asked me why you're here," the man commented finally, himself seated not too far away, reclining with his head propped up on a pillow. He looked into her eyes longingly, almost as if he…

…as if he *wanted her.*

"Why I'm here?" Anorra mumbled distantly, and looked down. Her thoughts raced. It was as if she were in a dark hallway, pressing against every door that met her hands, trying the handle. But none of them opened. She ran faster down the hallway, looking for the faintest sign of passage, but there was none. Then, in the distance, she could hear the whisper of scratching.

Someone was behind one of the doors.

She raced down the hallway, her heart pounding in her ears. She heard knocking, and then someone trying the handle. A door giggled. A muffled voice on the other side. She grabbed the handle and jerked it wildly. But it was locked.

"I brought you here because you are very special, Anorra." The way he said her name filled her with importance. She *mattered* to him. "*Very* special to *me*," he amended. "I have been watching you for a very long time. And I have decided something."

There was a pregnant pause. Anorra stared at him and held her breath.

"I want you to stay with me."

"Stay with you?" Anorra suddenly felt uncomfortable. But it wasn't all *bad*. She glanced around the room quickly. "Here?" she said with a nervous laugh.

"No, not here, my lily. But with me, to rule over my kingdom." He sat up and drew near to her. The fire popped and the heat grew more intense. "All I have," he whispered, "is *yours*."

Her stomach fluttered. He was getting very close. His frame was imposing, and the scent of his skin was intoxicating. His lips... *What is he doing? What does he want? This man really* wants *me?* Then the voice in her head changed entirely.

Anorra! What are you doing?

She sat upright and turned her face just as he moved in. The Prince paused and then withdrew. An awkward stillness filled the air, save for the rustle of the fire.

"I'm—I'm tired," she said.

The Prince took a moment to ponder her reaction. "Of course you are," he replied. "Let me stay with you."

"Nay, I prefer to be alone, c'symia."

"Very well, I shall leave you to your sleep." His tone was notably put off, but he resigned himself to her wishes and stood slowly. "Have my servants call upon me when you are rested." And with that he stood, turned across the room and exited through a grand set of heavy curtains.

Chapter Fifteen

FROM WHENCE THEY CAME

Only two ill-tempered Dylaithlok remained to plague the skies above them in Mt. Dakka. Boran and Benigan had dispatched the previous number, only to be left with the keenest; these, the brothers noted, had grown perceptive, focusing their attack on the sections of the city farthest from the watching towers. Boran descended the tower and summoned Gorn and a handful of warriors farther up into the city, while Benigan rejoined Brax on the ramparts, busy with a new breach.

"How many remain?" Brax shouted over his shoulder. He surveyed a large tear in the wall below. A great number of men and beasts sought each for the lives of the others, swords lunging into the calloused flesh of demon-hide and horns piercing the fragile human skin.

"Just two, my King."

"And Boran?"

"With Gorn in the upper city. The Dylaithlok have grown leery of the towers."

Brax only nodded, his attention fixed on the losing plight of his men below. The Dairne-Reih poured in through the broken section of wall faster than the soldiers could stay them off.

"This is the third break in the line," Brax said. "We cannot take another."

As if summoned by his fear, a massive fireball slammed into the adjacent wall across the divide, exploding into a fury of molten shrapnel. Carnage strewn with bits of men and demon alike flew into the air. Brax and his brother shielded their faces. The thunderous explosion was followed by souls in the throes of death and the crumbling of rock. A moment later, stillness.

Brax looked down in horror; the gap had doubled in size.

Those men that survived the blow struggled to their feet. But the demon horde was not so merciful as to let them stand. Crashing through the smoke and dust came a fresh charge from the outside that shook the ground. The charred ravine was filled with the sights and sounds of men crushed. But the push slowed as it met fresh legs and arms further in, spears at the ready.

The damage had been done. The Dairne-Reih entered in far enough that they spilled into the unguarded side streets and over the low rock walls that separated highly-traveled thoroughfares from dwelling passages.

"Come, brother," Benigan pulled at Brax's arm. "You cannot remain. To the palace."

Brax withdrew, but struggled to leave what he knew he must. The two of them joined the ranks of those retreating from the ramparts. With the wall breach now widened, the bulk of the enemy's attack would center there, leaving only a handful of stragglers attempting to mount the siege ladders; those demons that did were met by a loyal few, warriors who would not abandon their positions on account of their immovable allegiance.

Brax and Benigan weaved their way up through the city streets, avenues now filled with chaos. Captains shouted orders, orderlies toted supplies, and all manner of weaponry clattered along the stone roads. As they fled further into Mt. Dakka, soldiers peeled off from their retreat to take up supporting positions along the side streets; if they could not stop the hemorrhage, they would at least try to contain it.

The sounds of war soon ebbed until Brax and Benigan were far removed, gathering near to the palace. "Wait, Benigan," Brax slowed and turned around.

"What is it, my Lord?"

"I cannot leave them. And stop calling me that." He caught his breath. "If I am not able to stay with these men, then I am no King. I am a hireling."

"But Brax—"

"You know very well what I mean, brother."

Benigan was incredulous. "So you will meet the same fate as our father and bring this weight of rulership upon yet another? I don't think so. Not here. Not today." He reached for Brax's arm, but the younger twin pulled away and unsheathed his sword. He was walking back down the track.

"Brax."

The King stopped.

"Will you fight for a few when you are needed by many?"

Neither brother moved. The distant battle clash echoed up through Mt. Dakka's heights, summoning a great many souls to death with every toll of its haunting bell. Brax lowered his head but did not turn.

"How does a King measure his life, Benigan?"

"What was that?"

"How does a King decide between the needs of two souls, pulling him in opposite directions, when both are his people?"

"That is only for great Kings to face, I suppose, and even greater Kings to decide."

"Then I must confess I am not among them," Brax said.

"Not among them? Why, brother, you define them."

"Then tell me why I cannot decide which to favor?"

"Because a King who is not torn favors his own opinion rather than the needs of those before him."

Brax turned and regarded his brother. Benigan placed a strong hand on his shoulder. "May all Dionia's Kings be so fortunate to be watched over with such compassion."

"C'symia, brother."

Benigan caught a black smudge whisk across the night sky just above. Brax noticed as well and gazed skyward. "Dylaithlok."

"Aye. It's hunting," said Boran.

It appeared again, racing between two tall buildings, this time its yellowed eye gleaming as it passed.

"Quickly! We must draw it out," Benigan said. He and Brax turned and raced up the road into a spacious square. Dwellings bordered it on every side save for the gaps where the track led away in three other directions. A much taller structure to the left that served as a food storage building. Just then Brax spotted something unexpected: there on the roof…movement. As he peered more closely, Brax could see Boran lying hidden beneath a wool blanket, arm exposed and waving. Another similar lump just beside let Brax know Boran was not alone.

"Do you see him there?" Brax inclined his head but did not point.

"Aye," Benigan said. "Gorn will be with him, too, I wager."

A deafening screech seared across the night sky, and the brothers looked up to see not one, but two Dylaithlok dropping into the facing road and barreling toward them no more than a few spans from the ground. Their wings beat against the sides of the buildings as they tore up the avenue, a cloud of dust in their wake.

Both Brax and Benigan were stunned at the speed with which the beasts covered the distance. They barely had time to think as the next few moments played out. With swords drawn they took up position in the middle of the square. The two demon-birds opened their jaws and fixed on the pair, and then burst into the square. A moment later they surged forward, snapping at the two men. The brothers leapt to opposite sides, rolling out of harm's way, but the Dylaithlok were swift to pull up and out of the square, clearing the dwellings on the far side and disappearing into the darkness.

"It seems you may doubt your own importance, brother, but they certainly don't," Benigan said. "They want blood."

"Me?"

"Why pursue two when you could drink the blood of a host of men further below?"

"But I thought you said they were wary of the towers?"

"I know what I said, but they're after *you*."

Brax searched the sky in thought. Then he spun and looked at the storage building. *Boran.* "If I know him at all, Boran wants to fly a little himself."

"You mean—"

"Why else would they be camped out on the roof? Stargazing?"

"But that's impossible," Benigan objected.

"When did that stop any of us?" Brax faced the building and raised his voice. "We'll do our best to lure them down the road below you! Be ready!"

"You can't be serious," Benigan said. Then he noticed a number of other warriors emerge into the square, seemingly summoned by his brother's call. They were those accompanying Boran and Gorn.

"Stay where you are!" Brax ordered them. "No distractions. Wait until we have them down." He turned to Benigan. "Come on!" They raced across the square just under the storage building, standing in the middle of the lane.

• • •

The two huge Dylaithlok rose up into the night sky and circled around. The battle played out far below them, marked by countless fires and even more torches. The most intense fighting was now being played out in the three breaches along the southern and eastern wall. But that was of little interest to them now; they had found their target.

Centering on the meager square farther up Mt. Dakka's peak, the enormous birds banked into a steep dive, plummeting recklessly into the city below. The ground was racing to meet them when suddenly they pulled up, leveling out in the course of a narrow roadway bordered by buildings on each side. As before they honed their senses in on the two men, now obviously trying to escape from the square down an opposing route. Bloodlust consumed them; they would not fail a second time.

The Dylaithlok crossed the square with one powerful sweep of their wings, now a breath away from their prey. Mouths gaping and talons spread, the monsters lunged, but retrieved only air. And a violent burning in the back of the neck.

• • •

Boran was the first to leap off the rooftop. Gorn followed, flinging aside the wool blanket and drawing the sword of the Lion Vrie. They fell, both hands on the handles of their down-turned blades, careening toward the road. Boran landed blade-first atop the first Dylaithlok, Gorn upon the second, and their swords plunging deep into the base of each bird's neck.

Boran's foe let out a sorrowful moan and rose out of the road at first, only to falter about three tree-lengths above the city. The bird struggled to lift in the air as Boran buried the sword deeper, now protruding through the bottom of the beast's gullet. He could hear it straining against the pain, a rasping in the throat. The Dylaithlok lost flight and pitched forward. Boran was suddenly aware of the danger and held tightly to his sword's hilt. With the massive bird above him he would be crushed on impact. The ungainly pair hurtled down, only moments remaining.

Boran thrust himself to one side, willing the creature to roll. Its wings beat wildly, flipping this way and that. He could see the tops of the buildings below, and he knew death awaited him.

Gorn's efforts were met with more immediate results. He plunged his long sword in up to the hilt and then shoved it sideways, severing the spine and tendons to the wings. The Dylaithlok was instantly paralyzed and tumbled forward, slamming first against the side of a building and then into the road. Gorn tried to leap from the bird but a wing slapped him sideways into a stone wall. His body glanced off it and across the road and tumbled to a halt.

• • •

"Come on!" Brax yelled setting off down the road as the remaining warriors emerged from hiding and followed directly behind them. Just ahead was the lumbering form of the first Dylaithlok that Gorn had slain. Its chest rose and fell frantically, still trying to pump air into its lungs. The wings and legs twitched in the throes of death, breaking into wild spasms that kept either brother from getting too close.

Up ahead lay Gorn, silent and still.

"Gorn!" Boran shouted. They ran to meet him, prone in the street, blood pooling around his head. Brax knelt beside him and felt his neck for a pulse. "He's alive." He looked back over his shoulder to the warband. "Quick! Get him to the palace!"

"Where's Boran?" Benigan asked.

"We saw him fall that way," pointed one of the other warriors. "Just over that cluster of homes."

"To me," Brax picked out five of the warband to follow them and then set off down the track. They turned left down a side street, and then right onto a parallel avenue. Again, the band banked left at a fork and continued to veer south of the square. "Keep your eyes open for anything out of place."

The team followed their current course until it opened into another square. A quick survey of the outlying streets still turned up no sign of the missing man.

"We've got to get up top," Boran stated.

"Aye," Brax agreed. "Split up. To the rooftops."

The men raced to different dwellings, each searching for a stairwell leading above. A few moments later the band was again in the open air, now lightening in the west, a subtle sign of dawn.

"There!" came the call from one of the men. Brax was by the warrior's side in a moment. He indicated a dark mound on an adjacent roof. A wide street separated them, and the gap was too far to jump.

"Down!" Brax waved.

The team entered the dwelling's roof door and raced through the small living quarters, down the stairs, and through the gathering room. They burst onto the street and searched for a stairwell or door on the adjacent building.

"This way!" someone shouted. Brax and Benigan followed another warrior down a narrow alley and up a flight of stairs carved out of the mountain. They emerged onto the roof of a series of domed dwellings, chimney pipes protruding like tree stumps. And there lay a heap of deepest black, withered feathers scattered in all directions mixed with blood. Lying atop the dead bird with his hand still grasping the hilt of his sword was Boran, unconscious and bleeding from his mouth.

"Help me get him down," Brax ordered as he and Benigan climbed up the bird-corpse. Men surrounded the crushed heap and helped them remove their kinsman. "Gently! Watch his neck! Watch his head—"

"They've got him, Brax," Benigan said with a hand to his brother's shoulder. They looked on as the warband laid him on the rooftop. The brothers knelt on each side, Benigan wiping the blood from his face with a corner of his mantle.

Boran barely opened his eyes. "Dih-ie kill ih?" he slurred.

"Thoroughly," Brax smiled. A tear slipped down his cheek. "Rest, brother. We're taking you back to the palace—" But Boran's eyes rolled back in his head.

It was right then that something else happened. From deep within the ground, as if begun a long way off, a trembling arose that soon became a tremor, not all that different from those felt in recent days. Starting as a hum, the vibration soon became like the bellow of a ram's horn, a great and ominous blast blaring over the city like an oppressive tidal wave. The sound was low and dissonant. Loose clothing wavered. Hair stood up on the back of the neck. Rocks shook.

Brax held Boran in his arms, but his mind was elsewhere. "What in the great name of Athera—" But the sound consumed his words. And it grew louder. The men put their hands up to their ears and held their heads, squeezing out the noise. It went right through the chest and buried into the soul. Driven to their knees, the men bent over, desperate for relief. Their heads throbbed, and they grew dizzy.

Then, as it had come, so it departed, withdrawing back into the recesses of the ground from whence it came. Brax looked over to Benigan, and then down to Boran. He remained motionless. Benigan asked without speaking.

"I have no idea," Brax said without waiting. He turned to those men gathered around. "Let's get him to the palace with Gorn. Quickly!"

They carefully picked up Boran and carried him off the rooftop, up the road, and into the palace. Just beyond the King's Gate a runner from the battlefront stopped short.

"Lord Brax," he said, panting for breath.

"What is it?" Brax turned, torn between following his brother and this inconvenience.

"You must come quickly."

Brax noticed the concern on the errand boy's face, mixed with a certain relief. "Why? What is it?"

"I think you should see for yourself, my King."

"Go," Benigan said. "I'll stay with Boran. See what it is."

• • •

As Brax followed the runner further down into the city, something marvelous met his ears, something he had not heard in quite some time…
Cheering.

He picked up his pace beside the boy and soon overtook him, running faster down the main track until he crested a rise in the street with a view of the dwellings and wall below. And at the sight he fell silent—awestruck.

There stood the entire army, swords and shields and spears hoisted high, shaking with the shouts of victory. From up on the ramparts men looked over the wall, shouting and mocking their foe. And nowhere— not in the streets, not on the ramparts, and not in the breaches in the wall—could Brax see a single Dairneag, unless it was being beaten down or already lay slain.

Brax turned to the boy beside him, eyes never leaving the scene. "How did this happen?"

"After that strange noise," the boy replied in wonder. "They just stopped fighting and turned on their heels."

"They retreated?"

"Aye!" he replied enthusiastically.

"Just like that?"

"Just like that. First everything seemed to be falling apart, the walls broken, the enemy storming the city. Then they simply fled."

Brax was elated. Yet still, something didn't seem right. *Why would you work so hard to overrun a city only to flee in the face of certain victory?* He nervously massaged the pommel of his sheathed Vinfae.

"They ran before us, my King!" the boy added.

Brax stopped and looked at the boy. "What did you say?"

"I was just saying how they fled from us."

"No, you said they *ran*."

"Well, aye! Ran like dogs!"

"You don't run when you're winning," Brax said more to himself than for the boy's sake. He looked down at his men celebrating. Dawn would soon be upon them. And from the look in the sky to the west it might be the first day in many that they would actually see the sun. *Something's not right.*

Brax surveyed the scene again, trying to sort out the inconsistency. Turning to the runner he said, "Thank you, young man. Return to your post."

The boy departed, and Brax made his way down the track toward the main gate. Soon he was in the midst of the celebration, the men slapping him on the back and lauding one another. It was cause for celebration indeed, and Brax couldn't help but smile with them, even laughing when the occasion pressed him. Yet a sense of great dread and foreboding still tugged at his spirit. *I don't understand.*

He surveyed the breach beside the main gate, men pouring through it and onto the battlefield without. Rather than join them he turned aside and mounted the closest staircase to the ramparts above. As he peered past the crenellations he saw where the enemy had been but a short time ago. The ground was ravaged, a swollen and gory strand of muck. And further down, now well over the barren mountainside, the enemy horde ran. *South.*

He watched as the massive demon army drove up the side of the mountain opposite of Mt. Dakka. It moved like a black cloud, hovering close to the ground and leaving a dark stain wherever it went. He watched for a long time, the sky slowly becoming lighter, as the Dairne-Reih crested a final mountain peak that would take them over the horizon and out of sight. So quickly. Not like they are running away...

...but running *to* somewhere.

As the sun neared the western horizon on the Faladrial Ocean, Brax noticed that not every part of the morning sky shared the coming glow as it should. There to the south a dreadful blackness hung in the air, as if resistant to the sun's glory. Strange that a section of sky should not bow to the all-powerful light of day.

As the first rays of sun emerged from the far side of Dionia, the rebellious mass on the southern horizon took shape. And in that moment Brax knew what it was.

"The Sacred City. Great God—*they've found it.*"

Chapter Sixteen

THE GREAT SHAKING

The terrible storm had indeed wreaked havoc on the lovely island Luik and the other Dibor called home. At least every other tree had been uprooted, torn from their ancient beds and discarded in careless heaps. The Great Hall had fared reasonably well, save for a collapsed roof on the eastern side; a tree had been thrown through it like a javelin, speaking of the storm's terrible power.

It took some time for the warband to emerge from their subterranean shelter and find their way to the lift on the north side of the island. Dazed by the bright sunlight, they squinted hard at first, surveying the incredible amount of damage. Luik's tree house was nowhere to be seen, laid waste in a swath of destruction all the way to the north shore. Seeing the central square now, without its leafy arbor and canopy of vines and flowers, was almost more than he and the others could bear. It was as if the sacred space of their tutelage had never been at all.

Luik walked down the beaten steps of the Great Hall and knelt by the ruins of the fire pit. A light breeze sifted through the wreckage, water dripping from everything. He shoved a tree branch aside and picked up a handful of the ashes, swollen and lumpy with moisture. He massaged the mass until his fingers were black, soiled with the memories of countless stories. Everything seemed so long ago for him: his first journey to Kirstell, his first sparring session with Gorn. Now just memories held in black cinders, forever lost.

The only happy sight was that of the dawning sun in the west. Its warmth and glow was a boon to their souls, its simplicity, and its regular arrival now the only real sense of normalcy they could lean on. Luik stood and collected his thoughts, preparing himself for the next leg of their journey.

The Immortals, along with Luik's strongest men, helped the wounded down in the lift and to the rocks below. Once there, they needed to wait only a short time before the tide revealed the sandy strand leading to the mainland. And by midday the entire entourage was securely encamped in a grassy plain, the outskirts of Jerovah.

As the sun sank to its easterly home, Luik and Grinddr, along with Cage, Jrio, and two more of the Immortals, sat around a meager fire, the driftwood crackling and popping from too much rain.

"Our journey will be long with this many wounded," Jrio said. His discouragement was tangible and certainly not lacking company.

"Cage?" Luik inclined his head to the Horse King.

"On horseback, we could make the border of Tontha in little over ten days. But we're on foot, and with many who are in poor shape." He paused, thinking carefully. "Two tens and five."

"That's nearly a new liyde," said Donalik, one of Grinddr's men.

"Aye," nodded Grinddr.

Luik lowered his voice and said, "I fear many of the men will not last so long without the care of Mt. Dakka's hearth fires." None of them wanted to agree with him, but they knew he was right.

"Perhaps you and Grinddr should go on without us," Jrio suggested. "We'll stay behind with—"

"I will not hear of it," Luik interjected. "The Sacred Order is split up enough as it is. I honor you for your selflessness, brother, but it will not be done, not while I am High King."

Jrio bowed his head slightly.

A little wine was drunk as well as a little bread eaten, passed out to the entire camp. They retired shortly thereafter, stretching out on blankets and furs brought with them from Kirstell's underground bounty. The night was cool but gave way to a brilliant display of Athera, stars in abundance and the twin moons of Dionia elegantly drifting through their courses. Only twice was Luik awakened by the deep tremors that had been plaguing Creation. The ground shook, trembled with a jolt, and then settled back down. He wished Fane were there to explain it to him; surely he would know its cause. But, alas, Luik had made a mess of that, too.

His midnight thoughts began to drift into a sore state, doubting first himself and then, eventually, doubting the one person he knew he mustn't.

Just as light began to fill the western sky with a pink and purple splash of color, another sound pumped through the ground and awoke Luik with a start. It was another tremor. Or was it?

The rumbling soon clarified into a beating rhythm, a cadence with a familiar melody.

"King Luik!" someone shouted. "Look!"

Luik sprang from his pallet of furs and looked to the east. There, but a lean, dark line on the horizon, rode a sea of horses, a rising cloud of dust in their wake. Cage was by his side in an instant.

"Our rides," he said to Luik.

"Indeed," Luik said. "Indeed!" He looked back at the men. They, too, were standing to their feet, eyeing the horses. Soon they were all up, cheering at the provision of the Most High.

"May the Great God bless the ten that ride with them," Luik said. "I shall reward them richly." For indeed, it was Gyinan who had ordered the ten to stay behind with the nearly five hundred horses that had carried them out of Tontha on their journey to the Somahguard Islands.

"And if I'm not mistaken," Jrio added with a wide grin, "they will also be carrying our arms and armor."

• • •

By late morning the entire camp had been struck and everyone mounted in the saddle. Those who were too injured to ride alone doubled up. For them it was a little more strenuous, as the use of litters would slow the advance. But the sight of their mounts brought such joy that no one scorned the inconvenience. Especially Luik. Fedowah was first among the stallions to reach him, as Luik sought his ride out from among the throng. He whinnied, and Luik greeted him with open arms, slapping his neck and blowing in his nostrils. The exchange was brief, and Fedowah shook his mane with heartfelt glee to be reunited once again. Luik kissed his nose, savoring the sweet smell, and examined his saddle, still snug on his mount's back.

"It's good to see you, my friend," Luik said. "You up for a run?"

Fedowah neighed and stomped the ground.

The ten men left in charge of the horses had waited patiently on the shore, watching and waiting over the Somahguard Islands. The horses, while content to graze in the fields, never had settled down, presumably displaying their angst in the distant strife of their masters. It wasn't until the herd had begun to press south and then west along the coast that the men had had any real inclination that Luik and the warband were on the move. At first the herdsmen had tried to round up the stubborn animals, but when the entire pack had moved as one, they had been forced to accompany them or risk being left behind all together.

"So really, it wasn't our idea at all," one of the herdsmen recounted to Luik. "We just followed their lead."

"For once," Luik chuckled. "Either way, we are indebted to your courage, my friends. C'symia." The men received the praise and made the sign of blessing.

The warband rode hard, pressing along the eastern front of Grandath, rotating through the herd of horses in order to keep their legs fresh. The count was nearly two horses for every man. While this was indeed a great benefit, it was also a reminder to Luik and the others of their incredible losses. Less than half the men who left Tontha would return. This meant fatherless children would run to the Main Gate in tragic expectation, accompanied by women about to learn of their new status: *widow*. Luik's heart sank at the thought. As the waves of despair washed over him, it was all he could do just to remain in his seat.

He was convinced that his leadership had wrought all this. It was his inability to truly lead that had brought so much harm. If only he were wiser, a better suited King. But with those memories came a new plague, one of the future. What would become of Mt. Dakka? How did his brother Dibor in Ligeon fare?

He began playing scenarios in his mind, setting himself up for any number of calamities, all with their own conversations and outcomes. Beads of sweat formed on his brow, his heart trembling with each new image. He was worried. Worried about what would happen. Worried about *tomorrow*.

"My Lord," Grinddr rode beside him and pointed from his saddle. "Grandath."

The sun was sinking toward the eastern horizon, but the western sky was still all too dark. A heavy black cloud shrouded the distant trees and seeped upward, enveloping more of the western sky as they rode north. The column of smoke that Luik had seen just two days before had now billowed into a gaping monster that consumed most of the Great Forest, at least as far as he could tell. "They are searching for Ot," Luik assumed. "Morgui will burn it to the ground before he is satisfied."

"Surely he won't find it," Jrio said, but it almost sounded like a question.

"No, my brother. I think he means to."

"We can pray," Grinddr put in.

"Aye," Luik agreed. "That is all we can do for the time being."

• • •

On the dawn of the seventh day the war band had journeyed well into Trennesol, Jrio's homeland, and were in view of the western mountains of Tontha, still two-and-a-half days' ride out. The mountain peaks were shrouded in cloud cover, hidden from the rest of the world. Luik wondered what remained of his countrymen high up in their reaches. His eye followed the base of the mountains back down into Trennesol, where a gentle morning fog hung low over the western plains and slipped into the Great Forest. From there, the fog turned into a dark cloud of smoke that consumed the rest of the woodland, casting it in an ever gloomy hue of black.

He returned to lashing his sword and pack to his saddle when he felt the onset of yet another tremor. It began like all the rest.

"Hold on, men," he ordered. "It will pass."

But this one didn't. The ground heaved violently, a jolt that threw everyone off balance, and many right off their feet.

"Whoa," Luik said, steadying Fedowah. The horse was uneasy. Ears up, Fedowah looked around frantically, dancing in circles as Luik tried to calm him down. "Whoa!"

The vibration continued until another heavy blow issued from beneath them, this one much more severe than the first. Luik actually felt himself lifted into the air before slamming to the ground. Horses fell, and not a few on top of their riders. Soon everyone was shouting. But the sound was drowned out by the roar of quaking.

"Stand away!" Luik shouted, waving his hands to get the men away from their horses. But he could barely hear himself. "Stand away! Look out!" Even as he tried to get their attention, more horses fell, crushing many of the men in the chaos. Luik attempted to stand, but the ground shook so violently it was nearly impossible to get to his knees.

Although the tremor lasted for only moments, it felt like an eternity, each event unfolding with a slow, daunting pace. Men fell backward, thrown against the ground with ease; horses stumbled and bucked, terrified by the shaking beneath them. Bodies collided, the greater mass crushing the lesser into the dirt. Mouths agape let out noiseless screams; hoofs flailing for solid ground.

And then it seemed to ebb, the shaking ceasing much faster than before. Vibrations still carried through the ground, but the jolting had subsided as well as the noise. Now the air was filled with the cries of men, many of them trampled and broken. Most of the horses had gained their feet and ran wildly, ripping through the tall grass, unable to be caught.

"Attend those men there!" Luik ordered, pointing to a cluster of his warband on the ground. "And there!" he ordered some of the Immortals to another group. "Jrio—"

He was cut off. Another quake started, but this a monstrous one, paling all previous. The violent heave threw everyone down, slamming them hard against the solid ground. And then came the thunder of rock and soil splitting from deep beneath them. It cut to the soul of every man who heard it, a tearing of the deepest sort. Deafening the ear and tormenting the soul, the violent shaking continued.

Luik's head hit the ground, disorienting him for a moment. He rolled and then pulled his knees up under his stomach. With great effort he pushed his shoulders up and looked around. There, a great distance in front of him toward the mountain range, rock and dust shot into the air, flinging debris into the sky. The quaking continued, escalating as the ground began to contract against itself where he looked. Great segments of rock raised themselves into the air, protruding from the once seamless valley, now a disheveled battlefield of unnatural mayhem.

The ground was separating into a massive fissure that stretched from the Isthmus of Ninsessa all the way to Grandath. The ground tore more deeply with every moment that passed, the sound blasting their ears. Soon it incorporated a new sound: that of rushing water. Luik looked to his right. Flowing in from the north, like a wave from a broken dam, came a torrent of water pounding down the channel. It careened through the fissure with amazing speed, drenching both sides of the split, bursting over rocks and consuming mounds of dirt. The water was brown, carrying debris all the way from the Nollen Sea, blasting away at whatever was in its path.

And still the ground shook. Luik then noticed cracks appearing around him and his men, opening up into fractures large enough to swallow a man. Many did. And more than one horse tumbled to its fate.

"Luik! Help!"

Luik looked over his shoulder. Fyfler was slipping into a small fissure. He was grasping at tufts of grass on a section of tilting ground.

"I'm coming!" Luik scampered on his hands and knees, first climbing over the exposed plate of rock rising into the air. Then he slid down the other side, easing his way toward Fyfler. "I have you," Luik said, grabbing his wrist and pulling him up. But still the ground trembled, making the work laborious.

"Pull!" Fyfler pleaded. Luik fought against the inclination of the ground, heaving with all his might, but Fyfler's weight was too much. The grass in his left hand gave way, and the two of them slid toward the gaping mouth below. Just then, a hand caught Luik by the scruff of his collar. It was Kinfen.

"Need some help?" he hollered. Both men looked up into his face, a look of relief on their faces. Kinfen pulled them over the ledge and back onto more stable ground.

As soon as he could, Luik looked back to the valley before them, the crack now a growing, water-filled chasm. Rocks still shattered and moved wherever water touched the shore, sending up a spray of stone fragments. And in the channel, a maddening current churned, ever boiling in the rage of the quake. Soon the commotion ebbed, leveling off to a constant din, still loud, but manageable.

"The water is rising!" Quoin shouted, examining the growing body of water.

"Nay," said Grinddr, "I believe the land is separating."

"What?" Cage asked.

"That fissure is no mere crack," Luik added. Those gathered around him looked on. "Dionia—she's breaking apart."

No one said a word. They just watched as the space between what was now the northern side of Trennesol and the southern side of Trennesol moved farther and farther apart. The trembling continued, grinding away in the ears. Water filled the cracks that ran around the warband and soon spilled all over the threshold of the mainland, creating shallow pools. The men found themselves wading up to their knees, leading the horses back up to dry ground. And still water rushed in to fill the increasing space between the two landmasses. Grinddr had been right. The ground was separating; Dionia was breaking apart.

Luik felt a nudge from behind him. It was Fedowah. He swung into the saddle, and the horse led him over to a group of men struggling to get up in the shallows. He dismounted and helped them up, loading them on horseback, and then sending them off to dry ground. After everyone was out of harm's way, Luik led Fedowah to join the others, wringing out his shirt and running a trembling hand through his hair.

"You all right?" Cage inquired.

"Aye, given the fact that I just watched Trennesol get ripped apart."

Jrio sidled up to them on his mount. "It runs all the way into Grandath. Look." The small group followed the waterway south as it plunged into the Great Forest—now three times as wide as the Hefkiln River at its widest point. The massive trees that remained intact along the shore leaned over, dangerously low to the water, as if they would fall in at any moment. Beyond that, the men lost sight of the channel.

"Great God of Athera, help us." Luik looked skyward and squinted his eyes. The trembling in the ground labored on as the two landmasses continued to drift farther apart. The far shore was now so distant that many of them doubted they could even swim it. Eventually the swirling of the water seemed to dissipate, and before long the entire scene began to look as if it had always been, as if there were some name to this waterway, one which they had all forgotten. Finally the grinding ceased, and the tremors grew weak.

"So I have a new question," Cage asked, looking to those around him. "How do we get across?"

"I have an idea," Jrio said with a grin.

"Don't keep us in the dark, brother," Cage ordered. "We're all ears."

With the tumultuous churning of the ground beneath them finally subsiding, Luik and his warband looked out toward Tontha. The span between the two landmasses was broad, far from being fordable by men or horses. They needed ships.

Luik surmised that he would eventually name the waterway, deriving it from one of his men or a memory or some such thing, just as Ad had done when Creation was new. But for now he was still in awe of what they had just witnessed. The only explanation he could come up with was that Creation was doing its best to purge the evil within it, yearning in agony to be relieved. That, or perhaps Morgui—

No, he thought. *That is too grievous a notion. I will not think it.*

Jrio turned to the High King. "You wish us across with haste, aye, my Lord?"

"Certainly," Luik replied, only half paying attention.

"What about the dolphins?" Naron asked.

"They're surely still in the south. Warmer waters," Fyfler said. "No fish or animal could have survived that anyway."

"Right you are. Any ships are well out of reach as well, perhaps some three or four days away. And even then they must be in working condition and sailed back here," Jrio stated.

"Is this helping us?" Luik stared at him.

"Nay, but it proves we need a swifter method."

"And you have one?"

"Really, brother," Rab said. "Spit it out, man!"

"Aye, I do."

"And?" questioned Luik.

"Give me three days," Jrio asked. Luik looked at him. Jrio wore a curious grin, one which Luik knew all too well.

"Might I remind you that lives are at stake, Jrio? We have no time for reckless endeavors or faulty plans. This must be time well spent."

"I give you my word, O King; you will not be disappointed."

"Very well. Three days. Take what men and supplies you need. We'll make camp and take care of the wounded." Jrio nodded and turned to ride away. "Jrio," Luik caught him. "Three days. And no more. It's about *lives.*"

Chapter Seventeen

A NEW LOVE

Anorra awoke in the same room as before. The rustling fire had died, leaving behind a bed of embers. Candles flickered in their iron mountings, each one a few fingers shorter than they had been earlier. The princess stretched and sat up, pushing off the warm pile of furs and blankets. The room was just as it had been, save that the table was cleared of food, and that she was alone.

The sleep had been sound, free of pain; she was happy for that. Anorra felt somehow that she had much to recover from. But what, exactly, she couldn't remember. She'd been through something terrible... unspeakable. Yet it eluded her. Everything was just out of reach, like straining for a handful of mist, always visible, never tangible. Then the memories of her encounter with the man returned, filling her with unease. She knew him only as *the Prince*. But the emotions surrounding him, both awkward and somehow alluring, left her to feel that there was a great deal more to be known.

She stood and walked to the table, letting her fingers brush against the smooth board. The images of the sumptuous meal she had consumed filled her head. Her mouth watered. She was hungry again. Had she been asleep so long? But then another thought filled her head—one more intriguing than simple sleep or hunger. She gazed at the face looking back in the polished wood. It was if she had eaten at this table many times before. Perhaps many summers. She *knew* it—this space—like an old friend.

Anorra turned to look out the window. Then came a frightening realization: For all the beauty of this chamber, its furnishings, floorings, carvings, and candles, there were no windows. No portal into the outside world. It was in this moment she became afraid, aware that she knew not if it was day or night, dusk or dawn. She didn't know how long she had been asleep, or even, for that matter, how long she had been in this room. Had this bothered her before?

She searched her mind's eye and then became frustrated. There were no memories outside of this room. None before and only a few within it. But yet it *seemed* as if she had a history here, a long, even nostalgic affair with this place. She walked over to the hearth where she and the Prince had reclined, where they had stared into the flames and he had spoken of a great invitation. *To join him.*

She was *wanted*. She was *desired*.

Her heart fluttered and her face grew warm. Anorra took a step, backing away from the furs on the floor. *Why am I here?* There was a scratching at the door in her mind. She spun around. She knew that something had brought her here, some great hardship. She squinted hard, forcing herself to remember. *What was it?* Her hands were massaging her temples. But perhaps she had indeed been here so long that the past was too far forgotten even to will it back.

"Let me help you," he said.

Anorra screamed, and then spun around. It was the Prince. "How did you—"

But she had scarcely spoken when he began to laugh. Not a sarcastic, demeaning laugh. No. This was a genuine, *playful* laugh, one that a lover might bestow on his maiden, joyfully relishing their mutual folly. The sound of his voice was marvelous. She was terribly startled, yet she let out a sheepish chuckle; his only grew louder. Anorra felt her heart with her palm and recovered her breath. Soon she was laughing with him, her face and belly aching.

Between laughs he finally said, "I'm so sorry for startling you, my beauty." He wiped tears from his eyes. "I didn't mean to."

"It's fine," she laughed. "It's my fault, I was—I was just lost in thought, I guess." His light manner put her at ease, as did his handsome face. "I can't even remember what consumed me so."

"Well, then, whatever plagues you, it is gone now." And with that he cradled her cheek in his hand. It was as if everything that bothered her suddenly melted away. Now it was only he and she, alone in the bedchamber. "And you rested well?"

"Indeed," she said, gazing up into his eyes. All she could focus on were his impressive eyes. *So beautiful…*

"Then I am pleased my dwelling suits you, for I would implore you to stay with me, Princess. Have you forgotten my offer?"

"Your offer?" It seemed so long ago. *Was I not just asleep? Was he not here with me earlier this same day?*

"To join me as my bride, that I might share with you my kingdom. Everything I own, it is yours."

"Yes, I remember." She was astounded by his words. There was something about him. *So attractive.* Though she felt completely out of place, exposed and vulnerable, she still maintained at least some of her wit. "But while I know at least of the charm and beauty of my future husband, I do not know of this kingdom which he speaks so highly of, as if he offers me some great prize. How would anyone rightly reply to such an offer?"

"Ah, you are right, my lovely," he chided himself. "How nearsighted I am." He eased closer to her now.

Something quickened in her bosom—she couldn't help herself. Anorra felt something for him. He placed his strong hands on her shoulders and drew her ever close. He emanated power with every breath, and she found it captivating. She *needed* him.

"What would you like me to show you?"

Her body was pressed against him. She looked up into his face.

"Whatever you wish," she replied. She could hardly believe her own words. But it was so much easier just to let go. To give in.

She found herself lost in his gaze, surrounded by his magnificence. Everything was happening so fast. Whatever life she had lived up until now was forgotten. "You are my future," she whispered. Then she kissed him deeply.

Chapter Eighteen

THE CROSSING

As the sun reached the apex of its climb on the third day, a guard on the northern perimeter of the camp noticed horsemen coming in on the horizon. Luik was summoned and stood beside him, along with Grinddr and a few of the other Dibor.

"Jrio, my Lord," said the warrior on watch.

"Aye, but with too few men," Luik noticed. Of the two tens and five horses that drew near, only half of them bore riders.

"Something's amiss," Grinddr spoke up. The pack grew larger, a billowing dust cloud behind them. The shapes of the men became more distinct, and soon Luik noticed large packs on the backs of the riderless horses. His stomach churned.

"Bodies?" Cage questioned.

But no one spoke. They just stared and watched. Hoping. Dreading.

Men from all over the camp gathered around the High King. They spoke in hushed tones, but soon said nothing at all. The anticipation was palpable. Only the rhythm of horse hoofs beat through the ground. The dust was thicker and the scene more disheartening with every moment that passed. Soon the herd of horses was upon them, and the awaiting group could clearly make out the sacks slung over the animals. Yellow colored cloths were wrapped around man-sized bundles, each lashed to a board, presumably a litter.

No one dared say a thing.

Luik looked but did not see any sign of Jrio, nor of Fyfler or any of the brothers from Somahguard. He looked to the rider in the lead, moving toward him as he slowed. The man spoke before the King could open his mouth.

"Is all well, my King?"

Luik was a bit taken aback. "Aye, but I would ask the same of you."

"Forgive me, my Lord, but the whole lot of you looks as though you'd just watched your brothers fall in battle," the man replied. He then noticed everyone was eyeing the bundles quite hesitantly. "Ah! There is no cause for alarm," he smiled, quite relieved for them. "This is King Jrio's doing."

"He lives?" Cage asked.

"Of course he lives! Did you think us slaughtered in the King's own realm?"

"Well then, good man, is there a reason he is not among you?" Luik questioned.

The man beamed. "He said he'd prefer to trade the back of a horse for something more—how did he put it?—*exhilarating* is the word he used."

Luik looked to Grinddr and was about to speak when the man pointed from atop his horse. "Here he comes now!"

Luik turned to look along the newly carved coastline and walked past the horses. He blinked in eerie disbelief. The rest of the warband began mumbling among themselves, obvious curiosity in their voices.

"I can't believe it," Cage said. "I've never seen anything like it!"

In the distance were more than ten brightly colored yellow sails, flying like odd swooping gulls that dipped and rose in the wind. Each one was bowed, curved against the air and diving toward the sea as if about to plunge for fish, only to recover and surge skyward at the last moment. Barely visible to the eye were thin lines that led from each sail to a single man on the water, each erect, skimming along the surface and holding to a bar between both hands. Luik walked more quickly, a grin creeping across his face. Among the five men in the water, he noticed Jrio's form in the lead. His feet were affixed to some sort of board which he rode over the waves, a wake kicking up behind him.

"That's incredible!" Cage hollered and slapped the High King on the back. Luik glanced to his right and caught Grinddr's eyes. The Immortal simply shrugged with an awkward smile. Then all three looked back to the horses and everything made sense.

By mid-afternoon Jrio and his team had unraveled the packs on the horses, set up the *diji-hi*[6], or water flyers as Jrio called them, and laid out the wooden boards. The finely woven canopies were expertly crafted, the yellow fabric bearing the crest of Trennesol—a gull hovering over a leaping dolphin. This novelty was something Jrio said his clan was known for, though no one outside of Trennesol was familiar with the invention.

"It's something my father and I were working on," Jrio said proudly. "Our tribes took to the sport quickly," as any Trennesolian would with their long heritage in sailing. "I gathered these from a small village just north of us on the coast."

Thin lines made from terren root fibers were laid out on the ground and affixed to a wooden dowel about the length of a sword's handle and the width of a man's arm. Jrio demonstrated to everyone how to hoist the sail into the air and maneuver it by turning the bar. But when he passed the dowel and flying canopy to the others, everyone realized just how much power was at their control, and sometimes *not* at their control. One man was picked right off his feet, dangling from the bar and hoisted a tree-length into the sky before letting go and slamming into the ground. He was no worse for wear, but his pride was far from intact.

"It's all right," Jrio comforted as he raced to help the man up, others fetching the collapsing diji. "It's not easy. But you'll adapt sure enough."

Jrio and his team continued throughout the remainder of the day to give each man a turn with the sail and bar, more than one hundred diji aloft, all swooping like giant yellow birds. And before the sun set and the winds died, most took a turn with the diji in the water. Jrio demonstrated how to enter the water along the shore, diji aloft, and straddle the wooden board. As he steered the canopy overhead, plunging it toward the horizon, the bar jerked in his hands and he surged forward on the board. Within moments the plank was on plane and he stood, riding it just as many of the ocean-dwelling clansmen did; the only difference was that Jrio didn't have

---

[6] **Diji-hi** (*didge-EE-high*): *noun; singular and plural; modern Dionian for "flying water apparatus" (abbreviation "water flyers") consisting of a kite (diji) strung to a control bar, and a stand-on board (hi) designed to ride on top of the water when the rider was pulled by a sufficiently strong wind.*

a wave. With the diji-hi he *was* the wave.

Jrio rode about, carving water with the board by leaning back against the strong pull of invention. He swerved this way and that, even changing direction numerous times to stay close to shore so everyone could see.

"Now he's just showing off," Cage muttered.

"He certainly makes it look easy," Luik added. "Think everyone can learn?"

"If not, I'm sure Jrio will be glad to carry them across."

"But that may hinder his style," Luik mused, winking at Cage. As if on cue, Jrio pulled violently on the bar, whizzing the canopy in a wild change of direction overhead; the diji-hi hoisted him clear off the water's surface, but not before Jrio grabbed the board and brought it with him, twisting in the air as he went sailing skyward. Everyone held their breath as he continued to climb, suspended in mid-air, before gently landing back in the water and continuing on in his course. The warband let up a mighty whoop, applauding the feat.

"Correction," Cage added, "*now* he's showing off."

• • •

Just after dawn the next morning, Jrio and Luik had the men packed and ready. The winds were strong out of the northeast, making it an easy reach to the far shore. The horses were loosed of their burdens and tack, and then sent on their way back to their homeland in Jerovah; once on the other side of the new channel, the warband would have to make it on foot.

Based on everyone's performance the evening before, Jrio selected those who most easily took to the diji-hi and instructed them on the procedure for the crossing. Luik, despite his wounds, was one of them, and he listened eagerly. Because there were more men than there were diji-hi, each crossing would need half of the men to return, each bearing the burden of an extra board and rolled-up canopy. It was not impossible, but they would need the most agile and proficient riders to execute the plan. Those that simply couldn't manage the crossing were given the task of finding timber to construct rafts. But with scant few trees at their disposal, and Grandath still too far away to be of use, the rafts would be few in number.

By mid morning the first group was wading into the surf. The winds were picking up which, while making it easier to keep the sails aloft, also meant rougher seas. A number of the men were tossed about, falling off their boards, their sails tumbling into the sea. Jrio strode through the waist-high water, helping steady as many of the warriors as he could. With a little guidance and encouragement, the first wave was off, sailing across the channel on a single tack. Most stood on their boards, but more than a few remained seated, content to be dragged through the sea and not risk losing their balance.

In all, the first trip across was a success. Half the men stayed while the others returned with board and bundle tightly wound and carried under their arm. Maneuvering the bar with only one hand was much more challenging, many of the men choosing to sit down as standing was simply too awkward.

Upon their return, the bound diji-hi were rolled out, their sails hoisted skyward, ready for the next man. Luik steadied the sail and prepared to hand it off to a man just beside him. When only one hand reached for the bar, Luik instructed him.

"You'll need both hands," he said. Luik looked from the beautiful canopy soaring above to the man next to him. It was Sheffy, son of Wildaburn. He was suddenly embarrassed, but equally delighted to see him again, having not even noticed his whereabouts over the last few days. "I—I didn't mean—"

"No harm done," Sheffy said with a smile. "It's good to see you too, my King. I think I can manage just fine," he said, nodding at the sail above.

"Aye, that you will, Sheffy. Of that I have full confidence." Luik felt forever bonded to the little man, his conversion back to the land of the living a momentous miracle for all those who lived to remembered it. Luik knew this man had much to be grateful for and would never again begrudge an indecency against him. His was the joy of knowing his life was afforded him, and no more. Whether one less hand, or one less leg, it did not matter so much as long as he awoke another day to see the light of the sun. Luik studied him as he edged to the shore and, with no little effort, sat atop his board and set off across the channel, smiling as he went.

A gentle tug on his tunic startled Luik. He turned to see Fia behind him.

"My dear friend," he smiled and knelt down to her level. "How do you fare?"

"When do I get my turn?" she asked without room for argument.

"Fia, the task is one not even every full-grown man has the strength for, let alone a fair lady like yourself."

"You are calling me *weak*?" She balled her fists and locked her arms.

"Easy there, child," he said, resting a hand on her shoulder. "You are certainly far from weak. Still, I would have you ride with Jrio." Fia looked over at the King of Trennesol as he helped a sea-swollen man back onto his board. Jrio's handsome look brought the color to the little girl's fair face. "Will you mind the company?" Luik asked. She bashfully looked down between her feet. "As I said," he concluded, "you'll make the trip with Jrio. See you on the other side." He tousled her sandy hair with his hand and sent her running to the shore.

The air was hot; the sun soared high by the time the last trip was made. Luik and the remaining Dibor, along with the Immortals, who seemed equally suited for the diji-hi, raced along in the strength of the strong winds. Luik's board skimmed across the waters, cresting waves and ripping across the swells. He found himself quite enjoying the sport and wondered why Jrio hadn't shown him sooner. He raced west but found himself gazing to the southern horizon. Facing the Great Forest, Luik couldn't help but notice that the intense black that hung over the region was growing. Ever darker, ever wider. He knew Grandath was being consumed, and he could only assume that Morgui was on the hunt. The traitor wanted Ot. He knew it.

And yet the ground had torn, and the sea had divided the land. Was this rift in Trennesol simply a diversion? Was this Morgui's means of delaying Luik's warband? If so, his powers were far greater than Luik had imagined, possibly growing stronger. Or was Creation purging itself of disease, to extinguish the flames that burned her from within? If so the timing was far from optimal with regard to their journey home. Or perhaps, was this the Swift Sure Hand of the Most High, trying to keep Luik from returning to Mt. Dakka? And why would He do so? Was the city compromised and the greater need now in Ot? What did this mean for his companions?

Luik wrestled all of these thoughts in the span of a breath. Doubt filled his spirit, stirring up endless conflict. He was eager to get on with things, to know the answers. Now. He had never tasted the bitterness of anxiety as he had over these last few days. It was something he despised, like a rotting corpse inside his flesh. But even with the disgust, he could not shake it off. He could not *stop* being anxious. The more he entertained it, the stronger the grasp became. He hated it! But he could not resist it. It tightened around his throat, squeezing his chest. Even as the High King savored the sea air and the priceless moment of ease, riding across the waves, he knew his integrity as a leader was being assaulted once again.

Luik shook his head but could not pull his attention from the scene in the south, where black smoke blotted out the sky. Morgui would destroy the Scriptorium if he could. Even the Great Libraries, too. But Luik knew there was something more that Morgui wanted, something he wished to *uncover*; this, the means to an easy victory. And there would be no stopping him then.

Chapter Nineteen

IN THE MOUNTAIN'S SHADOW

Mt. Dakka was free that night, something Brax could hardly have imagined just a few days ago. He stood on the balcony of the King's Chamber with a commanding view of the southern city. He wore a plain white wrap around his waist and left the air to warm his naked chest. The streets were emptying of people, the clansmen retiring for the night, eager for the hearth fires and conversation. Their hard day's work deserved a good rest and the ministry of food and kin. Music had once more returned to the homes, lyrics and melody wafting upward through the chimneys with the curling smoke of the cook fires. A dog barked in the distance, and children ran through the streets, calls of mothers echoing after them. It was as if all was back to normal. But he did not share their revelry.

Brax stretched his arms and felt the numerous sources of pain throughout his body. The battle had taken its toll on his spirit and his flesh. He noticed in these recent days how he had become used to the ailments of his body; injury and pain seemed to linger far longer than when he had been a youth—than when he had been on Kirstell. He could remember Gorn's words.

Pain is the absence of the Most High's presence.

The King of Tontha lightly touched a large bruise that shaded his shoulder dark blue.

177

What did you replace Him with?

He moved the shoulder in circles, feeling the ache and clenching his teeth. He searched his heart. Where had he forsaken the Great God? Where had his vigilance failed? It had been so long since he'd felt the presence of the Most High, since he had heard the Master's Voice. He wanted things back to normal, not just because the enemy had fled Mt. Dakka, but because the enemy had fled Dionia; but with such a powerful home established deep within this world's bowels, Brax doubted it would be possible. He knew the enemy hadn't retreated.

Despite everyone's adamant declaration of Morgui's defeat, Brax didn't believe it for a second. Morgui had had them on the run. The city had been hours away from falling and the Dairne-Reih had simply *left*. They had taken Anorra. They had breached the City Wall. Morale had been low. Luik had been gone far too long, and there had been no word from Anondo in Ligeon. Tactically there had been no reason to flee—

—unless there was something greater to gain elsewhere.

In his spirit, Brax knew Morgui had found Ot. Maybe he wasn't *in* Ot, but he knew where it was. And it scared Brax. The fading light turned the pink clouds to purple, but the black in the southern sky remained ominous and ever foreboding. While Brax had never doubted the enemy's power or his intent, he had never really thought Morgui would overcome this beautiful world. Even when Brax had been taken from the High King's chamber during the council of the Gvindollion, even when he had been whisked away to Kirstell and all knowledge of reality been disclosed to him, even after the fall of Adriel and his induction into the Lion Vrie, he had never doubted his countrymen's abilities to vanquish the enemy; he had never doubted the Most High's strength and desire to uphold His Creation. But right now, standing here on the portico, he was suddenly aware that Dionia was in trouble. And there was little he could do about it. And little he saw the Most High doing about it...

"Beautiful night," Gorn said from behind him.

Brax remained fixed on the southern sky, his hands gripping the stone railing. "Aye, a beautiful night indeed."

Gorn came to stand next to him in silence. They listened to the inhabitants of the city playing out into the evening watch. Brax liked Gorn. Not just because of his tutelage or experience, but because he knew how to revere a moment; he didn't need to nervously fill every empty gap with words. Whatever he did say, he meant. There was no confusing his meanings. For this Gorn had earned the trust of many a king, Brax now one of them.

"She is in trouble," Brax finally said.

Gorn waited.

"I have never thought her in jeopardy before now," Brax continued. "Somehow, some way, I just knew we'd defeat Morgui. I knew we'd win. But perhaps I was naive."

Gorn placed his hands on the railing and leaned into the sky, gazing off in the distance. When he spoke, it was slow and even. "There is still time, my King. Remember, you are a Lord now, a ruler of the realm, and with it comes new understanding—and a new awareness. Things have not changed so much from when you were a boy, or even from the days of the First Battle. The threat has always been the same. But you *see* more now. *You feel it.*"

Brax pondered his words. There was a great amount of truth in them, and he had failed to consider the fact that he was now connected with the land. To him it was always more of a myth than a reality: a King *feeling* the needs of Creation. But now it made sense. It *was* true.

"Morgui has found Ot," Brax offered.

"I would say so," Gorn replied. "Why else would he hasten away so quickly?"

"Aye," Brax nodded. "And with the portal closed, we have no way to communicate with Li-Saide. How I wish he was here now."

"But I am," said a voice behind them both. They spun around and there, standing neatly in the doorway, was the famed chief of the Tribes of Ot, with his billowing, patch-worked hat and his bundled green robe. Brax found his presence an instant comfort.

"Li-Saide!" Brax sputtered. "What are you—? How did you—?"

"It's good to see you, too, King Brax." And with that he stepped forward, and Brax knelt and bestowed a large embrace, enveloping the dwarf.

Standing up, Brax turned to Gorn, who merely nodded to his old friend. "Li-Saide, it's good to see you again."

"And you, mighty warrior." Li-Saide edged closer to the railing and peeked above it, surveying the city and the gathering darkness in the south.

Neither man wanted to resume the discussion, fearing what news it might bring. So the dwarf did.

"Morgui has found us," he said.

The words were as a blow to the stomach. Brax dropped his head, and Gorn looked away.

"How long do you have?" Gorn questioned.

"Another day, maybe two." He stared off into the night sky, gazing into the blackness, as if seeing into the future.

Gorn and Brax both noticed the dwarf's eyes fill with a dark mist that swirled around his pupils. The air changed on the balcony around them, and when Li-Saide spoke next, his voice took on a strange quality, words carrying a mournful burden.

"*His* hounds *are very close and the shield that hides the Secret City will not hold against Morgui's powers much longer. He is growing stronger, the bloodlust full in his mouth. The barrier will break, and Morgui will cross over. Then the Dairne-Reih will pour into Ot and consume us. Nothing will survive.*"

Li-Saide continued to stare off in the distance, allowing the words their full weight, disappearing out into the night air. The joy of the reunion was traded for heaviness of heart. Although Brax knew the words were spoken in truth, he would do everything in his power to stop it.

"We must keep this from happening," Brax said. He looked at Li-Saide. "You speak the truth, I know. But as long as we have breath, we must confront evil, no matter how inevitable our fate."

"And this is why I have come," Li-Saide replied. "I will not give in so easily, even knowing how sure are the words of the Sacred Tongue. Of all those living, *I know*. But I will not bow my knee to *him*."

Brax had never heard Li-Saide speak like this. There was a transparency about him he had never seen. He understood in that moment that Li-Saide was not greater or lesser than he. The dwarf was his equal, just as reliant on the Hand of the Most High as he was. Just as he had seen Gorn as mentor and teacher, Brax now understood both of them were his friends—both with limitations and shortcomings.

"Nor will I," added Gorn. "And I will gladly give my life in defense of Dionia. As I have pledged, so I will do."

"You have my sword," Brax said, feeling a breeze rush against his chest.

"And you have my sword as well," came a strong voice behind them. The three of them turned and stared in disbelief.

"Luik!" Brax hollered and stepped swiftly. The two clasped forearms and embraced, giving up a mutual laugh for seeing one another again. "It is good to see you, brother."

"And you, King of Tontha." Luik closed his eyes. "And you."

"I say," Li-Saide leaned in to Gorn, "It is a night of grand entrances and reunions."

"Aye!" Gorn chuckled and then moved to greet Luik, followed by Li-Saide.

"How is your warband?" Brax questioned.

"Heavy losses," Luik said. "More than half." The three others lowered their heads in respect and made the sign of blessing.

"I'm sorry," said Gorn.

"They knew the price well," Luik said. "But their deaths will not be in vain. We adjust and carry on." He paused out of reverence. "And what news from Ligeon?"

Brax lowered his voice. "No news, my King." And he knew more bad news was coming.

"I see. And Mt. Dakka? The gatemen who let us in spoke of mighty tales. A victory for you already, King Brax?"

"The enemy departed, but it is not as they say."

Luik looked puzzled.

Li-Saide spoke up, "They have found Ot."

Luik's face flushed. "So it's true, then." He reached for the rail to steady himself. "How long?"

"We haven't much time," Gorn said. "If we move now, we have a chance."

"We've reopened the portals," Li-Saide added.

"Then we can have men there at once." Luik turned to Brax. "How many fighting men remain in the city?"

"Our losses were minimal."

"Then we leave immediately," Luik stated. The rest of them nodded, but no one spoke. Something was pressing them, he could feel it. He looked between them. "What is it?"

"There is more news to tell," Gorn said.

"Then speak it."

An awkward silence fell over the balcony. Luik looked to Brax. "What is it, Brax?" Suddenly his heart stopped beating.

He knew.

"We were defending the southern City Gate," Brax began. "It was late in the day when they began pummeling the walls with their fedchults."

"Where is she?" Luik demanded. No one spoke. His eyes darted between them.

When Brax looked away he grabbed him by the arms. "*Where is she?*"

"We told her to stay away from the wall, but she wouldn't listen!"

"*What did they do to her?*" he seethed. Luik began shaking Brax, tears flowing from his eyes and anger burning in his mouth.

"A ball of fire hit the wall beneath her—"

"*Tell me, Brax!*" He shook him violently.

Gorn stepped in. "*She lives*, as far as we know, Luik." He placed his hands on Luik's arms and tried to ease him away. "She fell over the wall and was carried away."

Luik turned his wrath on Gorn, glaring at him. "She—*she what?* You *watched* them carry her away? You didn't even try to stop them?" Spittle flew from his mouth as he spoke. The long, battle-laden journey combined with his injuries had made Luik uneasy as it was. But no one blamed him for his aggression. They would have done the same. "*How could you?*"

Li-Saide stepped in between them and touched Luik's elbow lightly. Suddenly a wave of peace washed over Luik, and his countenance softened. He looked down, now aware of the dwarf.

"What trickery do you play on me, dwarf?" But he could not move away.

"Only that which your own strength cannot afford you at present." He continued to touch Luik until his whole body felt refreshed, if even in the slightest. "A man ruled by his emotions alone is no use to anyone and brings with him a fate worse than he would normally wish."

Luik continued to feel the tension ease until he understood that his quarrel was not with his brothers. "We must get her back," he finally said with resolve.

"Aye, and we will," Gorn assured him.

"But we have a more pressing concern," Li-Saide admitted. Luik made to argue, but he knew the truth of the matter. "Luik, she will hold her own. She is strong. If she is to be saved, we must believe that the Most High will uphold her until we are able to intercede."

Luik bowed his head. The dwarf finally released his touch and gazed up into Luik's downturned face. "She lives, mighty warrior. And she well waits for your rescue. We will go to her, do not fear."

"Aye," he replied finally. He closed his eyes. "I'm coming for you, my love." There was a moment of silence that passed between them all, perhaps allowing Luik's message to take wings on the wind and fly to Anorra, no matter how far away she might be. Love would never fail.

"There is much to be done," Li-Saide finally said. "I move that we gather the remaining fighting men and prepare to defend Ot."

"Agreed," said Luik.

But Gorn put a hand on his shoulder. "You and those who traveled with you are to rest, however. We'll do the rest."

Luik started to object, but Brax spoke up. "My Lord, you are now in the Realm of Tontha, and according to Dionian Law, you are subject to the rule of the realm's King, even as *High* King." Brax noticed that Luik quickly glanced down to Li-Saide. But Li-Saide didn't falter in the least. "So," he continued, "I order you to take your leave. It would be ten and four days normally, according to protocol, but seeing as how we are pressed, we will leave at dawn."

No one argued, least of all Luik, who, truth be told, was grateful for the order and needed the rest.

"There will be much to talk about, and much time in which to say it, when we are all in the Great Throne Room, eh, brothers?" Gorn said with a grin. "For now, we are men of action! Come, Luik," he added, taking him by the arm, "I see that you are weak and will help you to your chamber. You do remember the way?" The two of them exited the King's Chamber, leaving the dwarf and Brax to themselves on the balcony.

"Taking to studying Dionian Law lately, Lord Brax?"

Brax smiled widely. "It must be a bylaw somewhere, don't you think?"

The dwarf laughed and patted Brax on the thigh. "Anything to get the High King to get some rest, or else we'll all be daft, bereft of our sanity!"

Chapter Twenty

TRUE SIGHT

Anorra awoke in the same room as before. The fire was long spent and the meal had been cleared from the board. She looked around and pushed the thick blankets down. Candles flickered. She felt as if she had lived this before, just a moment ago. But yet everything seemed so new. The fragrance of flowers filled her head. *How pleasant*, she thought. It reminded her of the sumptuous fare she had just eaten.

She stood and moved slowly to the table. Her fingers brushed against the smooth board. Images flashed before her. It was as if she had been here before—doing this very thing. Like a bad dream playing out over and over again. *But this can't be a dream*, she thought. *It's all so real—so peaceful.*

She gazed at the face looking back in the polished wood. Her eyes were soft and beautiful and brown.

She pulled away.

Something is not right. She felt as if she was watching herself from a great distance, standing on a hillside, observing a course like a shadow being cast from her true self, high on a ridge above.

Anorra turned to look out the window beside her bed. But there was none. She spun and looked to the far wall, and then beside the hearth. Suddenly she became afraid. There were no windows at all. She remembered this, too, as if something she had already lived.

But had she lived this only once before, or a thousand times over? She strained for memories. She knew she remembered *something*—but *what*, exactly, was beyond her grasp. She searched her mind's eye and then became frustrated. There were no memories outside of this room. Everything she knew, everything she had ever known, was right here. *But that's absurd*, she thought.

She walked over in front of the hearth where she and the Prince had reclined, where they had stared into the flames and he had spoken of a great invitation. *To join him.* She could see the flames dancing once again, the passion of the moment aflame in her bosom. She felt satisfaction in it. And yet...

And yet—

Something deep in her was left wanting. *Fire.*

She felt parched. She touched her lips.

The kiss!

She had kissed him! *The Prince!* She had offered herself to him! Memories, horrible memories of betrayal riddled her with guilt. Suddenly the terrible realization of what she had done filled her head. She had said *yes!* To a man she hardly knew—*but he was so beautiful.*

"What have I done?" she gasped aloud.

But betrayal? It ate away at her soul. *To whom?* All the images came to the front of her mind, of the Prince and his invitation. *There was no one else.*

Anorra felt confused. Everything seemed disjointed, as if she were missing some part of the picture, something significant. But how could she be forgetting something so significant? Important things are not easily forgotten. *Remember!* O, now her head was throbbing. It hurt to think. She reached up and began to massage her temples.

"Let me help you," he said.

Anorra screamed, and then spun around. It was the Prince. "How did you—"

Suddenly it was as if Anorra was watching herself in the same room—watching this scene play out as it had before. The Prince started laughing. And so did she. But she shouldn't. No, something was terribly wrong here.

"I'm so sorry for startling you, my beauty. I didn't mean to."

Something didn't fit.

"It's fine," Anorra laughed. "It's my fault, I was—I was just lost in thought, I guess. I can't even remember what consumed me so." But *she did* know. It was *him*; he didn't fit. None of this did.

"Well then, whatever plagues you, it is gone now." And with that he cradled her cheek in his hand.

But it didn't go away. In fact, Anorra suddenly saw everything for what it really was, as if a massive curtain had been pulled back to reveal a great mystery, now in plain view to all. She had been deceived.

"And you rested well?"

"Indeed," she said. His eyes weren't so beautiful now.

"Then I am pleased my dwelling suits you, for I would implore you to stay with me, Princess. Have you forgotten my offer?"

"Yes, your offer," she stated rigidly.

He tilted his head at her tone. "To join me as my bride," he said. "That I might share with you my kingdom and everything—"

"I remember," Anorra interrupted him.

The Prince's eyes narrowed. "And you have thought about—"

"Thought about who you are, *good Prince?* O, wait. *Good* isn't the word most reasonable people would give to you, now would they?"

The Prince stiffened. His eyes grew dark, and the room around them seemed to shimmer, as if ebbing from the realm of reality.

"You see, I am not so easily taken, Prince. Or do you prefer the name we call you? *Morgui.*"

But as strong as Anorra was, she was not prepared for what befell next. The beautiful visage of the Prince melted right before her eyes. The flesh peeled back and fell in clumps, swollen with blood, twisting muscles snapping. A rancid smell stung her nostrils, and she winced as bile rose in her throat. The creature's eyes grew stronger, blacker, and pulled back into the disfigured face, drawing her in with them. So empty. So devoid of life. Hopelessness overwhelmed her with one look, and she felt her heart give way, her eyes filling with tears.

The human form began to expand, soon bursting from within, the weak shell of a man revealing the mighty shape of a being much more powerful. A pungent cloud swirled about the black morphing mass, revealing a bulging, grotesque musculature, throbbing with veins. Once free of the flesh, Morgui stood looming above her and then bent down.

She stared up at his face, a hollow block of darkness, fangs protruding in ill fashion. There was no color about him, no hint of light, only swirling abysses for eyes and an eternally hungry hole for a mouth, gaping over her. There was not a single magnificent thing about him.

Anorra spoke first. "You do not frighten me."

When Morgui spoke, it was nearly unintelligible, ground out in a low, gravel-like thunder. "That is because I have not yet brought you harm."

She stood silent, not knowing what to say.

Suddenly a searing pain thrashed across her eyes. She screamed and fell to her knees. Her fingertips touched the burnt flesh on both side of her nose, going deeper into the place where her eyes once were. The sockets were charred and empty.

It was then that everything came back to her. The entire story of her life raced by her in a series of flashes, ending with Luik's face, the blue flame in the Lion's Lair, and the brilliant flash of light on the ramparts in Mt. Dakka. Luik's flame had been weak—had gone out. Hadn't it? She scolded herself now for not staying long enough to find out. She'd assumed the worst. Though there were no eyes with which to cry, her chest heaved as she sobbed in agony. He had tried to seduce her. He had tried to lure her away from the Most High.

But he had failed.

She was on her side now, curled up like a child. Whimpering.

Morgui neared her, his presence just a hand's breadth away. She could feel his emptiness. At least she knew this was reality.

"You are not thorough enough," she said in a whisper, choking in pain.

She felt him hesitate, knowing, though, that he would not reply to such a vague train of thought. But she would spite him. She would not afford him the pleasure of knowing he had won, that he could torment her. As a child of the Great God, made perfect in His image, she was superior. And always would be.

"I saw my reflection in your table. You were good," she chuckled, "but you weren't good enough." A shudder of pain momentarily halted her speech. "My eyes—if you ever took the time to see what the Most High made—are blue, *not brown*. I thought you should know for the next time you try to seduce a girl."

A rumble emanated from around her, growing in strength and rising in volume. But with the trembling came an increase in her pain. She moaned and tried to shove it away. It drilled into her head and then coiled around her neck, her chest, and soon her whole being felt like it was being crushed. She cried out once more.

But she couldn't hear her own voice. Just a ringing in her ears, an echo of the torment of her soul, so all-consuming that she asked just one request of the Most High, if He was even listening here in Haides: *Please, take me home.*

There was a flash, and a sudden flare of heat. Her face was mashed onto gravel, hot stones digging into her soft skin. A hot, sulfuric smell filled her head, and the pain lessened. Screams from without, mixed with creaking metal, stirring flames, and the lashing of whips, gave her to know she was back in her cell.

She tried to push her head up off the rocks, but she did not have the strength. It hurt so badly. Anorra could feel blood trickling down her neck. She clenched her teeth and growled to the air. She was so frustrated, so mad.

"I know you can hear me!" she screamed.

The demons listening must have assumed she was speaking to Morgui; even he, himself, was listening. But such an eroded being was far from her intended audience. She had an audience with the King of kings. With her Creator.

"If you will not rescue me, at least give me my sight!"

And then, for the first time in a long time, she heard Him.

My precious child, none of this is My wish for you. I have not forgotten you, nor is My hand short in rescuing you. But what you have asked, you already have been given. And your heart suffers for denying what you already own. Open your eyes…

Her heart soared. Here, in the deepest part of Haides, the place where she had felt He dared never go, she had heard Him. She had communed with the Most High. *He would send His presence even here?* Her spirit leapt within. And she had made up her mind: There was nothing she would not endure, no pain too wicked, no temptation too overwhelming, that she would ever doubt Him again.

And as for what He said, she knew it was truth. Why she had not seen it sooner, she did not know. But she would not blame herself; these were trying times.

Anorra lay there, her hands and face scalded on the gravel. She slowed her breathing and then allowed her mind to go back…

She saw herself atop her steed, riding through the fields of Ligeon. Gyinan was beside her, a noble smile on his handsome face. Their horses' flanks were soaked in foam, and the green grass was long and vibrant, shimmering in the sunlight. The animals lunged for every stride, hoofs beating the solid track ahead of them, nostrils snorting in the summer air.

Anorra laughed, feeling the warm sun beat on her face. She laid the reins across her horse's mane and spread her arms wide, basking in the glory of the moment. She was flying.

The moment passed in a flash, and she was atop a high peak. She knew it was Tontha. She stood there, one foot hanging perilously over a precipice. A blindfold was affixed over her eyes; she remembered the time well.

Another flash. Now she was bounding down the mountainside, leaping from rock to rock, racing down a river-worn track.

Flash. She was back on her horse, wheeling it around with her heels—one way and then back again. She lifted a bow and pulled the arrow to the corner of her mouth, lying backward over the horse's haunches. Then she let the arrow fly…

Dazzling white light filled her head and she steadied herself. Renewed life stirred in her veins. It was *Him*. She knew it was. She felt the strength to rise and pushed against the hot floor. And as Anorra lifted her head, she looked around her cell. The stones were a burnt red, as were the iron bars; she crawled forward and reached for them. Then, pressing her face between the rungs of her cage, she looked down into a vast sea of churning fire, and suddenly wished she had not had the gift she asked for.

She could see Haides.

Chapter Twenty-One

IN THE LIGHT OF TRUTH

Dawn came all too quickly for Luik. Even if he had had a whole summer to rest, Anorra's peril would have kept him from any sound slumber. But he *was* weary and did eventually manage to find at least a little rest before waking, bathing, and changing into battle dress. For today he was certain his sword would see blood.

Drying his face with a towel, he gazed southward out the window, staring at the mountain peaks on the horizon. He thought of his beloved Anorra, and his heart wilted. He longed to go to her—to rescue her if she still lived—and his heart said she did. But the heart was easily deceived in such matters, he knew. He thought of Hadrian and wondered how he fared in Mt. Dakka. And then of Fane, and regret returned to his soul. He wanted to make things right. And he would, if given the chance.

He walked to the massive chest that held his few belongings and examined the attire that had been set out for him. Luik took his time and donned leather breecs and boots and a maille shirt covered with a warrior's tunic. A new wide leather belt he wrapped and folded on itself and secured his sword frog to the left side. He slung a large cloak over his shoulder and pulled a shiny pair of gauntlets over his hands, newly forged by the Tribes of Ot. He then secured his sheath with the Sword of the Lion Vrie and picked up the helmet of the Sacred Order, holding it securely under his arm.

Today will be the day, he thought...

...the day that Morgui will meet the Lion Vrie face to face on the fields of battle.

Luik stood before a grand mirror in his bedchamber. He looked at himself as the light sparkled in his eyes and danced off his armor. The herald emblazoned on his outer tunic bore the mighty paw of The White Lion, the crest of Dionia's High King. And suddenly, in that moment, he was reminded of his dream.

He could see the massive creature standing over him, its hot breath spewing down. The Lion's yellow eyes glared at him. Luik couldn't move. And then the paw raised as it had countless times before in his sleep. The razor-sharp claws revealed themselves and glistened in the eerie twilight. And then it came—the deathblow. Then a knocking sound...

Luik snapped from the vision.

"My King, are you ready?" came a young lad's voice. Luik looked behind himself in the mirror to a lad peeking in through the doorway.

"Aye," he replied. Luik turned and straightened himself for the boy. "How do I look?"

The boy blanched, words escaping him. "You look—fine."

"Fine? Perhaps maybe I should have gone with the other breecs then?"

"Uh—" The boy hesitated and was clearly unnerved.

"Do not worry," Luik said, waving his hand. "Are the men assembled?" The boy nodded, glad for the interjection. "Very well. Let's be off."

He followed the boy down the grand hallway—as all hallways were in Mt. Dakka's palace—until arriving at a side room blocked by a heavy wooden door.

"The men are gathered in the King's Hall, but the others are here," said the boy. "Shall I wait for you?"

"Nay," Luik said, placing a hand on the boy's shoulder. He could see fear in the boy's eyes. He knelt down and looked in his face, suddenly feeling nostalgic. Could Luik have been this same age and size when he himself was summoned of to Kirstell? It seemed so long ago. "What is your name, lad?"

"Farquin," he said timidly.

"That's a strong name," Luik said. "And your father and mother? Are they here with you?"

"My mother is. My father left to fight in Ligeon with King Anondo."

"Ah, then your father is a hero."

"Pardon?"

"Anyone who fights for King Anondo is surely of the bravest sort. He is a hero, young Farquin."

"I suppose." Farquin wondered if he'd ever see his father, Fadlemir, again.

"Nay, suppose nothing. *Know* that he is and *believe*." Luik stared into the boy's eyes. "You are the future, Farquin. You may not understand now. But you will in time. You are Dionia's hope." Stillness filled the air. "And remember, the King is coming."

The boy looked at him oddly. It was this last phrase that perplexed him.

"Off you go," Luik said and turned him around. Farquin took off, and the High King stood. And then entered the council chamber.

Standing around a large wooden table were Li-Saide, Gorn and the remaining Dibor, minus the brothers of Ligeon. Boran remained seated due to his injuries but had refused to miss the meeting. Grinddr and three of his men were also present. All of them were dressed in battle attire, save the dwarf who remained as he ever was. They saluted Luik and made the sign of blessing as he entered, their faces displaying the honor due him, and glad for it. Then they began clapping and he joined with them. They were together again, but without four; Najrion they knew was lost, and Anondo and his brothers were still unaccounted for.

When the applause died down and reunions had been made, everyone settled into chairs around the room. Extra furniture had been brought in to accommodate the larger-than-normal council. Luik spoke first.

"It is so good to see you all." He looked carefully around the room. "We have been through much, and we dare not ask one another for too much detail, for our hearts could surely not bear the burdens we all carry. Just enough to move forward in wisdom. Yet we remain a brotherhood, a band of warriors bound by the Most High to protect Creation and to serve one another. As it is, it falls to us today to do the unthinkable, to defend the heart of our world and the center of recorded history. For that, I turn to Li-Saide of Ot, Chief of the Ancient Tribes." He inclined his head to the dwarf.

Li-Saide sat in a large chair with a raised cushion so as to be seen by all the rest. His fluffy beard moved when he spoke, and his eyes remained ever vigilant. "Morgui is at our doorstep, as bold as he ever has been. And I fear we will not last the night without a proper defense. And even then the future is not certain. But first I have news of my own that must be shared, and I fear the telling of it."

More than a few eyebrows were raised, and everyone felt a strange foreboding at Li-Saide's words. Things already seemed dire enough as they were, but to add more? Luik was worried for the news and not sure it was the best timing for whatever it was the dwarf was about to share. But then again, Li-Saide had never been inappropriate and had indeed taught him most of what he knew when it came to discretion.

"My first news is that King Anondo lives, but barely so."

There was a subtle gasp across the room. The Dibor leaned forward in their chairs and made to ask questions, but Li-Saide raised a hand. "Anondo's forces were caught off guard with a surprise attack from the north."

"The north?" Fyfler asked incredulously.

"How can that be?" Quoin added.

"The gates," Rab reminded them. "Even Luik and Anorra found one in the mountains above the Great Forest, remember?"

"That is the most logical explanation," Li-Saide continued. "The survivors of the attack fled west to Narin, pursued by the KiJinNard."

"The *hounds* of the dead?" Daquin asked.

"The same. Only more than a rank of them."

"So many," whispered Boran.

"Fadlemir, Captain of Ligeon's fighting men and armada, commanded three vessels from the Port of Narin northward in the hopes of landing in Tontha and returning to Mt. Dakka. But their landing was thwarted by a giant storm. A *cloud snake*, Anondo called it."

"It must be the same as what we encountered in Kirstell," Luik put in. "It ravaged the entire island and seemed to know exactly where we were."

"It very well could be," Li-Saide replied. "This storm hunted them all along the coast, at least from what Anondo could tell us."

"He doesn't remember?" questioned Luik. "Why not ask Fadlemir?"

"Because Fadlemir never made it. His last effort was to force Anondo's unconscious body into a small hole in the rocks. He never knew it was one of your *Sea Caves*, Luik. We were waiting there, praying he'd find us. We believe the Great Spirit drew him there. But we're sure he never knew."

A somber stillness fell over the assembly. Everyone sat in quiet honor of the man who had given his life to protect the King of Ligeon.

"I would have liked to have met him," Luik finally said.

"I'm sure you did," Brax said. "You would remember his face if you saw it. He was a good man."

"Aye…" Luik's voice trailed off. All of them had been good men. "Continue," he looked to the dwarf. "What of Thad and Thero?"

"That is another matter," he said, his face suddenly pensive. "But not for me to tell, as it was not their wish."

Luik looked to him and then to the others. "I—I don't understand."

Li-Saide slipped off his chair and walked to a side door, passing through it and returning a moment later with a tall man. His appearance was ruddy, and his eyes were deep-set and hard. At seeing all the men, however, he looked down.

"Do not be afraid," Luik said, rising from his seat. "Li-Saide?"

"This is Blandon, son of Aramos, a son of Ligeon. He was with Thad and Thero in their final moments."

"Their final moments?" Luik said. "Wait—"

"Blandon?" Li-Saide gestured him forward. Suddenly everyone in the room realized the gravity of what was about to be shared. Blandon stood uneasily before them until Cage offered up his chair. Blandon looked to thank him and noticed a single tear running down the Dibor's face.

"It's all right," Cage said. "You will honor them with your words, I know."

Blandon seemed strengthened by the gesture and sat accordingly. He took a deep breath and began the long account of their journey south into the Border Mountains. He shared about the tragedies in the mountain pass and their retreat down into Grandath. He related the dismal progress into the forest and the eventual decision of Thad and Thero, ordering the remaining ten men onward, not to "stop for anything, save the Dwarves of this realm."

"And so our scouts found them wandering in the smoke-filled forest," Li-Saide finished. "And not a moment to spare."

"They died heroically," Blandon offered up, knowing these were their closest kin and friends. "They served one another…served us all…right until the end." He lowered his head in sorrow.

"Do not fear," Luik said, placing a hand on the man's shoulder as all the others stood. "All is well, for they are in the Great Throne Room with the Father now. There is no weeping there, no sadness of heart." Then Luik embraced the man and thanked him for his faithfulness.

"Nay," said Blandon, "it is you we should honor. For you have been faithful to your people, to all of us. Thad and Thero were right—" his voice choked.

"About what?" Luik held him off.

"When they said you are the best of us all."

A somber mood filled the silence until Luik released the man and Li-Saide stepped in. "C'symia, Blandon, son of Aramos, you are dismissed." The man bowed and exited through the main doors.

Everyone settled back into their chairs, content to not say anything. The loss of their brothers was hard to bear. Of the original ten and eight Dibor, only ten and five remained. It felt as if they had lost an arm, knowing it was gone but expecting it to still be there to reach out for something.

"Might I remind you that the men are waiting," Gorn finally said.

Luik looked up. "Aye. That they are." He took a deep breath. "Li-Saide, what more is there to tell?"

"Our scouts report that the Dairne-Reih are encamped over Ot, filling the woods above."

"And Morgui?" Gorn asked.

"They have not seen him, but I'm sure he is not far off."

"Probably down in Haides with An—" Brax was cut off by a stern look from the dwarf. The comment, for all its truth, was inappropriate and misspoken.

Luik's face tightened. He could feel rage filling his head with the thoughts of his lost love, suffering in the fires of the underworld.

Li-Saide placed a hand on his arm and spoke softly, "We *will* retrieve her, my King. There is still time." He readdressed the men. "In the meantime, we will defend Ot with all we have. To lose the Scriptorium would be to erase the history of our peoples, and of Earth, breaking our connection and understanding with them." He paused. "But there is still more."

The men looked on intently.

"There is the issue of the Two Trees," Li-Saide said.

Everyone glanced around, but Luik raised his hand. "Let him finish." He turned to the dwarf. "Go on."

"The Tree of Life still stands, but if Morgui were to destroy it, our link to the eternal would be severed. Mortality would reign in Dionia."

"Mortality?" Fyfler questioned. "You mean we'd die?"

"Instead of passing from this life to the next at the Most High's command, we'd have a painful finite span," Luik clarified. "That and the dwarves—"

"You need not concern yourselves with us," Li-Said interrupted.

"Nay, I'd have you speak, friend," Gorn demanded, sitting forward.

The room filled with murmurings.

"Please, brothers," Luik lifted an arm. But still they talked among themselves. "Silence!"

The discussions ceased.

"Let—him—finish," Luik ordered, and then looked back to the dwarf.

"The Tribes of Ot were created by the Most High to serve and to protect the Sons of Ad. Knowing that we must maintain the knowledge of history, both here and elsewhere, we were granted a peculiar trait, a *gift* if it could be so called. We know neither death nor the calling home into the Great Throne Room. Our existence is and forever will be to serve Dionia. And our life's source is the Tree of Life. Without it, we are mortal. And given our age already, I do not know how long—"

"We understand," Luik interrupted this time. Everyone remained fixed on the dwarf.

"We've known that Morgui would return, bent on destroying the Tree, our tribes, and our history. Thus we inquired of you," he looked to each of the Dibor, "at the Counsel of Kings…the Gvindollion…to ensure our survival. And that is why we passed the secrets of our order, the Secrets of the Mosfar, on to another should we fall, to one Fane, son of Fadner."

The men were stunned, especially those who knew Fane personally. They talked among themselves, and Luik again had to calm them down.

"But, Sire," Boran looked to Luik then to the dwarf, "Fane is a traitor, is he not?" Heads nodded.

Luik was startled. He had not spoken such things to anyone. "So, word has spread?"

No one spoke.

"There were only two who knew of Fane's behavior. One is my love, and she was convinced of his innocence, and the other—" He paused, suddenly deep in thought, piecing everything together. Hadrian. "The other will answer to me."

"There is still the other Tree," Li-Saide said, looking to Luik.

Luik suddenly remembered their time in Ot together. He was taken back to the thick bramble path that led into the darkened cave. And there, the grotesque, charred ruins of an ancient beauty that held a secret power over the souls of man. He saw Li-Saide bending over and opening the flesh of the exposed root, revealing green within.

It lives.

"Tell them," Luik said. "We need to know."

Li-Saide stood and waved a hand through the air. But rather than a fruitless gesture, his hand moved through something like water, spreading ripples out over the table. The fluttering apparition began to shimmer and soon developed into a beautiful scene, a meadow filled with lush greenery dancing in the light of the sun. Flowers of every kind blossomed in that moment, and the sky was filled with radiance and the song and flight of birds.

The men sat spellbound at the miraculous vision before them. It looked so much like a place and time they fondly remembered but had forgotten.

Li-Saide spoke solemnly. "In the beginning, the Most High fashioned two trees to adorn the garden he made: one the Tree of Life, the other the Tree of the Knowledge of Good and Evil."

The scene showed two massive Trees stretching high into the sky, taller and stronger than any of the other trees in the garden. They were alive somehow, as if they could themselves talk and be heard by Creation. The Great God had given them life and was delighted in them.

"The one, the Tree of Life, was the source of mankind's hope, the sustenance that would see them through eternity. She was their link to Athera, the one that afforded paradise in this perfect world. If they ate of her, they would never die.

"The other, equally beautiful and strong, was the Tree of the Knowledge of Good and Evil. To her was given the fruit of the one thing that Ad was never designed to carry: knowledge of what his life would be without the Almighty. A sufficiency without the Great Spirit would mean death, and no true sufficiency at all, proving that without Him, mankind is nothing."

Suddenly violent flames leapt up and around the second Tree, consuming the branches and enveloping the image from trunk to leaves. And then a *crrrrrack* as the mighty foundation was severed and the Tree crashed to the ground.

"When Ad recognized the potential destruction promised in any failure to adhere to the Commandment not to eat of it, he ordered the second Tree cut down and burned. He watched and waited until the entire thing was gone—a blackened pile of coals and dust. If he could not be certain of his own ability to obey the Most High, then he felt it best to remove the temptation."

Jrio interrupted the vision. "So what's the concern?" The image slowly faded away, and the room was back to normal.

"That its seed has been slowly nursed back to health," Li-Saide said. "That it lives once again."

"It what?" Quoin exclaimed. The others looked on, incredulous.

"I've seen it," Luik added. "It grows deep within the ground, its roots firm, surely ready to burst out and fill the sky once more."

"So the fires weren't just meant to find Ot," Brax concluded.

"But to make way for a new tree," finished Jrio.

"Or a new *forest*," added Li-Saide.

The weight of the statement filled their hearts with dread. It couldn't be! *A new forest?*

"And if the Tree and its offspring are the *only* trees in Dionia's heart, then its fruit is also the sole product," Li-Saide continued.

"A fruit that would bring the Curse upon our entire world," Luik finished.

There was a long, drawn-out pause in the council chamber. No one moved, each man sitting pensively, left to ponder the plight they faced. Morgui's plan was revealed. He wasn't satisfied with the destruction of their heritage or an end to their immortal condition; nay, Morgui wanted it all. He wanted Dionia under his rule. He wanted mankind's habitation of this life *and the next*—with him in Haides.

Finally Rab asked what many of them had been thinking. "Who has been cultivating the seed? Someone must have."

"Ah, a valid question," Li-Saide replied. "We had long suspected an intruder, watering and giving nourishment to the remains of the Tree deep within Ot."

"One of your own?" Cage questioned.

"Not exactly. We suspected an outsider coming in through the portals."

"Then why didn't you close them off before this escalated?" asked Fyfler.

"Because if there was indeed an intruder in our midst, we wanted to catch him and stop him."

"Catching him in the act was the only way," Luik surmised.

"Correct."

"So you captured him? Why did you close the portals?" Fyfler asked again.

"Nay. We believe that the traitor was just the errand boy. He was about to bring Morgui himself, and we had to weigh which was more important: catching our watering boy or facing Morgui in a surprise attack."

"But after all this time, he didn't bring Morgui, even when he had the chance," Luik put in. "That's very strange."

"Aye," Li-Saide grew puzzled. "If this invader was indeed a traitor, he failed to carry through his most heinous act."

"Perhaps he was killed," Cage suggested.

"Possibly," Li-Saide said. "But right now we simply don't know and can't waste our time speculating. The Secret City is in its most perilous state and needs all of our help."

"And our help she shall receive!" Luik said, rising to his feet.

The rest of the men followed with a mighty "Hey'a!"

"Brax, Jrio, Fyfler," Luik listed, "you'll have command of the armies, answering to me. Grinddr, you will have the Immortals. Gorn, you command the Lion Vrie. After we brief the men, we'll head for the Lion's Hall."

"But the secrets of the Order?" Rab asked.

"If there is no Dionia, than secrets mean nothing. Today Morgui will know it all. The Lion Vrie. The life of my father, King Ragnar. Even the Mosfar. All things will be brought into light, and we will not sleep until we have victory."

"Hey'a!" the men shouted as one. They drew their swords and held them aloft.

"For the glory of the Most High God!"

"For the King's glory!" the men replied.

• • •

The Great Hall was filled with a grand audience. The massive stone arches and tall windows soared overhead, showering light onto a sea of expectant faces, all focused on the High King and his retinue that occupied the dais. These were the warrior men of Dionia, and only the Great Hall of Mt. Dakka was able to hold them all. Still they streamed out into the hallways and even into the main courtyard, completely silent, waiting for the words of their King to echo down the ancient halls. Not a man among them sat, and they each held a weapon in their hands. Some were no more than boys, barely able to hold swords, while others were well on in years; still, neither lacked in determination and heart. These were husbands, fathers, and brothers. These were sons.

In their eyes Luik noticed a familiar gaze, one of utter devotion, loyalty and zeal, but also of fear. Just hours from now they would come face to face with terrors no man was ever intended to witness. And those who had already stared death in the face, survivors of Adriel and elsewhere, knew they were about to revisit the nightmares of their past.

He saw many of the men he had fought alongside before, faithful men who had won great honor for themselves and their families; he saw men who had survived the brutal destruction of their homelands and the loss of their loved ones. These were his people—but more—these were his brothers.

"Men of Dionia, hear me! Today I look out over a multitude of faces and wonder how all this came to be. I see standing before me the inheritance of those who have gone before us, of those who would have given anything to see this day. For it is a great and terrible day. I see standing before me the legacy of the generations, a legacy which hinges on our actions and is borne on our shoulders.

"Morgui and his forces await us even now, encamped on the ground that hides the Forbidden City of Grandath, what we know as the Secret City of Ot, there to consume the records of our people and those of the Almighty's Creation. But his fires have ravaged the Central Forest and have cleared the way for something even more terrible, the latent key to a curse that would destroy us all. For the seed of the Tree of the Knowledge of Good and Evil has sprung to life, aided by a traitor from among us. If it blossoms, there is no stopping our people from eating of it, bringing upon them the curse which Ad himself tried to dissolve. For if we cannot remember the covenants of our forefathers, then we also cannot respect the curses that await us if we break those covenants. And fight to preserve those covenants we must!

"Men of Dionia, hear me! I see your courage, and I would speak to your fear: if there is nothing to be fearful of losing, then there is nothing to live for. If you see fear, it is only because you have much to love. You, of all Creation, have known His glory and perfection. You have *everything* to lose because you know what it means to truly live. Today we do not meet our adversary as mere mortals groveling at the feet of a tyrant, hoping to be given some quarter—hoping to be granted some feeble existence. Today we meet him as superiors, as Sons of the Blessed King! It is not mankind that quakes with fear, for we are those created in the image of the Most High! We hold the high ground! We fight for life! Today they meet the inheritance of every generation, the legacy that says, 'We will not surrender! We will not retreat!'"

• • •

In that moment, and for many more, the violent shouts of men could be heard echoing throughout all of Mt. Dakka. Every child on the street, every mother who busily cleaned at home to calm her nerves, every grandmother who paced in prayer, all heard the shouts and shut their eyes. It was the sound of defiance. The sound of rebellion to the fear that encroached upon them all, lurking in the shadows. And the shouting spoke: *We will not give up. We will not go down without a fight. We will not stop until the Mighty King returns.*

• • •

Luik joined with the men, raising his sword and shouting with all his might. The others with him did the same, their blood stirring from deep within. The deafening sound consumed the hall and shook their souls. It was magnificent.

When the roar finally ebbed, Luik once again looked out over his brave army, pride filling his heart. "By nightfall we will be well within the Secret City. There we will certainly find—"

There was a strange commotion in the back of the room.

Luik stopped his address. He strained to see what was the matter.

He heard one clear voice ringing out, and saw the throng of men near the doorway stepping aside.

"Make way!" said the voice. "Stand aside! We must see the High King!" More men parted and a path appeared through the middle of the expansive room. "Make way! Make way, I say!"

Coming into view were two men, one clearly older than the other and deeply troubled from a long journey. The older man's clothing and long hair were disheveled and soiled. He was hunched over and strained for every step. But the younger man Luik soon recognized despite his bedraggled appearance; for indeed he would have known his face and hair anywhere. It was Fane.

"Make way!" Luik cried out to the astonishment of everyone around him, and bounded down the steps of the dais. The men parted hastily as Luik pushed through them, running to meet his old friend. A mix of emotions filled his chest, from those of anger and frustration to others of deep conviction. He neared the redheaded, freckle-faced figure, wrapped in a dark green cloak swollen with dampness and stains of soot and soil.

"Fane!" Luik cried, his arms spread wide in embrace.

But Fane stayed back, halting two arm's lengths away. All those around were deathly still. Li-Saide was quickly to the King's side and stared into Fane's face, searching for answers in the unseen.

"Fane—what is it?" Luik was troubled. He followed Fane's stare to the man at his side, a sorry figure who was presently straining for great gasps of air. He looked even worse close up. The man's face was sunken and pale, teeth yellowed, and deep circles beneath his eyes. His hair was red with locks of grey, looking more like a rat's nest than a mantle of dignity. If Luik didn't know better, he'd say this poor creature had been of the *taken*.

"I am—" The man coughed himself into a fit, clutching Fane's arm. "I am Jadak—"

Time froze.

Luik glared at the man. Then at Fane. He felt his stomach tighten and his sight narrow.

Fane nodded his head.

"—Father of Hadrian."

Recognition lit in the High King's eyes. All at once the consequences of his actions became clear. It was *Hadrian* who had betrayed them. His redheaded friend had known that Hadrian had been lying all along. And Luik realized what Fane had done; if he could find Hadrian's father, he could prove his innocence to Luik. But more than that, he could prove that Hadrian was acting covertly. And Luik was certain now that it was Hadrian who had been sneaking in to Ot—for he was the only other one outside of the Lion Vrie that knew about the portals. About the Sea Cave.

Indignation filled Luik's head and he spun around. *Hadrian will pay.*

"Hadrian!" He looked to where his friend had stood moments before. But the space was empty. The men began talking amongst themselves. Luik bolted forward, running to the stairs, his eyes darting around franticly. "Where did he go?" But no one knew. They shrugged their shoulders and looked to each other. "Find him!"

Li-Saide was on it, summoning five of the Immortals. "If he is still in Mt. Dakka, we will find him," said the dwarf, and was off.

Luik turned back to regard Fane and Jadak with a heavy heart, the gravity of the situation setting in. He had granted audience with a traitor, shunning his closest counselor and boyhood friend. And without consulting the Most High or heeding Anorra's wisdom, he had aided a man who was secretly and, quite literally, watering the roots of evil under his watch.

More than being angry with Hadrian—a status not easily exceeded—Luik was angry with himself.

The men stopped mumbling, and the hall was quiet. Luik looked out among their faces, and to Fane and Jadak still standing in the middle.

"Fane, son of Fadner, my friend and confidant, has returned safely to Mt. Dakka and has undertaken a task which none of us, most of all myself, could ever repay. We owe him our lives for bringing a hemorrhage to light before it destroyed us further. We salute you."

The entire throng grunted a mighty "Hey'a" in affirmation and made the sign of blessing toward him.

"And to you, Jadak, for whatever wrongs have been committed against you, I am deeply sorry. And for whatever evils you have endured, may you see a thousand days of goodness for each single day of plight. For you have returned to the Land of the Living and stand once again in the Light of the Sun, though it be sickly and pale from what you surely once knew. For this, we salute you, and speak a blessing on your enemies' enemies."

Again, the warband saluted Jadak, the sound echoing throughout the palace.

"Men of Dionia, tonight we defend the Secret City of Ot. Things which have been hidden for ages will no longer be, and things that were once in secret will be shouted from the rooftops. I cannot promise you your lives, for I cannot promise what is not mine to give. But I can promise you that He, the Great God of Athera, will be with you, making your spears fly true and your shields hold fast."

Luik turned to the Dibor behind him. "Brax, Jrio, Fyfler—you have the floor. We leave on your command. I will see you in the Lion's Lair."

Chapter Twenty-Two

BATTLE FOR OT

Luik stood beneath the Tree, gazing about the cave. The space was a flurry of activity, the atmosphere nothing like it was the last time he had been there. The methodical changing out of the Scriptorium and orderly filing of the Archives had been replaced by shouting as thousands of dwarves busied themselves with the preparations for war. The garden floor was already beginning to flood with water and massive wooden spikes protruded high into the air. The lavish beauty of the garden had been pushed aside to prepare for the inevitable atrocities of war.

Men spilled in from the corridors that led from the portals, stumbling into the walls and collapsing in the ankle-deep water. The anxiety of travel was a shock to them, most heaving the contents of their stomachs or holding their heads in pain. Luik remembered the feelings all too well and pitied them, but the truth was that their turmoil was nothing compared to what was to come.

As the wave of agony passed, each man looked up, gazing at the miraculous wonder of the Tree that towered above them. Their eyes followed the massive trunk up into the leaves that disappeared into the blackness beyond, everything below them cast in its mesmerizing glow. But their awe was cut short as they took orders from one of the commanding dwarves. The guardians of Ot helped each warrior to his feet and then pushed them along.

"You've done that before?" Brax asked Luik, rubbing his temples. He walked slowly to where Luik stood in the garden.

"Aye," Luik said with a grin. "Too much for you?"

Brax just grunted and closed his eyes.

"Jrio and Fyfler?"

"They're coming," Brax said. "Just behind."

Luik looked just in time to see Fyfler double over and vomit, holding himself against a pillar with one hand. Jrio followed a few steps behind but managed to keep everything down.

"Everything's under way?" Brax continued.

"Aye, and moving along quickly. These dwarves are masters of efficiency," Luik said.

"So it seems," said Brax, observing the flurry of activity.

"Excuse me, King Luik?"

Startled, Luik looked down to his right where a small dwarf stood; he hadn't even heard him approach. "And you are?"

"My name is Spidanu, of the Tribe of Loy." He spoke very quickly. "Loy-Spidanu, really. But everyone tells me that's a mouthful. It is, I know. So everyone here just calls me Spid. Instead of Loy-Spi—"

"I'm pleased to meet you," Luik cut in, holding out his arm. The little dwarf met it before Luik could blink, shook twice, and withdrew his hand. It all happened so fast. The King was left still holding his hand in midair. "I see. *Spid*," Luik repeated his name. He looked at his hand and then back at the dwarf. Unlike Li-Saide's aged appearance, this dwarf looked incredibly youthful. His hair was short and spiky though he wore a similar robe as all the rest. "Well, what can I do for you, good Spid?"

"Your father summons you," said Spid.

"My father?" Luik was surprised. "Lead the way." And with that, Spid was gone, vanishing before Luik had a chance to see just which way he went.

Luik was astonished. "Well, I never—"

"You'll have to forgive him," came another voice.

Luik turned. A new dwarf stood beside him.

"I'm going to have to get used to all this commotion," said Brax. "I don't remember it being like this before. There are so many of them!"

Luik chuckled. "Aye, brother. That there are." He looked down at the new dwarf. This one was more what Luik was used to, portly and with a jovial round face, one that always seemed to be smiling no matter the actual emotion. He had red hair and matching beard, not as old as Li-Saide, but definitely Spid's elder.

"You'll have to forgive Spid," he said. "He is quite good at running errands—the fastest we have, in fact—but poor when it comes to having others keep up with him."

"So I can see," Luik replied.

"Ah, I digress," he thrust a hand out. "My name is Bi-Bablar." Luik smiled at the name. "I'll lead you to your father, as you'll surely find I'm a bit easier to follow than Spid."

"C'symia, my friend. My legs thank you."

Luik gave Brax a knowing nod and left him to tend to Fyfler and Jrio, who would then be helping assign the men to their posts. Bi-Bablar led Luik around through the garden in knee-high water and up one of the grand staircases that hugged the outer wall.

Luik could feel the tension in the air. The ground around them thumped and pulsed, a product either of the dwarves' activity or of the presence of their enemies above. But in any case Luik knew a tremendous battle was about to ensue. He tried to make small talk to ease Bi-Bablar's nerves. Or perhaps his own.

"So you like to write?"

What kind of a question is that? Luik thought. *He's a dwarf!*

"I like to ride," replied Bi-Bablar.

"Ride?"

"Horses," Bi-Bablar replied. "I believe that's what most people refer to when riding."

"And you would be correct," Luik nodded. "The error is mine."

"And I like to tell stories."

"Stories? Of what you write?"

"Of what I *see*," he corrected.

"Very good." The conversation wasn't helping anything, *especially me*, Luik thought. He felt it growing awkward.

"You know, my King, you ask many questions."

"It is my job to inquire, I suppose."

"You have no reason to be nervous, you know," Bi-Bablar added.

Luik was surprised at his forthrightness. *Can he see that easily into me?*

"I know," Luik said. "Yet I still am anxious."

Bi-Bablar stopped on a landing that overlooked the garden. "But the Great God is with you, my King. You have nothing to fear."

Luik stood thinking. All throughout the giant cave the dwarves were busy at work. Luik saw some of his men begin to integrate with them, lending their stronger arms to carrying supplies and readying the defenses, as he and the others had planned. "Sometimes all I can see is fear, Bi-Bablar. Sometimes I wonder if the Most High even hears my cries. These are—"

"Dark days. I know," said the dwarf. "But if you could only know what we know, what we see, then you would understand that the Most High does indeed hear your prayers. But long before you were born, and long after you are taken home to the Great Throne Room, He will still be dispensing the means of His will upon Creation. Whether your life comes or goes, it does not matter, so much as you were included, incorporated into His will with each breath you took. That is all He seeks. To have you a part of His masterwork. And most often that requires a feat of daring against those who would undo the tapestry of His legacy. You never know when your hardship means someone else's salvation."

They both stood staring at one another for a moment. Luik took great solace in the little man's words. He marveled at this race—so quirky and unusual—yet so instantly prone to being a friend. *Thank You, Most High.*

"Come," Bi-Bablar turned. "In here." He pushed on a heavy door, hinges fighting. They walked down a low, lengthy corridor lined with doors on either side. Thick candles fluttered in their wall mounts as they passed. The passage opened into a larger anteroom with a tall door set in the far wall.

"I will leave you here," said the dwarf.

"C'symia, Bi-Bablar," Luik said holding out his hand. "I trust we will meet again."

The dwarf snorted, "In the throes of battle, to be sure! And then in Athera, should the time ever come." He smiled widely and his round chest shook with a laugh. "Or I can just wait here," pointing to a small chair, "as I'm not allowed to leave you, yet I cannot go further."

Luik gave him a smirk. *Funny, too,* Luik added to his thoughts on the qualities of dwarves. He moved to the door and knocked with the heavy gold ring. The answer came as the door swung toward him and he slipped inside.

An attendant held the door and Luik thanked him before looking further into the room. It was decorated sparingly, as was Otian style, and was prepared for the Race of Men, as all the fixtures were much larger than normal. More relief pictures lined the walls, as Luik recalled were in his room when last visiting Ot, save that these were somehow much older. And this room, though Luik couldn't place it, had a personality about it—something distinct and almost royal—yet not without a certain air of leisure.

"It was Ad's room," Ragnar said, standing beside the bed. "His escape from Adriel, as if one could ever imagine it being needed." Ragnar was outfitted in full battle dress, a black tunic over his chain mail with a long sword strapped to his side; Luik knew it immediately as the Sword of The Lion Vrie.

"Father," Luik said, moving toward him. They clasped forearms and embraced.

"It is indeed good to see you, my son," Ragnar said, standing back to admire his appearance. "You look ready to slay Morgui himself."

"As do you," Luik replied.

Luik looked around the chamber.

"This room has been my home these many moons," Ragnar said. "And I find myself in good company, for the Spirit of the Most High has not been distant as my presence remains a secret for a little while longer." He walked over and touched the hard-packed soil beside a hanging picture. "Perhaps it is these walls, each one having sheltered my forefathers before me in times when they sought audience with the Tribes of Ot. Or perhaps it is the Tree without that reminds me of days gone by. But the time has passed quickly, and now you are here."

"I am only sad we could not spend it speaking more, or planning what adventure awaits us next," Luik replied.

"But what an adventure awaits us this day!" Ragnar spoke up. "Though my body is older now, my hand is still fit for the sword." He strode in front of Luik and clutched his arms. "And to meet my enemy with my son beside me," he sighed, "there is no greater day."

"C'symia, Father." Luik still felt that he wanted to know this man more. He knew him as King, yes; but as a *father*—that was something altogether different. Perhaps one could only know such a father as a boy, and so Lair would always hold that position. Luik felt that somehow this man, his real father, was much more of an acquaintance than an intimate. And while he pleaded with the Most High for the time to remedy such a circumstance, in his heart he felt that it would not be granted. Even worse, such an end meant that he would lose another father to battle—something he knew he could not bear again.

"What is it, dear boy?" Ragnar questioned. He looked deep into his son's eyes.

Luik thought of a dutiful answer. "It is the weight of Dionia," he replied, skirting the issue.

"Ah, a weight I know all too well." He patted him on the shoulder. "But you bear it well. And your battle plans are well formed."

"You have seen them then?"

"Oh, aye. And better than anything I could have ever fashioned. Your skill at kingcraft is equally fit to your skill in battle. It would seem that your tutelage under Gorn was well worth your absence from our world." Ragnar looked longingly into his son's face. "While I do not know you as I would, never doubt the investment made into your life. You are a Son of the Living God, an heir to His inheritance. And it was not I, nor the Gvindollion that chose you for such an errand. It was He, and He alone." Ragnar smiled then. "And I tend to think that He knows what He's doing."

"Aye, but sometimes I—"

There was a heavy pounding at the door. Luik looked over his shoulder, and then back to his father.

"You'll be fine, Luik. And remember that I love you. That's all I wanted to say."

"As do I," he replied.

"Enter," Ragnar called to the door.

"My King?" said Bi-Bablar.

Both Luik and Ragnar answered. "Ha, it's your title," Ragnar grinned at Luik.

Luik turned to the door. "Aye?"

"King Luik, the gate is breaching. Li-Saide has requested your presence immediately."

Luik looked to Ragnar.

"Let it be done," Ragnar said, picking up his shield and helmet.

They followed Bi-Bablar through the anteroom, down the corridor and out into the central cave. Once without, they passed up two more flights of stairs before stepping inside one of the lifts. Brax was waiting inside. No sooner was the gate closed than the lift lurched upward and sailed swiftly between the Tree's trunk and the side of the cave. The ground fell away at a hurried rate, and soon the large green leaves were racing by.

"Everything is ready?" Luik asked Brax.

"As ready as it can be."

"Good. Where is Li-Saide?"

"Waiting for you in the Surface Tunnel."

"And the men?"

"All to their stations. The portals are closed." Brax paused and looked down. "I'd say we're ready for a fight."

Luik took a deep breath. "We'd better be."

"We are, Son." Ragnar placed a hand on Luik's shoulder. "We are."

The lift came to a stop, and the gate was flung open. They were at the highest point in the cave, looking down to the Tree a great distance below. A low *boom* filled the air every few moments, and bits of dirt fell from the vaulted ceiling above.

Luik stepped onto the platform and looked up. There, just as he had drawn out, was an enormous net affixed to countless lift pulleys all over the cave's ceiling. It stretched out like a tightly woven blanket slung between tree limbs, ready to cradle anyone who fell in.

"I can't believe they made it," Luik admired.

"These dwarves are industrious beings," Brax said. "You said so yourself."

"Aye, it's just so big." He looked back down to the Tree's upper section. "And the archers?"

"Positioned and awaiting your command. Grinddr sent half of his men into the Tree as well."

"Well done." Luik looked to the tunnel. "Onward."

They marched up into a wide corridor, the same that eventually led to the surface. It was filled with men and dwarves, each busy with preparing the defenses as prescribed. The *booming* continued, and more soil and rocks fell on their heads. Luik brushed his hair of the debris and continued on. Long wooden spikes lay on either side of the floor, waiting to be inserted into the angled holes along the path, walls, and ceiling. And then he started to see the giant leaves attached overhead.

"They're bigger than I expected," Luik expressed.

"Aye, and swollen with water, just as you noted," Brax replied, moisture dripping down on their heads and sizzling in the torches. "They'll let them down and cover the tunnel as soon as we're done here."

"Good. And Li-Saide?" Luik asked Bi-Bablar.

"He's just ahead, my King," answered the dwarf, keeping pace behind them.

They climbed up the path, passing more layers of spikes and leaves until Luik could see Li-Saide in the torchlight. Fane stood beside him, examining the tunnel, which ended in a solid wall. Li-Saide was instructing a group of dwarves, each focused on a number of small cloth bundles being pressed into the tunnel walls.

"Li-Saide, I am—"

But the dwarf raised a silencing hand without even turning.

Luik stopped, as did the others. Bi-Bablar tugged on the King's tunic.

"They're setting the charges," he whispered. "One false move and..." the dwarf made an explosive sound with his mouth and spread his hands apart.

Suddenly the group of dwarves backed away from the dead end and Li-Saide turned to Luik. "It's all set," the Chief said confidently. "If they use the portal, they'll think twice on their next attempt. And if they dig through, they'll have a new mess on their hands." Li-Saide winked and put a finger to the air. "More digging either way!"

"Marvelous," Luik said. "I still don't know how this powder of yours works, but when have I ever questioned a dwarf?"

"Well, there have been—"

"Don't answer that," Luik put in.

They all turned back down the corridor.

"Is everything to your liking?" Li-Saide asked.

Luik nodded. Li-Saide waved a hand as they moved by the first set of spikes and leaves. The dwarves and warriors leapt to action, lowering the layers of leaves to completely cover the mouth of the tunnel, followed by placing the wooden spikes in a circular pattern around the tunnel floor and wall, all facing outward. If the Dairne-Reih came this route, and did indeed manage to dig themselves out of the cave-in resulting from Li-Saide's trap, the thick leaves would not only quench the fire of their enemies' torches, but hide the mouthful of spikes waiting to devour them in their rush for blood.

The six of them emerged back onto the landing beside the lift. Luik noticed men sawing away at the joints where the platform met the wall.

"The last ones through will pull her down," Li-Saide noted.

"If they get this far, they'll have a long drop," Bi-Bablar chuckled just thinking about it.

They stepped into the lift and descended.

"Only one question remains," said Brax looking to Luik. "Where do you want to be?"

Luik glanced at Brax, and then to Li-Saide and Bi-Bablar. "The Archives," Luik finally said. Li-Saide was all too proud. "If there is something to protect, it would be our world's history. The Great Tree will take care of herself, and I am no use with a bow. But give me my sword and my heritage to defend, and you'll have me in the right place."

"Then I'll join you," said Li-Saide.

"As will I," said Bi-Bablar.

"And I," said Fane. Ragnar nodded as well.

"And you, King Brax?" Luik asked.

"Ah, you know me," he said. "My men are in the garden and will tend to those who make it that far. With plenty of water to keep the fires at bay and spikes to welcome those who journey down? I'll only get in their way. Consider my sword yours."

Luik hit him on the back. "You are a faithful friend and a mighty warrior, Dibor. May our swords strike true."

Li-Saide pulled the line for the lift to stop at the next platform. They slowed and then adjoined the balcony and slipped past the gate. The landing was already filled with warriors extending down and up the stairs that bordered it on two sides, one set coming up from below and an adjacent set that continued upward, wrapping around the curve of the cave wall, each set on aiding Luik in his defense of the Library. In front of them was the familiar door of the Great Library and, beyond, the endless records of everything the dwarves had documented from the beginning of time, including the other worlds that the Most High had fashioned for His liking. Most notably, Luik remembered, the first world—*Earth*.

The three men and two dwarves exited the lift just before it was hoisted back into the air and raced to the Surface Tunnel above. Luik then turned to address the men now under his command. "We'll make our stand here," Luik shouted. "If we should fail, then we'll defend from within the Library."

"Defenses have been readied on the other side of the doors," Bi-Bablar reminded him. "As ordered, sir."

"Very good. Thank you for your diligence." He looked into the eyes of all those entrusted to his care. The loud thumping from far above grew louder. The enemy was near. "Meet your enemies with terror in your eyes and courage in your hearts," he exhorted. "Let your spears fly swiftly and your swords cut unhindered. This is our greatest hour, and *we—must—not—fail.*"

"Hey'a!" the men let up in unison.

Suddenly a horrendous explosion sounded from far above. The men looked directly overhead to see a puff of smoke and debris fly out of the Surface Tunnel and spew into the cave. The warriors and dwarves had not even finished cutting away the platform when the blast came, the shock wave blowing them and the platform off the wall. The lift swung wildly...

And then the line snapped.

The wooden crate along with the platform hurtled downward, bodies flailing in midair.

"Against the wall! Now!" Luik ordered. The men spread out along the inside of the stairs and pressed themselves against the wall as best they could. They watched in muted terror as the first of the fatalities played out before their eyes.

Within moments the wreckage flew past them, men screaming as they fell. Parts of the platform slammed into the balcony where Luik stood, shattering into oblivion. The scream of a man was silenced as he crashed into the upper staircase and ripped a portion of it down with him.

A dwarf landed with a sickening thud at Li-Saide's feet, appearing as a heap of robes and a smattering of blood.

A moment later the carnage met its end on the cavern's floor, echoes extending back up.

Ignoring the trauma that had just played out, Li-Saide said, "They're in."

There was a heavy pause as everyone in Ot became silent. All waited, listening for what would come next. No one stirred, or even dared breathe for fear of inviting what lay above them. Just utter stillness.

Then the *booming* resumed.

The Dairne-Reih were back to work.

"They'll be coming through the main ceiling very soon, I should think," said Bi-Bablar.

"Aye," agreed Li-Saide. And suddenly his eyes grew distant.

Bi-Bablar turned to Luik. "They've been digging down from the surface for three days. They're using Hewgogs."

Luik was confused, having never heard the word before.

"A giant Dairneag," replied the dwarf. "I've seen them with my own eyes. Gruesome creatures, to be sure."

Luik looked to Li-Saide. The dwarf was staring out into the distance, his eyes fixed on the Tree's trunk.

"Are you all right?" Luik asked.

But Li-Saide didn't move. Luik removed his gauntlet and placed a hand gently on his shoulder. The dwarf stirred.

"Where were you?"

"Something's not right," Li-Saide said quietly.

"What do you mean?"

"I feel something terrible is about to happen."

Luik knew Li-Saide never let his own fears get in the way of reality; he was a dwarf, after all, and they were immune to certain human dispositions. The statement worried him greatly.

"To what effect?"

"I'm not certain," replied the dwarf. "I just sense something in the spirit—" He squinted his eyes. Suddenly a look of great pain seized his face, and his eyes flashed back open. "O Great God!" he cried and fell to his knees.

"Li-Saide!" Luik knelt down next to him. "What's happening?" But the dwarf only groaned in pain. Luik heard more groaning from his other side. He looked and saw Bi-Bablar also crumpled on the ground.

"King Luik!" one of the men cried. "Look!"

Luik glanced up and noticed that any dwarf his eyes could find was doubled over, many of them weeping openly.

"Great God, what is this?" Luik whispered. Just then he heard Li-Saide trying to speak. He knelt lower.

"What is it?"

Then Luik heard Li-Saide say something he found unimaginable. "All is lost."

Boooom!

An explosion ripped through the cavern's ceiling, blasting through the final layers of rock with a deafening sound. Sunlight poured in through a gaping hole, streaming through the clouds of debris. Rocks and dirt showered down, most caught in the wide net overhead; but the larger bored holes right through the tight weave.

"Shields!" Luik cried and raised his shield over Li-Saide and himself. In the same movement he capped his head with his helmet. Rock fragments rained down, pelting their shields with pockmarks. But some pieces were much too large to be stayed off by weaponry and tore through portions of the wall-mounted structures, crushing men whole. Just to Luik's side he saw a man kneeling with his shield covering his head; one moment he was enduring the assault with bravery, the next he was pulverized, crushed beneath his shield, showering those around him.

The debris thinned, and the air was filled with men coughing, many groaning in their final moments of life.

"Look lively, men!" Luik hollered, standing to his feet. He glanced up to the massive hole above and the net filling with stone and dirt that seeped out like mud in a sieve. Then he remembered Li-Saide.

"Li-Saide!" he cried, kneeling back down. "Are you all right?"

The dwarf rubbed his head. "I'm no worse for wear."

"You were right, something was indeed about to happen. You must get up quickly."

"My King," replied the dwarf, as Luik helped him to his feet, "I was not talking about Dionia."

Luik paused as the dwarf brushed himself off; the comment disturbed him.

"O?"

"Something has happened on Earth."

Luik was stupefied. He didn't know what to say, although his heart was telling him something dreadful. Memories filled his head, images of what he had heard behind these very doors in the Library.

Images of a grave travesty…

…of the unexplainable.

For it pleased the Father to crush His Son.

"They're coming in!" Ragnar shouted.

Luik looked up to see the first wave of demons fill the space of the hole and block out the fading sunlight. They climbed through the opening with their claws digging into the ground. But as it crumpled in their hands, they fell headlong into the net. It was here that Luik's plans were set into motion. The Dairne-Reih scrambled over one another and tried to reach the edges of the net while others, toppling over on themselves, looked for places to slash through. But in either case, the demons were exposed and vulnerable from beneath. The archers throughout the Treetop and along the walls let loose a volley of arrows so thick they could be heard by the onlookers below. The missiles raced through the netting and found their targets, drilling into any number of the beasts caught in the net.

As the Dairneags continued to file through the hole above, the net filled with more and more victims, helpless as they tried to maneuver over the bodies. They growled and shrieked, filling the cavern with freakish sounds. Spotters continued to point out targets for the archers, shouting to be heard over the ghastly throes of death from above. Luik watched as the great net began to sag, filling with arrow-riddled corpses. The flow of demons was unrelenting, streaming in like giant spiders.

"It will not hold much longer," Fane noted. He held firm to his rowan staff.

Soon the net was so full that the archers could spy no new targets. The cords strained under the weight as more and more demons stood on top of their fallen kind. They raced to the edges and hung from the sides. But this proved fatal, as the bowmen unleashed their wrath. The Dairneags were met with mortal wounds, their fingers slipping from the net, their bodies hurtling to the spike-ridden ground far below.

"She's going to give," Brax shouted.

As if hearing his admission, the main cords of the net began to unwind, their lengths spinning wildly, snapping under the increased weight. Like sinew popping from too much stress, the bonds gave way one at a time. The pulleys squealed as lines raced through them, smoke pouring from the blocks.

"Take cover!" Luik ordered. Once again the shields went up and everyone knelt against the wall.

Just then the final cords tore free and snapped back like whips. The net churned one last time and heaved sideways, spilling its contents out into midair. A black mass of demon corpses issued forth like a wave pouring over a waterfall. There was nowhere to go but down. Dairneags that still lived shrieked in terror as they flew through the air, hurtling to their end. Most seemed to pour into the top of the Tree of Life, careening into branches that broke their bodies further, many impaled on the smaller upturned limbs.

But now the message was sent to Morgui's forces: only those demons with the ability to climb could come through the hole. Luik and his men stood closely against the wall as bodies bounced off and flew past them. Then his eyes turned to the Surface Tunnel entrance. He saw wreckage spill out of it, and dirt fling into the air.

"They've dug through," he said to Li-Saide.

"Aye," replied the dwarf.

Back at the main hole, demons crept down from the surface and peered into the vast cave. Their gathering forces pushed down from above, and a few unlucky beasts were shoved free, screaming as they fell. But most studied the cavern and plotted their course. They reached around the edge of the hole and climbed along the ceiling with their claws dug into the hard-packed ground. The archers had no problem picking them off, watching them climb along and then dropping them with well-placed arrows.

Again, Luik noticed movement from the Surface Tunnel. He pointed up as a Dairneag emerged and stepped out into the open air. The men watched it fall, flying past their balcony. It was large and, from the bloodied body, had clearly borne the brunt of the spikes within. The demon also released an extinguished torch as it fell; the damp leaves had served their purpose.

Another demon followed behind the first, stopping just short of a fatal fall, but the pause was temporary. The Dairneag coming behind it did not slow and shoved the first out into the open, following with itself and a few more. Luik could hear the horde still in the cave begin to click and chatter, certainly passing along a warning.

"The first wave is over," Luik surmised. "They know they can't just barge in."

There was a lull in the commotion as the Surface Tunnel activity ebbed, as did that pouring in from the hole above. But everyone knew the battle was far from over.

The archers readied their next missiles.

Luik drew his sword, a sound followed by countless more of the same. He squinted up through the cavern, now filled with a dusty haze.

A single coil of rope, tethered from above, shot down through the main hole, followed by four of five more. They unraveled speedily and dropped into the canopy of leaves. A moment later, the largest Dairneags Luik had ever seen descended through the space.

"Hewgogs," Li-Saide cursed.

"What?" asked Luik.

"What we were telling you about," Bi-Bablar reminded him. "The giants of Morgui's army."

"I've never seen such creatures," Luik mumbled.

"That's because they are something new," said Li-Saide. "Morgui created them."

"But I thought he can't make anything new?"

"Ah," Li-Saide corrected himself, staring up at the rappelling giants, "he *bred* them."

"Excuse me?" Luik was disgusted.

"Can we save the lesson for later?" Brax interrupted. "Look!"

The Hewgogs, riddled with arrows, dropped from the ropes and fell into the uppermost branches of the Tree. As they met the canopy, branches cracked and ripped apart, leaves flying out from within. To Luik and the others it looked as if someone had reached in and shaken a bush with their hand. Luik noticed the sounds of countless bowstrings *thwipping* through the air, followed by deep growls. More crashing and then screams—

—of men.

Bodies fell through the upper limbs, bouncing around like pebbles, and then appearing in midair underneath the canopy of leaves.

"Look out!" Brax hollered down below. But the first few bodies surprised the warband beneath the Tree and landed among them.

Just then another wave of demons slid down the ropes, but these were the typical Dairneags. Luik imagined them moving easily through the limbs and working in conjunction with the Hewgogs. Without adequate swordsmen to protect them, the archers would not last much longer. More of the Dairne-Reih filled the tree, and soon a full-fledged battle ensued within the branches. More limbs cracked and bodies fell out of the leaves.

And the battle was moving—down.

Luik heard a great commotion in the lower branches. Men were shouting, dwarves barking orders. And just then a lift descended from the canopy, lowering swiftly to the garden below.

"They're retreating," Fane said.

Luik looked back to the hole. Not only were more demons descending through the hole, but the more agile had resumed their method of climbing down along the ceiling. So many came, in fact, Luik could not count them, the effort immeasurably overwhelming. Even from the Surface Tunnel they came, crawling out of the tunnel and racing down the wall—*right for them*.

The lanky, swifter demons moved with remarkable speed, covering the distance in no time, as if running on level ground on two legs. They seemed to defy gravity. Luik was astonished. But equally pleased.

"Ready the ropes," he ordered. Li-Saide raised his hand and the warriors all around reached for any of the number of ropes that dangled against the wall. Farther up, the lines attached to the wall, linked to something fixed within.

Luik squinted through the slits in his helmet and squeezed the sword in his hand. The Dairne-Reih were picking up speed. And they could see him—Luik knew it. They wanted King's blood. There was nothing better to them.

"Hold!" Luik ordered.

Dirt was raining down on Luik's warband as the wall was eaten away. Like a black shadow spanning across the ground, the crawling demons spewed out from the two holes above and blanketed the entire ceiling, pouring down the walls.

"Hold!"

He could see their mouths flare, teeth exposed.

Luik held his breath. Eyes keen.

"Hold!"

There must be legions of them, he thought. And then he thought no more…

It was time.

"Pull!" he hollered.

Li-Saide lowered his hand, and the warriors heaved with all their might. The lines snapped taut. From above, more wooden spikes, hinged from their bases, angled out from the wall. The demons had no time to react and plunged into row after row of the deadly dowels, jerking back violently. The force was tremendous, many breaking spikes in half, only to fall into the next set. Those not impaled jumped out from the wall. They sailed over those hanging in the spikes, but tried in vain to pull themselves back into the wall and fell to their deaths in the garden below.

Wood and flesh drifted down on top of Luik and those around him. The first charge had been stalled. But those pouring in from the tunnel and the hole continued with a second wave. It appeared like a coating of black oil that oozed down from the ceiling, covering the cave entirely as it went. Those that could not climb slid down the ropes into the Tree. And Dairneags were picking through the spikes above Luik's head, regrouping for an assault on his platform.

He looked across the cavern and slightly below to where the Scriptorium platform was. The warriors were just now releasing the wall spikes above their location with the same devastating effects. But as the countless beasts filled in from the sides, Luik imagined the entire balcony to be swallowed whole in a matter of moments.

But then Luik noticed something else even more disheartening, something that stopped the breath in his lungs, something he had not noticed before: the light of the Tree was dimming.

"Li-Saide, look," he pointed to the canopy.

"I know," replied the dwarf.

The Tree of Life was not as it once was. The mesmerizing glow that gave light to fill the cave, and eternal life to the dwarves, was diminishing.

"Swords ready!" Brax commanded. Luik glanced up. The Dairne-Reih were on top of them.

A Dairneag left the wall and sailed down, horns and teeth bared. He crashed into a cluster of men, chomping on their swords and exposed limbs. Another landed beside Luik, thrashing wildly. He met him with a powerful jab in the side.

Suddenly Luik was smashed to the ground, weight bearing down on his shoulders and chest. His head slammed against the platform, rattled in his helmet.

He looked up.

The grotesque face of a Dairneag growled just a hand's breadth away, staring him right in the eyes. The monster's hot breath stung his skin, drool slipping in through the helmet's breathing holes. His body was on the alert and didn't even notice the pain as the monster squeezed its claws into his chain maille. He tried to twist away beneath it, but the effort did nothing to deter the beast.

Time slowed.

Luik felt the Spirit rise in his body.

All his training flashed before him and then stopped with Gorn in the Lion's Lair. *The Tongues of the Dibor.*

He glared back at the demon on top of him. This monster would not win. Morgui would not win. So long as Luik had breath to breathe, so long as the Most High still sat upon His throne…

He recalled Gorn's words. "It is not an accomplishment you are looking for, but a flowing with His Spirit to arrive at a place within His Will."

What came next was less than an action and more of a thought. *Die.*

Luik grabbed the creature around its throat with his left hand and then brought his sword up into its gut with his right. He whispered the Sacred Tongue and, in one swift motion, drove the sword all the way through the demon.

The action was so devastating that the Dairneag was torn in two, exploding all over Luik's body.

Luik lay there, the power surge still coursing through his veins. He caught his breath. He remembered how his sword had decimated the granite rock in the Lair, and it was almost as if he could hear Gorn speaking to him now. *Well done.*

Time raced back, and he looked up to see more Dairne-Reih besetting the platform. He pushed himself up and noticed more coming up from beneath them, climbing over the balcony.

"There are too many!" Brax yelled out, swinging at a Dairneag and wresting it of its arm.

Luik engaged another beast, this time the Tongue coming more easily. He brought his sword back and swept across the demon's midsection, speaking the words as he swung. His sword cleaved the demon in half, the upper section toppling over and onto the floor. A demon nearby examined the severed corpse and then looked at Luik.

For the first time Luik could recall, the demon stopped—and looked at him with *fear.*

"Brax!" Luik yelled over his shoulder.

Brax disemboweled a foe and then spun to Luik's aid. He saw the demon Luik was staring at and noticed its expression. Ragnar and Fane also stole a glance. As Brax drew closer the demon looked over at him, now taking a step back.

"What did you do?" Brax asked, and then he looked to the ground and saw the carnage.

"The Tongues of the Dibor," Luik replied, eyeing his new opponent.

"Of course!" Brax brightened, slightly frustrated why he hadn't thought of it sooner. *Too much reliance on the natural.* He spun and met his next adversary.

An agile monster leapt from the wall and drove at Brax. But he sidestepped, sending the demon off balance, and swung hard, willing the words to his mouth. But the lack of practice had a price. The Dairneag leaned away from the sword and jabbed a horn-knuckled punch at Brax's head. He ducked, and then tried the words again.

Time slowed down.

Brax could sense the Spirit increase.

He drew his sword back and lowered his head.

Then he whispered.

The words boomed into a shout as his sword plunged into the demon's armored chest, and then out as the beast flew clear off the balcony and far into the cavern.

Luik caught the motion out of the corner of his eye—his opponent did, too. And it was cause enough to take another step back.

Luik moved forward. The Dairneag looked back to him. Luik raised his sword, and the demon flinched.

"We've got them," Luik said quietly, his words filling his helmet.

Suddenly the commotion on the platform ebbed as other demons noticed the standstill between Luik and the Dairneag. The beast was at a loss.

Luik began whispering the Sacred Tongue again. His hands tingled.

"O, no," came Fane's voice.

Luik glanced over. Fane was fixed on something high above…

…a glow in the mouth of the main hole…

…brighter than daylight.

There, issuing rapidly, came a river of fire, as if made up of thick oil or, worse, molten rock set aflame. Luik's eyes widened. The flow cast an orange glow into the cavern, and all turned to watch it. The torrent was wide, catching demons around the hole and swallowing them instantly. It streamed down, filling the air with flames…

…and then, the unthinkable.

The liquid fire gushed onto the upper portion of the Tree, drenching the canopy and folding the leaves down. Instantly the branches were set ablaze, the greenery leaping with flames, white hot, leaf edges running with black lines. The lava cascaded downward, splashing off the Tree and showering the sides of the cavern.

Luik heard shouting and looked to the lower limbs. Men, dwarves, and Dairne-Reih alike stared up with terror, caught between the fire's devouring appetite and a mortal fall to the garden below. While many chose the fall over burning alive, most did not have time to think. Luik watched in speechless horror as the liquid fire raced down the wood and poured over those in the Tree. His mind burned with the images of men holding hands up against the heat, dwarves covering themselves with their robes. And even demons who, consumed by the treachery of their own Lord, screamed upward into the flames, molten fire filling their gaping mouths. Even the mighty Hewgogs tumbled down through the flaming carnage, their bodies rolling through the mix and spewing out into the open air below the canopy.

The cavern filled with the scent of burning flesh and sulfur mixed with charred wood. The Tree limbs burst, propelling flaming fragments into the platforms around the cave. The entire space was cast in a lurid orange glow, a far cry from the once shimmering beauty of the Tree of Life. The demons around Luik and the others turned upon them with renewed aggression, feeling their victory now secure.

Luik forgot the words he was about to speak and was suddenly flung back against the cavern wall, his head slamming against the inside of his helmet with a jolt. Tiny specks of light danced across his dimming gaze. Sound was ebbing.

A sword flashed in front of him, and blood was spilt.

"Get up, Son!"

The words wafted toward him as if on a gentle breeze. Luik blinked, trying to clear his head. A strong hand latched under his arm and jerked him up upright.

"We must get out of here!" he heard the voice again.

Luik gained his feet beneath him and looked around. The sounds of battle returned, rushing at him full speed. There fighting in front of him was his father, Ragnar. He paused long enough to give Luik a wink and then continued slashing at the beasts nearest them.

"To your left!" Brax yelled.

Luik turned to meet an imposing foe, a Dairneag three times his size who, by the look of its hands and mouth, had already indulged in the flesh of numerous men and dwarves. Luik felt his sword strong in his hand and found the words of the Sacred Tongue without so much as thinking.

"*Kee a-tah shuhe tey ahm-a—*" and then the blast of his sword interrupted the speech, boring a hole the size of a man's torso in the creature's chest. With no lungs to even issue a scream, the demon dropped to its knees and collapsed before him.

But it was replaced by three more. Luik looked around. The platform was assailed from above and below, and his forces were being overwhelmed. The demons were pouring over the wall spikes and converging too quickly. The stairs leading down to the garden were flooded, and in the distance far below he could see a black mass of Dairne-Reih scaling the walls and closing in on the lower ranks.

"I suggest we make for the Library, as you've prepared, my King," Li-Saide yelled above the din of battle and fire. "It's our only hope." He turned toward the giant doors.

Brax and Ragnar drew near, as did the remaining men and dwarves, defending their retreat toward the Library. Li-Saide and Fane gapped only one of the heavy twin doors, hinges groaning, and slipped inside. It was just enough for men to slide through, but not enough for the demons. Luik heard something thud on the opposite side, presumably a beam to keep the door from opening farther.

Suddenly Spid's head popped around the corner. "Varos, High King!"

Luik was surprised to see him but had no time to dwell on it. He grabbed the closest warrior to him and shoved him through the gap, prompting more to go as Ragnar and Brax busied themselves with fending off the encroaching demons.

Within mere moments the platform was overrun with Dairneags, and the three kings were tested by the role of being the last ones through the door. Over their heads a few demons scratched at the gap in the doors, reaching their arms in, trying to squeeze through.

"We need to clear some space," Ragnar hollered. "We'll never be able to close the door!" He parried a thrust with his sword and blocked a horned fist with his shield.

"When I say duck, do so," Luik ordered. "But for now, cover me." Brax and Ragnar nodded and took up a position directly in front of him, their backs to the door. It was two against a multitude, but their swords went right to work.

Luik brought his sword back over his head, hands twisted over and the blade pointing out in front of him—*high guard*. Normally, it was a poor defensive position.

But he wasn't playing defense.

He closed his eyes and tried his best to quiet his spirit. Everything was so loud around him.

He could hear Brax grunting…

…his father's sword striking bone.

Demons clucking and hissing.

The fire chewing away at the Tree.

Men screaming in the throes of death.

Most High, I need you now.

He searched his heart and looked for The Presence. He felt as if he was wandering in a solemn maze, each turn presenting more of the same barren corridors, more of the same prize-less dead ends.

He took a deep breath and waited for the Spirit to fill his hands.

The maze presented a new turn up ahead. He ran toward it, eager to pass the corner. He could feel it. He could feel *Him*.

"Any time now," Brax yelled over his shoulder.

But Luik was not listening. He could feel the Most High—he could *see* his prize.

The Spirit touched his hands, and Luik felt warmth move in his stomach, like a river stirring deep within his gut. It was the Living Water. He knew he must yield to it—that is how it worked every time: to relinquish control and give himself over. Not in a passive, apathetic way, but in a deliberate invitation to move with it. To *dance*.

He summoned the Sacred Words again, whispering.

The river of water in his stomach suddenly turned hot, as if liquid fire like that which burned the Tree—save more intense. Invisible flames ate up his chest and surged down his arms. Fire shot up in his bones. His hands felt as if the flesh would melt right off them, but he could not let go of his sword. Suddenly the blade resonated, humming with the power he felt within.

He opened his eyes.

The Dairne-Reih moved slowly, unaware of his state. He had time to look from one to the next, taking in their features with ease, time all but standing still. Brax's blade was inching through a victim in mid-stride; Ragnar was deflecting a blow and soon to jab upward. But time for Luik was fluid, his actions as if nothing hindered them.

"Down!" he yelled. But the response was slow.

Brax painstakingly dropped to his knees while Ragnar finished his thrust and rolled to his side. When they were clear, Luik drew in a breath…

He was suspended in the moment.

Inhale.

Everything froze. The Dairne-Reih were still, some glaring at him, others at the two men on the ground. His entire body was alight with fire, his very marrow set aflame.

Exhale.

The Sacred Words issued forth, drenched with the Fire of the Spirit. His sword swung across, sending a blast with it much like a wave that rippled through the water, but this through the air. The concussion careened into all those standing, passing through them and then suddenly obliterating them into complete carnage, their forms decimated into oblivion.

But time still lingered.

Luik's sword finished its arc and still trembled in his hands. He looked up to see those demons scratching at the door. With both hands firmly on the hilt, he thrust it upward, still well below the monsters. But the distance meant nothing. Sent from the tip like a lightning bolt, a flash of light leapt into the cluster of beasts gathered atop the doorframe. Their bodies shot up and away, pulverized by the blast, and collided with those above them.

Seeing the platform was clear, Luik ceased the words. The fire deep in his belly suddenly withdrew, and time accelerated to the present. The force of the return sent him off balance and he caught himself on Brax's shoulder. An echo of the blast still resounded off the cavern walls, sounding as if thunder just boomed in the space.

"W-what," Brax stammered, his eyes surveying the platform, "was that?"

Ragnar pressed himself up to a knee and stood wearily; his ears rang. He looked at his son. "What did you do?"

"I don't know," Luik said, helping them both to their feet. "But we need to get moving."

While Luik's actions had certainly bought them temporary reprieve, the bloodthirsty Dairneags were already feeling the lust in their tongues and regrouping up the steps and down the walls. Ragnar slipped through the gap, and Brax followed. Luik entered last and gave a final look back into the cavern. The Tree was now completely consumed in flame, the intense heat burning his face even as he lingered. Charred corpses hung in the limbs, leaves now only embers drifting through the air. And all around the cave Dairne-Reih poured over the walls like a wave of grease glazing down the sides.

He couldn't see to the garden floor, but he could imagine the carnage that his eyes would have met: mutilated bodies consumed in flame, burning on spear point, or floating in the flood waters. Those who were not crushed from falling debris and corpses, or burned alive by the fiery flow, were now fighting for their lives, surely running back toward their only means of escape—the portals.

Luik was pulled away from his vision and gave the order to close the door. The hinges groaned for a final time as the ancient wood locked shut. The scene was gone—though not from Luik's mind. The Dairne-Reih clawed ravenously on the opposite side, their shrieks and clicking evidence of their frustration. Luik leaned in, his helmet against the door. It vibrated with the violence. Brax, Fane, his father, and Li-Saide were among the only ones he knew as friends—as brothers—who had survived. Where his other Dibor were, Gorn and even Grinddr, he could only guess. And the guesses were not pleasant.

His thoughts were quick and clear. The battle for Ot had happened swiftly, and ended even more so. Luik had fought many a battle against Morgui: Adriel had been slow but total; Somahguard had been swift but fought with the *taken*. But this—this had surprised him. He had thought they at least had a chance. It was, after all, the *Tree of Life*. Who could have ever imagined her succumbing to the hand of Morgui? Who could have ever imagined the Most High allowing her to fall?

A violent crash came from the other side of the door, and Luik's head popped away from the wood.

"They're attempting to breach the door!" Bi-Bablar exclaimed.

"Correction," said Li-Saide, "they *are* breaching the door."

Luik and the others turned to the Chief of the Tribes, now leader of a race of homeless dwarves. The High King took off his bloodied helmet, the metal slipping in his gauntlets. His eyes swept the corridor that opened up into the first of the Great Library's countless vaults, stacked to the ceiling with their prized scrolls. Then it dawned on him…

Not only had they lost Ot, and soon the entire texts of their civilization, but they had absolutely nowhere to run. Morgui had won. And Luik had never felt so alone. It was, indeed, the end. A fear unlike any he had ever known laced its tentacles around his chest and squeezed. There was no way out. This would be his grave.

"We're trapped."

Chapter Twenty-Three

FORGOTTEN SOULS

Anorra clung to the bars of her cell, white knuckles and trembling arms racked by fear and exhaustion. She peered with her Second Sight out into the vast sea of horror before her, her face half hidden in the shadows of the hot steel. The cracks in her flesh were scabbed over, and her eye sockets swollen with infection. But she couldn't feel the pain in her body. It was her heart that hurt the most.

The cavern in front of her was a tumultuous sea of writhing limbs swirling wildly like a forest on fire, beaten by gusting winds. Hands, feet, and arms stretched into the air through metal grates that covered massive pits in the ground. She could only guess what matter of vile fury lay below as billowing smoke and bits of molten rock shot upward, bringing horrific screams with each blast.

The screams, however, seemed familiar. Those of people. She studied what she could make out of the extremities more carefully. She saw individual fingers. They were indeed human hands, grasping at the air. For anything.

The anguish she felt then threatened to crush her chest. *Dear Most High!*

When the infernal shrieking seemed to reach a climax, the entire cavern trembled with a subtle quake. A churning pool of molten rock then flooded the floor below. It rushed up through the prisoner-laden cells and spewed between the grates overhead. The captives disappeared beneath the torturous deluge, and the room had a new floor, a churning mass of boiling lava that burned cherry red. All was calm.

It was then Anorra noticed the watchmen, demons standing along charred pathways that looked over the giant pool. They strode back and forth, eyeing the bubbling surface below with keen stares. They each carried a long whip in one hand and an overlong spear in the other: a breed of Dairneag with enough hand-articulation to carry weapons.

A deep *clunk* echoed up from the depths, and the lava began to recede. It seeped back down through the grates, and the cavern resumed its former appearance, save for the captives. All was silent.

But she assumed too much too soon.

Miraculously, a lone hand rose up from between glowing red bars, fingers gnarled and twisted. *Surely no mortal could endure such a horrific bath!* But the victim seemed undeterred, though at least wary. Resilient perhaps? Or, from what happened next, perhaps just new to the order of things here…

Swiftly one of the watchmen nearest the unlucky victim sent its whip trailing through the air like a snake's tongue. The length of the weapon uncurled and snapped at the outstretched arm, lashing around three-fold. Then with one sharp yank the whip jerked taut, and the captive hollered as joints separated and ligaments tore. Anorra covered her eyes instinctively, but the action availed no relief. Her spirit saw it all with unending clarity.

Trying to save the one, other hands reached up and endeavored to free the victim, fingers prying at the bond. But the watchman was keen and ready for this. A flip of the wrist, and the whip end was loose again, only to be answered by a jeering howl of voices below. But their revelry was short-lived as the guard's spear shaft was sent swinging over their heads in an instant, cutting through flesh and bone like a scythe through ripened wheat.

Soon the severed limbs were joined by the masses and, amazingly, the plight of those encaved below resumed just as it had before, the cycle complete.

Anorra sank to the floor of her cell, unable to bear the scene any longer. And for once, her Second Sight obeyed. She coughed. Her broken ribs stole her breath away, and she tasted blood in her mouth.

She needed to hear Him again. She needed His presence. If not, she knew she would be no different from those poor souls caged up in the pools below, writhing monsters with the blood of Ad still running in their veins.

I need you now, my daughter.

Though she could barely discern the words, more prompting than audible, she knew it was Him by the way He spoke. She had always known Him. And even here in this place His voice was not foreign. If anything, it was more welcome.

"Aye, my King. I am ever yours." The words slipped from her swollen lips, heard by no one but her Maker.

Her vision opened once more, projecting the writhing arena as before. Then, as if carried on the wings of a bird, the image in her spirit moved out the far side of the cavern and into another twice as large as the first. Smoke filled the room, and she could taste the sulfur in her mouth. Burning bodies swung from the ceiling on metal chains, and watchman slashed at them for a game.

The room passed, and she traveled down a long corridor. Enormous stalactites and stalagmites grew from the ceiling and floor, like enormous teeth waiting to feed on any who passed by. She hovered between them and raced down the length of the tunnel and into a strange room, wide and tall but extremely shallow in depth. Small cells were pock-marked all along the wall in front of her like swallow nests in the side of an embankment. Except these chambers had no access and their gates were permanently sealed: the inhabitants were never intended to leave.

She cast a long stare down the length of the corridor, the cells stretching on out of sight to the right and left. Anorra could feel that there was something much different about the atmosphere in this room; these souls were unlike those in the lava pits. None of them screamed out; no hands reached between the bars. Everything was silent. She passed up through the small chambers, passing row after row, looking into the shadows. Lurid eyes stared back but never recognized her—their once-gleaming faces now barren and haunted, full of despair. Full of defeat.

It was then she understood.

These souls were forgotten.

Her view raced on along the wall, high up now. She cast a quick glance down and suddenly wished she hadn't, for the floor far below was swallowed in darkness. Then her progress slowed and she hovered before a cell that bore no bars.

"What is this?" she asked of her Creator. She peered into the darkness but saw nothing.

Look closer.

She edged nearer.

A set of old eyes opened.

Anorra lurched back in her cell, but her vision did not move.

These eyes were different again. There was something about them…as if this being could *see* her. It was gazing back at her! All at once a man's face appeared. Sallow and grave, he fumbled forward. Seeking rescue? A gnarled hand stretched forward, just bones beneath seared flesh. Anorra screamed, hearing her own voice echo in her cell.

The vision vanished.

She sat against the far wall of her cage, listening to her own labored breathing. "Who was that, my Lord? Why show me such a thing?"

I want you to rescue him.

Chapter Twenty-Four

THE READING ROOM

"Reinforce the doors!" Luik ordered, standing with his back against them and sheathing his blade. The clawing and screeching increased as the demons without increased in their lust for a prize. Men and dwarves picked up the giant beams, anchored them in their newly-fashioned floor mounts, and let them drop into place, slamming them down with a heavy *ka-thunk*.

"If they don't break through soon, the fires certainly will," Ragnar pointed out. They could feel the heat penetrating even then.

"Come," summoned Li-Saide. He ushered the men down the entry corridor and into the first of the large archival rooms, lit by only a handful of torches. Many of the warriors limped or carried wounded dwarves in their arms. More than half their numbers had been cut down in the short assault on the platform.

Luik leaned down to speak privately with the dwarf. "We cannot make a stand with so few men."

Li-Saide regarded him.

Thud. A muffled blow struck the doors from the outside. Dust fell from the ceiling.

Bi-Bablar walked over, as did Spid. "What would you have us do, Mighty Chief?" they inquired.

234

Thud.

Fane drew near as well. "Sir, we have a number of men who need attention." Luik looked over to those indicated, studying their painful expressions. Blood already stained the wood and carpet, their moans mixed with the terrors outside.

Thud. It came again, followed by a *crack!*

"My Chief," Bi-Bablar pressed. The doors were weakening. But Li-Saide was deep in thought, focused far away, as if searching the Great Library from within his mind, for something. Anything.

The sounds coming through the door grew louder, the shrieks of the demons now prodded by the flames that devoured the Tree. Luik looked over his shoulder, testing the integrity of their defenses with his eyes. Brax nodded. "She won't hold much longer."

Luik turned to Li-Saide. "My Chief? I need options."

Thud-crack!

"We must make it to the Reading Room," Li-Saide finally replied.

But Bi-Bablar looked to the injured. "Chief, that is a great distance from here. I'm not certain that—"

"Save it," he glared. "They will make it."

There seemed to be a small commotion among the dwarves, and Luik grew uneasy. "Where is this Reading Room?" he asked Li-Saide.

"It is the first room Ad had burrowed out for the Library when she was originally fashioned—the farthest away from here. It's a long story. Must I?"

Luik shook his head.

"C'symia." The dwarf turned to their small warband. "We have far to travel," he announced. "But you must endure. It is our only hope of survival." Everyone just stared at him. Survival by fleeing farther down a dead end? It was madness. For what, a few more precious moments of life?

"I trust you have a plan?" Luik asked the dwarf. He nodded warily. Luik sighed. "You heard him, men! On your feet! Let's go!"

As if his words needed further backing, another *thud-crack* pummeled the doors, this time with a sliver of orange light seeping in through the middle. The warband glanced at it and leapt to their feet. Dead end or not, they were certainly not interested in being devoured here on the floor.

"Quickly now," Bi-Bablar coxed, helping dwarves to their feet and pushing them along. "Heads up. Stay together." Brax picked up a man who nursed a hacked leg, pieces of chain maille sunken in the wound.

"I'm not sure I can walk," said the warrior.

"You can," replied Brax. "You can, and you must." The warrior limped awkwardly at first, wincing in pain. He turned to look back at Brax. The King winked. "You can do it."

Luik glanced up at the doors now that most of the men were on their feet and moving. Li-Saide regarded the deepening damage as well. "How long do you think we have?"

"Only moments," Li-Saide said. "Those are Hewgogs, infuriated and scalded ones at that." He turned to Luik. "They can smell you."

"Comforting," Luik said.

Another blow to the doors sent the beams jouncing in their mounts. The crack widened.

"Come," said the dwarf. "We must be off."

• • •

Luik and Li-Saide easily caught up with the warband, half limping, half running down the dimly lit interior of the Library. Only the first room had been illuminated as usual; the rest were darkened, the wall torches and chandeliers extinguished for battle. Li-Saide, Bi-Bablar, Brax, and Luik carried torches now, with Luik and the Chief leading the way.

They moved between row after row of the legendary shelves, each at least five men high and crammed full of scrolls. But unlike Luik's last time here, each enormous chamber room was as black as night, save for the fires in their hands. The orange glow reflected off the lacquered mahogany and shone only partially down the red-carpeted aisle before them. The warband skirted the meticulously-kept reading tables and passed underneath the low archways that separated each grand room from the next.

As the glow of the first chamber faded away behind them, so too did the sounds of the Dairne-Reih. The *thudding* was now a gentle thump and gave way to the warband's patter of feet on the thick wool, as well as their labored breathing. The air grew cooler as they went, and the pungent smell of old parchment filled their nostrils.

A man stumbled; Luik caught him under the arm.

"I can't go on," he said, pleading. "May we rest?"

"Nay, brother," trying his best to keep the man upright. "We must move along. There will be time for resting in Athera." But as Luik said the words, he suddenly wished he hadn't, implying that they were all headed *there* shortly.

Brax eyed him and then joined in helping the warrior to keep moving. "Couldn't you have picked another location for resting?" he chided the High King.

Luik smiled, feeling the humor of the moment and allowing it to encourage him. "I was thinking of the beds in Mt. Dakka, but they're much too hard."

"Not as hard as the bread baked in Bensotha," Brax added.

For that single moment, bantering back and forth, Luik felt like he was back on Kirstell, engaged in one of Gorn's contests or sparring with the other boralee. It was a feeling of great comfort, one that he enjoyed so thoroughly, he grew sad when it slipped away into the blackness.

Craaaack!

The sound echoed down the hallways, racing through each chamber. The warband stopped.

"They're through," Li-Saide offered.

The chase began.

The men took off at a run. Those who labored before now bounded down the corridors, defiant of their pain. Some carried a dwarf on their backs; others cradled one in their arms. Luik noticed the sweat coming down his forehead and struggled to carry his shield, helmet and torch. So he discarded his helmet and opted for his shield. It would be more useful.

They raced under an archway and into the next chamber, which appeared exactly as those before it. Their firelight danced across the rows of shiny cases and tables; their feet were cushioned on the lush red carpet. Halfway through the room the warband heard the shrieks of pursuing demons.

Luik shuddered. "How much farther?"

"A ways," Li-Saide said.

"A ways is far?" Brax asked, panting.

"Aye," said Bi-Bablar.

"We need more time," Ragnar grunted.

"We need a diversion," Li-Saide added and came to a standstill. "Keep going," he ordered Ragnar, Fane, and Bi-Bablar. "Luik. Brax. I need you." The advisor moved the group along, now under the light of a single torch.

Luik and Brax slowed and wondered at the dwarf's choice of tactics. "What's your idea?" Luik asked, mindful of their approaching enemy.

Li-Saide glanced upward and whispered under his breath. "Forgive me, O Most High." Then he held up his torch. "We place one in the corner of the two rooms. Different spots."

"Start fires?" Luik asked.

"Not at first, but they will catch quickly. And they'll think we've stopped to hide, following the glow. At least for a moment. We'll use the third torch, however, to set the scrolls on fire."

"But the records?" Brax asked.

"They're ruined anyway," said the dwarf. "What does it matter if it's by our hand or theirs? Luik, you run to the third room ahead. Light everything that will burn." Luik just stared at him, unable to believe what he was hearing. But he knew it was the only chance they had to gain more time. "Brax, place this torch back in between the walls at those cases," the dwarf indicated a tight grouping of tall shelves that would hide the torch, but not its glow. "I'll plant the next one."

They nodded, and Luik turned and raced down the room just as another series of shrieks echoed through the corridors. The Dairne-Reih had come much closer.

Luik passed through the next chamber quickly, ducked under the archway and bounded in. He stopped, torch flame flickering in front of his face. "Great God, forgive me for what I'm about to do," he prayed. He ran to the first case of scrolls and held the flame to a protruding, ragged papyrus edge, yellow with age. Luik could make out ink marks and figures just within the first curl of the bound page. He cringed. The fire licked up the parchment and blossomed upward, casting light all around him. He watched as the ravenous tongues spread and within moments enveloped a wall of scrolls in front of him. He stepped back, horrified by what he had done, and then turned to run across the aisle.

His hands trembled as he held the torch to another bundle of scrolls. The shelf's contents erupted in a wall of fire, and thin embers broke off and floated up around him. He heard the screams of the searching demons rip through the air again. He stepped back into the central aisle, observing how quickly the fire spread through the room. The heat increased, as did the smoke, making it harder to breathe. He covered his mouth and then turned to look back through the arch, eyes searching for his friends.

The flames spread to the remaining cases in the hall and forced Luik to retreat toward the next room farther in. He looked back again and caught sight of a figure running through the smoke toward him.

"They're coming!" Brax shouted, one hand over his mouth, the other waving Luik on.

Luik caught him by the shoulder, "Where's Li-Saide?"

"He's not with you?" Brax looked around.

"Nay," Luik said and then coughed.

The room roared with fire, torrents of spinning fury twisting off the shelves and consuming the ancient documents, now but ash flung in the air. The two kings ducked to avoid the smoke and winced at the extreme heat. The massive shelf nearest them snapped in two and one portion fell toward them. Brax pulled Luik out of the way as the wood slammed against the floor in a spray of sparks.

"We've got to move on!" Brax said.

"But Li-Saide! I will not leave without him."

"Luik, we must go," Brax pleaded, shouting over the noise of the fire.

It was then Luik saw something moving through the fire behind them. He nodded, and they both peered through the distorted air. Frantic hands waved in the smoke, and a billowy hat appeared, flames set upon it.

"Quick!" Luik shouted and sprinted toward the dwarf, Brax on his heels.

Li-Saide stumbled through the flames that devoured the carpet, his robe and beard on fire. Luik grabbed him by one arm, Brax under the other, and together they raced back down the aisle. Their exposed flesh smoldered, smoke bringing tears to their eyes. Li-Saide struggled against the heat that licked his face but didn't so much as whimper.

Once under the arch into the next room, the Kings dropped the dwarf to the floor and smothered the flames about him with their tunics. They helped him to his feet and, seeing that he was able to stand, turned and watched the raging inferno in the room behind them. There was nothing but intense heat and a white-hot glow feeding on the legacy of written pages. Li-Saide bowed his head.

"We must move on," Brax suggested as the heat stung their faces. "This will not stay them forever."

"Agreed," Li-Saide said, lifting his head. "We must catch up with the others."

"And when we do?" Luik asked as he peered down into the dwarf's face, his once regal beard now a charred thicket.

"A secret passage," Li-Saide replied, still maintaining his ever-present sense of mystery. "If we make it in time, it will secure our retreat. Come." With that he turned away. Luik and Brax followed, the light of the fire illuminating their path through the next room. And not too soon, as deafening screams chased after them, a multitude of Dairne-Reih infuriated by the delay the flames presented.

The three of them bounded under the arch and into the next room, and the next. Sweat poured down their faces and soaked their undergarments. Up ahead they could see the faint glow of flickering torchlight: the rest of their warband plunging through the darkness. Moments later they had caught up to the group, and Li-Saide pressed ahead to the front of the pack.

"This way," he shouted and, once under the next arch, turned abruptly and ran along the inside wall. He grabbed a torch out of the closest man's hand and raced ahead. He reached the side wall and then turned to run along its length as well, stopping halfway down.

Brax was right behind him. "What is it?"

"We're here," he replied and thrust the torch into Brax's hand.

The dwarf knelt down and ran his fingers along the boards, searching for a seam. He summoned the torch closer and blew dust away to reveal a small aberration in the wooden floor's pattern.

"What is it?" Brax asked.

As if to answer the question, Li-Saide's fingers found a metal ring layered in dust and pulled it up. With a firm tug, the outline of a small door appeared. Brax and Fane helped him pull it back and made to toss it aside.

"Nay," Li-Saide caught his arm. "We'll need it to cover our escape." The dwarf held the torch into the hole: a set of steep stone stairs leading down into blackness. "Get everyone down," he said as he handed the torch to Bi-Bablar. "We'll follow shortly behind."

More shrieks filled the chambers behind them, but nearer. "They're through," Luik gasped, eyes alert and searching the shadows behind.

"Quickly!" Li-Saide took the last remaining torch from a warrior's tense grip and raced to an adjacent shelf. He lit the scrolls in front of him then passed the torch to Luik. "Light those," he pointed, "and then toss it across the aisle."

Luik waved the flame across a broad section of the old parchment and then tossed it fluttering through the air, to land beside another shelf on the other side of the room. He watched as the torch flame seemed to ebb, flickering on the ground; but a moment later the carpet runner caught flame, as did the scrolls nearest the floor.

"Draw swords!" Luik ordered. The remaining warriors pulled out their weapons, blades running against scabbards. Spid helped the warband through the door, pushing their heads down as they ducked into the tunnel. More screams tore through the air.

The last of the dwarves slipped into the stairwell, followed by the other men. "Let's go!" Li-Saide turned and slipped down the stairs followed by Brax and Luik, just as the heat from the shelves became overwhelming. From below Brax moved the lid back over the hole and seated it securely.

They stumbled blindly down the stairs, for only the one torch far ahead gave any light. The tunnel was dank and musty, unused for ages. Luik's feet continued to miss steps. He put his free hand up to run along the rough walls. The light ahead disappeared around a corner, and their course turned to the right. *Where is this taking us?*

As they rounded yet another bend, a heavy *thud* echoed through the tunnel from above. The group stopped to listen further. *It could be a collapsing shelf,* Luik thought. Another impact. Li-Saide shouted, and they resumed running. Labored breathing, clanking metal, and the chaos of footfalls traveled with them...down...down into the tunnel. *Was it their own, or that of the demons behind them?*

No one dared speak, only descend hurriedly, taking three or four steps at a time. A few men stumbled, caught by those behind them and carried along until they could find their feet again.

The air was growing cold; Luik felt a chill move up his spine. Or was it that the enemy neared? He cast a quick look behind him, catching Brax's eyes and then further past into the black.

The stairs ended and the path leveled. The warband raced along and eventually came to a wooden door as tall as a man. The group packed up close to it, everyone studying the intricately weaving knot work carved into its surface. Bi-Bablar held up the light and produced a small key from within his robes. He inserted it into a slender keyhole and then turned it.

The key snapped.

Bi-Bablar's eyes widened. He turned, trying to hide his surprise, and looked for Li-Saide.

"What is it?" the Chief asked, noting his brother's worried stare. Bi-Bablar held up the broken piece of the key.

"What does that mean?" one of the warriors asked, panic in his eyes.

"It means we have to break it down," Luik answered, pushing his way amongst the men. Brax followed.

Another heavy *thump* echoed from above them.

"Defend our retreat!" Luik ordered those with swords. "They'll be through sooner than later, I wager."

Bi-Bablar stepped aside, and Brax and Luik both rammed the door with their shoulders. While it may have been old, it was far from weak; the door didn't move in the least. They doubled their efforts but to no avail.

"It's too strong," Brax said, massaging his shoulder.

Everyone heard a muffled shriek go up from above. Then a loud *crash!* of wood splintering into the tunnel.

Luik held his sword in both hands and addressed the door. He gazed at the rich wood carvings that danced in the firelight. Then he closed his eyes and began speaking in the Ancient Tongue, his mouth finding the words afresh and anew each time. His hands tingled, and an inner prompting rose within him. He felt the climax burn within and released it, opening his eyes as he drove the sword into the door.

The wood filled with white light, cracks splintering through the surface. Everyone shielded their faces. Then the door burst into fragments, showering them with smoldering bits of timber. The remaining torch flickered, but did not go out.

"Everyone inside," Li-Saide prompted.

The warband needed no further instructions and raced in, Bi-Bablar holding the torch. The illuminated room was a grand, circular chamber with a domed ceiling barely visible in the firelight. A large, round rug was centered on the floor, while lavish chairs were spread throughout; some were even elongated, able to hold many people. Luik had never seen such furniture.

Low tables sat next to each chair surmounted with large iron candelabras. And beyond, massive paintings hung along the walls, thick wooden frames bordering each piece of art.

Luik's eyes searched the walls, scanning for a door. But instead they fell upon a startling image. There, hanging on the far wall, was a painting of a great white lion, paw outstretched and claws extended. Its fierce yellow eyes looked down upon a helpless man lying on a white marble floor, a starlit sky above him.

Luik walked toward it, taking in the man's stricken expression...

...his sandy blond hair...

...the way the armor was worn...

...and the emblazoned mantle, markings of Bensotha, and then of Casterness.

Luik's heart stopped. This man was Dionia's High King. It was *himself*.

Chills ran down his arms and legs. He noticed he wasn't breathing and stumbled back, unable to take his eyes from the painting. *How could this be?* Countless questions entered his mind. This painting was surely generations old! He bumped into someone. Li-Saide caught his hand and turned him around.

"It is as you have seen it?" the dwarf asked calmly.

Luik stared into the Chief's eyes and nodded. It *was* him. "What is this place? How could—?" But Li-Saide only shook his head knowingly.

"Those are not the questions you should be asking, Good King."

"How about the question of how we're getting out of here?" interrupted Brax.

Shrieks and clicking raced down the tunnel and spilled into the Reading Room.

"Everyone to the center of the carpet!" Li-Saide shouted. Luik had turned and looked back to the painting, oblivious to the commotion. "Take a last look," Li-Saide said. "We may yet have time for talking later." Luik nodded, the image burning into his mind's eye, mirroring the same image from his dreams.

The group stood in a huddle now, swords drawn and facing toward the destroyed doorway.

"That's it?" Brax inquired toward the Chief, voice strained. "We make a stand here? Like this? That's the plan?" He was incredulous. "You're the Chief of all dwarves with the wisdom of the ages—and this is your plan?"

Li-Saide cast him a lethal stare, and Brax withdrew. The Chief walked to the edge of the carpet and reached out to one of the candelabras. He chose an iron stem and then pulled it down. It was then Luik remembered the entrance to the Lion's Lair.

Li-Saide walked back to join the others. "We'll be going for a ride," he said casually. The group turned from the door and balked. But the distraction was short-lived. A ruckus drew their attention back to the opening.

The first Dairneag appeared deep in the tunnel, the torchlight bringing out its demonic eyes and gaping mouth. It raced forward and screamed with a twist of its head, rows of razor-sharp teeth displayed.

"Brace yourselves!" Luik readied them for the impact, swords lowering.

But it never came.

The floor dropped away beneath them. An instant later they were sailing downward, plunging toward the carpeted floor that seemed to float just below. They left the Reading Room above in blackness, and Bi-Bablar floated with the torch in his hand, the flame whipping about.

A scream echoed above, and Luik looked up. To his utter astonishment one of the demons was falling down with them, presumably the one in the door moments before. Its arms were tucked to its sides, diving headlong after them.

Accustomed to free flight from the Lion's Lair, Luik reached over and took a spear from one of his men, the sorry soul tumbling about in midair. Then he looked back and pointed the weapon straight up toward the flying Dairneag.

"We're coming to the end!" Li-Saide shouted above the *whoosh* of the air. "Watch for the floor!"

As the mechanical protraction of the floor neared its end, Luik could feel the carpet touch under his feet and his weight return to his legs. Likewise, Luik braced the end of the spear against the floor and aimed the head at the ever-nearing Dairneag. Without the aid of the floor to slow it down, the demon closed in, aware now of the spear shaft. It had nowhere to go, eyes terrified.

The floor slowed further, and the spear point penetrated just under its chin into the neck and then up into the chest cavity. The Dairneag screamed, arms and legs flailing wildly like a beetle slipping down the shaft of a pin. When the floor came to a jarring halt, Luik rolled away as the monster fully impaled itself on the spear and crashed into the ground.

"Well, that was easy," Brax chided him.

But any joy in their escape was short-lived. Despite their rapid descent, they heard the frustrated wails of the Dairne-Reih closing from above. Those that could climb raced down the walls and would be upon them within moments.

"This way!" The Chief indicated a narrow gap in the wall, a crack formed in the rock just big enough for a man to slip through. The injured slid through first and then the dwarves. More clicking traveled down the cave. Brax and Luik looked up.

"My Kings!" Bi-Bablar called to them. "Your turn! We must hurry!"

Bits of rock and dirt showered down over them, dislodged from the walls far above. Brax went through, but Luik turned and noticed Li-Saide standing back by the candelabra; the Chief nodded to Luik knowingly. The High King slipped through the opening and heard the twisting and grinding of gears. With the system in motion, Li-Saide raced across the carpet and into the crack.

Then all at once the air was sucked out of the tunnel as the floor shot upward. Their ears popped, and they gasped for breath. But a moment later they breathed more easily and heard the distant sounds of bodies breaking against the speeding platform as it returned to the Reading Room.

Brax grabbed Li-Saide and stared at him in the torchlight. "That was a good plan."

Chapter Twenty-Five

LEAVING ALL BEHIND

"Where are we?" Luik asked.

"Very close to the portals," Li-Saide replied. "This way, but we must be swift. And quiet."

The path they followed was much more a rocky trail weaving through a deep cavern than the hand-made tunnel leaving the Library. Water dripped from stalactites in the ceiling, pooling on the ground, each plop echoing softly in the warband's ears. Their footfalls reverberated hollowly, and wind moaned up ahead like a melancholy lost soul. The walls closed in around them, jagged rocks reaching out in suspended motion. Then the path opened up moments later into a large thoroughfare. The team continued on, moving deeper and deeper into the cavern, skirting around boulders and massive chunks of rock that had departed from their roosts in the ceiling long ago.

They walked quickly, never uttering a word, until Li-Saide held up a hand. Luik could hear a commotion up ahead; the path forked and he could see a faint light reflecting off the ragged wall in the next turn to the right.

"What is it?" he whispered to Li-Saide.

"The Cave," replied the dwarf.

"You mean—?"

"Aye," Li-Saide nodded. "I said we were near the portals. But I need to see the garden…" his voice trailed off. "I need to see what's been done."

Luik swallowed, knowing how hard this could be. He turned to the warband. "Stay here. Ta na, Brax, Fane, Bi-Bablar, Spid—with us."

The seven of them left the group and moved on up ahead. As they rounded the next turn, Luik and the others hid behind a rock outcropping. Luik peered into the main cave, and his eyes met a sight that stole his breath.

The focal point of the room, as always, was the Tree—or what was left of her. She listed completely to one side, leaning against the cavern's wall and dismembered of her limbs, each one burned or ripped from the trunk. Her base had been completely severed, cut through by a massive saw that still lay upon the stump. The bark was a mutilated covering, one charred by ghastly gashes that exposed the flesh beneath. Demons crawled along her form, and Luik noted their utter satisfaction with their work. Her once magnificent shape was now a playground for the vile, the Dairne-Reih's pride evident, their defiling complete.

In the garden beneath the Tree, Luik and the others were horrified to see not a man or dwarf among the living. Water and lava mixed together as smoke drifted upward, the smell of sulfur and burnt flesh filling the air.

"They've—they've cut her down!" Bi-Bablar said with tears in his eyes. Spid grabbed his friend as Bi-Bablar began moving from side to side with his eyes closed. "Nay, nay, nay!" he bellowed, and then repeated it over and over again as if trying to will the image out of his mind.

All at once the cave shook around them; dirt and rock fell from the ceiling. Luik braced himself but could not look away from the Tree. Soon the quake subsided and he turned to the Chief. But the dwarf was overwhelmed.

Li-Saide gripped the rock in front of him and pulled back from the scene, his knees weakening. "Luik, I—" he faltered. And then he looked up into the High King's face. Steeling his resolve, he cleared his throat and regained his composure. "We must move on," he said, looking back out over the scene and indicated the stone archway that led to the portals.

"It's a long ways," Luik stated, figuring they were on the far side of the cave. Things could not be worse. "I thought you said it was close?"

"Closer than we were before," Li-Saide forced a shallow smile, trying to find some humor.

It was right then that Luik noticed a change in the dwarves' demeanors; not only were they stricken with obvious grief, but something else had changed—something that foreshadowed their lives altering. Of their lives *fading*.

Li-Saide slumped back against the rock, holding his chest and gasping for air.

"What is it?" Luik pleaded. "Talk to me!" He knelt down in front of the Chief.

Fane looked to Spid and Bi-Bablar, also acting strangely, above and beyond any expected shows of sorrow. "Something's happening to them, Luik," he said.

"It's the Tree?" Luik offered, trying to get Li-Saide to look him in the eyes. The dwarf nodded solemnly, his brow furrowed in pain. The cave began rumbling again, this time more violently. They all reached out to brace themselves and shielded their heads from the failing debris. Then, as before, the shaking ceased.

"We'll…be…we'll be fine, my King," said the Chief.

"Just wait here," Luik offered.

"Nay!" Li-Saide held up a hand. "We must continue on. Morgui will destroy everything! We cannot remain. Lives are more important than scrolls or trees."

"And the others?" Brax asked, noting the absence of the bulk of their fighting force.

"We must assume most of them made it out alive, pushed back by the lava flow," Ragnar offered. "And that we will rejoin them in Mt. Dakka soon enough."

Li-Saide reached for Luik's hand; the King helped him stand. "Spid." The little dwarf was still holding his head and weeping softly. "Spid, I need you to get to the other side," Li-Saide ordered.

But Spid still didn't respond. Luik stepped over to him and squatted, placing a hand on his shoulder. "Spid, listen to me. I need you now; your country needs you now."

"She is lost," he whimpered. "She's gone."

"I know," Luik said. It was eerie how he heard the Tree's end drawing nigh even as he spoke. "I know, and there is nothing you can do about her. But you can do something for us—for your people. They need you." He paused. "I need you."

The dwarf looked up, trails of water streaking down his cheeks. "You need me?" he repeated, surprised.

"Aye. I've seen how you move. I need to know what's on the other side, in the cave to the portals. I need to know what enemies we face and how many. Only you can get over there. No one will ever see you. And even if they did, who could catch you?"

The dwarf grinned and wiped his face with the sleeve of his robe, smearing hot tears and mucus across his face.

"All right," he finally said, pulling up his courage. "I'll do it."

"Right you are!" Brax said and slapped him on the back. The dwarf stumbled forward, and Luik caught him.

"Easy," Luik mouthed to Brax, eyes wide. Brax smiled and apologized sheepishly.

"As fast as you can," Li-Saide instructed. "No delays. Find out what lies in each of the corridors and who guards the pools. Then return here at once."

"Very well," replied Spid. He offered up a slight smile and then lowered his head.

The next instant he was gone.

The five of them leaned around the rock outcropping and watched as a faint wisp dashed along the raised ground and weaved between unsuspecting Dairneags. The men gasped as demons lumbered about, swinging tree limbs and wreaking havoc in the garden, sure Spid would be struck or worse. But the little dwarf never once faltered, able to move around the Dairne-Reih as if they were but statues oblivious to his presence.

And then he was gone, lost in the caves beyond.

"He made it," Brax sighed and patted Luik on the shoulder. "He made it!"

"Aye, let's see what he finds."

They waited impatiently, counting the time that passed with unease.

"Well, it's pretty much empty of demons," came a voice behind them.

The group turned in surprise. Spid was standing right behind them.

"Hey'a—how did you—?" Brax was stunned, as were they all.

"Pretty much empty?" Li-Saide inquired.

"A few demons wander through the corridors, but they clearly don't know what to make of the portals and appear very disinterested."

"We have a chance then," Fane put in.

"Li-Saide?" Luik asked for the Chief's next suggestion.

"Crossing through the garden will be too dangerous. We'll be exposed. There are many tunnels that the Tribes never developed. They should lead us to the portals."

"Should?" asked Brax. "I don't like the sound of that."

"But crossing the garden—it's too risky," Ragnar surmised. "We'll be easy targets, and we don't stand a chance against such numbers."

"Aye," agreed Luik, rubbing his temples. "And these tunnels?"

"Back where the men are waiting," Li-Saide pointed. "The left fork takes us into the catacombs, an undeveloped network of natural tunnels we've used for burying the dead."

"I thought you didn't die?" asked Brax.

"We don't," he glared at him. "You do."

"And all your animals," Bi-Bablar added. "You think we leave them in Grandath?"

But Li-Saide raised a hand to his assistant. "It's not the time. Come," he addressed the group. "We must be moving. The cave won't last much longer."

• • •

A Dairneag busied itself with moving a heap of corpses, both demon and man, into a standing pool of liquid fire. It watched the bodies sizzle and pop, sending up thick black smoke that reeked of burnt flesh. Soon, however, its task was finished and boredom set in. Another creature bumped into it, carrying a load of bodies; the former lashed out viciously, shoving the monster aside, and the morbid load tumbled to the ground. A small skirmish ensued, but soon the first Dairneag left the other to collect its work and move on.

It looked around and studied the havoc encompassing the cave; the devastation was complete. Dairne-Reih scoured the walls, tearing at elegantly carved railings and porticos. They ripped doors from their hinges and threw furniture from the interior rooms, casting them down into fire pits. Anything they couldn't extract, they burned. Columns of smoke emanated from doorways all along the cave's interior like little chimneys that vented smoldering hearth fires.

Then the Dairneag detected a new scent on the wind...

...something still alive.

It turned its head to discern the source, and spied a small crack in the wall not two tens of paces from where it stood. Its eyes narrowed. Easing itself down from the small mound, it worked its way through the putrid liquid that now rose to its upper legs; the demon avoided the lava that glowed beneath boiling blood and water, swirling together in morbid beauty. Approaching the wall, it slowed and crept more stealthily. Hands wrapping around an outcropping, the beast glared into the darkness of the tunnel and inhaled. The long, cool breath brought the scent of warm flesh and sweat. It sniffed the rocks and touched the floor; the presence was but moments old.

The Dairneag spun around and clicked forcefully; five other demons in the immediate vicinity answered the call. It turned its glare back into the tunnel and moved forward to stalk its prey.

• • •

The warband weaved its way through the massive network of tunnels, Spid often running ahead to navigate the paths that Li-Saide had forgotten from lack of use. The speedy dwarf would return just as the warband came to a chamber that presented multiple routes. He'd indicate which route brought them closer to the portals and then vanish once again.

Not long after they set out, however, the quaking resumed. But this time it was much more forceful; many men were cast into the rock walls, others crashed to the ground.

"Watch yourself!" Ragnar shouted and shoved two men aside as a large rock dislodged itself from the ceiling. The warriors sprawled on their stomachs, and Ragnar narrowly missed being crushed.

A fissure burst open underneath them, and a blast of hot air sent rock shards bouncing off the walls. One dwarf screamed as the fragments stung his eyes.

Fane scooped him up, blood staining his cloak. "We've got to move!" he shouted.

The sound of rock grinding against rock was deafening, like thunder, boring into their heads.

Luik steadied himself, a hand on the wall. "Quickly, men!" He turned to Spid, the little dwarf sidestepping back and forth just to keep his balance. "Which way?"

"Through there," he yelled, indicating a low passage up ahead.

Above the rumbling came another sound—one they could not forget. A series of shrieks bounced off the walls behind them.

"We're being followed!" Fane hollered. "Biea Varos!"

"This is unbelievable," said Brax. "Don't they ever give up?"

Li-Saide helped a tribesman gain his legs and then plunged ahead. Luik caught up and aided two more injured men to their feet. The group bounced around and then started forward again. Spid stayed a few paces ahead, leading the warband through narrow turns and selecting the fastest routes. They ducked under massive boulders and squeezed between pointed outcroppings, Brax catching his shoulder for a moment and more than one dwarf hung up by their portly girth.

While passing through a large chamber, another fissure ripped open, and steam shot up from the ground. The floor heaved and tossed one man over, sliding down toward the opening.

Brax dove and grabbed the man's hand. But the hot air scalded the warrior's legs and he couldn't hold on; he slipped over and was swallowed into the chasm below.

Brax lay there for a moment, struggling with the man's passing so suddenly.

"Come, Brax!" He felt Ragnar's hands around his ankles, hoisting him away from the fissure.

Another series of shrieks cut through the tunnel, and Luik stepped aside. "Keep going!" He shouted to Li-Saide and Spid, pushing men on past him. "I'll meet you at the portals!" More dwarves and warriors passed, and then Brax and Ragnar.

"What are you doing?" Brax yelled.

"Defending our retreat! Quick now, draw swords!"

The three of them began covering the end of the line, racing forward but glancing over their shoulders every few steps. "Let me take the rear, Luik," Brax said, letting his King pass by.

The walls continued to shake and rocks fell, slamming into their shoulders and denting their armor. More than one hit them in the head, bringing stars to their eyes and blood trickling through their hair.

Brax stepped over a newly-fallen rock and felt something dig into his back. He twisted away from the pain. But the pressure remained and then pulled him backward off his feet.

"Luik!" he screamed.

Luik and Ragnar spun around, shocked to see a Dairneag holding Brax up in the air by his armor. "Nay!" Luik yelled. He ran back, hands tight around his sword.

The monster glared at him, curious.

Brax struggled to get away, swinging his sword frantically behind him.

The demon eyed Brax...

...then looked back to Luik.

"*Naaay!*" Luik shouted, running as fast as he could, mumbling the Tongues of the Dibor. It was then Luik could actually see the demon *thinking*...

...and Luik realized he just wasn't fast enough.

Eyes fixed back on Brax, the demon reached its free hand up to his chest and drove horned fingers into the plate armor, piecing metal and bone in a single plunge.

Brax's eyes widened.

The demon looked for a reaction from the High King.

"*O God!*" Luik screamed.

Brax tried to say something, mouthing empty words. He looked down from his lofty position and stared impassively at the hand dug into his body.

The cave rattled like a child's toy. Luik tripped and fell to the floor. He glanced up.

Brax was smiling.

The rocks quaked violently, and then a huge boulder shook loose from the cave ceiling above.

Luik reached out as if to stop it—but its course was fixed.

Brax looked longingly into Luik's eyes, and then he was no more. The boulder slammed down in a spray of rock and blood and sealed off the tunnel.

Luik could hardly see through the tears filling his eyes.

Brax had saved his life. Had nursed him back to health. Had been his closest friend in Mt. Dakka.

He was his sword brother.

Now he was gone. In the blink of an eye. There had been no time to say goodbye. No time to thank him. No time to tell him that he loved him.

Ragnar reached down and grabbed Luik's shoulders, hoisting him to his feet.

"Let me be!" he sobbed.

"We must go, Son! Now!"

"I can't believe it! I can't leave him here!" The thought of Brax being buried in this *tomb* tore his heart.

Ragnar struggled to turn him.

"Son! We must leave!"

"Nay! I will not leave him here!" Blackness filled his heart. It was worse than fear.

It was dread.

"Luik! We *must* go! You have a people to lead!" Ragnar twisted him around, rocks crashing down everywhere.

But Luik resisted. Ragnar slapped him across the face.

Luik finally looked into his father's eyes, stunned.

"You must carry on! There is more life to live! Let him go! There is nothing more you can do!" He paused. "But I can't force you!"

Luik hesitated, and then relented, falling into his father's arms. Ragnar turned him forward, and with one arm under his shoulder, helped him exit through the tunnel ahead.

They had taken no more than ten steps before a voice echoed through the tunnel. But not one they knew; it was louder and stronger than the men calling from up ahead. It was fuller and carried a dark emotion… on a dark wind…with a dark purpose.

"*Do you not know?*"

The voice hissed the words, sweet and slow. Luik and Ragnar paused. They looked ahead but saw no one. They turned to one another.

"*Do you not know that I have won?*"

It was Morgui.

"Don't listen to him," Ragnar said.

As if hearing the suggestion, the voice laughed slow and long, echoing throughout all of Ot.

"Don't you know victory is mine? Why do you even flee? Don't you know?"

This time Luik stepped forward and freed himself of his father's assistance. "Let's go."

"Don't you know that I've killed him?"

The two men stopped. Icy chills pricked across Luik's flesh.

"Don't listen to him, Son."

"Nay," Luik raised a hand. "I will hear him out."

"Don't you know I've killed him? I've slain the King's Son myself!"

Ragnar meant to move them both forward, burying what he, too, had read long ago. "He couldn't possibly—"

"Wait," Luik thought.

He paused there amongst the imploding cavern, rocks bursting all about him. Time slowed, and the sound faded away.

He was with Li-Saide in the locked room of scrolls, poring over the pages. The story of Earth played out in his mind's eye as he heard the ancient prophecies read aloud...

...the story of the King's Son.

And of His death.

"He's right," Luik agreed. "The King's Son is dead."

Chapter Twenty-Six

INTO OBLIVION

Try as she might, Anorra's pleas with the Most High went unanswered. Despite the urgency of His last instruction, she did not have the strength to rise, let alone come up with a way to serve Him in the requested task. Rescue him? How was such a venture possible, even with all her strength restored? Surely this was another of the enemy's ploys to draw her into submission, to catch her in an act of defiance—an act surely punishable by death.

But was she not already on death's door? If Morgui wished her gone, would he not have already sent his minions to dispatch her? Or even do the deed himself? The fact that he lingered so long disturbed her. Why wait?

Another searing jolt of pain seized her head. The ache was unbearable. Had she still had her eyes, she would have squeezed them shut. She pulled up her knees, but the movement pressed on her broken ribs and stole her breath away. Anorra gasped for air, and then choked on her own bile. She coughed violently, her poor form writhing on the stones. The pain in her head grew stronger, and her stomach retched though there was little enough to come up.

"Where are you, my God?" Just the effort to speak was exhausting.

"Why do you not answer me?"

Then a voice spoke inside of her—less like His and more like her own.

But He has spoken to you.

Her body trembled from the recent outburst, but she managed to keep herself under control, preventing another wave of torment.

The question remains. Will you obey?

She shuddered. The stones were hot against her skin, yet somehow she felt so cold. So alone. Sweat soaked her skin, her torn clothing clinging to her body.

If it was Morgui that prompted this, was she not already dead anyway? Whether now or later, in an effort to defy him, it made no difference. But if this was her Maker—if this was indeed the voice of her Beloved—she must not keep Him waiting. And His Swift Sure Hand would supply for what His Voice had commanded.

"I am Yours," she replied. "Always. And forever more."

Lying there in her cell, nothing changed. She felt no warmth, no comforting shaft of light. No voice replied in recognition of her noble words. And for the briefest of moments she doubted if it was really He who had spoken at all—apparently failing to respond in kind. But she knew better. For even if it was the voice of the enemy that prompted her, she trusted His Hand to protect her in the midst of her ignorance. He was that good.

She strained to sit upright as the stones bit into her palms like thorns. Every muscle in her slight body ached, and it was all she could do to resist the urge to vomit once more. And then she focused on *seeing*.

Her Second Sight came more easily to her this time, the image of her cell snapping to life inside her mind. Her gaze wandered over the bars in front of her, searching for a gap. But she saw none. She turned around slowly and looked for some space in the rock wall behind her, a crevice in the floor. Anything. But the chamber was sealed up tight. She thought to look up, but that too was a thwarted idea as the ceiling was solid rock.

"Most High," she said under her breath, "You know my heart. I am Yours. But I cannot go where You don't provide a path. Help me. Please."

Doubt filled her mind. Had He helped her at all since she had been taken into the bowels of death? Had He been there when she had stood before the Demon Lord himself? Had He been there when her vision had been stolen from her atop the wall?

"I believe," she said. "I still believe."

A subtle *click* shook in the lock casing on her cell door. She glanced toward it. The metal bars seemed to be slightly offset in their hanging. *Could it be?* Not wasting a moment, and not entirely sure she could trust her feelings, she scrambled forward, shoving the pain out of her mind. She stopped short in front of the gate and raised herself to one knee. Then, like a mouse investigating a crumb, she eased out her fingers and let them settle on the iron.

Then pushed.

The door swung open just a hand's breadth. Anorra gasped and stole her hand back as if not believing it was true. But it was.

"O, Great God! You heard me!" Surprised by her own loudness, she shrank back and glanced sideways. She held her breath, waiting for something to happen. But nothing did. *She was free.*

She stood, pushed the gate open further, and then slipped out.

Glowing red light flickered against the rock ledges and cast shadows against the walls beside her. The stalagmites looked like teeth gaping for prey, and she edged around them cautiously. Just below she could clearly see the sea of liquid fire that continuously swallowed its victims, only to drain once more revealing the writhing mass of souls bound beneath the grates. And above them stood the guardians, spears and whips in hand, dispensing their wrath to restless sufferers.

She shrank behind a rock ledge just as a whip snapped, lashing out and producing a shriek from far below. She remembered her pain then and slid down the rock surface to her knees. Fear reached for her.

You will get caught. Turn back to your cell.

"No," she pressed her hands to her temples. "I will not go back. If I perish, I perish. But I will not go back."

She took a deep breath and found her feet again. She glanced down to the sights of the sea below and studied the demons who looked down from their ledges. None of them had noticed her presence. She turned back toward her cell. Nothing. Then she surveyed the path in front of her. A narrow escarpment climbed its way higher, hugging the rock wall of the cavern and moving into the next room. She waited for the chaos below her to escalate before making a move into the next chamber. Racing up along the path, she ducked behind pillars of rock, glancing quickly to make sure she hadn't been seen, and then continued on up the track. Her body screamed for her to cease, to turn back. But she willed herself on. The sea below her had filled and receded twice before she summited the path and turned into the next cavern, this one much larger than the first.

Hanging directly in front of her, suspended over thin air, were the mutilated remains of a poor wretch, beaten to the pulp of his innards— yet still mumbling in a morbid stupor. She looked away, and this time her Second Sight obeyed, hiding in the cover of her arm. She moved farther along the path, now descending along the wide cavern wall. Once out of direct view of the living-corpse, she stepped inside a crack in the wall to catch her breath.

She could hear her pulse in her ears and sucked in deep breaths. Her muscles ached, and she knew she was losing blood from somewhere on her mangled body. The bruising internally was severe, and she was aware it wouldn't be long before her energy was spent.

What will you do even if you reach this lost soul? came the voice in her head.

She hadn't thought of that.

But her Maker would see her through, she reckoned. He had opened the gate, after all, had He not? Surely He of all people could see her through to whatever means He so desired.

Wouldn't He?

Shrieking suddenly filled the cavern, and Anorra mumbled under her breath. She had been found out, surely. She waited there, hidden in shadow as the shrieking grew louder. Was she being pursued? She wanted to cover her ears against the terror, but she dared not make the slightest move for fear of being noticed. So she stood there utterly still.

When the screaming finally died down, Anorra edged closer to the opening and peered back down the path. She knew more guardian demons and tormented souls lay below; she had seen it in the vision. And if she remembered correctly, the long tunnel leading to the prison chamber lay at the end of this cavern.

She drew in a deep, caustic breath and then emerged back onto the path. The sulfur burned her nostrils, but she preferred it over the smell of burning flesh. She quickly moved down the sloping track and hugged the cavern wall as best she could. She stopped from time to time, hiding behind a rock outcrop and timing her movements with the rise and fall of the lava below. A few times she was sure she had been spotted, but then realized the demons had nothing else to do and were not accustomed to be on the lookout for princesses wandering through their lair.

Every step brought her closer to the far side of the cavern, and every movement sent pain shooting up her legs and rattled her ribs. If her eyes could have produced tears she would have been weeping. But she supposed not crying was one dignity she had been allowed to keep.

Eventually she moved out of the large cavern into the long, toothy tunnel. Happy to be beyond the lava pits, Anorra quickened her pace and moved more freely along the unoccupied corridor. The going was a bit more tedious, as this path snaked its way among the massive teeth that grew out of the floor. And it was clearly less traveled than the other.

More than once she tripped on a large stone, landing on her face and driving her hands into the ground. She winced in pain, but found that she was getting used to the constant agony that her body endured. That, or she was losing feeling.

One particular fall toward the end of the tunnel caused her immense pain, and blood flowed from a fresh gash under her chin. She hit hard on the rocky floor and felt a new wave of fatigue wrap around her body. It drew her into the darkness, and her Second Sight faded. She was so tired…

…so weary…

And then she was asleep. Blood pooled around her face as she lay on the jagged ground. She lay there alone and exposed, her broken body in the middle of the meandering path. She did not dream, nor did she get much rest, for not long after she was awakened by a piercing scream…

Anorra lifted her head off the ground, congealed blood clinging to her cheek. The deafening sound cut through the space like a sword, ringing throughout the caverns like a warning bell. It cut the air above her head and echoed out beyond into the prison chamber. And then, all at once, it ceased. And she was sure of why it had come. They had found her empty cell.

She pushed herself up and stumbled forward into a run. Her first few steps were too short and she fell into a large boulder, bouncing off to one side. She made a few more before hitting the left wall with her head and shoulder. A fresh cut opened on the side of her head. But she didn't even notice. The Dairne-Reih were coming.

Moments later she moved out into the high-ceilinged room full of pigeon-hole cells. Heart beating quickly, she looked up, searching for the gateless cell she had been shown. After the fifth or sixth level, the wall was swallowed by darkness. She willed herself to remember the image of the cell. It had been very high up, so high that the ground below was swallowed in black. But lack of light was not an issue for Anorra. For with spiritual eyes, a soul can see in the dark.

"I'm coming, lost one," she offered up.

The subtle sound traveled up the wall and rang through every cell. All at once there was a rustling from overhead. Something above her was moving. *A great many things* were moving.

She took a few steps toward the wall and then reached out, letting her fingers find their first hold on what would be a long climb. She stretched higher with her other hand and met a rock, and then her feet followed. In a few swift motions she passed beyond the second tier of cells, and then past the third and fourth. While her body resisted the expenditure of energy, she knew she had to keep moving. Her enemy was very near.

Anorra's left foot slipped, and she let out a grunt. She heard her voice echo through the space, answered this time with more rustling. Movement. It seemed to be coming from within the cells.

She reached up with her right arm, her fingers searching for their next hold.

A hand grasped her around the wrist.

Anorra screamed.

Suddenly the entire hall burst into a cacophony of shrieking, arms straining out between the bars of the cells, grasping toward her. She screamed louder and tried to wrest her arm free. But the hand would not let go.

Another hand reached out and grabbed her left ankle from below. The jerk downward was sudden and tore her foot from the wall. Her right foot slipped away too, and she dangled five levels above the floor, held only by her left hand.

The hall was racked with another long, angry shriek from back through the tunnel. The Dairne-Reih were closing in. The outburst had a sobering effect on the prisoners, however, who darted back into the darkness of their cells in total silence. Anorra did not need another invitation to settle herself back on the wall and made quick work upward.

Moments later the lost souls braved the world outside their cells again and strained to reach her as she climbed. Hands brushed against her arms and tugged at her hair. But she managed to fend them away with a blow here and a sharp kick there. As demonic as it all seemed, she noticed that the hands reaching for her had strangely human qualities to them. Somehow, she felt, these beings were her kin.

Anorra kept moving higher and higher up the wall, making quick work of the heights and losing count of how many levels she had passed. The hands continued to search her out, but she retaliated as best she could and pressed on. Her arms and legs screamed for relief, so badly wanting just to stop and rest for but a moment. But she knew it would mean her death. She had come too far. She could not give herself any quarter—her enemy would do no differently.

When she reached the level she thought the gateless cell was at, she heard a familiar clicking sound fill the chamber floor far below her. They were here. The prisoners once more retreated into the safety of their rooms, and all was silent. She didn't dare move.

Very slowly, Anorra peeked between the gap of her arm and hip, looking straight down to the ground. Five demons milled about, looking all around. Another three joined them, and then more spilled in from the tunnel. They began walking along the base of the wall, peering into the cells and jabbing prisoners with their long spears. The sorry souls bellowed and howled but did not produce what the Dairneags wanted.

Anorra glanced back up and searched for her prize. She allowed her mind's eye to pull away from the wall where she clung and get a larger view of the upper cells.

There.

One more level up and three over to the left. She could make out a hole in the wall with no bars over it. That was her room.

Could the demons climb this wall?

Ever so slowly she reached for her next handhold and pulled herself up, supported by her feet. She passed over the next set of cells and then began the tedious lateral traverse to the open cell. She paused only once to spy on her pursuers, all of which seemed busy moving along the length of the wide-reaching wall, apparently not even considering that their prey would be high above them. What prey moved further into captivity?

A few moments later she arrived at the cell and paused, just beyond sight, to the right side. She took a deep breath, sure that the demons beneath could hear her shaking muscles racked with fatigue.

"Help, Most High," she whispered, barely audible. "I need You."

She reached a hand around the corner of the cell and, finding a hole for her fingers, brought her foot in as well. One more motion and she was standing on solid ground, now towering high above the chamber floor that crawled with a prowling host of bloodthirsty demons.

She stared into the darkness, and there her eyes made out the form she had seen in the vision…what seemed to be a man crouched at the far end, shaking, with an arm swung over his head. He wore a red tunic, torn and soiled, and the tattered remains of a purple cloak that hung lifelessly from his shoulders. His skin was scabbed and stained with grime, not a clean patch anywhere to be seen. And his hair was long and wild, as was his grizzled beard. When the man had enough courage to look up from his cowering stoop, he cast a fearful eye toward Anorra.

Unsure of how he'd respond, all Anorra could think to say was, "I am Anorra, daughter of King Thorn of Ligeon. I am here by the prompting of the Most High to rescue you."

The man only stared at her with his one visible eye.

There seemed to be a commotion from among the demons below.

"I am here to rescue you," she said again.

Tell him I am coming soon. If he wants freedom, it will be granted.

The words confused her greatly. Panic was squeezing in her chest. What could He possibly mean by that?

Do as I say.

"The Most High is coming," she said, not quite convinced herself. "If you desire freedom, He will grant it to you."

This time the man turned to face her and made to move forward. His fragile voice cracked in the air.

"Ife de veirsin ti leq shemaeh?"

Anorra froze. She was amazed he could speak.

"Leq shemaeh? Ife de veirsin ti leq shemaeh?"

She merely gazed at him, unsure what to say. Clearly he had something he was trying to tell her. But she couldn't understand him. And his tone was growing more urgent. The Dairne-Reih would hear him.

The tongue he used was old, older than any she knew. *Probably first Dionian*, she suspected. Fane had taught her some words over the summers, as had Gyinan. She tried to work it out in her head.

Shemaeh—high mount. Her mind raced.

"Ti leq shemaeh?" He seemed to be begging her now.

Horse. Something about a horse. He was clearly mad.

"Ife de veirsin ti leq shemaeh unua meh frestehk?"

Have you seen my horse?

She could place it all. But he was getting more animated. She raised a finger to shush him and took a step forward.

Suddenly he lunged toward her and caught her by the wrists. Anorra made to step away, but the open air was all that was behind her. The man pleaded with her again, now louder.

"Ti leq shemaeh?"

"Hush, sir. You'll get us both caught. I don't know what you're saying."

"Ti leq shemaeh! *Leq shamaeh!*"

"Nay, I haven't seen your horse! Please," she struggled against him. "Let me go!"

This wasn't at all what she expected. This man didn't want her help. He was crazy! What was the Great God thinking?

She leaned out and away from the man, though he was the only thing keeping her from falling back into space. She looked down and saw a Darineag stare up at her. Recognition dawned over its face, and it screamed out, drawing the attention of the others. The rest looked at her and immediately started up the wall with lightning speed.

"Sir! Please! The Dairne-Reih are coming for us both now! Please let me go!"

But his grip remained fixed. And his eyes were intent. She was aware of his stink, the foul stench of waste and bile and death.

"Tadellis," he finally said, softening. "Ti ama pelleh Tadellis ap Trinade."

Anorra was arrested. Her heart stopped.

The demons were halfway up the wall.

"*What did you say?*" she cocked her head sideways in wonder.

"Ti ama pelleh Tadellis ap Trinade."

"Your name is *Tadellis…son of Trinade.*"

It was then she realized exactly who the Most High had sent her to rescue. And they regarded one another in silent awe as the first demon stretched out its hand for Anorra's leg.

Chapter Twenty-Seven

HAIDES CALLING

"We are leaving now," Luik stated firmly. Fatigue and sorrow seeped from his eyes, his losses now far outnumbering his gains. The others gathered around the council table shared his woe. But never the same gravity. And they knew that standing up to him was pointless, yet they had to try. A good friend would.

"My King," Gorn spoke up, "I think I speak for all of us when I say you're in no shape for another battle."

"Blast it, Gorn!" Luik slammed his fist into the board. Luik cast him a hard stare and then withdrew it, regaining his composure. Did they not see? Could they not understand? "What more do I have to lose?" He looked in the faces around him, searching. No one responded. "The fact that I still cling to my own life humiliates me. I have offered it to the Most High countless times, and yet He has not taken it." He grew cold, recalling his bitter dream. "Instead he bids my brothers to die and my love to torment."

"Luik, that is unwise talk," Li-Saide said.

"Is it?" Luik's temper rose again. "Is it *truly*, dwarf?"

"Son," Ragnar raised a calming hand.

"I can't take this!" Luik stood to his feet and cast his chair back.

"We cannot ask the men to go on another errand," Jrio spoke up, ready for Luik's retribution.

"I'm not asking them to go!"

"But you cannot go by yourself, brother," Fyfler added. They had been over this already.

"Then the onus is upon you and not me. Why is this so difficult?"

"Because, Luik," Li-Saide said, louder than he had ever spoken before, "*we* have already lost many kin today and cannot bear to lose you, too. To think you are alone in your grief is pride that I dare not have to point out. You know what I speak is true."

Luik looked to Benigan. Uncomfortable, he turned away, sought to right his tumbled chair, and then brought it back to the table, sinking heavily into it. He blew out a mouthful of air and laid his head on the board.

"Forgive me," he said to one and all, looking up.

"It is well received, King," said Fane. "And understood among us all. But you are but one man, and spent at that."

Luik's desire to fight this through ebbed, and his thoughts went to his beautiful Anorra. He wanted nothing more than to see her again, to hold her and breathe in the smell of her hair. The thought brought tears to his eyes—even more so the thought that she would be suffering this very moment. He knew she was alive. He could feel it. Barely.

Luik looked up and stared his father hard in the face. "Would you sleep if you were me?" He turned to Gorn. "Would you waste any time?" He looked to Boran. "How would you eat a meal?" To Li-Saide. "Or drink a draft of mead?"

A long silence followed. Everyone contemplated his words and knew they would say nothing to the contrary if in his position.

It was Benigan who first stood to his feet.

"If it is Anorra you wish to save, I have already lost my life once today and fear not losing it again." He laid his sword upon the board.

Luik lowered his head as tears welled. He looked up and mouthed the word *c'symia*.

Fyfler stood next, drawing his sword, laying it on the table without a word. Jrio unsheathed his blade, and Fane laid his staff flat. Gorn shook his head but stood nonetheless. Li-Saide followed, and before long all those at the table were on their feet. Although a great many men had been lost in Ot, only Brax's seat at the table remained vacant. Tontha was without a king, and before the end of this day Luik feared the rest of the realms would be no different. He was not asking them to go with him, but he knew he couldn't go alone.

Morgui had destroyed the Tree of Life, razed Grandath to the ground, and surely killed the Great King's Son, just as he had boasted. Dionia's way of life was forever changed, and they could not go back to what had been, or expect it to return to them. And Luik simply could not allow the last remaining passion of his life to go unsought. He had to find her—even if for one last look. Even if only to bury her.

"Well," Jrio spoke up. "When do we leave?"

• • •

The battle for Ot had ended far worse than anyone cared to recount. So it was understood that the carnage witnessed and the suffering endured would not be spoken of…not for a very long time. Suffice it to say that those who had battled in the garden beneath the Tree had been forced to retreat through the caves and press into the portals, returning to Mt. Dakka. A great many of the dwarves had been lost, however, choosing to stand against the molten lava to their own destruction. Those who had seen it would be forever haunted by the image of the noble race, unwilling to leave the treasures they had sworn to keep. But many of the ill-fated dwarves had been pulled from their posts by warriors not willing to see them perish. The men had dragged them away, the dwarves flailing their hands and feet all the while, demanding to be released, constrained to die for Ot.

The warriors had defended their retreat back into the pool to Mt. Dakka, throwing the dwarves into the waters and beating off the Dairne-Reih. When all were safely through, the demons had lingered, batting at the water but never entering. They eventually had grown bored and returned to the main cavern, joining their brethren in destroying the Secret City. When Luik and the others had finally managed to connect to the portal caves, the pools had been empty, and their escape had gone unnoticed.

The High King's return to Mt. Dakka was met with both sorrow and rejoicing. It was the strangest mix of emotions any of the Dibor had ever experienced; they were overjoyed to know that so many had survived, but Brax's death and the destruction of Ot was more than they could bear. Any embrace of welcome was quickly stalled by weeping.

The council meeting over, each man was off to solicit the help of those willing to join their lost cause. Luik checked in on Boran, still nursing his wounds and barely able to stand.

"You will be of more use here to lead the city's defense when you are well, than to needlessly perish with us in the fires of Haides," Luik said, dismissing Boran's adamant plea to join them with a wave of his hand. The Son of Tontha would have argued more, but it took too much strength even to talk.

Luik wandered through the halls then and out into the garden, needing time to think. To clear his head. He had yet to change his clothes, gore-smeared and blackened with soot and sweat. He paused only to take a drink of water and steal a hunk of warm bread from the refectory. He ambled down the stone paths, his legs and back weary from fighting, chain maille slinking over his shoulders.

The flowers tried their best to smile at him, but he was sore with the memories they stirred up. Just there he and Anorra had lain, gazing at the starlight and talking of the future. And beside that fountain they had sat, their fingers entwined, the murmuring of the water soothing their fears.

He passed through a wrought-iron gate and into another larger garden, dancing with the scents and smells of summer. The deep longing in his heart was overwhelming. The silver-green leaves fluttered in the light breeze, and tall grasses swayed back and forth in lazy rhythm. He remembered this space all too well: snowball throwing in the winter, meetings with the Dibor late into the warm evenings of summer.

The sun beat down on his head and forced him to find shelter beneath an elm, the cool shadows revealing just how tired he was. He sat down then, his back against the tree, and closed his eyes. The leaves rustled each time the wind picked up, air kissing his skin, hot and bruised from war.

"Is this all?" he whispered. "Is this all, Most High?"

A single tear seeped from between his eyelids, starting down his cheek. "You made me for this? To be born? To live? To suffer and then have everything in my world taken away?" He inhaled deeply, a tremor in his chest. No answer. "So this is it." The breeze picked up. He paused and took a defeated breath. "Then I accept it. Just give me the strength to do what I must. To see this to the end."

He waited then, thinking he might hear the voice of the Great God reply. Thinking He might speak. But nothing came. Only silence. Silence that mixed with the leaves, the babbling fountains, and the singing birds… silence that wooed him to sleep.

• • •

"My King," a familiar voice called from far away. "The men are ready. We leave at your command."

Luik looked up. His slumber hung heavy on his eyes, and his head was thick. Jrio was standing over him, a hand on his sword, the other behind his back.

"The men," Luik repeated, remembering. He ran a hand over his face, blinking. "Then we shall leave at once." He made to get up, and Jrio helped him to his feet.

"Are you sure you want to do this?" Luik asked him, holding fast to Jrio's forearm.

Jrio smiled. "As sure as I am living and certain I won't see another sunrise." Then he chuckled. "You know, I've been asking myself, 'What else is there to live for?'"

Luik thought the question oddly familiar. "And?"

"And I haven't thought of anything. To live for this beautiful thing called life, or to die trying to hold onto it. Either way it's meaningless."

"Meaningless?" Luik eyed him narrowly.

"I mean, without *Him*. Without His love. And without people to love as He loves us." Jrio looked up into the brightness of the afternoon sky and then back to Luik. "You know, Luik, my life used to be so simple. I mean, as boys. You remember?" Luik nodded. "Working our lands with our parents, dancing in the festivals, and playing rokla whenever we could steal away from sight of our mothers."

"I have many such memories."

"As do we all. But the thing I miss most—the thing whose absence haunts me in my sleep—is not the sorrow of those past times long gone. I thought it was. For a while, I did. But nay, it is meaningless in and of itself. My parents, bless them, were meaningless. My friendships, including yours, are meaningless. Then it hit me. Whom have I but the Great God? If He is not, then what is? Without His voice, without His presence: is there really anything more satisfying? More worthy to die for? If He betrays me, though I have my life, I have nothing." Jrio took a deep breath, his eyes settling on the grass between his feet. "So you see. What does it matter that I lose my life this night? If I remain here to endure the absence of His voice, I will fight for its return. And if I am taken away, gored on the hands of my enemies, then I speed to the Great Throne Room and see His shining face for myself." He looked back to Luik. "Either way, I live for no other. I live for Him. And if it's love you long to rescue, may we demonstrate the power of His love which He is about to reveal."

Luik was moved by his words. He admired this man…this friend. They had walked together from the beginning, from leaving the Gvindollion to this very moment. Faithful. And now his words spoke of something yet to come, of something eternal. And Luik knew each word he spoke to be true.

"Whatever love we have, whatever we feel, it can only be from Him," Luik said. "The very fact that we, flawed and abandoned, should be able to partake of it in this, our weakest state, only speaks of His mercy. For though I cannot hear His voice I cannot deny love. And somehow, dear friend I see it in you. Now. I see *Him*."

They embraced there in the garden as warriors do, but even more as friends.

• • •

The hike south was swift. No provisions were needed, as no one intended to stay long, nor ever to return home. They brought a few skins of fresh water and only what they could carry in weaponry: swords, shields, spears, bows and arrows, and polearms.

They ran most of the time, single file, moving along the craggy trail that dipped from one mountain peak to the next. No one spoke. The only sounds were those of heavy footfalls beating against the ground, adorned with the clink of metal and tap of hardened leather.

Two hundred men in all made the journey…two hundred who harbored no illusions about returning. It was a death errand that no one had ever done. But with everything already lost, even the defending of

Mt. Dakka seemed a failing chore. So most who had the heart and energy reasoned it would be better to meet the enemy face to face than to die with their backs against a wall. And so they joined Luik and the others, devoid of fear.

By the time the sun dipped low toward the eastern horizon, the Sif Gate appeared on the peak of the next mountain. The warband picked up speed, raced down the narrow track and then wound back up the opposite side, pressing toward the monolithic stone structure that rose above them.

"It still stands," Fane said as they neared.

"And looks intact," replied Li-Saide, moving closer to the aged stones.

Fane knelt to examine the dirt on the north-facing side. "It's been used recently."

"A good sign," said Gorn.

Li-Saide stretched out his hand and moved it slowly toward the structure. When his fingers touched the cold stones, he jerked his hand away. The men nearest just stared at him.

"What is it?" Luik asked, doubt suddenly filling his chest.

"Evil," the dwarf said. He reached out to touch it again.

Fane moved to the opposite column and applied his hand. The stones were cut at right angles and bore strange markings as if etched by the hand of a tormented writer. Demons most likely, the warband thought.

Fane could feel the power, too—a dark, foreboding mood sweeping over his spirit. He closed his eyes and fought to stave the force off. But the cloud edged closer and closer. Try as he might, he could not keep the impending evil at bay.

"It's too strong," he called over to Li-Saide.

"Remain focused," the dwarf replied, eyes also shut. "The power in you is far greater. *Remember.*"

The evil seemed to be surrounding Fane now, coming at him from all sides. He wanted to pull his hand away. He wanted to run.

Suddenly he felt a hand on his back. "Remember."

It was Luik.

And then another hand. "Remember," Gorn added.

All at once the burden was lightened. Not eliminated. But lessened. In his mind's eye he could see the black clouds halt that loomed over him, their progress arrested by a contrary wind. Lightning flashed. Something was moving them back…something was *scaring* them.

"It's working," Fane lit up. "It's working!"

"Aye, now stay fixed," Li-Saide ordered.

Together they worked, their hands on the columns, willing the wicked to bow. Li-Saide squinted with the effort, and Fane's brow glinted with perspiration. They pushed their spirits forward, interceding with all intent to win. To overcome. *To reveal.*

While no one else heard anything but the evening air washing through the mountains, Li-Saide and Fane heard the crashing of thunder and the howling of violent winds.

They watched as the death clouds gave way to a rock wall adorned with a single hole. Li-Saide knew it at once.

"The key hole," the dwarf shouted. "Do you see it?"

"Aye!" said Fane. Then paused in frustration. "But where's the key?"

"Reach for it, with me!"

Fane strained in his spirit and there before him appeared a black key, deathly ominous, intermittently illuminated by flashes of lightning. It was suspended in the air, held aloft by an unseen force. But as he willed it forward, the key did not disappoint.

"Keep going," Li-Saide urged. "Guide it in to the lock!"

The clouds rumbled overhead, threatening to swallow Fane whole at any moment. But the key was so near, edging ever closer. He felt more hands on his back and then Li-Saide's voice in his ear.

"Insert the key, and twist. You can do it."

Fane was startled by the dwarf's being so near. Perhaps that was only in his mind. It made sense. But they worked together, forcing the black key into the hole and then with a sudden jerk, twisting…

Fane fell back from the columns and gasped. The others caught him and he looked around. There beside him was Li-Saide.

"But I thought you—"

"Nay, you didn't need me. In fact, I couldn't help. Only the pure Mosfar born of Ad, Keepers of the Sacred Words, can open these gates."

"Then why—"

"Hush." Li-Saide motioned toward the gate.

A white spark flickered in the center of the space between the stones. A chill prickled everyone's spines. Then a loud pop: and a thin, transparent wall of brilliant blue appeared that stretched from column to column, from ground to spanning arch above.

"Well done," Gorn said, hitting Fane on the back. Those nearby congratulated him in like kind.

"Why so eager to thank me for your deaths?" Fane inquired. The congratulating stopped.

"Come," Luik stepped up. "Li-Saide, how does it work?"

"Honestly, I've never gone through. But I would imagine it is a portal into the second natural state, the *supernatural* as some would say. We simply *walk* through."

"Like the Sea Caves?" Fyfler asked.

"Hopefully not as painful," said Jrio.

Benigan pushed everyone aside, his imposing size making ample room before the gate. "Nothing's going to be as painful as being run through by a Dairneag. So let's get on with this." He looked to Luik.

"After you," said the High King.

Benigan drew his sword and lowered his head. "For Dionia," he said softly.

"For Dionia," they all replied.

The hulking man strode into the blue wall. The edges of his form caused ripples like those in a pond. A moment later the shimmering wall enveloped him and he was gone.

"Great God of Athera," the men muttered.

"Next?" Luik piped up.

"Well, I'm not letting him win my kills!" Kinfen pushed past everyone. "Let me through." And without another word the blue wall closed in around him.

The rest of the men formed up and drew their swords. Luik eyed them all and thanked them for their bravery, their steadfast resolve. Then he turned and led them through the Sif Gate.

Chapter Twenty-Eight

IN THE MOUTH OF THE ENEMY

The first thing Luik noticed was the heat, stifling and oppressive. Each breath of the caustic air proved a task just to draw in. And once within it caused the lungs to burn. If anything indeed lived in this place, he wondered how it survived more than a single night.

But worse was the smell. He had almost grown used to the stink of burning flesh and rot, yet nothing had prepared him for this. As the warband closed in behind him, tucked around a large cluster of boulders, he heard many a man issue the contents of his stomach up onto the scorched cavern floor.

Soft red light flickered on the rock walls around them, Luik acutely aware of voices up ahead. Voices of the tormented. It was then his heart went out to Anorra. Is this where she had been taken? How could anyone survive?

"So what's your plan, Dibor?" Fyfler edged closer to Luik, wiping his mouth of bile.

"Not to stay here," Luik smiled. He looked to Li-Saide and then to Gorn. "I guess I'll take the first look."

He held his sword up and edged around the closest boulder until he neared the wall of light coming from the large chamber up ahead. Then, ducking low, he peered around the corner.

A horrific scene of tortured souls played out in front of him. Their labored cries and flailing limbs met with the lash of whips and spears, answered moments later by a floor of molten lava. The heat was so intense against his face that he withdrew back into the shadows. His eyes simply couldn't believe the atrocity they had just witnessed.

A hand met his shoulder. "It is great evil," Li-Saide said softly. "It's supposed to concern you."

"Concern is too formal a word, Chief." Luik gathered his thoughts and then gave the chamber another long stare, watching the entire drama unfold another time before returning to address the men, eager to know what foe lay beyond.

"Archers," he pointed at six men. "There are two Dairneags, one on each side on raised ledges that overlook a pit. Unless there are other hidden eyes, which I'm sure there are, these two guards are our only threat."

"That's all?" Jrio asked.

"O, watch out for the lava," Luik added. "I suppose that'd be unpleasant. I see another larger chamber beyond. We'll take the demons one at a time." His men nodded in reply.

The six men with bows stepped forward and paired off, the first set taking a knee, the second set hunched over, and the third erect, all with bows extended and arrows nocked and drawn. They remained in the shadow and waited for Luik's command.

He listened for the wailing to be drowned out by the rising lava. The guards would be fixated on the swirling pool, and Luik's men would have the least distraction. When the silence came, he lowered his hand, and the archers swiveled out into the room.

Each man picked his target, arrows impaling demon flesh at the neck. The nearest demon was carried clear off the ledge and sent sprawling into the molten pool below. The other fell backward against the wall and struggled to stay upright. It was clearly shocked beyond belief and looked around in wild confusion. Just when it noticed the six men standing in the cave entrance, a fourth shaft pierced in between its eyes and pinned its head to the cavern wall.

"Quickly!" Luik ordered and took off running along the perimeter of the room. The men followed him in short order as they skirted the pool on the narrow ledge above. The warband ran in single file, taking great care not to fall to certain death.

They passed by numerous iron-barred cells, each containing prisoners of uncommon quality: men and women whose faces were deranged with terror, some with limbs missing, most trembling in the corner.

One cell remained empty, the gate ajar.

"Anorra has been here," Fane nodded to Luik.

"What?" He stopped and retreated to Fane's side. He peered into the shadows, his stomach tight with anger. How much had she endured?

"She has been taken elsewhere," Ragnar surmised.

"Or escaped," countered Li-Saide.

Those gathered eyed the dwarf, only hoping it was true.

The lava began to recede back through the grates in the floor, and the men noticed hands emerge out of the flow.

"Don't stop!" Gorn hollered. "Keep moving! Keep moving!"

The liquid fire emptied further, and soon the cavern floor was a mass of writhing hands and arms, made all the more furious once the men were noticed.

The hall erupted into a frenzied din, the captives' shrieks ringing in the air.

"Keep moving!" Gorn yelled again, but his voice was drowned out.

One man stopped, terrified by what he witnessed, and was bumped carelessly by a warrior behind. The first man lost his balance; his foot slipped off the ledge. The warrior in back reached for his arm, but sweat made it too slippery, and the man tumbled over. His body landed with a thud on a grate below. Though he tried to stand, he was immediately arrested by a throng of grasping hands...hands that pulled him down through the bars in bloodied pieces.

"Great God of Athera," Luik muttered in horror as the screaming in the cavern intensified. He looked back at his men, who had all stopped, and then began waving his arms frantically to draw their attention back. The warband regarded him with pale disbelief, but eventually heeded his desperate calls to move onward.

Surely the entire underworld had been alerted to their presence now. Luik knew they had precious little time to do what they had come to do.

The ledge curved along the hall before bending sharply into the next cavern, this one significantly larger. But their arrival was no surprise.

Four Dairneags stood on their ledges eyeing them curiously, having been warned by the commotion. But surely they had not expected to see a warband of men! And they were far from suited for the battle, as their whips and spears were no match for the far-reaching arrow shafts that found their marks in the demon flesh.

The corpses tumbled down, this time into the hands of the captives, eagerly devoured in a short-lived fit of vengeance.

Luik did not pause to watch but made his way onward, running through the room and toward what looked to be the opening of a tunnel. Soon the screams of the tormented were joined by other familiar sounds: the clicks and shrieks of the Dairne-Reih.

The ledge neared its end and soon spit the warband out into a long tunnel filled with jagged teeth of minerals and rock. And just beyond they could see movement and the faces of demons.

This is it, Luik thought. *My last battle.* Everything he had learned, all the lessons he had earned through failure, came down to this defining moment. How would he live this poignant flash of life? His body cried out for rest. He was bruised and broken. He was tired of spilling blood. Of war. He loathed the day that he had first drawn his sword and cursed those who had felled his brothers. He wanted no more. And he would meet his end here and now.

With battle-hardened determination and nothing left to live for, Luik tilted his head forward and began the charge.

The two forces drove at one another, racing past stalactites and bounding over rocks as if two opposing dams had broken, emptying into the same tunnel. Nothing could stop them. Legs pumped, weapons raised by one league, spikes and bared teeth by the other.

Luik held tight to his Vinfae and a spear, running up the side of the wall as the enemy neared. His brief moment aloft gave him a full view of his prey in the dim tunnel light: about three tens and four demons ran toward them, far fewer than he expected.

He pressed off from the wall and sailed overhead of the first line, driving and withdrawing his sword from the neck of a tall demon in one swift motion, and jabbing another in the skull with his full weight behind his spear. The spearhead popped through its target, and Luik landed nimbly on his feet, adrenaline now driving every trained motion like a precision dance of death.

He whispered the Tongues of the Dibor and swirled around, severing three Dairneags at the waist with his blade before leaping again to the curved wall of the tunnel, picking his way farther back into the fray. The shrieks of the dying monsters joined with those of the captives, a deafening sound that none of them would soon forget.

Luik continued to speak in the Ancient Tongue, his weapons charged with the endowment of power. He swung left and right as if clearing a wheat field with a scythe, hacking his enemies to their knees.

And then, all at once, *she* was there, slung like a bag over a demon's shoulder, a man slung over the opposite shoulder. A soiled mat of hair swayed in the air, and her arms were limp and bloodied. But it was Anorra.

Luik's throat squeezed shut, and rage overtook him, the kind only warriors feel in the most unjust of battles. Three more Dairneags stood between him and her captor.

He summoned a surge of power that shook his arms and then heaved the spear out of his grip with wild force. The oak rod quivered as it flew, stirring the air overhead. In the same moment that the spearhead impaled the face of Anorra's subjugator, Luik tucked his sword against his side and leaned forward with all his strength. He barreled into the first demon and screamed in the Ancient Tongue, his words summoning the might of Athera itself. He passed right through the beast in an explosion of carnage that showered the walls. The next two foul monsters met the same end, and all at once Luik stood before his love, her body crumpled in a heap over the shoulder of the slain demon that carried her.

She was completely still.

He did not cry out her name, nor did he look to his right or left. What demons weren't cut down by his following warband were too frightened of his manifestation of power to take another step toward him.

He dragged his sword in the rocky dirt, growing delirious with rage. Suddenly all was silent in his ears save for the pounding of his heart. He was infuriated, caught up in a frenzied state of hate and loss, now sure that his love had met her end here in this vile abode. He screamed out, but could not hear his own voice. Luik swung his sword around his head and then hacked the demon corpse as his body succumbed to utter exhaustion.

The handle slipped from his fingers as he knelt by the body of his beloved, his soon-coming bride. But she did not respond to his touch.

At least not that he could feel.

. . .

From far away she could hear screaming. But these were not the screams of the captives she had become so quickly accustomed to. Nor were these the eerie shrieks and clicks offered up the inhabitants of this realm.

Nay, this was something altogether different. And yet strangely familiar. There was defiance there, a cry that came from a thread of life she could follow…follow up out of her despair.

But it was so dark here. And alluring. Her body no longer hurt; she could feel it slipping away from her. She wanted to stay and rest a while. Just a while, and then she could go on.

But to what?

The memories swirled about in her mind like shadow paintings dressed with dim colors, each canvas whipping around in a fuzzy haze.

The darkness grew stronger then, willing her away from the sounds and the colors. Calling her to rest. To lay down her woes and give in.

But the screaming grew louder and louder. Somewhere, she was quite sure, a man was screaming. A man she may have known once. But that would have been so long ago.

Fight.

Anorra shook when she heard it.

Fight, my beloved.

She could see the words drawn out across the blackness, a silvery ribbon that led forward. When she heard *fight* for the third time she decided to grab hold. Her hand shakily reached out and caught hold of the ribbon's tail.

It was all she could do to hold on, her hand aching with the effort. But holding on was all that was required. For He would do the rest.

The silvery ribbon became a cord and matured into a strong rope that accelerated forward through the darkness. Light and color raced passed her as if she were traveling down a tunnel of brilliant clouds. Wind stirred her hair and made her eyes burn. The rope threatened to slip out of her hands, but He was there to make sure it wouldn't. For He was holding on with her, one hand on the rope, the other wrapped with a Strong Arm around her waist.

Anorra turned then and noticed His strong embrace. She raised her chin and looked up into His face, searching for His eyes. She knew this One. Her Beloved. She had seen Him so many times in her heart. But somehow right now, right here, He was the most real. It had cost her everything to find this moment. But she decided that it had been worth it.

Her God had saved her.

In the blink of an eye, the vision was gone; and reality, a dimmer reality, came racing back to her. She did not want Him to leave.

But she knew He would never be far.

And then the scream. This time just above her.

It came from someplace deep, a heartache that she could not fathom. From deep within the soul of a man, a scream that stirred her immensely. She knew this man.

"Luik?" she asked weakly. But the Warrior King could not hear, too distraught himself. Battle still ensued, and beyond that the chaos of the captives echoed loud in her ears.

She made to move her arm. It seemed as if it were on fire. But she did it anyway. Her Second Sight became alive just then, but only in her immediate vicinity. There, not a hand's breadth away, was a man her heart longed for, a man who owned what parts of her heart the Great God had allowed her to give away.

But he looked so sad. So defeated. *But I'm here!* She beckoned. "Luik!"

Still he cried out with his head lifted upward, mouth agape.

She willed her hand forward and, for what felt like the first time in her life, her fingertips touched the skin of his forearm.

• • •

Luik's face froze, and he slowly lowered his gaze, letting his eyes rest on the distorted face of the princess he had loved as a boy. His heart all but burst when he saw the blackened spaces that had once held her beautiful blue eyes, now no more. She looked as one dead, her body beaten and maimed. But a hand hung on his arm, suspended by its own strength. Her fingers were cold and shaking, but were there all the same, holding to life by a thread.

Suddenly filled with a flood of emotions, he grabbed her hand, and then reached for her fragile form. He slipped an arm carefully underneath her head and another beneath her knees and cradled her against his chest.

"My Anorra, I have come for you. Everything is going to be all right." Tears choked his next words. "I've got you. I'm going to take you home." But he suddenly realized they had no home. And they were in no situation to make it out of here alive. But they had to try.

To his amazement her hand moved up and touched his face, hugging the contour of his cheek with the gentlest touch. Undeterred by her marred visage, he looked to her torn lips and kissed them gently. Though he could barely hear himself in the ruckus, he leaned in close to her ear and whispered, "I have missed you so."

And words came back.

"Why did you come for me?"

Surprised by the power that her voice gave him—weak and frail as it was—Luik found some of his old spirit, if even for a fleeting moment. "I rescued you once; I can rescue you again."

He watched as what resembled a meager smile crossed her face. Out of the corner of his eyes he noticed blood staining his arms. He thought it was from the demons at first, but quickly noticed Anorra's tattered and red-stained clothes and assumed the worst.

"Hold on," he said, summoning up a bit of renewed strength, "I'm going to get you out of here."

Luik rose to his feet with Anorra in his arms and turned. His men had made quick work of the enemy host, and Luik thanked them silently with his eyes.

Fane knelt beside the man who had been on the demon's other shoulder. He wiped his face with the edge of his cloak and spoke gently over him in the Tongue of the Mosfar, urging life back into the man.

"Who is it?" Luik asked.

"I know not, but he is on the edge of death." Fane continued to minister the healing words.

"He is Tadellis, son of Trinade," Anorra offered.

"Son of Trinade?" Li-Saide turned to walk toward the man. "Third son of Ad." The dwarf's mind raced. "Can it be?"

"You know him?" Fane questioned.

"He was the first to be *taken* more than ten ages after the Great

Battle ended. We lost him in the Great Forest, right out from under us," Li-Saide remembered.

"He is a Lion Vrie," Gorn added. "One of the first."

"I think you'll know his horse," Cage smiled.

"His horse?" Luik puzzled.

The ground beneath them began to tremble. The screams of the captives suddenly died away, overwhelmed by the thunderous approach of footfalls. Then heart-sinking shrieks and clicks.

"More Dairne-Reih," Li-Saide said flatly.

"And from both directions I'm afraid," Gorn added, looking farther down the tunnel and then back from where they had come.

"And from the sounds of it, we won't have the force to fight our way out of this one," Li-Saide conceded.

Luik looked down the tunnel one way, and then the other, and back again. He could see the distant outlines of the familiar enemy racing toward them. He looked along the tunnel walls for an opening, a small fissure—*anything*. But there was nothing. And he was far too tired to fight; any romantic heroics he knew would be just games at this point.

Had they come so far and achieved so much only to be defeated here like this? But he had found his love, and alive at that, which was more than he could have hoped for.

"If we perish, we perish," Luik shouted back to Li-Saide and Gorn so the others could hear. "But they will taste our cold steel and the Spirit of the Great God long before our lives have been snuffed out. We lived together, so shall we die!"

"So shall we die!" the warband replied as one, swords and spears aloft.

"In the center, both of you." Gorn drew Luik into their midst. "Circle!"

"C'symia," Luik said, unsure Gorn could hear him given the noise. The demon host would be upon them in moments. The warband circled around Luik and Anorra, and someone slipped Luik's Vinfae into his hand. It did him little good, but he would die defending what he had come for. Standing here. In Haides. Never thinking it would be he and Anorra in the middle of the war circle, the formation they had learned on Kirstell so many moons ago.

"I think they're upset we broke into their house," Jrio said to the side.

"Oh, aye, brother," Fyfler replied. "Mightily upset indeed. 'Tis an outright shame so many of them are going to have to die."

"Hush now, boralee," Gorn said. "Our end is upon us. Let us go down as the legends you've become."

And without another word, every man raised his weapon and called upon the name of the Most High with a final breath.

Chapter Twenty-Nine

STAND OFF

Just when Luik and his men were sure their destruction was imminent, the charging mass of Dairne-Reih slowed and held short. The change of intent was baffling but didn't keep a few of the archers from loosing a number of well-placed shafts into the advancing masses. Even with this taunt, the demon army remained in check and stood but five paces away.

Their jeering calls and noises also subsided. The last echoes faded out to the ends of the tunnel, and the entire length of the corridor was filled with an eerie stillness. The warband stood ready to defend, hands shaking with the expected clash of battle, now absent, most likely only delayed. Why did they tarry?

The closest creatures loomed twice as high as any man, leering down at the warband, pure hatred in their eyes. Luik could feel his arms burning, Anorra growing heavy in his grip. But he would not let her go. Not this time, not ever again. He turned slowly to eye the demons on the other side. They were surrounded, yet not overcome. What strange turn of events had merited this?

A murmur arose from somewhere far back toward the main cavern they had come through. A cloud of swirling black blotted out much of the light at the tunnel's mouth, and an ominous figure crossed within it. The being stood three heads above the demons and made its way slowly down the tunnel. The Dairne-Reih parted and bowed to let the newcomer through.

"Morgui?" Gorn proposed.

"Aye, I believe it is he," Li-Saide replied.

"Funny, I've been wanting to meet him for some time," Kinfen laughed nervously. "Just to tell him what a thorn in our flesh he's been."

"Hush now," Li-Saide motioned.

The fallen lythla seemed to float down the passageway accompanied by the swirling black fog. Not a sound was heard except the labored breathing of the host of demons and the beating of each man's heart, the blood pounding in their ears.

The final rows of demons stepped aside, and there stood the fallen form of Morgui, once Prince of Athera, now an eternally tormented being.

The warband stared up into the creature's expressionless face. Two holes for eyes, a toothy, gaping mouth, and black flesh that more resembled roughly polished stone than anything human. His body was black as well, rippling muscles displayed in some show of prestige. Yet Luik and the others noted how distorted his form seemed, uneven and lopsided in parts. Massive leathery wings were folded behind him, poking beyond his shoulders. But they, too, were a shadow of their former selves, now torn and tattered.

The Demon King, the Dragon of Haides, took a step beyond his cohorts and looked down into the center of their cluster, eyeing Luik and Anorra—that is, if he *had* eyes.

No one stirred.

They simply waited for whatever would happen next.

A long, strained, and uneasy silence passed. Then, startling them all, Morgui threw back his head in laughter. The sound was thick and loud, like massive boulders dragged slowly over one another.

Luik's flesh prickled. He hated standing here doing nothing. But he had nothing left in him. Empty. Tired of battle and weary of games, he just wanted to die. He wanted to see Athera's Great Throne Room and leave all of this forever. He knew Anorra would join him, and together they would dance in the Great Hall of the King. Brax would be there. As would Thad, Thero, and Najrion. Dear Gyinan would welcome them, as would Lair, the beloved man who had raised him, and Anorra's father, too.

Luik could not take any more and resigned himself to the fate that awaited him. He would not be robbed of one more moment of his eternity by this thieving, lying excuse for a *leader*. Luik spat on the ground. Morgui had already taken everything else. What more was his life? Luik realized it was indeed nothing. His life was nothing. And Morgui could have it. All the sooner he would be in the presence of the Great King.

"Let it be done" he said to Gorn. "I'm sick—"

"So this is who has come to rescue the Princess?" Morgui's tone was incredulous, each word low and twisted, filled with spite. He turned his head back and forth, studying each of them carefully. "This is the mighty Luik, High King of Dionia?"

He let the last word hang in the air before another laugh issued up from within. Suddenly he raised his head and looked up. Screaming at the ceiling he said, "*This* is all you have to pit against me? You send me *this?*"

Then his laughter grew to its height, shaking the air around them. Luik saw Anorra shrink back, face contorted in agony. He would have covered his own ears but for holding her. Morgui howled and bellowed, shaking a hand toward Athera in defiance. Then he returned his gaze to the trembling throng.

Luik waited, ready for their fate to be delivered without quarter. He looked to his men, each standing with their weapons poised. He had never been so proud of any warband in all his life. Here they were, standing before the face of greatest evil, ready to lash out and go to their deaths with kingly valor.

Morgui made as if to open his mouth to speak...

...but nothing came.

Luik remained calm, looking intently to the Traitor of Athera. But still the wretch said nothing. For his attention had shifted slightly...

...to something beyond them. Farther down the tunnel.

Luik made to turn, but to his surprise, demons were backing up into him, completely unaware of his presence. He stood then, lifting Anorra with him. More demons bumped against him, backing up toward Morgui, their heinous gaze fixed on something far away.

What was happening? Luik tried to seek out Gorn in the mess. Jrio was also being jostled, and Li-Saide was trying to avoid being stepped on. A breath later the entire rear guard of Dairne-Reih was making for cover, now shrieking and utterly terrified, as if startled by...

Luik and the others did all they could not to be carried away or crushed by the retreating throng as the last demons fled down the tunnel and left the warband alone. A brilliant shaft of beautiful light met their faces and blinded all but one of them; Anorra lifted her head then and stared down the tunnel, seeing easily into a light far stronger than the sun.

"He is here," she said.

Could it be?

Anorra spoke again, "And He is beautiful."

In that single moment, awe and wonder completely overtook them. Intense feelings, indescribable then or ever after, rose in their hearts and moved them to their knees. The action was natural, uncontrived, and easy to do. Luik felt tears well up in his eyes. He was exhausted and facing death itself. He had been fighting for so long, not knowing peace since the rule of his father. And he had seen no hope.

Until now.

The Mighty King had come! He was here at last to save them all. And it was too much for his heart to endure. He held Anorra limply in his arms and wept openly.

It was over.

All the sleepless nights, all the crying out to the Most High. All the unreturned cries for help and the lonely battles fought without His presence.

None of it mattered now. In one instantaneous, unexpected, glorious moment, the King had returned.

Luik could hear the sobs of his men beside him, their bodies racked with pain and exhaustion as was his, their hearts overwhelmed by the silent presence of their King.

Luik squinted against the light and looked down at Anorra. A tiny hand reached out and touched her on the forehead. Li-Saide said, "Everything will be all right now, Princess. You have nothing to fear." Luik heard the dwarf sniffing back tears as he spoke.

"Aye," Luik joined, "there is nothing to fear now."

The warband knelt there together in the tunnel, hidden in the very bowels of Haides, but now not alone. Abandoned no more. Luik was aware of the Great God's presence as never before. As it had always been in the times before Adriel's demise, but even nearer.

He attempted to open his eyes, wincing against the overwhelming light. And there, directly in front of him stood a magnificent white Lion, head touching the tunnel's ceiling.

It was the Lion from his dreams.

His yellow eyes burned as if on fire, and His lush coat gleamed with the light of the stars. He was not intent on His enemies, staring down at Morgui or the host of Haides. Instead His eyes were affixed on Luik and the others, kneeling in His majestic presence.

Anorra was the first to speak. "You came," she said weakly, barely holding to her life.

The reply, as if making His presence felt all the more, was the most thunderous roar ever given up in any realm of Creation. His massive mouth gaped open, teeth sharp as razors. The air rippled in front of Him, unable to withstand His power.

Luik's chest trembled, and every muscle in his body threatened to give out. Yet somewhere deep within, the sound gave rise to a newfound strength. It was the roar of hope. The roar of destiny.

It was the roar of *victory*.

And though Luik could not see it, every demon knelt, some collapsing and toppling over, all others willfully resigning themselves to the superiority before them. Even Morgui himself, the defiant blasphemer of Athera, was forced to bow his head and kneel.

The roar continued, as if threatening to crush each man's chest beyond endurance. Every breath that Luik managed in the wake of the roar brought renewal to his spirit. He remembered his dream then, and wondered as to its meaning. He stood atop no gleaming white pearl here. No open sky full of stars. Quite the contrary. And he held his love in His arms; would the Mighty White Lion slay her, too?

Truth be told, his whole life had been lived in fear of this moment, yet he did not feel afraid. If visions were true, then he would breathe his last in but a moment, the Lion's paw gouging deep across his breast and slashing through his heart. But to prove what point? That his life belonged to the King? Had that not already been displayed in every battle where he risked life and limb? Luik did not understand.

All at once the powerful roared ceased.

No one, not man nor demon, dared to move.

When His Voice spoke, it was warm and strong, beautiful in every way yet commanding the highest respect. Luik and the others had heard it before…

…but never like this.

"My Name is The Lion of Judah, the Redeemer of all Creation." His words shook the walls of the tunnel, and every heart quaked in kind. "This day you shall know that I Am.

"My enemies have long tormented My people and I have heard their suffering. I have come to be their Deliverer and never again shall they be without Hope. For all who call upon My name will be saved. And I will make My enemies a footstool underneath Me, and their plans will be brought to nothing. So it has been said; so it is done."

His words reverberated down the tunnel and into the caverns beyond, through every prison cell and past every grate. The lakes of fire were stilled, and every ear heard clearly what had been declared.

The White Lion cast his intense gaze upon the quivering form of Morgui.

"Fallen One, I have come for what is mine. You know of what I speak."

"Yes, Your Majesty," Morgui replied, not daring to look up.

"Bring them to me in three days' time. On the dawn of the third day we will meet on the plains of Jerovah, and you will hand over what is mine. There you will do battle against the Children of Light, and they will exact the recompense they deserve from you for your atrocities, and take back what is rightly theirs."

"As it is declared, so it will be done," the demon replied, a pained expression on his face.

"Today, I will take all those who belong to me. And to all those dead who wish to live once again, today I give you Life."

At His Word, the ground beneath them shook. So violently, in fact, that all fell to their faces. Metal strained against rock, and bars burst from their hinges in the distance. Voices yelled and began calling out to one another.

Luik held Anorra tightly as the ground jostled them back and forth. He stole a glance upward and noticed that the Lion was looking into the distance. He was watching.

Watching for who would come.

The quake subsided, and peace fell over the scene again. Luik got up on all fours.

"Sons and Daughters of the Most High," the Lion finally spoke, "gather yourselves."

Luik looked down to Anorra and then cast Fane a sideways glance; Fane merely raised his eyebrows in wonder. They stood slowly, their bodies sore and battle weary.

Demon movement caused them to turn around. The entire enemy host parted, Morgui included, and there walked a line of men and women, streaming in from the network of caverns beyond.

"Look," Anorra said, staring back behind the Lion. Luik turned. More people were streaming in from the far end.

"He's setting the captives free," Luik uttered in amazement.

"They are free to go if they want to," Li-Saide said. The Lion looked down to confirm the dwarf's statement.

"If they so wish," the Lion added.

"But who would not wish to?" Li-Saide said, voice cracking.

Suddenly the Lion's face saddened. "There are some. And there will be many more."

Li-Saide saw the White Lion's eyes, staring off into the future. Many summers into the future, he could see. The Lion whispered as if to Himself, tone full of a strange sadness, "There will be many who do not want my Life."

"Then why offer it at all?" Morgui dared to speak up from down the tunnel.

The Lion rose up then, eyes snapping back to the present, and glared hard at the fallen lythla. "Because it is Mine to give and not yours to take, wicked spirit! It never was! For I gave it freely! Are you so foolish that you could not see My power? And have you so quickly forgotten the power of my Father? Death cannot hold Me!"

With that He issued another roar to conclude the argument.

"You have defied me for the last time, traitor. And I have come to answer your pitiful question. Are these all I have to send against you, you ask? I do not send My Creation to do King's work. So I have come Myself. And the host of Athera is at My command. You will mock Me no more. Three days, Morgui. Then My work here is finished, and you will be one day closer to your imprisonment."

Luik and the others looked on in amazement. Not in their wildest dreams could they have foreseen such an encounter.

"Come," the Lion said then. "It is time for us to go."

"Go? Go where?" Luik asked.

"You have an inheritance waiting, and a people who need your guidance, Luik," He replied. "You should not leave them waiting any longer than they need to."

As Luik gazed up into the mysterious eyes of his Lord, the light around him grew more intense, steadily increasing until he had to look away. Even through his eyelids the light grew. It was inescapable. He was wrapped in pure light, swept up into the presence of the One his heart longed to see, and he left Haides far behind.

Forever.

PART THREE

Chapter Thirty

RESTORATION

The warband returned from Haides in a flash of light. As quickly as the piercing radiance swept them away from danger, it likewise dissipated, dissolving into the dark and delivering them under an open, twilight sky. Luik had never thought the stars looked so beautiful…

…neither had his heart's love looked so beautiful. Though he could not see her face, Luik was sure Anorra slept soundly in his arms, breathing steadily, slumped against his chest. He turned quickly and realized the entire warband was with him, all in the King's Garden, the portico and secret passage just to one side. They were back in Mt. Dakka, standing in the shadow of the palace.

"We're—we're home," Jrio said. They all looked around in wonder.

"Aye," Gorn replied, gazing at his hands and arms, turning them over and over. "That we are." But those who knew him could hear the concern in his voice.

"Gorn, what is it?" Luik asked.

The warrior turned and held his arms up. He took a few steps forward and Luik noticed wet trails glistening on his cheeks in the starlight.

"Gorn?"

But the man simply continued to examine his forearms. "My scars," he said. But there was more. "My—my *pain* is gone."

At first no one understood.

Luik stepped forward to meet him. But the movement seized him. He met Gorn's intense stare. "My leg," Luik said softly. "It's—"

No one spoke. Everyone among them began to check their bodies, moving limbs and rubbing wounds.

Luik's heart leapt. Could it be? His first thought was…

Hot tears fighting to cloud his vision, he knelt and laid Anorra on the soft dew-covered grass. She stirred.

"Luik. Luik, is that you?"

Luik's heart clutched in that moment as he searched her face for…

"Luik!"

Her eyes opened beautiful and bright in the starlight. Very stars themselves.

"O Great God!" Luik yelled and pressed his forehead against hers. "You're healed!" He sobbed heavily, and she wrapped her arms around his neck.

"We're all healed," Li-Saide added. Patting himself with little hands he said, "His presence has made us whole. Even my beard!"

All the wounds and bruises, all the ailments and breaks—*everything* had been touched by the Master's Hand. Luik tried his best to regain his composure, but it was impossible. The flood of emotions was too great. For Anorra as well. Others gathered around them and shared in their overwhelming gratitude to the Most High. Surely He had done this.

Their cheers and cries made such a commotion that lamps flickered to life in the palace windows. Soon those abiding within joined them in the garden.

It was Benigan who spied him first. "Anondo!"

Everyone turned to see Ligeon's King striding through the garden with his two other sisters on each side. A dazzling smile danced across his face as he surveyed everyone, their armor bloodied but their countenances bright.

Someone began clapping, and soon the throng was cheering for the wounded king, now whole. The healing power of the Most High had swept into the land of the living. Luik wondered how many had been touched by his Swift Sure Hand.

Anondo moved through the crowd, embracing each of his countrymen, kissed on the neck by the Dibor and beat on the back by the rest of the Lion Vrie. He looked to Luik and saw a blonde beauty standing beside him. Though her hair was unkempt and she wore a thick blanket to cover her tattered clothes, he knew her glowing features all too well.

"An—Anorra," he stammered, overcome with joy. "You live!" He stumbled toward her with tears streaming down his face. He hoisted his sister aloft and spun her around. "Anorra, we have not lost you after all!" He kissed her face and nearly squeezed the life out of her. But she returned the embrace, happy to see her brother and sisters once more. Happy to see anyone.

Analysia and Lana immediately started stroking her head and attending to her like busy maids, asking her dozens of questions and comforting her in any way they could. Their empathy poured out of them like cool, calming waves over a sandy beach, for they too had once known captivity by the enemy, all too well. Now it was their time to minister heart-healing.

Even good Sheffy bustled into the garden, not one to miss out on the revelry. He brandished his new hand in front of the crowd, tears pouring down his cheeks like all the rest. He waved his arm in front of Luik and embraced the High King. "C'symia, my King. You have done it!"

"Nay, He has done it all," Luik corrected.

Many hours were spent reveling in the Redeeming Hand, stories shared and their miraculous end, until finally those wishing to be reunited with their kin said farewell and disappeared down into the city. Around the same time, fatigue drew each of the warband to their beds, and the gathering disbanded.

They would speak again at breakfast. For the first time in a long time…too long a time…there was a new day to look forward to.

• • •

Luik and the others slept deeply that night, unlike any sleep they could remember in a long time. Such peace enveloped them that no one stirred until well after the sun rose twice its height above the western horizon. No nightmares, no restlessness. Just pure rest. And no one bothered to wake them, either. No knocks at the door and no noise in the hallways. The entire palace atop Mt. Dakka, from Great Hall to outer gardens, was like a becalmed sea after a storm had passed.

When the Dibor finally woke, they shuffled down the hallways in robes and sandals, led by the smells from the kitchen. Coming one at a time, they gathered around one of the massive preparation boards between the hearths. Luik arrived at last, joined shortly after by Gorn, Li-Saide, and Fane. A number of the Lion Vrie entered as well, mostly those without wife or children, who had preferred to sleep in the palace rather than return to an empty dwelling.

"Good morning everyone," Anorra greeted the group in the kitchen, but her eyes were fixed on Luik. She smiled sweetly.

Gorn stood, his action bringing the rest of the men to their feet. Luik stepped forward and looked her in the eyes. He had never cried so easily, taking a deep breath and then wrapping his arms around her slender body. She returned the passion in kind, and the room filled with clapping and laughter. They all had a second chance at life.

"Sleep well my love?" Anorra spoke in Luik's ear.

He nodded, his chin hugging her shoulder, and then withdrew, staring in her eyes. "I can't remember the last time I've been this happy."

"Nor I," she beamed and went up on her tiptoes to kiss him.

Luik blushed, and then Anorra turned him around and they addressed the group, who cheered all the louder.

The accolade was followed by the clap of the master cook, who forced bowls of steaming soup into everyone's hands, and then laid trenchers of hot bread on the board. They all broke their fast together and bunched up on the benches, Luik never once leaving Anorra's side.

Neither of them had much of an appetite, too full from staring into one another's eyes. Those around didn't mind the couple's distraction in the least; they had fought for this moment as much as they had fought for the people of Dionia. Luik and Anorra, of all people, deserved such a warm reunion. And truth be told, it rekindled love in all of their hearts. Seeing the two of them together brought longing into their souls and put them in mind of what they knew Luik had wanted if he were to ever see Anorra again. Her hand.

Li-Saide called for hot mead to be served and then stood on the bench. "Here's to Luik and Anorra," he said, mug raised, "King and future Queen of Dionia!"

"Here, here!" everyone shouted and then tipped back their draughts.

Luik drew her close and couldn't help but kiss her, to the shouts of those gathered. How he had longed for this day! To be with her again!

"So, how about it?" Anorra finally asked him. Everyone went silent.

"How about what?" Luik replied.

Jrio pegged Luik in the ribs from the other side. "I proclaim, man! You are as thick as a waterlogged hound." The others chuckled.

Anorra took his face in her hands. "You said that once we were back together…" her voice trailed off, and Luik gazed at her in spellbound amazement.

The Most High had done this. He had done all of this. One moment Luik had been at the end of himself, running headlong into the face of death with his men—the next he was sitting beside his beloved, both healed of their wounds and ready to face the future.

"Anorra, my love, I have never had eyes for anyone but you. It seems that all along I knew you were my rib, even as a youth. And now, unsure of what tomorrow will bring, I want nothing more than to meet it, and whatever days that follow, with you beside me. It is my soul's desire."

She gazed into his face longingly, tears filling her eyes.

"Anorra, I've asked this before, but not in the clearest of ways. I—I…" He hesitated. "Will you be my wife? Will you marry me?"

"Oh, aye," she giggled and pressed her forehead against his, hot tears streaming down both of their faces. "It is my soul's desire as well. I am yours!"

Luik laughed and the two embraced, accompanied once again by shouts and toasting. It was a long time before the congratulations subsided, each man taking his turn at kissing Anorra on the cheek and pounding Luik on the back, making their way around the board.

When everyone had eaten and drunk their full, Li-Saide raised a hand and called for silence. A sobriety fell on everyone, the echo of their revelry dying away down the halls.

"While I couldn't be happier for the new couple, I need not remind us of the task ahead. Time is of the essence, so let us not tarry needlessly. Luik and Anorra," he faced them, "words cannot describe the overwhelming joy we all share at your proposed union; truth be told, I don't know a man or woman among us who did not see it coming." The

CHAPTER 30 | RESTORATION

men grunted in acknowledgment, pounding their fists on the board. "But, as you can imagine, it must wait yet a little longer.

"The White Lion has rescued us. The Great King has stepped off His throne as was prophesied in the days of old, and has come to set His Creation free. But more, He has come to confront our enemy and defeat him. He has come for the Keys of Life and Death."

The group looked at him and then to each other. No one had ever heard of the items—these *keys*.

"What do you speak of?" Fyfler inquired.

Li-Saide turned to Fane.

"The Keys of Life and Death," Fane spoke up, "hold unspeakable power. They command the destiny of all created souls, enabling the Keeper of the Keys ultimate authority to judge the living and the dead. Until now, Morgui has held them, given over to him when Adam fell on Earth. But the White Lion has come for them. They are rightfully His. But He had no right to acquire them until the debt was first paid in full."

"What debt?" Jrio asked.

"The peshe debt," Gorn put in. The group looked at him. "Did I not teach you enough?" Gorn looked surprised. "Luik, what happened to you when you rescued Rab on the strand outside Kirstell? And Rab, how many times did you rescue Luik in kind? All our doubting, the places we made for fear and disobedience against the Most High, forged an everlasting debt, evidenced by pain and the absence of His Spirit, a debt only paid by blood."

"Blood?" asked Rab.

"Life is in the blood," Li-Saide said. Seeing no one understood, he continued. "When we grieve the Great God, we effectively kill the very thing that He breathed life into. Relationship. Because of our disobedience, even in the smallest way, we deserve to die—to shed our imperfect blood. Then it must be atoned for by *perfect* blood. The only way we even have a chance at living is if one life is exchanged for ours."

"Thus His sacrifice," Luik muttered.

"What was that?" Jrio asked.

"His sacrifice," Luik said. "He gave up His perfect life on Earth to meet the requirements of those who peshed. He gave His life in exchange for theirs."

"Not just for those on Earth," Li-Saide said. "For us, too."

"But we never fell," Jrio said, trying to grasp everything.

"Nay. We *did*," said Li-Saide. "For it was written that the Great God would die to reconcile unto Himself both things below and things above, both in Athera and on Earth, *all* of Creation."

"Ad did not fall away," Fane put in. "He chose life for us all. However, each of us still had the choice *for ourselves*. And it was only a matter of time before one of us entertained the thought. As Morgui's presence increased, so too did our propensity to withdraw from the presence of the Most High. It was not *because* of Morgui, but he was certainly an influence. Just another hand on the hammer."

A pregnant pause filled the room. No one stirred as eyes looked down, searching the table and the floor between their feet. It was Luik who spoke next.

"So even we, Dionia's pride, are in need of a Savior. Even without Morgui, we would have eventually chosen a path leading away from the Most High. Is that what you're saying?" He looked to Fane, and then to Li-Saide.

"That is what I am saying, for that is the truth of it," Li-Saide replied. "He is Good. We, my friends, are not."

"Which leads us to the battle yet to come," Gorn spoke up. All eyes turned to him. "The White Lion rescued us from Haides. Yet do not forget his command to Morgui."

"Morgui is to bring these Keys to the plains of Jerovah then?" Jrio surmised. "Is that what He spoke of?"

"I believe it is so," Li-Saide said.

"But if the White Lion has commanded it, then why a battle?" Anorra asked.

"Aye," said a few of the other men.

"Because Morgui will not bow quietly," said Li-Saide. "He is too proud. He thinks he has won, but he knows his end as well as any who have read the Ancient Texts. The White Lion will crush him beneath his feet, and the serpent will bruise his heel."

"Then we can't lose," Jrio piped up.

The dwarf didn't reply.

"Can we?"

"The White Lion will not lose," Fane spoke up; "however, that does not mean we will be invulnerable." Fane seemed to want to say something else, but closed his mouth.

"The White Lion will claim what he has come for," said the dwarf. "And He will champion us at His side. But—" He paused, searching for the right words, looking to Fane, and wondering if this was the proper time.

"Go on," said Luik.

Still the dwarf hesitated. Finally: "I do not think He will stay."

There was a look of confusion shared among all those present.

"Whatever do you mean?" asked Anorra, unconsciously clutching Luik's arm.

Panic suddenly sprang to life and spread with ruthless speed. The Dibor gazed at Li-Saide, trying to put it together in silence, knowing better than to question their teacher.

"Aye, what is that you say, Chief?" asked one of the men in the back.

"What do you mean He won't remain? Where's He going?" asked another.

"Going to abandon us?"

"Why wouldn't He? He never came to our rescue before when we needed Him the most. Look at everything He allowed to happen!"

"Say, where is the Lion now?"

The observation sent a murmur throughout the rest of them, small conversations sparking everywhere. As Li-Saide watched, wishing he had remained silent after all, an onslaught of questions erupted to the point that Li-Saide could not silence them.

Something was happening. Something they could not foresee, but could feel. Fear was tearing into their hearts like the head of an arrow. Where just moments before there had been hope for the future and joy in feeling renewed life, it had been overrun like a storm front, giving way to a rain of doubt. So fickle is man.

Luik looked to Gorn with a nod.

In one swift movement Gorn withdrew a long dagger from beneath his robe and buried the point deep into the board in front of them. "Enough!" he roared.

Every man closed his mouth.

Luik waited for the group to compose themselves before speaking. "I will not tolerate such behavior among you." He eyed the lot of them. "You are the Lion Vrie. Together, we are the last hope of Dionia. Further,

301

I will not let you defame the Name of the Most High by entertaining arguments and gossip. The day of the White Lion has come, and He will not leave us without giving us what is needed to succeed. He is faithful. Anyone who wishes to disagree with that statement may retire to his home now. I have no use for the weak-minded."

No one dared move. The King had spoken, and they suddenly felt ashamed.

In truth, the power Morgui wielded was more far-reaching than they had dared admit. His strength was not just seen in his vast army of Dairne-Reih, but took wings in the unseen realm, plaguing the minds of any man or woman not attentive to his ventures.

"The White Lion is loose in Dionia," Luik said at last. "And when He roams, the enemy quakes. If we have ever felt the sting of our adversary before, it will be a fond feeling compared to what will be unleashed. He fears the White Lion. And his fear will drive him to be more heinous than we could ever imagine. For fear without regard for self-preservation is hate…more dangerous than any other evil.

"The Most High *will not* leave until He is sure the battle is won. Do not be dismayed. And do not be bought by the tactics of the enemy. His days are numbered, and the King has come at last."

He searched the room for doubters, his eyes staring deep into their souls. He glared at each man, willing contention to rise up. But none surfaced, and all remained calm. He knew that if they were to succeed, if they were to follow the White Lion into battle, he must keep a tight rein on his men and their thoughts. With victory surely within their grasp, the battle would now be in the mind. And Luik was sure Morgui was well ahead of him. Despite the warband's miraculous healing, their gratefulness would be lost in an instant when the faithfulness of the Mighty Father was questioned.

Morgui had won this skirmish. And Luik was fed up. "We will reconvene tonight in the Great Hall. You are dismissed."

Chapter Thirty-One

FACE TO FACE

Luik had begged Anorra for an hour alone. As much as it pained him to leave her for even the blink of an eye, he had questions that could only be answered by One. Although he had hardly sensed the presence of the Most High since—well, since longer than he could remember—he reasoned that perhaps the White Lion's presence meant a new dawn for Dionia. Perhaps, he hoped, even returning to the way things used to be.

Anorra eventually conceded but maintained that Luik was not to go beyond the King's Gate but remain within the palace. So he took his leave in the gardens.

Despite the chaos that seemed to entwine its fingers into the fiber of the land, summer had returned in full force. The streams welled up from inside the mountain and fed all the pools and fountains in the gardens, the vibrant sound of water massaging the air. Birds added the much-loved melody of summer, and the leaves rustled in rhythm as the breeze coaxed them to song.

Fragrant flowers blossomed under Luik's gaze, and all around him the grass was lush and green. He walked steadily down the pathways of his forefathers, feeling the cool stones underneath his feet. The track inevitably led him into the King's Garden and along the ancient portico.

He found a comfortable place beneath an aged ash and closed his eyes, allowing the warmth of the afternoon to soak his skin before the breeze brushed the heat away.

Luik's thoughts swirled about him. The events of the past few days seemed surreal. Everything had happened so quickly. Dionia had deteriorated faster than he could cope with, and then had halted in a single moment. Haides itself had swallowed him whole, only to spit him out. And now everything felt so close to an end.

But what bothered him the most was the sudden appearance of the Most High. While his heart was grateful for the presence of their Mighty King, a deep emotion plagued him, one he was at odds with. And truthfully, he was afraid of admitting it.

His memories filled with visions of Adriel, once gleaming high atop the peninsula, now a charred pile of rubble, razed to the ground in a single, nightmarish day. So many had perished. So many had given their lives in a battle that would be but the first of many. The Kings of the East had been swallowed by Morgui's power. Lair and Thorn had perished together. Even Hadrian had succumbed to evil over time.

Narin would forever entomb the souls of the children he had wept over. The memory was one of his most bitter and brought the taste of death to his mouth even now. He would forever curse the well in Trennesol and scorn the Somahguard Islands for taking Najrion and Gyinan from him.

Kirstell—his beloved Kirstell—had become a place of mourning. Once filled with the joy of his youth, the island was torn asunder and marred by the hand of the evil one.

And Grandath. What could be said? The ancient halls were now barren, their contents but dust. Thad and Thero had found their resting place in the flames above, and Brax was entombed below; the Tree of Life was destroyed, prostituted and then devoured by the hate of the enemy. The remains of so many were mixed with the ashes that covered her, their memories forever stained in blood.

So many questions plagued Luik's mind. Unanswered questions that deserved replies. Demanded replies.

The White Lion had healed the wounds of his body, and those of Gorn and Li-Saide and the rest of the warband. Anorra's eyes had been completely restored. Anondo had been touched even while lying in his bed high in Mt. Dakka. And countless more had surely found their healing in the night. Yet others had perished, his kinsmen fallen in battle. Would the White Lion bring them back to life? Was His hand short in that he could not restore life to the fallen? To Lair and Thorn? To Brax and Gyinan?

Luik had thought he had no more tears to cry, yet more came. For what he could not understand—what he simply could not wrap his mind around—was why, of all times, the White Lion had come *now*.

Why now?

"Why did You not come sooner?" Luik screamed. "How could You stand back and let this happen?"

Luik pounded the air with his fists, suddenly overwhelmed.

"Where were You? Were You not watching? Did You not see?"

The heat in his face was strong. Shame broke over his head. For the very thing he had admonished his men for was what he himself had hidden in his heart.

"How could You let so many die? You let them perish! And then what? You come at the *end*? For what?"

Luik curled up and fell to his side, lying on the ground. He sobbed, gasping great breaths of air only to loose a tirade of tears and mucus.

"Where were You?" He shouted. "I needed You! Where were You when I needed You?"

He beat the soft ground with his fist as the full extent of his desolation burst over him like an ocean wave.

"*We* needed You…needed You…"

Soon his words became unintelligible. His chest heaved but all that came out were whimpers.

And of all things, he could not figure out why he was still alive. Why plague him with a dream that does not come true? What sick manipulator prophesies death only to take the lives of others but leave the subject untouched?

"I want—to die," Luik finally said in a long, troubled exhale.

His body relaxed, and the torrent of emotion subsided. His chest rose, drawing in deep breaths that then left through clenched teeth and spittle. He moaned softly under the powerful wave that pressed him further into the grass.

He had seen more than any other before him. He had endured more than the Gvindollion could have ever dreamed in their worst nightmares.

Had they foreseen this? Would they still have gone through with training the Dibor if they had? Luik had carried the weight of a nation on his shoulders and had seen her through her darkest hour.

Through it all he did not even see that the White Lion had slain him just as he had dreamed; not physically, as he'd presumed. But in heart. And in soul. And perhaps there had been no other way than this: that if the Mighty Father would not spare His own Son to accomplish His aim, how much less would He spare others for another pursuit?

Was it all for Luik? Perhaps not. But was Luik for the slaying? That is a more worthy question. A wounded man is of value to the Maker.

Such slaying of the soul does not come as man expects it. And it does not leave us in any condition we could have imagined. For surely any foreknowledge of such events would melt even the strongest heart, and any purported outcome would distract the most resolute will with its value. For it is the mind He longs to offend—not for hating it—but for revealing the heart. The heart, which He values far more.

"I am a dead man who yet breathes," Luik said at last.

"And that is what I wanted all along," came a powerful Voice from above.

Luik's eyes spread wide, and he gasped.

The White Lion stood over him, gazing down onto his trembling form. Luik fought to sit upright, unsure if his eyes betrayed him. He squeezed them shut and then reopened them, wiping away the tears with the back of his hand. The Lion was real.

Luik's heart thumped in his chest like a boulder careening down a mountainside. Had his King heard the animosity in his questions?

But it didn't matter. He would know anyway. Nothing could be hidden from His gaze. Rather than hide, Luik fumbled forward, blundering headlong into the tumultuous issues of his heart.

"Where were You?" he asked in a strangled voice, the tears welled up his throat again. "When I needed You? When *we* needed You?"

A long silence filled the garden air, interrupted only by the fragrant sounds of summer. Luik knew for sure he had offended his Creator. Discipline would come. The White Lion sighed, heavy warm breath washing over Luik's body. He shuddered. Finally, at long last—Luik hanging on every beat of stillness—the White Lion spoke.

"Where were you when I made the stars, Luik son of Ragnar?"

The Lion's Voice was firm yet not without compassion. Yet the question hung in the air like a gauntlet thrown.

Luik could not accept the challenge.

"And where were you when I created the land and filled the depths with water? Did I consult you for counsel or seek you out for instruction? Who guided my hand when I formed you in your mother's womb?" He paused. A beat. "Did I ask you for your opinion when I knit your very soul together?"

Luik looked on, dumbfounded. He did not know what to say.

The Lion waited.

Luik finally looked away, shame heavy on his shoulders.

"I—I..."

The magnificent Creature exhaled again, something heavy on His heart. Luik heard through the action and looked up. "I plague You, I know," was all he could offer. Words spoken in true humility.

"It is more than that," the Most High replied. "It seems that My Creation forever asks me questions, yet never stops to answer those that I first ask."

A surge of remorse spread through Luik's body like ink, staining the far reaches of his conscience. "I am—forgive me."

"My ways are not your ways," the White Lion said, not yet acknowledging Luik's apology. "And My thoughts are not your thoughts. My ways are above your ways."

He lingered there. Then went on.

"But there is coming a time, very soon, when you will have My mind—My heart on the needs of your day. Forever changed, you will be. That is, *if* you remain in Me as I will be in you."

His words were mysterious, yet Luik felt he discerned the meaning in his heart. He received the impartation.

As if hearing Luik's true thoughts the White Lion said, "I am sorry for your losses, Luik, my son." The kindness in His voice brought tears to Luik's eyes. "It was never My heart for you to suffer. For any of you to suffer." The Lion looked up then, a sense of regret in his tone. "Nor was it ever My will for you to choose as you have—you and those before you. Those beside you."

"Your will?"

"My will is good. Pleasing. Perfect," said the Mighty King. "I do not err and I do not change. And yet, I cannot create a man to love Me. I cannot make him do what I want."

Luik thought. "I don't understand."

"Luik, you ask Me questions yet do not answer My own. In the same way, you question why I have permitted mankind to endure hardship. Why I have allowed hardship, even atrocities to occur. Why I have let men go down to Haides, even sent them there myself.

"Yet I want to know, was it I who welcomed evil into this place? Was it I who opened the doors for the enemy? Am I the one who controls man when I myself made him with a free will?

"Mankind speaks of control and blames Athera. Their pride causes them to point a finger at Me, when it is they that have chosen their own course." The Lion's voice suddenly grew louder and Luik shook. "Again, I say, answer My questions. Where were you, son of man?"

Luik quivered in his skin. He felt naked and open. There was no place to hide. He could not retreat nor fake a reply. The Great Lion would not move until Luik spoke.

He gave up. Who was he to question the Maker of All Things?

"I was not there."

"Nay, you weren't."

And that was the truth of it.

It was then and there Luik realized his great misconduct. Of all those to blame, he had betrayed the One who least merited it…who, in fact, remained blameless. The actions of Creation did not warrant one act of grace, not one sole merciful deed. They had disobeyed. That they were even left to live was clemency itself.

"I am sorry," Luik uttered, looking into the Lion's blazing yellow eyes and then hiding his face in his knees, unable to match His gaze. Luik could only hear the pounding of his heart in his ears and the rustle of the leaves above. Time stood still as he waited for the verdict. The Righteous Judge had every right to slay him for his treason; Luik's dream foretold it. The White Lion's wrath was equal to the task, and Luik knew he had erred greatly. He had insulted the very One whose Name he had sought to guard. He had been weighed, measured, and found wanting.

He deserved…

"I forgive you, my son."

A breath.

Those words…

…those amazing words…

…were all he needed to hear.

"And I love you. I have seen your every hardship. I have ever been near you. Yet now you know what it means to die."

"I do?" Luik questioned.

"A man dies a deeper death by living with what he knows than dying with what he doesn't."

"So, You're not going to slay me?"

The Lion looked as though he grinned. "Your dream was meant to serve one purpose, Luik: to bring you to a place of surrender, where it was no longer your will driving your life ahead…but Mine. And more than that, know this: that your dream was not meant to speak of your death, but of your *dying*."

Luik grew puzzled. "I don't understand."

"You have come to a place of true surrender, to My life and will being accomplished through you. Even *in* you. But do not be deceived. For before you reach Athera, you will die many more times. Daily.

"In Dionia you began with Me in control. Yet over time you gave way to fear—to your own will. Control. You relied on your own strength and not Mine. And that is the tendency of all flesh: to do it in their own power."

Suddenly all was clear. At last Luik understood. This life, every breath, was not even meant for him…for his own pleasure. It was meant for the Most High's. Anything outside of that was an offense to the Great God.

"So then, what You're saying is…" Luik mulled over his thoughts only briefly, "…that all You really wanted was *me*."

"That's all. In life or death. Just you. For he that finds his life will lose it, and he that loses his life will find it. For when you lost your life—there in that place—you found Me.

"I know how you have suffered, Luik. I was not far from you. And I have suffered in kind. Even today, I have known ultimate suffering. For one reason: to say that I have done everything necessary to win My Creation back to Me. I have suffered more than they ever will. I have taken their errors upon Me and thus also paid their penalty for their wrongs."

"On Earth? Then Morgui killed You indeed?"

"Far from it!" replied the White Lion. "He stole nothing. For My life was not his to take—but Mine to give."

"Then You did suffer?"

"At the hands of My Creation, aye. Morgui thought he had won. But he did nothing short of releasing Me to forever amend the breach between My Beloved and Me. Death has no more victory. I have stolen its sting."

"Then You have come for the Keys of Life and Death?"

"It is as you have spoken. I have paid the price for them, something Morgui could never do. He was never a threat to My will, only to My Creation. And if they will die to themselves and find life in Me, than his roaring threats will be seen for what they truly are. Empty. I have made a way where there was no way."

Luik hadn't noticed, but his strength had returned. The deep sorrow in his soul had been replaced, filled in by an indescribable peace. He made to rise and stand before his King, brushing his tunic out and squaring his shoulders.

"So there remains the issue of these Keys. May I inquire of You, my Lord?"

"Morgui has taken possession of something of Mine. And I want them back. Adam took the Keys into his own hands, by his own choice, ultimately surrendering them to the enemy. I have paid the price for them by offering My own life for their return. But I want Morgui to remember who suffered the penalty for his theft. So I will not be the one to finish the battle here in Dionia."

"You—*you won't*?"

"You will, Luik."

"I will?" Luik was dismayed, hand to his breast.

"I must make sure that all men know what has been done for them. No longer will death swallow them whole or keep them from My Father's presence. To ensure this, I will prove that the enemy has no hold on Me, nor those who call upon My Name."

"But the enemy wages war *here*, Most High. Here in Dionia. What better place to defeat him? Why leave?"

"My son, let Me ask you. What better way is there to defeat an enemy that has slain you?"

"Why, to defy him in death," he thought aloud. "But is that possible?"

"For Me it is," the Most High replied. "For I intend to rise from the dead."

Luik felt the words shudder through his body; unspeakable power resided in them. "So You have been defeated on earth, yet You live here?"

"I live here only to secure the future of My Creation, your future and of those that follow. In two days I will return to Earth and do what the enemy does not expect. I will conquer death itself."

Luik's thoughts raced, trying to wrap his mind around everything. "Then, we can defeat Morgui without You?"

"You will hardly be without Me, dear Luik. Until now you have felt My presence around you. You have known Me daily, and I have filled your world with wonder and life. Yet you have not known Me to the fullest. Surely I walked with you. I have always been among you. But that Presence, even what you see before you now, can be taken from you, as you have felt…as you will see. But I must leave so that you may know Me in fullness. Before I was *with* you, but soon I will dwell *within* you."

Luik hardly understood the full import of His words, yet he somehow took great comfort in them. He trusted whatever the White Lion said, though he did not understand it in the slightest. And he knew better now than to question Him.

"In two days time we will meet Morgui on the plains of Jerovah. There you will fight him."

"Me?" Luik replied. "But I am just a man."

"And he is just a fallen angel, one whom I have bested."

"How long can You stay?"

"I will stay to watch it begin."

"But, Lord—"

The White Lion growled with intolerance.

Luik stepped backward, almost falling over.

"My grace is sufficient for you, Luik," the Lion uttered in a deep voice. "Did you not hear Me? I will be with you *always*, for when I leave I will be *in you*. And then, only then, will you be unstoppable. Unshakable."

"I'm sorry, my King."

"Do not be sorry. Be victorious. Give everything. Endure anything. Just as I have done. That is the way of my Kingdom, that is what I've called you to. Nothing less."

"Aye. Nothing less." Luik bowed.

"I will return to you tomorrow, to the Great Hall. We will discuss the battle plan together. I have some ideas. But I want to hear yours."

Luik stammered, thinking he misunderstood his Maker. "You— You want to hear mine?"

"I did not create your genius for naught."

"Right," Luik grinned between red cheeks. He looked up longingly to the Lion's eyes and noticed that, despite their strength, there was a deep softness there. "Tomorrow then."

"Tomorrow."

The massive Lion drew in a deep breath and then turned away toward the center of the garden, His fur rippling like a soft tide.

"Where will You stay tonight?" Luik spoke up, surprised at the sound of his question.

The White Lion stopped and looked back. "I have no place to rest My head tonight, Luik. But I have not seen Dionia in a time and look forward to roaming the lands I once made with Ad. As I recall, the starlight that soaks Bensotha valley is particularly lovely, is it not?"

All at once Luik was taken back to the days of his youth. He remembered midnight walks under the starlight with Hadrian and Fane and Anorra during Jhestafe-Na. Long after the festivities had subsided for the evening—participants exhausted from eating and talking and playing— he and the others would steal away into the cool night air and lie out, just watching the stars glimmer. Captivated by their beauty.

Standing there with the Lion, he did not remember the last time he had seen the valley, soaked in the blood of his countrymen, riddled with their corpses and bones; he did not recall the streams running red, or the trees hewn and burnt black; he did not feel the immense loss that bit into the flesh of his soul.

He only saw the magnificence.

"None lovelier," Luik said distantly.

The White Lion nodded and then turned to leave once more, pausing a last time.

"I'm proud of you, My son," he said. "Well done."

The words had the effect of an ocean wave washing over him, and brought him to his knees. Emotion welled up from deep within. He sobbed for the ultimate fulfillment of all he had endured. Of all he had faced. The comment was so unexpected. So fleeting. Yet it carried the power of eternity in it.

The pride of his King. Of his Creator.

Well done.

Luik felt as though chains had bound him for such a great length of time that he couldn't remember a day without them; now, in light of the King's words, they were gone. Released from his neck, wrists and ankles, falling away to nothing. Nothing.

Luik was free.

It was all he could do to speak through the hot tears. "C'symia." He looked up, but the White Lion was gone.

Chapter Thirty-Two

TREASURES BEFORE THE STORM

"I spoke with Him."

Anorra pulled away after the warm embrace. "What?"

"I spoke with the Most High in the garden," Luik added. He brushed a strand of her blonde hair behind her ear.

"That's good, my love," she said, pulling herself back into his chest. "I knew you just needed some time with Him."

"Nay, I mean I spoke with Him, face to face. He came to me."

Anorra leaned back again and stared him. "You mean—"

"He was in the garden, Norra. He stood with me there."

Her eyes glowed in wonder.

"He was magnificent. I never imagined Him so captivating."

"What did He say?" she asked as if a little girl again, delight singing in her countenance.

"We spoke of many things. Of things past and things to come."

But his response made her impatient. "Like what?"

"Like Earth and why He must leave."

"Leave?" She reeled. "Whatever do you mean?"

The two of them sat on a seat mounted high atop one of the palace turrets, watching the sun set under the eastern sky. He told her everything he could remember of their conversation in the garden and spared no detail of the majestic Lion's appearance. She hung on his every word; before her was her second love speaking of her first Love.

Her life was full.

The day had been primarily consumed with the affairs of the city and its people. There was much celebration for Anorra's return, and that of the Lion Vrie, despite the tragedies suffered in Ot. But by far the news of the day was the appearance of the White Lion. Though only those in Haides had seen Him, and now Luik—which no one other than Anorra knew about—word spread quickly of the Great King's arrival. And what an effect it had!

The tide had turned.

Dionia had been slipping into a dire state, one in which people were ruled by unseen fear. Anxiety lingered in the doorways of every home, both the dwellings of the living and those empty, their owners deceased or *taken*. Battles were lost more than they were won. Women and children shrieked at their losses when the warbands returned, their husbands and fathers and brothers absent. The presence of the Most High was a faded memory, a story only told to doubting children, conveying what life *used* to be like. Not what it was. Or ever would be again. It seemed that everything had been lost. And if there was indeed anything left, it too would be stolen. Of that they were certain.

But everything had changed now.

In a single day, the crushed spirits of those in Mt. Dakka had been set ablaze. Though they had not even seen Him with their own eyes, merely the rumor of the Most High's physical return to Dionia had become a beacon of absolute hope. Pure hope.

Their eyes were bright again. Children gathered around hearth fires that evening, listening intently to what their parents had learned on the street. It was all that was talked about around the board, and all that was discussed in the markets. Anorra had been rescued, and she was whole. Luik was safe within Mt. Dakka with his warband. And all the free peoples of Dionia were gathered together, awaiting the commands of their kings, with Benigan taking the place of his fallen brother, Brax, as King of Tontha.

It seemed the overwhelming thought was a simple one: Nothing was impossible.

When Luik finally finished recounting his visit to Anorra, she sat for a long time in awed silence, picturing the encounter as if she had been there herself. She longed to see the great White Lion. To touch Him. Perhaps she could sit with Him tomorrow when the battle plans were discussed. Surely Luik would permit it. But for now her thoughts lingered on the man before her, the one she had come so close to losing.

"Will you be my bride, Anorra?" he spoke up.

"Why, Luik," she paused dreamily, "you already asked me this."

"I know, but I wanted to ask you again. You were lost, Anorra. And now you are found, and I want to ask you again. I want to hear you say it again."

"I would marry you today," she exclaimed, "but for the battle ahead. You would not be fit to fight."

"Then let it pass, and I will be yours forever."

Anorra took on a pseudo air of authority. "So be it," she ordered in a low, kingly voice.

They were left undisturbed atop the turret as a brilliant canopy of stars appeared above them. The city below sparkled with lanterns, and singing could be heard coming from the Great Hall. All was as it should be. And even though so many questions remained unanswered, the people of Dionia knew that everything was going to be all right. Their King had returned. Yet…how long would He stay?

• • •

The next morning went much like the previous, save without the verbal contention. Everyone gathered in the kitchen and embraced the others as bread was broken in genuine thankfulness. But what was not asked aloud was surely asked in secret. Doubt is a bitter enemy, one hard-fought.

While many a man would have seized any chance to speak up and voice the fears of their heart—fears Luik had voiced to the White Lion only a day before—one simple thought held their tongues: The White Lion would meet with them all today.

But before He did, there was one relationship Luik needed to reconcile.

Luik found Fane just where he suspected, browsing the shelves of one of the only remaining libraries left in Dionia. Now that Ot was destroyed, whatever scrolls could be found elsewhere would be a precious rarity, prized among the people.

Mt. Dakka's Royal Library was not as large as some, but had other characteristics that made it unique. Built in the round, its domed ceiling was made completely of glass, fashioned by the Tribes of Ot on order of Tontha's first King. It was covered with steeply slanted boards during the inusslen to keep the snow from breaking it. Mahogany reading tables sat in clusters in the middle of a heavily carpeted stone floor as four balcony levels towered overhead, each abounding with scrolls.

Luik allowed the heavy oak door to latch behind him and moved into the center of the library. The hall was still, filled with the comforting smell of aged papyrus.

A voice floated down from up above. "Come to do some reading?"

Luik looked up and spun around. Fane's head stuck out over a railing on the second tier.

"I heard there were some things worth perusing here. Any recommendations?"

"The Wisdom of Kings," Fane pointed clear across the room to the other side. "Third level. They are exceptional."

Luik followed his direction and nodded with assent.

"Although I left a few on the tables just there. Feel free…" Fane waved his hand.

"C'symia," Luik replied and moved toward the tables. He found a few scrolls laid out, pinned down at the corners with clear balls of glass, flat on one side. He slid one of the stools out and sat; one was never meant to be comfortable while reading the ancient words. A plush chair would have been an insult to those who penned the lines. The words were the focus, never luxury.

Luik scanned the page and began reading. The text offered line after line of profound insight. After only two or three sentences he had to stop, searching out their meaning and dividing its truth. He was impressed at how the words probed his heart and soul. How any man could digest more than but one line in a day was beyond him. Surely these were written over great spans of time by great men, tested and tempered by the trials of life.

Avoiding the conviction each line brought, he pressed on, scanning down through the document. Then his eyes stopped after reading a particular statement, one which he reread aloud.

"A king's lips are the mouthpiece of the Great God; they should never betray justice or righteousness."

Luik heard his own voice echo up through the tower and dissipate into silence. He felt the sound convict his heart, realizing that these words were not just for any man, though they could be, but were for him as a King. Dionia's High King.

He lowered his head and knew then, as he had before, that he was guilty of this fault where it concerned Fane; he had betrayed his friendship with his brother by not listening to wise counsel.

A hand rested on Luik's shoulder. He raised his head.

Fane looked down at him, a peaceful expression on his face.

"I am indeed sorry, my friend," Luik said.

Fane did not reply, knowing there would be more.

Luik went on, "I have wronged you in this way. As it says here, I have done what a king should never do. And I am sorry for it." He sighed. "You would forgive me and have me as your swordbrother once again?"

Fane squeezed his shoulder and easily replied, "I forgave you the day you spoke the words of harm to me. They harm me no more. All is right."

Luik stood then, embracing his childhood friend and savoring the restored friendship, though it had never been broken in Fane's mind…only in Luik's. Whether they know it or not, it is the heart of the offender that breaks the most deeply; for theirs is not only broken with the cutting, but is the broken heart that merits the cut.

"C'symia," Luik said and then released Fane. "I am sorry for not trusting you…you who have been ever faithful to the Most High and to Dionia. I should have never—"

"It is done," Fane said. "We will speak of it no more. And anything spoken of this event will only recall this day, of restoration and forgiveness."

"So be it," Luik conceded.

They stood smiling at one another until there was a knock at the door.

"Come," Luik spoke up.

The door moved open and a small face peered through the crack.

"Fia!" Luik exclaimed.

Fane looked between them, and then said, "I will leave the two of you alone." He bowed his head before Luik and then turned to the door, letting the girl in and closing it behind him.

"They said I would find you here," she said. She wore a purple dress and a white ribbon around her head to keep her blonde hair out of her face. Fatigue had racked her the entire trip from Kirstell to Tontha, and Luik could only imagine what she had endured to follow them to Kirstell in the first place. But now she looked rested, and her eyes were full of life.

"Fia, it is good to see you!" He knelt to hug her.

"As it is to see you, my King."

Luik held her off at the shoulders and examined her. "You look lovely today. Ready to meet the White Lion, I presume?"

"I had hoped so, only if…"

"If what?"

"If you'd allow me."

"Allow you—why, child, since it is a rare wonder that any man would follow his King across dangerous land simply to look out for his safety, how much more than a little girl."

Fia looked indignant at being called "little girl."

"A daughter of Eva," Luik corrected.

She smiled.

"Of course you shall meet Him, heroine of Dionia. You will be among the first!"

"Really?" Fia giggled then threw her arms around his neck. "Oh, c'symia, Luik!"

Luik chuckled and then pulled her away.

"Ta na and Na na always said you would favor me one day," she said. "And that's when I would know."

Luik was confused. "What do you mean?"

"That's when I would know it was safe to give you this." Fia reached behind her and withdrew a small blanket tucked in her sash. She handed it to him with a big smile. "They told me the story of how you found it in the tree and returned it to me."

Luik's heart beat fast in his chest. He had touched this blanket before. He knew it just by the feel of the fabric.

His fingers intuitively searched the corners for…

…R.M.C.

Ragnar-Meera-Ciana.

"Ciana?" Luik said, almost in a whisper. He looked up.

"Aye," Ciana giggled and shrugged her shoulders.

"But you—I mean, you were—" he reached out to touch her face. "It was always you?"

"I'm your sister."

"Then you always knew?"

"Aye, I told you I could keep a secret," she grinned, remembering their first meeting.

"But why didn't you ever tell me?"

"Father said it was better that Morgui thought I was dead, as he could not bear the thought of having another of his children in harm's way."

"But Fane told me you had been killed by Morgui!" He remembered the garden meeting with the Dibor and Anorra.

"He never told you that," she corrected him. "You concluded that yourself, and Fane let you move forward with your conclusion to keep me hidden."

"So they kept your existence a secret," he concluded. "As did Meera." *Amazing woman*, he thought.

"Aye, but no longer."

"No longer," he echoed and took her into his arms. They wept together, swaying in the library.

• • •

When Luik and the others opened the doors into the Great Hall, the White Lion was already there, standing beside the dais.

At first no one moved in. They stopped in the doorway and looked on with awe through the massive room. Luik collected himself and strode ahead, the others in the warband eventually following, never once taking their eyes from the Most High. They didn't know whether to fall prostrate or cry out and run to Him.

Luik moved forward, locking eyes with his Maker and smiled at the reunion, now the third time he had seen Him face to face.

"My King, allow me to introduce my men to You," Luik said and turned.

Every man was on his knees, heads bowed, as were Meera, Pia, and the young women in their midst.

Luik knelt as well. The short moments that followed were filled with wonder as Luik heard sniffles go up from those gathered. He had had his moment; this was theirs. *He* was here. Standing before them. There was no way to calculate one's own reaction. There was no preparing for such a moment, no reciting memorized lines or offering gifts as was often spoken of. Nor was it expected. One minute they were walking toward the Great Hall, the next they were in profound awe.

"Arise, Sons and Daughters of the Living God, Your Light has come!" The Lion's voice boomed in the Great Hall like thunder across the sky. His words filled them all with a sense of relief. But more. With hope. There was something so fulfilling about the Great God's voice... something that left them *complete*.

One by one they each stood, slightly lightheaded and most not daring to look up. But the White Lion commanded their attention, and soon each was looking at Him square in the face as if they were the only two beings in the room; many wiped tears from their eyes with the backs of their hands.

"I am honored by your presence, My people," the Majestic King said at last. "Thank you for coming." He turned His head and indicated the tables and chairs set up around the throne, still in place from the last planning meetings that had sent the warbands to Ot.

The people found their places among the seats, and the Lion insisted that Luik take his seat on the throne. He made to argue but thought better of it. The White Lion stood tall, towering over the throne and those seated like a living statue, marble white.

"I am sorry for each of your losses," he began, looking around. "I would have it known today that your misfortunes were never My desire, nor My intention. But such is the risk one takes when offering the gift of freedom. There are always two roads, one leading to death and the other to life. Without such a condition, there is no true demonstration of love. Even for Me."

The meaning of His words dawned slowly on the listeners. While they had been focused on their own decisions as of late, they never once considered the ramifications of His decisions. For them, He had chosen death so that they might live.

It was in that moment that all their issues with Him, whatever they may have been, were swept away. For none of their arguments, none of their complaints, drew the scale to their side in the slightest when compared with what He had sacrificed. With what He had endured.

"The days of mourning, however, are behind us. The days of victory are dawning. That is why I have come." The declaration sent a ripple through the crowd, each of them suddenly alive with a fire that burned in their bones. "Morgui has had his way with My people for long enough. They have suffered under the hand of his tyranny and today, I say, it shall be no more!"

And with that everyone stood up and shouted! Cheering filled the Great Hall from wall to wall. It was the release of a generation's suffering, of parents who had lost their children, of children who had lost their brothers, of a country who had lost their hope. Today, all was reconciled.

The White Lion allowed the victory cry to resonate and only continued speaking when the people sat back down. "I have come for what is Mine, The Keys of Life and Death, the keys to My Creation which Adam—Earth's Ad—took and eventually gave up. And I have come to make things right, by proving once and for all that death has no power over Me or those who call on My Name.

"Tomorrow at dawn we will meet the enemy on the Plains of Jerovah. I have come to Earth in the East, and so to Dionia in the West. As the sun rises, we will gather upon our foe with valiant force as the light meets the darkness. Morgui will not prevail."

He looked down at Luik.

"Gather all the fighting men in the city to the streets before the sun rises. Those women wishing to tend to the wounded may come as well." He looked to Anorra, and she smiled. "Daughter, your bow will be welcome. But stay by My side."

She bowed.

"Begging your pardon, Majesty," Luik said, "but Jerovah is many days away."

"I know your question, but we will not be traveling on foot. Just before dawn we will attack the enemy, but not as he suspects."

The White Lion then went on into great detail, sharing his strategy and then asking Luik and Gorn for their thoughts. Li-Saide also added notable wisdom, as did Fane, before the meeting was finally adjourned.

"If I am to remain by Your side, how long will you stay?" Anorra interjected as they were dismissed. Everyone hesitated and then discreetly sat back down. "I must know. For if You should leave," she alluded to the rumor spreading among them, "by whom should I stand then?"

The White Lion did not scold her for her indirect question. "I will stay for as long as I'm needed, until I am called elsewhere by My Father, to a field of greater importance. The truth is, Anorra, that I do not need to be present at all. I do so only for you—for you to see your vindication. For you to see justice served for the lives of those the enemy has taken." He let His words settle. "Know this, that when I do leave, I will send One after Me who will be with you always. For this reason, among others, I must depart."

Insisting that He be the last to leave, the entire company exited before Him, but not before Ciana ran up and threw her arms around the Lion's right leg. He lowered His head and nuzzled her, His whiskers tickling her body. She rubbed her face against His fur and then looked up, high up into His large eyes.

"I love you," she said so that only He could hear.

"Me too," He replied with a wink.

Anorra called for her, but the Lion gestured for the Princess to come to Him as well. Not one to disobey, she stood beside Ciana and embraced the same leg. He pressed His mane down so that it enveloped them both. His warmth surrounded them, and Anorra was overwhelmed with an emotion she could not put into words. It was…it was just too much. For how does one explain something never felt before but by comparing it to previous experiences, ones insufficient in their description of the new?

Before long Anorra and Ciana withdrew to where Luik stood waiting. The three of them walked to the exit, cast a last look to the White Lion, and then closed the doors to the Great Hall.

The next time they would see Him would be on the field of battle.

Chapter Thirty-Three

THE GATHERING

Luik hadn't slept at all.

He lay restless on his bed, anticipation stirring his mind. He was thinking through all that lay ahead of his people, all that he would face. And yet for all his worrying the outcome still eluded him.

Dusk was still a long way off when he rose and sent the messengers out on their errands. He figured it would take most of the pre-dawn hours to assemble all the warriors.

The messengers raced from the palace and spilled through the streets, knocking on doors and delivering the King's orders:

To Men of Dionia fit to fight: Be ready for battle within the hour. Meet outside the City Gate. Women wishing to tend the wounded are welcome.
~By order of the High King of Dionia, Luik son of Ragnar

Luik donned the armor he had worn only days before, now cleaned and mended. Despite the repairs, the rings of his chain maille shirt were stained with patches of rust and blood that no brush could ever remove, much like the memories he bore. The leather scales of his courbouilli were mixed and matched, the old and new blending together in a battle-weary vest. And the great helm of the Lion Vrie was far from its pristine beginnings, now a scratched and dented shell. No amount of buffing would ever remove the gouges on the metal—or the pictures in his mind.

He wore a red cape slung over his shoulder and strapped his sword belt around his waist. He fingered his Vinfae's handle and tried to repress the fear that came with it. So much blood…

Would this be the last battle he would fight? It seemed a meaningless goal, too long for the way things used to be. One could only swim upstream for so long before relenting to the pervading current and allowing it to carry a defeated body away. Exhausted. That was how he felt. Even with the promise of the Most High, he was tired of fighting. And truth be told, he did not want to fight today. It was the Luik of an earlier time that had longed for the battle, to charge headlong into the fray. Standing here now, all he wanted was to sit beneath a shade tree in Bensotha Valley and eat a piece of fruit. Talk with his family. Play rokla with his friends. And kiss his soon-to-be bride.

He looked at himself one final time in the long mirror.

"Perhaps today is the last battle," he said to himself. "Perhaps today it ends."

• • •

"A fine day for a fight," Jrio said as Luik entered the King's Counsel Room.

"Day? What have you seen of it, Jrio?" Kinfen asked. "It's as black as a Dairneag's soul out there."

The small group chuckled.

"And dawn will be coming all too quickly for us to see enough Dairneags," Gorn added. "What say you, King Luik?"

The warband welcomed him, and they moved around the table together, each man arrayed in battle dress. As per Luik's request, only the Dibor and a few of the Lion Vrie were gathered.

"I'm not sure where to begin today," Luik replied at last, "save that I hope we will see the inside of plenty of those black souls."

"Hey'a!" they all affirmed. He continued after they settled in their seats.

"I must confess I do not want to fight today." A hush fell over everyone. "I do not want to fight ever again. For all the knowledge I have gained, for which I am indeed grateful," he eyed Li-Saide and Gorn, "a part of me wishes I had never known it. However, my will has little to do with anything, and I am content knowing that.

"But if it is one more battle that sees Morgui to his fate, one more swing of my sword that brings freedom to the children I have yet to see, then I will rise to the occasion with zeal as if it were my first day. Truly, men, I have never been more proud of any group as I am of you. We have seen the face of death together, and yet we live. You have dared to place your lives in harm's way too many times to count, yet you sit here at my invitation ready to draw your swords again. I am honored among kings to serve with you. Ready to spill my own blood if called upon.

"These are humbling days for me to be sure. Never has my life meant so little…meant so much. But I recognize it is not about me. It is not about each of you. Our lives are but vapors, here one moment, gone the next. And what is our purpose? What is our destiny?

"I have never had such a full understanding of my life as I do today. I have been handed a gift, a chance to breathe, to love, to make decisions. Even to die. But it means nothing apart from one Person. The Great God.

"Unless my life—our lives—are lived in Him and for Him, they mean nothing. In and of themselves, they are meaningless. Even our greatest exploits, our fame and our legend, are what in the coming ages? Memories? And when memories fade? Then what?

"I confess to you all this day that my life is not my own. If the Great Father would require His own Son to go to death—His life in exchange for ours—then I can offer nothing less than my own life. Anything else would be an insult to His Name and bring disgrace to His Offering."

Luik caught the eye of his father, Ragnar. He saw fatherly pride in those eyes. And he longed for it. But recognition was not what Luik wanted; acknowledgement was not what he sought. He had had that.

"It is not my pride that brings Him honor; my pride is an affront to Him. It is not my convictions that earn Him honor; for that is pride again. It is not acts of heroism nor my righteousness. They, too, are dismissed when compared with what He has given up.

"Nothing can compare. Nothing. With what He has accomplished? With what His will has forged among the legacy of men? Our offerings are stale compared to the life He has laid down. The King of Glory sent to die in exchange for our freedom!

"I said that I do not wish to fight. But the truth is that I don't have to. The Most High is doing it all from here on out. My life is nothing to me if I do not have Him. If He wishes me to die, then so I die.

"Some might say I have given up. But I realize, this day, that I have given in."

Luik stared each man in the face, taking his time as he did so. He was measuring them—each of them—not against himself, but against the Most High. And each one was found lacking. He could see it now. Despite all their efforts, there was nothing to compare with the Great God. Nothing to compare with who He was...what He had done.

"My life is not my own," Luik said at last. "I am dead in Him. I don't even want me inside of me." He closed his eyes, not understanding what he was saying. But he had to say it. "I want Him inside of me. If it's me, then what do I live for? But if His Spirit lives in me, then I live for everything...I live for His sake...His will."

Silence once again consumed the room, and each man was left to his own thoughts. Luik gave them some time—gave himself some time—to think about what he had said. He felt as though no other words were important as these. As a King, there was nothing more imperative he could mandate than this.

Finally, Luik stood from his seat and the others followed. He withdrew his sword and said, "I am dead to myself, but I am alive in the Most High."

The men drew their swords and repeated the same words. In that moment they became invincible, in the present life and the next.

• • •

The Dibor walked the route out through the King's Gate and into the city below. The buildings lay in shadow, the only light cast upon their darkened exteriors coming from the lanterns scattered among the windows and a dark blue twilight waking in the western sky.

As they walked, the warband met up with other men headed south to the City Gate. Wives were kissed goodbye and children embraced. Soon the main thoroughfare was bursting with people, onlookers standing on the rooftops for a glimpse of the warriors. These were their fathers and brothers. These were their heroes.

All at once someone began cheering. Like a wild brush fire spreading through a dry valley, the praise took flight and sparked every street corner, open window, and rooftop until the entire city was ringing with tribute.

Luik and the others passed under the massive outer wall through the City Gate and into the open, stopping then to stare at the sea of men that had gathered. Countless heads turned to them as they stepped into the field, their faces consumed in the twilight. Before them were the valiant men of Dionia. Her protectors.

"I never knew she had so many," Quoin said from behind.

"Nor I," Jrio whispered, not wishing to disturb the majestic sight. "Nor I."

The warband slowed to take in the sight while the men of the city continued to pass beside them and find their places amongst the growing throng.

"They are so quiet," Fane spoke up, the only noise coming from those cheering within the city behind them.

"They're waiting," Li-Saide answered Fane's unspoken question. "Look."

They followed the dwarf's outstretched finger and examined the faces of the men more closely. They were not so much looking at Luik or the others as they were *looking around*. Their eyes searched the sky above, the mountains peaks to the south, and the western sky.

"They're looking for Him," Luik said.

"Aye, wouldn't you?" Kinfen asked. The Dibor looked to one another and smiled.

"Aye, I would," Jrio put in. "Most surely, I would."

Luik and the others remained just outside the gate, standing on the stone bridge while the final ranks of men descended and joined the army. The women and children in Mt. Dakka pressed up to the gate and flooded the ramparts, their eager faces looking out expectantly.

Luik raised a hand, calling for silence. The cheering subsided and the entire warband gave him their attention.

"Men of Dionia!" He listened to his voice echo out over them and drift into the mountain passes. He felt each pair of eyes fix fast on him. "Sons, each of you. Fathers, many. We wait for the sun to dawn on what will be the Day of days for our land, the beginning of a new freedom for our people. A new reign. You have seen Dionia through her darkest hour, and yet you still stand. For this, I can only commend you. Although I cannot guarantee your success individually—for no man knows what his next breath may bring—I do know this: The White Lion has come for us, to set us free, and to liberate us from the affliction of our enemy!"

He thundered out the last line and raised a fist skyward. The warband cheered as one, hope kindling afresh in their hearts.

Luik then turned to his leaders. "You know your orders," he said above the cries. "Be swift and mighty."

"Swift and mighty!" they said as one, making the sign of blessing as they departed to their places among the warband.

Luik faced the throng once more. He could see the sky lightening in the west. But something else caught his eyes to the east...

Fane followed his gaze. "A storm," he said.

"Aye, and a dark one at that," Luik added.

"Morgui controls the elements as before," said Li-Saide.

Luik nodded and then continued in his address to the rest of the men. "I am sending your kings and leaders among you. Listen to them as you would me. You each have a role to play, and you honor one another with your lives."

Luik could see the Dibor and Lion Vrie moving amongst the warriors, giving orders and grouping them off in hundreds and thousands. It was a strenuous task to be sure, but Luik had confidence in his men. They were, after all, the best.

Orders were passed back through the ranks, the details echoed over and over so each man could hear. The leaders explained the strategies just as they had been explained to them. The news was passed on until even those in the farthest reaches of the field had heard.

The western sky continued to lighten and Luik wondered if the task would be complete in time...before *He* arrived...

He felt a touch on his elbow, too graceful to be a boy's, too gentle to be a man's.

"I will be by His side," Anorra said softly.

"And your arrows watching my back," Luik replied without even turning.

"To be sure," she said. "There are a number of women who wished to come along. To help."

"We will be grateful. Keep them out of harm's way."

She hesitated. "I will…"

Luik sensed the concern in her voice and turned at last. Her yellow hair was bound in a tight braid, her face the essence of beauty to him. She wore a silver tunic that shimmered in the dawn light, made up of countless tiny plates that moved with her. Below that, leather breecs tucked into her tall boots and a knife lashed onto her belt. Her bow was in her left hand and two quivers were strapped to her back. He caught his breath, speechless in her presence. "I will be as the Most High wants me to be," he said finally.

She was not pleased with his response, but she knew it was as it must be. "I know." A half smile curled in her cheek. She would be glad when this day was through.

Something tugged at Luik's sleeve.

"It is time, my Lord," Li-Saide said. "He comes."

Luik turned toward the western sky and watched as an orange glow warmed the canopy, driving out the black of night. He was reminded of his dream just then, of the single star moving through the illuminated sky on its own. First it was hardly noticeable. But soon it gained speed. And descended.

"Hear me now!" Luik hollered over his army. "The Most High will meet with us in the blink of an eye, and we will be caught up with Him into the sky. When you open your eyes, you will see the enemy before you. Do not hesitate! Do not delay! Exact the vengeance that the blood of your children cries out for! Give him no quarter, and do not spare a thought for yourselves. This day must be won. And remember, He is with you always!"

Luik clutched his Vinfae and pulled it out slowly, with the sound of the blade drawing against the metal throat of the scabbard. When it was held aloft, the single sound was repeated thousands of times over, producing a song of war.

"What happens next?" Luik asked Li-Saide over his shoulder.

"How should I know?"

The candid response brought a smile to Luik's face. How should any of them know?

It was right then that everything slowed down—almost froze. Luik's vision panned outward as if leaving his body and swiveling out over his men. Then the angle pitched upward and addressed the western sky.

He could hear pounding in his chest.

His heart beat.

Or was it something else?

It beat like drums in the ground. Running.

Something was running toward him.

The intensity of the light beyond peaked, a single flare of sunlight piercing the darkness like a sword. Then everything around him turned white, bathed in light, until he had to shield his eyes. It was too intense.

He was too intense.

Chapter Thirty-Four

THE PLAINS OF JEROVAH

Morgui strode out from the burnt ruins of Grandath with his entire host of fallen lythla. As far as the eye could see, from one end of the Great Forest border to the other, countless Dairne-Reih emerged from the wreckage like black ghosts resurrected from the ashes. Their grotesque forms moved in measured rhythm, beat out by some distant drum. They marched into the eastern plain of Jerovah like giant locusts trampling tall grass. Their line was unbroken and deep, not a gap between them, stretching endlessly back into the charred remains of Dionia's Secret City—secret no more.

Morgui fixed his gaze on the massive army that lay across the horizon, a thin white line against the fading night sky. With every step he measured his opponent, seeing that they numbered far less than he had expected, a notion that pleased him. He counted the standard bearers and watched the small shreds of colored fabric wave against the pre-dawn sky. Men-at-arms stood in the front, mounted warriors behind them, and surely archers in the rear. It was poor judgment to let the men-at-arms lead. Ignorant. He would punch a hole through their center as if driving a spear through a corpse.

The commanders of Morgui's army, his warlords and generals,

flanked him on either side. Morgui acknowledged them with a nod, and they surged forward, running ahead. The mass of Dairne-Reih matched their pace and pulled away from their dark leader, leaving him in the rear.

Morgui stretched out his arms as wave after wave of his minions passed beside him. He could sense the power of his forces coursing through his veins. He could smell victory and the blood of flesh staining the soil of the ground. It would not be long. He had beaten the God of Athera once. It would end here. He would finish it today.

The gap between the two forces narrowed as the warm glow of the rising sun kissed the western sky. The enemy warband on the horizon was now a strong presence, the faces of men, half covered by their helmets and armor, eager for the battle clash.

The Betrayer exulted with expectancy, longing for the bloodlust to consume his head. He anticipated the sounds of battle as a child yearns for his mother's evening song. War drove him. Possessed him. He had no deeper desire than to destroy. To kill and steal, aye, but even more to utterly erase the memory of his foes' existence. To soak his fingers with their blood and hold their hemorrhaging bodies in his hands until their last breath was spent.

He had convinced so many that he did not exist, that he was not a threat. Some, even, that he could help them. Give them power. He laughed at the thought. What fools!

What ignorant fools…

When the last lines of his army passed him, Morgui began to run. He watched with insatiable greed as his demons spread out over the plain, greatly outnumbering the children of Dionia. And where was their great leader? Where was the Lion he had slain on Earth? Nowhere to be seen. A coward. Or perhaps dead in the spirit as well as in the flesh? Morgui could only hope as much.

As his Dairneags accelerated, anticipating the kill, the ground beneath Morgui's feet trembled. Horned feet smashed the tall green grass and tore at the dirt. A wake of broken field was all that was left behind. Jerovah would be burned before the day was through.

The two forces neared each other, both picking up speed. Morgui could see the heads of his leaders lower, their spikes and horns lunging forward, unsheathed from their folds of calloused skin. The monsters shrieked and clicked, the air alive with terror. Only a few moments more…

Up ahead Morgui saw the men running to meet the enemy, spears lowered and shields up. The cavalry followed behind, weapons poised to finish what the men-at-arms started. As if their feeble weapons would be a match for the power of Haides. Had they not seen what he could do? Not only in brute force, but in deception; had they not understood they were inferior in every way? Morgui, the Prince of Darkness, would remain supreme.

Just then a brilliant white light flashed against the backs of his hordes, so bright he had to shield his eyes. Blinded for but a moment, Morgui reeled around. He looked back toward Grandath. All he could see was the sun breaking the horizon, countless times more concentrated than he ever remembered. When had the sun ever been so powerful?

• • •

Gorn gripped the reins of his horse with two hooked fingers, his feet swishing against his horse's belly with ease. He held a long spear in his left hand and a sword in his other. It was not his custom to use a shield. Half of the other Dibor rode beside him, and the Lion Vrie led ranks of spearmen in front on foot. It was a good day to war.

As Morgui's demons appeared out of thin air, materializing on the outskirts of Grandath like vapors, he heard gasps go up from his men. It was an unsettling sight, but nothing he hadn't seen previously. He had slain them before; he would do so again.

Gorn had been given charge of the eastern flank, and he would not fail. As the demons formed up on the horizon, Gorn gave the order to march. When the enemy had spilled completely from the ash heap, he gave the order to run. The horses jogged slowly behind the men-at-arms, each beat of the hooves, each stride of the legs, bringing the warband closer and closer to the enemy host.

Gorn picked out Morgui at last, remaining in the rear of his hordes. The coward. The surge was led instead by Morgui's warlords, each imposing in its own right. He noted the extra pieces of metal armor they wore, even dull helmets that covered their faces, metal ported for their horns.

Gorn glanced over his shoulder. Countless archers kept pace behind the cavalry, bows held ready. Before the spearmen killed a single demon, the archers in the rear would be his first line of attack. And it must be timed perfectly.

The gap between the oncoming force and his was narrowing with every heartbeat. He felt the weight of his weapons rest easily in his hands, the reins running through his fingers. This was his moment. This was what he was meant for. Had been bred for. Though Dionia was not his home, he was prepared to die for her.

He called for the pace to increase, and his warriors did not disappoint. The men-at-arms reached for longer strides, and the horses switched to a slow lope. The archers remained close behind, ready for the order to draw and loose.

The enemy hordes greatly outnumbered his force. But the battle would not be played out here. His was but a single part. And if he died this day, he would die a King of Dionia. He couldn't have been more proud to breathe.

The warband was now at full speed. His timing was of paramount importance: too soon and the enemy would not be able to hear what was coming behind them. Too late and the plan would be wasted.

Gorn could see the horrific faces of the enemy, their eyes aflame and hungry for blood. They would spare nothing in the coming clash. They knew the White Lion would be among them. Likewise, their terror would be relentless.

Gorn braced for impact.

And then it happened.

• • •

Light consumed Luik's entire being.

He could see nothing else. Feel nothing else.

It was as if he was caught up in a cloud, suspended in midair by an unseen power, floating in brilliant white with no sense of direction. He thought he could hear music, even voices. But as soon as he found the melody, it changed. Or moved on.

Then a voice saying, "I am with you, Luik. I will always be with you."

He turned about, looking for the source. But his eyes met only a piercing bright light.

Just then his feet touched solid ground. It sloped away, and he had no choice but to run downhill or risk tumbling head over heels. He moved quickly and noticed the light betraying shapes up ahead, undulating forms in dismal hues of grey and black. He looked down. Long blades of grass were broken and trampled in dirt.

The thumping of his footsteps beat loud in his head, challenged only by his beating heart. Suddenly he was aware of others running beside him. Behind him. The ground leveled, but his pace increased in a strange exchange, as if it was no longer he that ran, but something beneath him.

Fedowah.

The sound of the animal's heavy panting filled his head, the rise and fall of the horse's head plainly in view.

The light that had consumed him moved forward and now illuminated the dark figures up ahead.

A flash of radiance.

Dairne-Reih.

He would know them anywhere. And there in their middle was a being he had first seen only three days ago. He would never forget.

Morgui turned around. Luik noticed something amazing: a look of sheer terror.

Morgui was afraid.

The brilliant flash diminished, the light of the dawning sun taking its place. It cast a yellow glow over the demon horde and covered over the eastern plain of Jerovah.

It had happened in an instant. Luik and the majority of Dionia's strength lay between Grandath and Morgui's army…

…directly behind them, and completely unexpected.

Luik raised his sword and screamed with all his might. He kicked his legs against Fedowah's ribs and the stallion lunged forward, reaching deep inside for each gain. The mass of mounted warriors to either side responded in kind and raced toward the back of their enemies.

They had them.

• • •

Morgui was furious. Furious that his enemy had tricked him. Furious that he had been caught off guard. Furious that he had been bested.

Furious that he was afraid.

Reacting more than thinking, he spun away from the advancing cavalry behind him and ran forward. He flung demons to his right and left just to make space, to advance farther into his pack and buy time.

The first battle clash was not the one he had been anticipating. It was not in front, but behind. The sickening sounds of metal slashing through flesh and bone met with the demonic screams of his minions as they were cut down in mid-stride.

Finally gathering his thoughts, aggravated that he had run, Morgui let loose a guttural command heard by all his forces. They slowed and looked to their leader. Then back to the ambush behind.

They were caught between two advancing armies of Dionia.

The next battle clash was Gorn's. And it was devastating.

• • •

It couldn't have been more precisely executed if they had practiced it a hundred times. Morgui's outburst caused such a freakish amount of disorder in the demon host that even those in the front of the advance slowed, most turning to address their leader.

It was all Gorn's smaller force needed to punch through.

The men-at-arms suddenly stepped aside into neat rows and allowed the skillful riders to slip by, horses reaching a full gallop with open space before them. At the same moment the archers planted ten shafts into the dirt and drew back their first arrow. They aimed high into the sky and loosed when the order came.

Thousands of black missiles sailed through the morning air with silent terror. They moved as one like a black cloud of death descending on the enemy. The projectiles found their marks, striking the heads and bodies of the Dairne-Reih with massive force. Demons were pummeled into the ground, shafts driving into skulls and pinning feet down where they stood. The monsters cried out in pain, only to find another shaft cutting through a gaping jaw or driving between a neck and shoulder. Joints split apart like eggshells, and bodies flew back like leaves blown by a gust of wind.

It was then that Gorn and the mounted warriors struck.

Their charge was furious, an attack without restraint. Gorn's mare dove headlong into the fray, fearless and bold. As she kicked and reared, Gorn plunged and slashed. He became a madman, swinging his blade at anything that moved. He could not find enemies fast enough and demanded his horse move on. But she needed little encouragement.

His spear met the soft neck of a mammoth Dairneag who spun and threatened to break the shaft in two. But Gorn was quicker and replaced the spear point with a sword blade under the armpit. The monster cringed in agony and fell sideways just as Gorn's mount brought him away from the fall.

Gorn heard the men-at-arms plunging in behind him, their polearms keeping the enemy at bay, gouging and slashing as they came. With each new foe the warband met, the demons seemed unsure whether to fight or pull to their master.

At last, Gorn thought.

• • •

Luik was surrounded by demons, but fear was nowhere in sight. Fedowah pressed forward through the crush as Luik hammered out blows with unrelenting tenacity. Most of the demons he met were terrified at having seen their warlord flee, so they emulated him. But when the forces became too compressed, they resorted to climbing over one another. It was here that the cavalry met them, dismembering them in their panicked attempt to escape.

Luik's Vinfae severed spinal cords and gashed the backs of necks, leaving heads bending forward over the chest until the demons stumbled over their own body parts. Fedowah jumped over each mangled heap.

All along the rear, the cavalry drove deep, digging a wound that would never heal. Dionia's warriors cut without quarter. There was no mercy in their blades. They had one chance and lived as if it was their last.

Luik heard another sound from deep within the pack—an order from Morgui. He could feel it.

He continued to serve his lethal pass to oblivion, catching even the swiftest demon with his whizzing blade. All of a sudden a face appeared between two demons in front of him. A face he did not know personally. But he didn't need to.

It was a man.

Morgui was sending the *taken.*

• • •

From the center of his surrounded army, Morgui looked to his warlords and gave the command to release the *taken*. It was early still, but he could feel the enemy's power dominating. He needed to do something. And quickly.

He would turn the tide.

Hidden in the initial emergence from Grandath, the *taken* had walked in the middle of Morgui's host, out of sight from any angle but above. They had been given weapons retrieved from the massacre in Ot and were more loyal to the ways of evil than ever.

Morgui grinned.

Luik would not know what to do. And when he finally figured out that there was no returning these souls to light, it would be too late. If Morgui could not crush their bodies, he would crush their spirits.

• • •

Gorn was in mid-swing, slashing at a Dairneag's neck, when he spied the first glimpse of a man's face somewhere in the tumult ahead. At first he thought it was one of his own men too far along in the advance.

But the man was not fighting. The Dairne-Reih ignored him.

Gorn's hesitation gave the demon enough time to shield against the blow. His sword bounced off the bone-armor. He ducked as a horned fist flew over him and collided with his horse's skull. The horse lurched forward, fighting the urge to slip into darkness. Gorn swung his leg over the side and leapt sideways as a second blow from the demon landed on the animal's neck. The horse dropped to the ground, broken.

Gorn took two bounding leaps, one to the left, one darting back to the right, and then leapt at the trespassing Dairneag.

The beast reached for Gorn.

But Gorn was too quick, dodging the death grip and inserting his sword between two ribs. The monster screamed and grabbed at the sword—but it was gone, only to appear on the other side of its body between another set of ribs. A third and final jab from his spear completed the task, and the Dairneag fell.

Its life was not equal to that of his steed, but Gorn was satisfied and wiped the blood from his brow. All round him his men fought, slashing at their marks. Arrows continued to soar overhead, riddling their targets with death.

Gorn looked back to the *taken* he had seen earlier. The lifeless man stood five paces away, now with two other men beside him. Their clothes were torn and limbs muddied. Sunken yellow eyes, bloodshot from no rest, peered out from twisted faces.

These were once his brothers…

Once.

These men had once eaten at table together. They had drunk from the same goblets of Dionia's choice wine. More, they had known the presence of the Most High.

Gorn had always been adamant about his stance against the *taken*. Destroy or be destroyed. They had forsaken grace.

But Luik had proved him wrong. And somewhere in his heart, Gorn wanted to prove himself wrong.

These were once his brothers…

Once, and perhaps again.

He lowered his sword.

"Come back!" Gorn yelled above the din. Battle raged all around him. "Come back to the Light!"

The three men stood as they were, their swords poised to attack.

Gorn tucked his spear shaft beneath his arm and stretched out his free hand.

"Come back, brothers!"

There was a pause.

Then the leader took a stride forward, sword listing to one side.

Gorn's eyes widened. Hope kindled in his heart.

It was working.

These were once his brothers…

• • •

Luik finished off two more demons before stopping short of a man standing by himself, left alone by the retreating throng. From atop his horse Luik looked down at the man and eyed him narrowly.

He had been fooled before. He would not again.

"I give you quarter, my friend," Luik hollered. "Come with us if you wish."

The man did not move.

Luik looked up and noted that the retreat was slowing. This exchange was costing them.

"I ask you again, come with us and fight again for the Most High."

Still the man looked as though he did not understand. He clutched a sword in his hand. Luik knew the blade.

Sword of the Lion Vrie.

It had been taken from their defeat in Ot, Luik surmised. Morgui had outfitted the *taken* with the spoils of battle. But how was this man holding it? It was meant only for the Great Warriors!

"For the last time, come back!"

Luik looked again to the churning mass of Dairne-Reih in the center. Something was happening.

They were regrouping.

Luik looked back to the man before him. The *taken* opened his mouth and tried to speak; finding the words seemed a task in itself. When he finally spoke, thick dregs of spittle dripped from the man's blistered lips.

"I do not know the Light," he replied and lifted his sword.

Luik watched as the man ran toward him, a strangled cry coming from his throat. He nudged Fedowah back in a turn, trying to avoid the wild attack. The man leapt forward, swinging his sword at Luik's legs.

Luik kicked hard and landed a blow on the man's shoulder, knocking him to the ground. Then Luik looked up to the army. They were coming: a slow advance now headed his way.

"Come on, man! Why do you resist the Most High?" Luik spun Fedowah around. But the man spit in the mud and struggled up.

"I do not know the Light!" he seethed. He swung his sword again, coming short of Luik.

"You are Dionian! You have tasted His Goodness! You have known His Love!"

The man swung again and again.

"Stop fighting!" Luik yelled. *Can he not see?*

The man stared up at Luik, rage twisting his face. His chest rose and fell in gasping breaths; blood dripped from the corner of his mouth.

Luik moved forward, the army marching toward him, more *taken* now in the front lines. This was insane.

"He'll take you back!" Luik yelled.

But the *taken* man was possessed beyond understanding. He raised his sword and lunged forward. "I do not know the—"

An arrow shaft drove through his neck and stopped halfway, lodged in bone. The rest of the arrow's energy spun the man backward off his feet and onto the ground.

Luik looked behind him. An archer waved, Fane standing beside him, guiding the shot. Fedowah reeled around, uneasy with the situation, and Luik nodded a doleful thanks to the pair behind him.

"My King," Jrio cried, "watch yourself!"

Luik brought his attention back to the enemy's new advance. For every two demons, he saw one of the *taken* between them. Another strange sound from the center of the circle, and the advancing line broke into a run.

Demons shrieked, men screamed.

He wanted to talk with each of the *taken*. To reason with them.

He hesitated.

"Luik!"

There was no time.

"Luik, give the order!" Jrio implored. "Now!"

The line of demons and *taken* was at full speed.

"*Luik!*"

In that moment clarity came. The lives of those who still lived—those who had chosen life—were the ones he must reason for…the ones he must have the heart for. The *taken* had selected their path willingly. Despite his desires for them, their own desires were greater. The truth was, he loved them dearly. Each of them. They had been his people at one time. He offered them salvation if they wished it. But he could not force it upon them.

All at once he understood what the Mighty Father felt.

It all made sense.

He knew what must be done.

"Charge!" Luik bawled. His Vinfae lunged ahead, invisibly driving the line of warriors with it. The entire western flank bore down on the advancing enemy; within five strides the horses galloped at full speed.

They would not be stopped.

• • •

Morgui looked to the west as he saw the enemy line surge forward to meet his minions. All expendable. He had seduced them with power and ruled them with force. And they loved him for it. Or at least were fearful.

The sound of the battle clash was deafening, reaching Morgui like a thunderclap booming off a mountainside. Debris flew into the air above, cloaked in a crimson mist. While the *taken* had not delayed Luik as long as he would have liked, Morgui knew it must be killing him. Literally.

Morgui turned to his left. A man stood, sword in hand, surveying the progress.

"Are you ready?" Morgui asked him.

The man looked up. "As you wish, my Lord."

"Go to him," he gestured. "Win him if you can. Deceive him. Kill him if you must."

"As you have spoken, so it will be done."

• • •

These were once his brothers…

…but no more.

Gorn waded through the enemy masses, slashing with a grieved heart. The first man had come within arm's reach, and at the last moment raised his sword to strike. Gorn deflected the blow, still not willing to retaliate before he had exhausted every option.

He did not know the man. But he was born of the womb. He would listen to reason.

"What has Morgui given you that is worth dying for?" Gorn asked, blocking a second blow. He took a step back.

"Do you know how it feels?" the man asked.

Gorn blocked yet another blow. The man was weak, but not inept.

"How what feels?"

The army was regrouping around him. More *taken* moved out from the demon ranks and confronted the warband.

"How it feels to be free to pursue your desires? No bounds," the *taken* man slashed at Gorn. "No limits." He slashed again. "To give in to power. To your lusts." Three more blows rained down on Gorn's blade.

"In exchange for what?" Gorn countered, shoving away the next blow with his spear shaft and knocking the man back a few steps. "Mortality? Death? Look at you!"

"You have no idea how it feels," the man said.

"Oh, but I do," replied Gorn. He stared hard at the man until the eyes averted from Gorn's intense glare. "Come back," Gorn said. "I know what it is to see the darkness of your own soul. The Light is stronger. But you must let go of your pride. Of your fear."

The man's mouth gaped open. Light flashed in his eyes. "I—I—"

"You can." Gorn felt hope.

There was a beat.

"I won't." The *taken* man grasped his sword with two hands.

"Nay," Gorn shook his head. "Don't do this."

The man did not reply. He moved forward and aimed his sword at Gorn's face.

"Don't…" Gorn whispered. He would fight for this man, but not more than he would fight for the innocent. "Please don't."

But the *taken* man disregarded his pleas and lunged forward.

In a single movement, Gorn bobbed his head out of the way and slashed the man across the stomach. Not enough to kill him. But enough to give him one last chance before bleeding to death.

"Come back," Gorn said again as the man doubled over and fell to the ground, sword tumbling away.

"Nay," he quivered, curled up in a ball.

"You can be healed. Forgiven. Life can start afresh for you." Gorn stood over him, weapons at his sides. The front lines were almost upon him.

This must end.

"I will never come back," the man spat. In a violent move, he leapt up from his cowering and slashed at Gorn's face with long nails. The action was a surprise, and the fingertips drew blood from Gorn's cheek. A flash of metal and a swift *kuh-shunk* sent a severed hand tumbling to the ground.

The man screamed, clutching his stub of an arm.

"Come back!"

"*Never!*"

The *taken* man wavered on his feet but had enough strength to reach for his sword. Then he charged Gorn. The Teacher of the Dibor ended the exchange with a blow that could not be parried.

• • •

Luik and Jrio warred side by side. They fought mercilessly, dispensing wrath on any demon that dared raise a fist to them. Attacking the *taken* was a great deal harder, however. The pair killed them more slowly than they would Dairne-Reih; not that their deaths were more painful or drawn out—quite the contrary—but that they deliberated a beat longer when delivering the deathblow.

The added conflict meant the Dionian warband would hack through the Dairne-Reih more slowly and give Morgui an added edge. Luik congratulated his foe on a cunning tactic. But it stopped there. For everything else about it was offensive and made him want to vomit.

Though the eastern and western flanks warred relentlessly, each warrior hesitated before striking one of the *taken*. The error worked to the enemy's advantage, and soon the killing came from both sides. Luik noticed the cries of some of his own men as they met their fates, gouged by the horns of the enemy and driven into the ground.

Allied arrows rained in from the rear like black clouds, showering over the enemy lines and striking those farther back. Luik wondered how many shafts they had yet to free. He was sure his warriors could go on fighting for days, even if their supplies ran out. This was the greatest battle of their lives. And they fought like it. Everywhere he looked his men worked valiantly at their craft, dispatching the enemy like a scythe through wheat. Morgui himself had come out to meet them and they did not disappoint. But the fallen lythla's presence did not thwart their cause; they knew the White Lion was among them. Somewhere.

A thunderclap shook the air behind Luik, a flash of light turning the entire battlefield white. He did not need to turn around to know what it was. He could see it in his enemies' faces. Their pupils tightened, and a white glow reflected in the black center. The Dairneags blanched and suddenly forgot where they were.

Luik did not hesitate, delivering blow after blow, hewing the demons where they stood, oblivious to their oncoming doom; what their eyes met beyond overwhelmed them past movement. Luik's path became so crowded with corpses that he eventually dismounted Fedowah and sent him back toward Grandath. It was easier to fight on foot here. He swung relentlessly until a powerful wave knocked him forward.

• • •

Gorn continued to wade through the thick of battle. He stayed the larger enemies off with his spear and used his sword to parry and cut those closer. Fyfler and Cage had found their way to his side, working together as they carved a trail toward the Demon Lord.

A thick haze of dust hung over the entire field of battle. Morgui stood in the midst of his Dairne-Reih, surveying both fronts. He seemed to command them without speaking, turning this way and that, ordering them with silent power. His black body glistened in the morning sunlight, muscles flexing with every turn. Though his form was hideous to behold, there was a strange beauty about him. Something that lured—that played on the lusts of mankind.

Gorn studied his opponent and wondered what he was thinking. Feeling. And how what would happen next would affect him. Gorn stared westward when…

…a flash of light blinded them, arms raised to shield their eyes. As soon as it happened, they knew He had come.

A shock wave burst out from the epicenter of the Most High's appearance and rippled out over the entire scene like a white wave cascading from the center of the ocean. Men and demons alike stumbled back, struggling not to fall. Even Morgui fought to keep his legs beneath him, shoving his generals aside.

"He has come," Cage uttered in amazement.

The fighting ceased. All eyes turned.

The Great King stood on the field of battle.

Gorn gazed in awe at the majesty of his Lord. The White Lion stood, dwarfing all others, a white haze lingering over His form.

The yellow eyes stared directly forward, glaring at Morgui.

No one breathed. They just watched.

The din of war ceased, a long silence hushing the slaughter. Armor rustled and bones creaked as men and demons alike regained their feet, never looking away from the God of Athera.

Then a Voice boomed out over the entire plain…

• • •

"I have come for what is Mine," the White Lion said.

A shudder went through those gathered: His authority demanded respect; His eyes never left Morgui.

"What is it you wish for?" came a snarling voice from the center.

"The Keys of Life and Death," He replied.

Everyone looked to Morgui.

But the Demon Lord did not reply.

Suddenly there was an uneasy feeling in the air.

"Answer, you scoundrel," Jrio said under his breath.

"Hush," Luik insisted.

"But he is—"

"Hush."

The White Lion spoke again. "Do not make Me ask again," He boomed.

"His patience wanes," Quoin whispered.

"This is not patience," Fane put in. "It is anger held at bay for but a moment longer."

Finally the Dark Lord's shrill voice replied.

"If you want them…"

He paused.

Nothing moved. All was completely still, awaiting his reply.

"…then come and get them yourself! *Attack!*"

His last command ripped through the air like metal screeching on stone, sending his minions off into a frenzied drive toward the White Lion. Massive Hewgogs erupted from underneath the ground, and made their way forward as well, the land shaking with every step they took.

"Is he mad?" Jrio spat, the front lines now turning on them with intense aggravation.

"Aye!" Luik replied, raising his sword. "Mad and about to die on the point of my sword!" He uttered the Tongues of the Dibor, a brilliant glow emanating from his blade.

The first Dairneag he met slashed left, and then right. Luik ducked, and then brought his Vinfae across the demon's chest, disemboweling the monster and lighting it on fire. Its entrails burst into flames and black smoke poured out.

"Back to Haides!" he screamed and stepped around the burning corpse to his next victim. He felt the ground rumbling. Just as he raised his sword, he heard a voice cry out.

"Luik!"

He spun around and looked to Fane. The ground shook even more. His finger was pointed.

By the time Luik spied the Hewgog barreling down on him, he knew it was too late.

• • •

Anorra stood beside the White Lion, hardly able to contain her excitement.

When the flash of light faded she found herself standing on the mangled remains of the Great Forest's edge. Charred tree stumps and ash heaps spilled out into the marred fields of Jerovah. Ahead of her she saw the armies of Dionia and Haides pitted against one another. But their lethal conversing had ebbed. They struggled to stand erect as all eyes turned in absolute awe of the White Lion.

She felt so proud in that moment, standing beside Him like that. Despite the terror beyond her, she knew she was safe. Nothing could touch her as long as she remained beside Him. As long as she obeyed His orders. She would never disobey again.

The scene before her was so magnificent, she hardly listened to the replies of the enemy. That Morgui would ever disrespect Him to His face had never even crossed her mind. Yet when the Demon Lord finally defied her Master, and further sent his legions of demons bounding toward Him, she unconsciously withdrew an arrow shaft and snapped back to reality.

"Prepare for battle," the White Lion said.

"Anorra," he turned and gazed down at her. "You will be safe here. Remain here even if I move forward. Keep the women with you. Understood?"

"Aye," she said.

"Now, defend your man," He ordered.

With that, Anorra looked out to the sea of warriors engaged in combat and searched for her love. It was easy to find him, right in the center, sword clashing.

She spied a Hewgog racing toward Luik, bashing Dairneags out of its path.

Luik dispatched a demon, lighting the wretch aflame, smoke floating upward.

Luik was unaware.

She saw Fane scream.

Faster than she could think, her arms pulled the wood and string apart. Her fingers relaxed, and the arrow was away.

It raced across the tops of the warriors' heads, parting hair and skimming helmets. Swift as a diving falcon, the arrow slammed into the forehead of the massive Hewgog and snapped its neck backward.

• • •

Luik was trapped, unable to escape the onrushing foe, sure he was breathing his last. He looked up at the racing giant that loomed overhead, towering above, when a thin dowel cracked through its skull. The demon arched backward while its legs continued forward, kicking out from underneath it. All at once the beast slammed into the ground, crushing two of its lesser cohorts beneath it.

Luik felt something wet spray across his face before spying the arrow shaft protruding from the Hewgog's forehead. Three red stripes on the feathers.

He spun around and saw Anorra in the distance, standing just to the left of the White Lion. She was already aiming at another target but cast him a quick nod and dispensed wrath on her next victim.

"Luik!" a voice cried out.

Luik spun again, anticipating another giant. But he was in no immediate danger; the warband was holding the enraged enemy at bay. He searched the throng for the voice.

"Over here!"

Luik saw a warrior dressed in fine clothing, face sallow and strained, black hair slicked back.

Luik's heart raced.

Hadrian walked toward him, hands to his sides.

"I should kill you now," Luik said loudly.

"After all we've been through? Please."

"Do not patronize me," Luik replied, bringing up his sword. The shouts of his men met with those of the Dairne-Reih. Metal and bone struck one another with measured rhythm.

Hadrian raised a hand against Luik's bloody blade. "Luik, I've been working on your behalf. I want to help the White Lion obtain the Keys."

"Then you would have brought them yourself." His muscles tensed. He did not want to do this…

"I had to speak with you first," Hadrian replied.

"Speak with me?" Luik wanted to believe him. He loved this man. His friend. Everything in his head screamed *danger*, but everything in his heart longed for forgiveness. He knew he had betrayed Fane's confidence. Not to mention Anorra's trust. Yet he knew there was *something* inside of Hadrian. Something worth fighting for. Something true.

"What would you speak with me about?"

"Why I have done all that I have," Hadrian said.

"Here?" There was something off. "Now?" This was not the real Hadrian speaking. He would not seek forgiveness this way.

"Aye, I was wrong in how I went about my return. It was poor judgment on my part."

"Poor judgment? Hadrian, do you confuse me with a fool? What are you talking about?"

"I speak of repentance. I want to make things right." He took a step forward.

Luik countered with his blade.

"Look, I carry nothing," Hadrian held his hands out.

Luik hesitated. He wanted to forgive. He wanted restoration with his childhood friend. Nothing would make him happier.

Hadrian held his hands out to embrace him.

Luik lowered his sword. He would forgive.

The two stepped near. And embraced.

A knife slipped from Hadrian's sleeve and into his palm, fingers enclosing the handle, arm swinging in over Luik's shoulder blade.

The metal found its way between the rings of Luik's shirt and glanced off bone before sinking into the back of his lung. He gasped, pain seizing his chest like a horse standing on his ribcage.

Luik gazed into Hadrian's possessed face. "What are you doing?"

Hadrian leaned closer. "Exacting payment," he seethed into Luik's ear. Unlike Morgui, Hadrian knew Luik could never be won, lulled to the ways of evil. He was too distracted, too blinded. So Hadrian forewent his master's first command, and went straight to the second. He would finish him.

Luik felt his muscles spasm. He tried to order his Vinfae up, but his arm wasn't responding. The knife was wedged in such a way that any movement on Luik's part brought excruciating pain.

"Luik," Jrio yelled over. "You all right?"

To anyone else it looked as though the two were embracing. Reconciliation in the midst of battle.

"Oh, c'symia, Luik!" Hadrian hollered, trying to put Jrio's worries to rest. Jrio nodded, not wanting to interrupt the reunion.

"Why?" was all Luik could think to ask.

"You took my father."

"Took your father?" He coughed and tasted blood in his mouth. "That's what this is about?"

Hadrian paused.

For a moment, Luik's head cleared. He needed to speak to Hadrian. His friend, Hadrian, not the possessed.

"I followed him," Hadrian finally said, driving the knife in a little deeper. Luik gasped. "He led me to power. Deep within myself, I found true power."

"True pow—Hadrian. Listen to yourself." Hadrian did not reply. "Hadrian, you have become like *them*. A monster."

"Be that as it may, I am exacting vengeance."

"But we did not take your father!"

"Aye, you did!"

"He came back, Hadrian."

"Nay—"

"He came back!"

Hadrian shook the knife, and Luik's knees buckled under the pain. "*Naaaay!*"

Luik whimpered, losing strength. "He came back...his own choice." He could not say it any other way. He felt heat traveling down his back. His vision was blurring. "Hadrian...he loves you." Luik was losing consciousness, but felt Hadrian wince at his last statement. He would press it further. "I love you."

Hadrian jerked away. He let go of the knife and moved back. Luik slumped forward and fell to the ground.

In the space of two breaths Hadrian was surrounded. No more than ten and five men-at-arms, as well as Fane, Jrio, Rab, and Li-Saide, pointed weapons at the man who had mortally wounded their King. Even Anorra, watching from afar, had her bow trained on the traitor, having never believed his approach genuine in the first place. And now she scolded herself, her desire to preserve the lives of those tending to her love—should she miss—her only reason for not releasing her arrow at present

Fane and Rab made to help Luik up, but Li-Saide cautioned them. "The blade is poisoned." The pair looked to the knife and then looked to Hadrian.

"What have you done?" Jrio blurted out, glaring at Hadrian.

Luik raised a hand toward Hadrian. "Do not harm him!" he shouted with his last bit of strength.

"My King, do not speak," Fane said.

"Nay," Luik slurred, head drooping. "There is still greatness in him," and then slumped into unconsciousness.

"Hush," Li-Saide added.

"What have you done?" Jrio demanded of Hadrian again, getting in his face.

Rab dropped Luik's shoulder and aimed his sword at the traitor. "You shall die!"

"Do not dishonor our King's word," Fane called after him.

"There is no greatness here!" Rab retaliated. He had fought many times for Luik's life; to see it end here and now—not by the hands of Morgui, but by the hands of a childhood friend—was more than he could stomach. His sword point was pinned against Hadrian's throat, a bead of blood appearing on the flesh.

No one moved, nor did they blame him for what he was about to do.

"Stay your sword," came a new voice from behind the crowd. "Luik is right." The men turned to see who spoke. "There is still greatness in my son."

• • •

Gorn made out the exchange between Morgui and the Most High with baffled disbelief. How could the Great God tolerate such arrogance? Such audacity?

The demons turned on him with renewed animosity. They tore into the warband's lines, spurred by the rebellion of their leaders and the sudden emergence of the Hewgogs.

"Hold the line!" Gorn shouted, ducking under a swinging arm. He answered the over-eager attempt with a swift attack to the demon's midsection, breaking ribs and gouging the flesh. Three more filled its place, however, and soon he was fighting for his life.

He wondered if the opposite side was faring as they were. Was the White Lion helping? How were Luik and the others?

Gorn glanced beside him, dispatching yet another Dairneag. Cage manhandled a downed foe that fought to wrest him of his sword, kicking the beast in the eye and then cutting into its hand. Others fought against the mounting attack, fending off encroaching demons from every side.

"Hold the line!" he ordered again, if nothing more than to let the men know he was there. Keeping their morale up was vital.

Two Dairneags in front of him suddenly flew aside.

Gorn ducked as a stray leg nearly took off his head. Before him was one of the Hewgogs, enraged with the scent of blood. It focused on Gorn and barreled forward.

Gorn spoke in the Tongues of the Dibor and ran forward. He met the giant in a small clearing and leapt up…

…the monster's arms reached for him…

…Gorn lunged, both spear and sword points driving through the beast's palms and into the bones of the forearms.

The Hewgog screamed as it watched its hands glow a brilliant blue and cracks of white light splinter across its skin toward the elbow.

Boom!

Its arms were obliterated, the body tumbling backward. Gorn landed and rolled to one side. He dealt the deathblow to the neck and then looked up. A wide path had been cleared by the advancing Hewgog, leading to within a few paces of Morgui. And then he saw it. Opportunity.

"Men of Dionia!" he rallied with a wave of his sword. "To me!"

A moment later he plunged down the narrowing alley flanked by Dairne-Reih, aimed for the Demon Lord.

• • •

Morgui looked on as Luik was carried back to where the White

Lion stood. Hadrian had done his job. The young man was more useful than he had anticipated. Morgui figured the White Lion would most likely heal the poisoned king. If they got to Him in time. But even still, the wound had been delivered. Betrayal was complete.

He glanced up at the White Lion who stood watching the battle. Look at him! Would he not dare to venture out to help his men while they sacrificed their lives for him? Would he simply stand there in complacency? Not willing to mar his lovely white coat? He was a coward after all.

Morgui compared himself to the Almighty. He scorned him. At least *he* was in the midst of his army. At least *he* was not afraid to go into battle with his forces—

"Face me, enemy of the Great God!"

Morgui turned in surprise. A dark man clothed in armor stood behind him, sword and spear in his hands.

"Gorn."

"Morgui."

Somehow Gorn had run right up into the center to meet him, a sizable force covering his advance and warring against the Dairne-Reih in the open path. Morgui smiled at his boldness. At his ignorance. He could use a man like this. There were other worlds to conqueror, other Created Peoples to deceive.

"You have tormented Dionia for long enough," Gorn declared. "Your tyranny ends today."

Morgui chuckled. "Does it now? And who ends it?"

"The Most High."

"Ha!" Morgui jerked. "The Lion? Look at him," Morgui pointed a finger behind himself. "He stands when He should be charging, letting His lessers spill their blood for His cause."

Gorn did not flinch.

"Even Luik is carried back to Him, wounded," Morgui added. He could see Gorn's eyes flicker then. He had touched him. He knew Gorn wanted to look over the heads of the Dairne-Reih and prove the Demon Lord's words false. But it was impossible. It was a battle of wits, and Gorn had taken the bait, struggling even now with the truth of the matter.

Morgui towered over him and took a step forward. The hook was set, now it was time to bring him in. "Why serve a leader who allows His subjects to perish on His behalf?"

A beat.

Gorn's eyes flashed, and Morgui suspected he had won.

"My King does not need to fight," Gorn paused, "when He can send me to fight for Him!"

Gorn bared his teeth and lunged forward. Morgui was surprised at the tenacity of the warrior but saw defeating him an easy chore. He extended his right arm and opened his hand. A blast of energy emanated from his palm and sent Gorn flying backward, tumbling into a heap of dust.

"Do not think you can best me, Gorn. You have no idea whom you are dealing with." Morgui laughed as Gorn struggled to his feet. The demons stayed back with a wave of dismissal from their master.

"Need I know anything more than you are a traitor?" Gorn replied, and then charged again.

Morgui watched as Gorn made up the distance between them and once again extended his arm. As the wave came, Gorn rolled sideways and dove behind a Dairneag. The energy slammed against the monster and sent him tumbling to the ground.

Morgui looked for Gorn but he had vanished, only to appear a moment later on his left, barreling toward him with weapons poised.

Within striking range, Gorn jabbed with his spear at Morgui's face. The Demon Lord leaned away and responded with his own attack, grabbing Gorn's head in his fist. He used Gorn's momentum to pull him forward and threw him, slamming his head into the ground.

"Join me," Morgui offered. "I have use for one as tenacious as you."

Gorn once again found his feet, shaking his head.

"I will make you powerful and wealthy! Surely these are things you desire?"

"Is this how you woo all your lovers?" Gorn spat in contempt.

Morgui did not reply.

It was then that Gorn saw Hadrian walking to a cart just behind Morgui. Morgui noticed the shift in Gorn's eyes and made to move.

• • •

As Gorn was tossed aside and rolled in the dirt, he glanced back and saw Hadrian approaching the cart. Morgui turned to look at the dark-haired young man he had lured to his side. Hadrian, however, looked up in panic, one hand on the cart, the other hand fumbling with a lock of a wooden chest.

Gorn was confused. Morgui seemed to be eyeing Hadrian with contempt. But Hadrian was...

...perhaps no longer one of them?

...perhaps he had returned?

Suddenly Gorn felt he understood. At least a little.

He reached to his side where Morgui had tossed his spear. He grabbed the ash pole and called out, "Morgui!"

But Morgui was walking toward Hadrian.

"Blast!" Gorn said to himself. He hefted the spear once in his hand to feel the weight, gauged the distance, and then heaved the weapon through the air.

• • •

Hadrian didn't know how to respond when he saw his father standing there outside the circle of men—men surely about to kill him for what he had done. He had been sent to lure the King to the darkness, and if not that, kill him. He thought he would make his master proud...

...but would it make his father proud?

It was a question neither Morgui nor Hadrian had thought he'd encounter.

"I see greatness in you, my son," was all his father had said. That and, "I love you still."

There was something about those words. Something that made him feel...

...like a child.

He was taken back to the days of his youth. Before he knew of evil. Before lust.

Things were simple again. It was all about him...

...and the Most High.

Visions of how things used to be flooded his mind, cascading over him like a torrent of rain, each drop a memory. He was bathed in a deluge of pictures.

Hadrian longed for those days again. How far away they seemed, no one but Hadrian could tell. If he could get them back, he would.

But it was impossible.

It was, at least, until his father stepped through the throng of warriors and stood before him.

"My son, come back."

Hadrian just stared. His father did not look like usual. He looked more like...

...what he *used* to look like. Whole. Healthy. Full of life.

"Ta na?"

"Aye," Jadak replied. "'Tis I, and I alone."

Hadrian knew his father had returned to the Light. And he had scorned him for it. Yet he did not anticipate what he saw now. He did not anticipate *life*.

His father stretched wide his arms. "Come."

In that moment Hadrian made a choice. The one he wanted to. The one he knew was right. His father drew closer, and Hadrian fell into him, throwing his arms around him.

"Oh, Ta na!" he said into his father's shoulder, his chest heaving with great sobs. "I'm so sorry! What have I done?"

"There, there, my lad," said his father.

"What have I done?"

"Nothing that cannot be undone," his father said. "All is forgiven."

Hadrian wept deeply. To hold his father once again in the face of all he had done was overwhelming. He had betrayed Luik, tortured Anorra's sisters, and conspired against the Tribes of Ot. It was too much to be forgiven.

"Nay, Ta na. There are some things that cannot be undone," Hadrian said, pulling away.

"My boy, all is well. You are back!"

"I have done many things, father. Things which I can never return from."

"But, Son—"

"Nay," he lifted a hand. "There is too much."

His father made to speak, but Hadrian stared him down. Silence passed between them, and the warriors were growing restless.

"I know what I must do," Hadrian finally said. He turned to Li-

Saide. "I know it will be hard to forgive me for what I have done," Hadrian said. "It was I who kept the roots alive, not Fane." He looked to Fane and then back to the dwarf. "But perhaps what I am about to do will ease your bitterness."

"I hold nothing against you," Li-Saide said solemnly.

"Nay," Hadrian winced, holding up a hand. "Just—please. Nothing more. Morgui still has more to his plan. Send axmen and torches back into Grandath."

"Grandath?" Jrio wondered.

Li-Saide silenced him with a look.

"The other Tree lives, and Morgui will use it before this day is done."

"Very well," Li-Saide said. "But what are you going to do?"

"I am not so ignorant to think I can atone for the wrongs I have done." He looked back to his father and mouthed the words *I'm sorry.* His father smiled. "But I can still make my life count for something." He addressed all those surrounding him, weapons poised. "If you will allow me, let me go."

The men mumbled to one another and looked to Li-Saide. This was foolishness!

"Please," Hadrian turned to the dwarf. "Let me go back to Morgui. Give me one more chance."

The dwarf thought hard. He looked to Hadrian's father and then to Fane. He looked over to the White Lion and the women attending to Luik; Anorra was right beside him.

"I will not fail," Hadrian said at last.

"For your own sake, you had better not," Li-Saide answered. "Varos!"

"What are you doing?" Jrio yelled.

"Peace, Dibor!" Li-Saide pointed a finger. "Have you learned nothing of grace?"

"Grace? This is madness!" Jrio contested.

"Madness?" asked the dwarf. "Is it truly? Or is a man asking to walk back to the Lord of Darkness himself greater madness? You know as well as I that Morgui will kill him. It is a death sentence either way."

Jrio had nothing more to say. But the dwarf continued.

"So if he is to die, let us think the best of our brother and only remember him under the anointing of the Most High."

The last word made Hadrian turn. "C'symia." He looked back to his father and embraced him a last time.

"Go," Jadak said. "Make me proud."

"I have stolen your pride, Ta na. But I will bring Him glory with my last breath." He eyed the White Lion in the distance. To Him he whispered, "I will see You in Athera."

· · ·

"What do you think you're doing?" Morgui asked Hadrian.

The words had no sooner left his mouth than a terrible pain ripped through his abdomen. Morgui glanced down and saw a spear protruding from his belly. He spun back and saw Gorn running forward.

"Fool!" Morgui shrieked. He raised both hands and filled the air with a shock wave that hurtled toward Gorn. But this time Gorn was prepared, and the Ancient Tongues were already in his mouth.

Morgui's attack rippled through space and suddenly split apart, diverted like a river around a boulder. Gorn was still running ahead. In three more steps he leapt at Morgui, his sword driving for the demon's head.

Morgui was late in reacting and just barely avoided the point, but not before the blade carved a line across the side of his face. He screamed and whipped his arm across Gorn's body. Gorn grunted against the blow that sent him flying off into a mass of demons. As he rolled to the ground, he looked up to see Morgui looking for the traitor.

But Hadrian was gone, the wooden chest left wide open.

· · ·

Hadrian ran for all he was worth. His legs pumped, and his heart beat loudly in his ears. He didn't dare look behind him. He was too terrified.

The demons he squeezed between were far too consumed with the battle to even notice him. But still he felt as though the entire world was watching him. He had resigned himself to the fact that he would surely lose his life with this action, but for a moment he almost felt like he would survive. Like he would live.

His lungs burned, and his legs were tired. He could hear the sounds of battle up ahead, the front lines drawing close. Could he make it?

The Keys in his hands were heavy and far larger than he had expected. They shone a brilliant gold in the morning light, and while he wanted nothing more than to return them, he was tempted to sit down and admire their beauty. These were valuable, he knew. Why, exactly, he did not know. But they were worth living for.

Worth dying for.

Almost there, he thought.

Up ahead he could see demons engaged in mortal combat, exchanging blows with armored men. The eerie clicks and shrieks he had grown accustomed to suddenly seemed repulsive and detestable. He wanted nothing more than to burst through the lines and head to safety. To return these keys to their rightful Owner. He wanted to live.

A few more strides and he was against the backs of the foremost Dairneags. He ducked to avoid their swinging elbows and arms and searched for a gap to slip through unnoticed.

There!

He spied a beast just cut down by the sword, stumbling backward and pushing those away that vied for its place. Hadrian was there in an instant, thinking only of escape, and bounded over the demon's corpse.

The group of men on the other side were quite surprised to see Hadrian and raised their weapons, thinking he was one of the *taken*. But Fane shouted an order Hadrian could not make out. The men stood down, and Hadrian was through. He had done it!

But the same men who had watched him pass through suddenly grew pale as their eyes filled with terror. Hadrian looked in their faces and turned…

Racing forward was the pent-up fury of a legion of Dairne-Reih in the form of one demon—Morgui. He strode with lightning speed, smashing Dairneags on either side and flinging them high into the air.

Morgui's eyes were fixed on Hadrian. The men around him backed away, stumbling in fear, until Hadrian stood alone.

But he was not finished.

Realizing he would never make it to the White Lion, Hadrian looked to Fane and threw him the Keys.

• • •

Everyone watched as the dazzling ring of golden instruments glittered through the air. Fane reached out his hands and caught them, eying the Keys in amazement. He looked up and saw Hadrian's face, now adorned with a brilliant smile.

Hadrian had succeeded, just as he had said he would.

Fane smiled back, a look replaced a moment later with a look of terror as Morgui set upon Hadrian from behind.

One moment Hadrian was there, smiling at Fane; the next he was pummeled into the ground with one thrust of Morgui's palm, the air filled with dust and blood.

• • •

Morgui stared at Hadrian's remains with pleasure. But a moment later his lusts were craving again. He looked up and saw Fane.

Men fled from Morgui in all directions, scattering like ants in a rainstorm. Fane did not move, however, and stared back at the demon with defiance.

Morgui began stepping forward, his breath heavy.

"Give me the Keys, weakling," Morgui demanded.

"Did someone make you the owner?" Fane replied.

Morgui stopped, appalled with this little man's audacity. "I will pretend you did not say such a thing and tell you again. Give me those Keys."

"Last I knew, they didn't belong to you," Fane said as Morgui marched forward. "You see, Someone else bought them. Apparently His offer couldn't be matched."

Morgui was seething now, words slurring in his mouth. He drew closer and closer to Fane. But the red-haired man did not move. Not in the least.

At last Morgui was upon him, and warriors were shouting for Fane to run. Morgui was waving off flying spears and deflecting a barrage of arrows. Nothing would keep him from his prize, certainly not this puny man before him. He towered over Fane and drew his arm back to strike. Strangely, Fane still did not move.

"Die!" Morgui screamed.

The blow came...but was stopped short. Morgui's hand slammed against an unseen barrier just above Fane as if driving into solid granite. The concussion sent a wave of agony rippling through Morgui's body. He let out a deafening yell, more from frustration than pain, and then looked down at Fane.

Fane, on the other hand, remained calm and stared up at the Lord of Haides.

"Didn't you know I was a Mosfar born of Ad? I thought someone would have told you by now. You can't destroy me so long as He is alive," Fane pointed over his shoulder to the White Lion.

Morgui was furious. "Give me those Keys!" He shook with rage and started slamming his fists at Fane. But each blow came only so close before bouncing off the invisible shield around him.

Fane then turned and began walking toward the White Lion, Who yet remained away from the front lines. Morgui followed each step, breaking his hands in midair above Fane's head. Nothing he could do allowed him to touch Fane in the least. He followed the little man blindly until Fane held fast.

Morgui looked up and all at once found himself standing before the Great White Lion. The battle stopped.

"I believe these belong to You," Fane said and offered up the golden Keys to his Master.

Chapter Thirty-Five

THE OTHER TREE

The White Lion acknowledged Fane and the Keys, and then glared at Morgui.

"Give them back," Morgui hissed.

"Hold your tongue," the White Lion said.

Morgui made to speak but found his mouth could not utter a single word.

"I made these Keys," the Most High began. "Adam took them into his own hands. Then you stole them. If anyone should be asking for them back, it is I. You did not have the strength or courage to take them from Me directly, so you took them from Adam. You coward. I, on the other hand, have both the strength and the authority to take them back from you. And now I give them into the hands of My Creation.

"Behold," the White Lion raised his voice for all to hear. "Today I set before you life and death, the Keys with which to enter each. Choose life. While it is still called Today, I urge you—*choose life.*

"As for you," He regarded Morgui with distaste, "you thought you could kill Me? Well, know this: Today I give My power and glory to those I have died for. It is no longer I alone that you wrestle against, but every man and women who calls upon My Name. They will crush your head each day they breathe. They will be a thorn in your side until the day I return, able to resist you whenever they so choose. Such is My power in them."

While the White Lion spoke, the armies of the Most High were closing around, and the Dairne-Reih were backing away. Morgui was surrounded. The Dibor and all the Lion Vrie were wading through their enemies; even Gorn and those from the east were coming through.

"Kill him now!" Jrio whispered from a little way off, willing the White Lion to finish the job. Li-Saide shot him a stern glance. Jrio shrugged his shoulders. "What?"

The White Lion turned to Luik who now stood healthy and whole beside Anorra. "Luik, son of Ragnar, the time has come."

A profound silence fell over everyone. Then murmuring.

Morgui tried to yell but found he was still mute.

"You are leaving us alone?" Luik wondered.

"Never alone," said the Great King.

"But Your Majesty…" Anorra pressed him. Her thoughts were spinning wildly. "Now is when we need—"

"Peace, child," He replied. "Your fate is in My hands, and My hands alone. Do not be afraid. You do trust Me, don't you?"

"Aye," she spoke softly. "I do trust You."

He then turned to Luik. "Know this: I must go and finish the work that I started on Earth. But you, here and now, must finish what you started. This is your battle, your war. And I will not rob you of the honor of seeing it to its completion. Go and do what I've empowered you to do. In my Name."

"In your Name," Luik repeated and bowed his head.

The White Lion turned back to Morgui. "And you, enemy of Athera, I leave you in the hands of Luik the Mighty and the peoples of Dionia; you and your kind are theirs to do with as they please. You will remember this day, awaiting another when I will return. And when I do, the Armies of Athera will accompany me."

Then the White Lion raised his head into the air and let out a thunderous roar such that Dionia had never heard its equal before. All the warriors let out a war cry with Him, shaking their fists and banging their weapons together. Luik shouted with all his might until he thought he would tear his voice from his throat.

Gorn and Cage met up with Li-Saide and Fane, each of them

shouting in each other's faces, victory pumping through their veins. Quoin shook Fyfler by the shoulders, and Kinfen beat his chest like a wild man. They had waited for this moment...longed for this their whole lives. The Great King had come.

All the training—all the work—had come down to this moment. All the heartache, the separation from family and loved ones, and the loss of dear friends, had made them long for this day. The Dibor roared like lions, screaming into the air for those they had lost, for the children who had been murdered, for the families that had been torn apart. The blood that rusted their swords and stained their skin was not in vain. They yelled for Najrion...for Brax...for Gyinan. They even hollered for the *taken*, knowing that there was still hope for the lost.

And then they screamed simply because they were alive. They exulted that they had breath to breathe, that they had been to Haides and back. And now their Great King had seen death and defied it. If Morgui could not stop the White Lion, then nothing was impossible.

They roared because they could.

With the enemies of the Great God stumbling backward, a dazzling light flooded their faces and made them turn away. Luik was consumed with light as well, shielding his eyes with his forearm. The White Lion was glowing with light...

...rather, He *became* light.

The White Lion's roar grew louder and louder until Luik's ears rattled in his head. He tried to shut out the light, but it permeated his mind. He couldn't hear himself shouting anymore...

...just the roar of the Lion.

A thunderclap shook the ground, and all at once the light was gone. The roar faded away until all was still.

Luik pulled his arm away from his face and blinked his eyes. At first he couldn't see anything. All was as night when compared to the Light of the Great King. Then shapes and shadows began to form until he was looking out at the plain full of demons and warriors. Morgui was a few paces away. Luik's men looked to him as their sight returned.

The White Lion was gone. The Dairne-Reih were confused. And Morgui was...

"I think he's really angry," Anorra said.

It was then they realized just how alone they really felt. Morgui and his entire army stood before them, fuming as if a child had shaken a beehive. A breath later the entire plain was transformed back into a nightmarish scene.

Luik's men formed the battle lines and prepared to face their enemy once again. Gorn, Li-Saide, and Fane stood beside the King as Morgui glared at him.

"So that's it?" Morgui was incredulous. "That's all your King could do? Frighten us with a little roar?" He laughed.

"Watch your tongue, Morgui!" Luik countered.

"Fools!" Morgui spat. "You serve a weakling for a King! If he could not kill me, what makes you think you can?"

"Kill you?" replied Luik. "You know He would not kill you here, Morgui. Humiliation is a far better vengeance."

"I disagree," Morgui said, and then coughed. The wounds on his face and stomach still bled black. He swung his arm forward, summoning his hordes to action. Within moments the men of Dionia were flung back into war, swinging their swords and blocking a barrage of renewed hostility.

Luik raised his sword and shouted orders. Captains raced to regroup their men, and archers loosed their arrows once more. Luik then turned to Anorra. "Quickly, head to Grandath! Keep the wounded and women with you. Use the stumps for height and help us where you can."

"But Luik—"

"Norra, there is no time. Varos!"

She nodded, gave him a kiss on the cheek, and was away.

Morgui retreated back into the folds of his army. He barked orders in his demonic tongue, his generals moving throughout the throng with ease. Luik watched him take up a position amongst his legions and gloat in his opportunity for victory.

While Luik trusted the Most High, he could not see how his departure was prudent. It only gave renewed zeal to the enemy and filled the rest of them with doubt.

Questions filled his head as he engaged the first Dairneag that dared cross him. He ducked under a swinging arm and then lashed out, severing the limb from its host. The creature swung with its other arm only to feel a blade pierce its ribs. When the beast had fallen, Luik looked to Morgui and thought he saw him smile.

Gorn and the others fought alongside Luik, dispensing wrath and making the most of each swing. With the White Lion gone, they knew it would be a long battle.

Perhaps, too long.

• • •

Anger consumed him. What was the Most High doing? Show up for but a moment of the battle only to revive the wounded Luik? And this *roaring*...was this supposed to frighten him?

Morgui was furious. And frustrated.

If the Most High thought this pitiful army of men was strong enough to conquer him and his Dairne-Reih, he was wrong. Perhaps they were stronger. Perhaps they were braver. But Morgui was more cunning.

He knew what must be done next. It would take all of his strength and concentration. But he had waited for this, plotted long years, and lured many into his service for just such a feat. Hadrian had been instrumental. But he had been expendable, as were all of his servants.

Morgui knelt down and placed his palms on the ground, lowered his head, and closed his eyes. A grim hum came from his chest, and within seconds met with a harmonic drone from somewhere underground. His generals stepped away and watched as every muscle in Morgui's sleek, black body began to tighten.

• • •

The axmen had wandered into the ruins of Grandath just as Li-Saide had ordered. Still not sure of why he had sent them on such a mysterious errand, they longed to return to the front lines where the *real* battle was being fought. Their countrymen needed them. This felt more like retreating than following wartime orders.

They continued to walk west, picking through the ash that covered the ground. Everything they saw was black. Black tree limbs, black stumps, black piles of rock. The pungent smell of smoke still permeated the air.

Wispy trails rising skyward marked small, smoldering fires. An intense heat still emanated from the ground, like the stone around a hearth fire long after the meal had finished cooking. Despite Li-Saide's instructions, the men could not imagine how anything could have survived the fire, let alone continued to grow.

"This is absurd," one of the axmen complained. "This is a fool's errand."

"We should be back with the others," said another.

The man in charge spoke up. "Then why don't you go back to the dwarf and explain why you think he doesn't know what he's talking about?" No one replied. "We move on until we find the tree he spoke of."

"And if we don't find it?"

"Then we wait to be relieved. Li-Saide will not forget about us. He is a dwarf. They do not forget."

The band of men walked on in silence, searching the horizon for anything above head height. The entire forest had been utterly leveled. It was a horrific sight to behold. Their feet were black with soot and their faces were already dirty, ash mixed with sweat.

It wasn't long after that the men felt thirst rise in their mouths and knew it had been a while since they had drunk anything. They were reminded that they had entered Grandath without any provisions; this was to have been a short errand. It wouldn't be long before the all-too-familiar pangs of hunger gnawed at their stomachs.

"Spread out," the leader ordered, trying to get their minds off their lusts. "Let me know the moment you spy anything out of the ordinary."

The men fanned out in a long line, picking their way through the dismal setting. The deeper they got, the greater their thirst grew. No distraction could quench it. They desperately wanted to turn back. How long must they be on this feeble exploit?

"Over here!" one of the men yelled. The leader was running toward him in an instant. The rest followed.

"What is it?"

"I tripped on this. Look," the scout pointed to a thick root protruding from among the cinders. He then took a knife and pried apart the flesh to reveal green meat beneath.

"It lives," uttered the leader. "How is that possible?"

"It must be very strong to withstand such an intense heat," said another of the axmen.

"Aye," agreed the leader.

Suddenly the first man's knife was pulled out of his hand. "What the—" He stepped back in disbelief as the root moved.

"Stand back!" the leader yelled, unsure of what was happening.

"My knife! That's not possible!"

All at once the root submerged beneath the soil and was gone.

"It lives," said a few of the others.

The ground began to tremble, and the men moved away, stumbling over charred stumps as the quake grew worse.

"What's happening?"

"I don't know," said the leader. "I think you disturbed something."

"Perhaps it's the tree Li-Saide spoke of!"

"Perhaps," replied the leader. "Hold on!"

The ground shook more, and the axmen reached out to keep from being knocked down. It felt as though something was moving beneath their feet.

"Look! Over there!" the leader shouted, pointing a finger toward a rupture in the ground not ten paces away. What appeared to be long, snake-like fingers burst from the ground and curled onto the surface, extending from the hole.

"Ready your weapons!"

The roots searched blindly, moving over rocks and around stumps. One man got too close, and two long fingers discovered him. One wrapped quickly around his waist, the other punched a hole through his chest. His life ended with a shriek of terror.

"What is it?" a few of the axmen shouted.

"I don't know," said the headman. "But stay clear!"

They stepped back and continued to watch as the long roots moved outward and then all at once drove back into the ground in a circle five paces from the original hole. The ground continued to shake, and the roots snapped taut as if pulling something up from the deep.

From the center hole emerged a slender shoot adorned with small green leaves—a welcome sight in the bleak ruins of Grandath. The greenery rose higher until the men realized it was not a shoot, but the image of a tree. Limbs fully laden with leaves snapped out into the air, feeling the relief from being pinned down below. The roots continued to pull the tree up from beneath until they vanished back into the ground.

Higher and higher the tree soared until the men ran away, the ground breaking apart all around them. The sound was deafening. Rocks split like eggs, and stumps were uprooted and discarded as if driven by a massive plow. The axmen tumbled haphazardly, rolling in the soot, smashing into all manner of obstacles.

When at last the tremors subsided, the headman rolled over and looked skyward…

•••

Luik and the others tumbled over as the quake shook away their balance. Demons sprawled everywhere, and swords and shields clattered to the ground. The sound of fighting was replaced by grinding rock coming from somewhere within the charred ruins of Grandath.

"What was that?" Jrio finally asked when the ruckus subsided. He sat up and looked around, watching the first of the Dairne-Reih regain their feet.

"Great God," Gorn said in a hushed tone. "What is that?"

Those near him turned, following his stupefied stare westward. Illuminated from behind by the rising sun stood a massive tree stretching toward Athera.

"The Tree of Life!" Fyfler exclaimed.

"Hardly," said Li-Saide. "It is—"

"I thought it was destroyed?" said one of the soldiers near them.

"It was," replied another, one of the Lion Vrie. "I was there when it burned."

"Then how—?"

"It is not the Tree of Life!" Li-Saide interrupted, aware that the demons were still hungry for blood. "Do not be diverted! To arms!"

Luik was staring back at the magnificent creation, captivated by its beauty, when the words *To Arms!* pulled him back. He turned around in time to see Gorn sideswipe a Dairneag that would have caught him by surprise.

"C'symia."

"Keep your head in the fight," Gorn reminded him. "We can't lose you now."

"Aye," Luik nodded, "or ever, I hope." Gorn smiled and was off again, sword and spear swinging. "Hopefully your axmen are doing their job, Li-Saide." Luik cast a last glance to the tree.

The dwarf studied the creation and then looked at the King. "Let's hope so."

• • •

"Step away!" ordered the headman. "Or I'll kill you myself!"

The three men just ahead stopped in their tracks and looked back. Their chief held his ax at the ready; he would do as he said without hesitation. But the giant fruit at their feet was so alluring.

The massive red apple had fallen during the tree's powerful rise into the sky, and had burst open when it hit the ground. The tender white flesh was lined with moisture, adorned with black seeds.

"I'm warning you one last time! Step away!"

The men looked to the fruit once more and then conferred with one another.

"What are you doing?" the leader demanded, now walking toward them.

In the blink of an eye, two of the men turned their axes on the headman while the other one knelt and carved out a piece of the fruit with his hand. He turned and lifted the dripping morsel.

"I told you…"

But the fruit looked so amazingly wonderful. The leader could not resist at least *considering* if it was good to eat. He was, after all, terribly thirsty, and now quite hungry.

"Let us try it at least," said the man holding the fruit. "There is enough for everyone. Enough to bring back to King Luik and nourish the men. Perhaps it is what the Great God intended to sustain us during the long battle fought in His absence."

"Does it not look just like the Tree of Life?" said one of the two bearing their axes. "Perhaps the dwarf was misinformed. He said Hadrian had told him that this tree needed to be cut down. Was not Hadrian a traitor many times over?"

"I sense a great reward for us if we return with such a bounty," said the one holding the fruit.

Still the leader hesitated.

"Come now, how could something so beautiful be so evil?" the fruit bearer continued. "Are not the most beautiful things in all Creation fashioned by the Master's hands alone?" With that he brought the fruit to his mouth and bit deeply.

"Nay!" the leader cried. The other two held up their axes.

Juice from the apple's flesh ran out the corners of the man's mouth as he chewed. His eyes closed, and he groaned with the taste in his mouth. The other three watched.

"It's amazing!" said the man. "It is the Tree of Life!"

"You see?" said the other two, lowering their axes and turning for their own share.

The headman remained motionless, still weighing everything in his heart. A moment later the rest of the men were diving into the massive fruit and eating handfuls as fast as they could.

Nothing seemed to be happening to them. No death. No torment. And they certainly weren't acting as the *taken* might. He watched as they gorged themselves, admitting that his own mouth wanted nothing more than to join them. He was so thirsty, after all.

So hungry…

"Come!" said the first. "Li-Saide will wonder why you denied yourself if you do not return to him with joy in your eyes."

The eyes.

"Look into my eyes," said the head axman.

The first man just stared at him before asking, "What?"

"Look into my eyes." He remembered something his father had once told him. The eyes…he searched his memory. *The eyes are the window to the soul.* "Let me see into your soul."

But the other man went back to his feasting.

The leader reached out and grabbed his man's arm.

The head whipped back, and his eyes went wild, teeth bared and snapping at the leader.

The headman leapt back and brought up his ax blade. But three men beset him from behind.

"Eat with us," they said, pinning his arms to his sides and moving him forward.

"Nay!" he cried. "This is not the Tree of Life!"

"O, but it is! Taste and see," said the traitor. "Taste and see!"

"I will not!" he replied. "I'm going back to Li-Saide!"

"Not eat?" The man scratched his chin and fondled another piece of fruit. "Then you shall die." He turned to the three men holding their chief. "Kill him."

• • •

Morgui had been humiliated. And what was worse, none of his plans seemed to be working. It was maddening.

But he still had the Tree.

"We must push the Dionians back," Morgui said to those few generals that remained. "Get them as close to the Tree as possible. I don't care how many we sacrifice."

"But Master, our forces are already dwindling."

"I don't care!" he seethed and turned to his generals. "Push them back now!"

• • •

Luik went to work, hacking at anything that resembled demon flesh, and advancing farther into the enemy line. But as the moments wore on he sensed a change in the flow of battle: the demons became more aggressive, pushing forward with a strengthened resolve, albeit carelessly. Luik and his men met the challenge with tenacity and did their best to carve a swath deep into their ranks. Dairneags fell in untold numbers. But despite mortal wounds, they flailed in their death throes, reaching for one more strike. More than one unfortunate soul was undone by a downed demon. Enough men met their end that Luik and Gorn called the warband to stop their advance and defend their position.

The defense, however, only lasted so long.

• • •

Anorra tended to a young lady who had sustained a deep head wound. The quake had tossed all of the women around like puppets, crashing into the wreckage of the broken forest. She tried to stop the bleeding, but try as she might, the cut would not slow the red flow that soaked the fabric she held in place.

"Can you hold it?" Anorra asked the girl.

"I think so," she said weakly.

"I really need to see if King Luik needs me," Anorra reached for the bow beside her.

"Go, Princess. I'll be fine."

"Very well." A moment later Anorra was atop the wide burnt-out bowl of an oak, drawing a nocked arrow to the corner of her cheek. She searched for Luik's form and found him battling one—two—then three Dairneags all at the same time. It was unusual for him take on so many at one time. They swung wildly. Anorra identified the most aggressive and then let her weapon do the rest.

Luik did not seem to acknowledge her signature arrow as before, most likely because the demon Anorra felled was instantly replaced by another. And then another. She saw Luik stepping back.

"Princess!" one of the young women yelled up.

"Not now," Anorra replied, waving the call off. Luik was in trouble.

"But Princess—"

"I said not now!"

She had already nocked and loosed another shaft, sending it on its death errand. But Luik still retreated.

"I think you must really see this!"

This girl is relentless! "What is it?" Anorra glared. The young woman was looking off in the distance, staring at something in the west. At first she had no words, and then, "Where did that come from?"

"I don't know, Princess. Is it—"

"The Tree of Life?" finished another woman.

Anorra hesitated. "Nay—nay, it can't be."

"He's sent it to give us strength!" cried a girl. "It's a sign!"

"It's hope!" said another.

Anorra glanced back at the warband and searched for Luik. Her heart stopped. Eyes searched frantically. *Where did he go?*

"Come, let's go! We'll be safe!"

"Nay!" Anorra shouted, turning back to the women. "We must stay and help the men!"

"But Princess, the line is retreating!"

"I can see that," she looked back to the battle. The enemy was gaining ground. They were getting closer to the edge of the plain.

"We must seek safety," pleaded the young women with the head wound. "Please."

Anorra looked down at her.

"Please."

374

She looked back to the line. She saw Gorn signaling. *Retreat.*

"It can't be," Anorra whispered. "We're not supposed to lose this one." She fought back tears. Luik was nowhere to be seen. "We're not supposed to lose—"

She watched as an enraged Hewgog swung its arms like a scythe, flinging a dozen Dairneags and men into the air. Another few steps and it burst through the front line and deep into the warband's center formation. Here it went unhindered, flailing without restraint, turning the bloc of soldiers into a tumult of destruction.

"Princess, we must go!"

Anorra nocked another arrow and aimed at the giant's bulging head. Its neck was already riddled with spears, yet it still stood, possessed.

"Princess!"

"Die," she whispered and loosed her razor-tipped shaft.

Anorra watched it sail past the black ruins and pass over the heads of the warriors to its mark. The Hewgog glanced up…

…and raised an arm.

The arrow sank into the demon's flesh, lodging in the bone of its forearm.

Anorra didn't move. She had never—

The demon lowered its arm and looked across the warriors and into Grandath, right into her eyes.

"Princess! Can we go?"

"Aye," she said, not looking away from the giant. "To the Tree."

• • •

The fighting was the most ferocious Luik had ever encountered. Whatever demons could not engage warriors in the front lines simply leapt past, finding targets farther back. Within moments Luik was overrun and separated from the others, demons passing to his left and right, leaving their demonic brethren to finish their deadly work alone.

Luik was pressed backward. When a demon would fall, another behind would leap upon the corpse and jump down at him, barreling ahead at full speed. Head down and arms thrusting, the Dairneags no longer cared about their own welfare; in battles past there was some sense of strategy, some semblance of caution. But now they were careless, driven like a crazed herd of horses. Luik uttered the Tongues of the Dibor unceasingly and dispatched his enemies. But he could not hold out forever.

His arms were growing tired. He could feel the burn in his hands and shoulders. And he was alone, cut off from his men. In addition there was no cover out here, no place to retreat to. Only Grandath behind. Had the White Lion accounted for this? And why had He left if He had known the fighting would only get worse? Perhaps He hadn't known...

The ground trembled under the heavy footfalls of an infuriated Hewgog. Luik glanced up from his latest kill and watched as the giant flung men and demons high into the air. Despite being riddled with weapon shafts like a porcupine, the overgrown beast charged forward, cutting deep into the center of Dionia's fighting force. A moment later nearly every Dairneag around him rushed forward, following the Hewgog's lead.

"Retreat!" Gorn yelled a short distance away. Luik turned, relieved to see Gorn, the black warrior swinging his sword over his head. "Retreat!" he said louder.

"Retreat?" Luik hollered back.

Gorn looked around before spotting Luik surrounded by Dairne-Reih. "Luik! Hold on!"

Luik parried a wild blow at his head, stumbling back from the concussion. Two other demons took advantage of his misstep and lunged. Luik fended off one attacker, but the second was too quick for his blade.

But not Gorn's.

Gorn's sword flashed, emanating a dazzling light just before cutting through both of the Dairneag's wrists. The fleshy stumps rammed up against Luik's chest but did little more than push him aside and mar him with dark blood. Luik finished off the foe with a slice to the back, the demon sprawling face first in the dirt.

"Come on! We must get back!" Gorn pulled on Luik's shoulder.

"Aye," Luik nodded. Neither of them wished to remain in the chaos any longer than need be.

The pair made quick time running just behind the advancing Dairne-Reih. They kept steady pace as the demons pursued the fleeing warriors, never passing, just three steps behind. Eventually the terrain under Luik's feet turned from trodden grass to black ash and a cloud of heavy soot rose into the air. Up ahead he could see his men fleeing into Grandath. Some took up defensive positions among the rocks and stumps, archers doing their best to keep the attackers at bay. But the Dairne-Reih were hysterical in their pursuit, trampling when they could not hit, tossing aside when they could not skewer.

There was little Luik could do but keep pace with the charging demon horde. The two men needed to get farther into Grandath and turn against the enemy again when rejoined with their brothers. Luik ran hard, pumping his legs and arms. Arrows whizzed by their heads. Suddenly Luik's foot landed on something soft; he looked down as he stepped through the flattened remains of a man. A brother-in-arms. He thought of Hadrian, pummeled into the soil. But there was no time for grief here.

It was then Gorn called Luik's attention to the Tree that loomed high above them. The enemy's pursuit slowed, and both men prepared to engage once more.

"Look," Gorn yelled, his spear pointing up. "Men in the tree limbs!"

"Archers?" Luik wondered.

"Let's hope so."

• • •

"Stop!" Anorra commanded and batted a woman's hand away. They stood beneath the shadow of the massive limbs above.

The frightened lass coddled her hand and turned from the Princess.

"No one touches the fruit," she ordered, staring each of her ladies down. "Do you understand?"

"But they—"

Anorra glanced over at the axmen who indulged, almost unaware of their presence. Unaware of everything.

"I don't care how good it looks!" Anorra's anger flared. *Did they not see?* "Do *not* touch the fruit!"

She waited for someone else to talk back.

Satisfied she had been heard, she continued, "Now, make a place to treat the wounded back there." She indicated a large flat patch of burned-out grass west of the Tree. "The men will be here any moment, surely taking up defensive positions around us. Treat who you can, invoke the power of the Mighty Hand for those you cannot."

The women could feel rumbling under their feet; *they* were coming.

"Understood?"

Everyone nodded and was away.

Anorra strode to a large boulder and swallowed her fear. She knew she would see Luik running toward the Tree with all the others. Just one look would put her weak heart to rest. Anorra clambered up the rock face and froze.

The retreat was in full progression, a dark cloud of soot hanging over the host. A sea of warriors rushed toward her, fear in their eyes. And behind them…

…a black wave of death, flowing over the terrain and devouring those farthest back.

"Great God, help us," she whispered. *But He had already come. What help there was has already been given. And then He left…*

There was no more help.

The rock shook beneath her as the armies advanced, one after the other.

Shunk!

Anorra turned around and saw a large apple split open on the ground. Three more were shaken from their perch high above, hit and broke open. The fruit was as big as she had ever seen. And so enticing.

She shook her head. *This is war! Not time for feasting!*

She jumped off her rock and ran around the tempting food, headed back for the clearing. The sound of the retreating line rose behind her as she reached the ladies. They were all huddled together, looking at something between them.

"What are you doing?" Anorra yelled.

Two of the ladies looked to her and blushed. The whole gaggle seemed agitated at Anorra's presence and moved uneasily as if hiding something.

"What have you done?" Anorra demanded. She strode forward and yanked one of the younger girls up.

There on the ground was a large piece of apple.

"I told you!"

"But they brought it to us!" screamed a girl, pointing to the axmen. "Said it was fine! Said it would help us in the fight!"

"Fools! Have you any idea? This is not the Tree of Life! The Tree of Life is dead!"

"Then what is it?" another woman asked. "Because it makes me feel—"

"I don't care how it makes you feel. It's not the Tree of Life! It's another Tree!" She threw the first girl down and stepped in the middle of them, pushing them away. "Get back, all of you! Get back, I say!"

Just then she heard men yelling behind her. Anorra spun around and saw that the first of the retreating warriors were coming into the shadow of the Tree. Archers.

"To the limbs!" they cried.

Anorra watched as a few of them stopped to examine the massive apples that lay split on the ground.

"Keep moving," she whispered, willing them not to stop.

"To the limbs, men!" one of the lead archers yelled.

"Aye, to the limbs," Anorra answered and was off and running to the base of the Tree. Her bow would best be used aloft, so she would join them.

As she drew near the colossal edifice, she noticed for the first time that this Tree did not glow like the Tree of Life. She had thought it had at first sight, but realized now it was just the rising sun. From this angle, the Tree was as bland and normal as any other Tree. That was, until she touched it...

The moment she pressed her hand against the bark to find a handhold, something pricked her fingers. A sensation. Of something leaving her. Of something drawing life...

...away.

She pulled her hand back. Uncomfortable. Awkward.

"You there!" an archer called. "We have need of your bow! Come with us! Are you not the Princess of Ligeon?"

"Aye," she said distantly, still eyeing the bark.

"No other has eyes like you," he went on. "Help us defend this, our last battle."

Anorra looked over to the man, placing his bow over his shoulders and preparing to climb. Others were already mounting up, scrambling for the lower limbs.

"Please," said the man.

"You have my bow, good soldier," she finally replied. The man smiled wide and started his way up.

"The Princess of Ligeon joins us!" he shouted up the Tree, which brought a rousing cry from those above.

Anorra grabbed the bark again, the prick still biting her hands. Embarrassing her, like knowing something she wasn't supposed to be privy to. Violating her. But she ignored it and willed herself to climb on. And climb she did, distancing herself from the charred ground below. Every glance she took of the oncoming armies below showed them gaining on the Tree.

She worked each handhold and wedged her toes into the nooks of the bark. Arms pulling, legs pushing, she finally made it to the first enormous branch when a hand reached down.

"Take my hand!"

She didn't even think and thrust her arm up. Caught around the wrist, she was hoisted up. Another hand caught her belt and a third her bicep until she was standing on a wide limb, surrounded by archers waiting to take their turn to ascend the next route.

"Glad to have you with us, Princess," one of the captains said.

She wiped the sweat from her forehead and smiled quickly. "Mind if I keep going?"

"Not in the least," replied the captain and raised his arms. "Have at it."

Anorra stepped to the trunk again and began to climb, and then stopped and looked back. "Captain."

"Aye?"

"The fruit on this Tree. It's not safe. I'd advise your men not to eat it."

The captain gave her a funny stare, but then said, "C'symia, Princess. I had no idea. Is this not—?"

"Nay, Captain. That Tree is no more. And this one is far from safe."

• • •

When the advance finally halted and the fighting recommenced, Luik and Gorn took advantage of their precarious position and dispatched the unsuspecting Dairneags in front of them. They hacked into their backs without mercy and felled as many as nine demons in the space of a few breaths. But their presence was noted, and the Dairne-Reih behind them grew incensed.

Luik and Gorn turned, their backs once again covered by their brothers in battle. Their faces were spattered with gore, and their swords were slippery in their hands. Out of breath and nearly exhausted, Luik readied himself for another charge. Fight or die, he had no other choice.

The demons charged at him, and Luik made the most of every swing, speaking in the Ancient Tongues and watching his sword turn into a flame of fire. The effects were staggering, and even his winded body gained strength by watching the ease with which his weapon worked. Dairneags were lit ablaze, sent careening back into those behind them, while others were cut in two, falling apart in mid-step. Others simply exploded.

Yet for all his feats, Luik was only a man, and soon fatigue reined him in.

"Come with me!" Fane yelled and grabbed Luik's arm. "You need to rest! You, too!" he yelled at Gorn.

Both men acknowledged the call and did not resist. They stepped back from the front and were replaced by fresh swords. Fane led Luik deeper back through their lines, a subsequent calm resting on those awaiting the foray. It was then he realized Dionia's plight was not as hopeless as he had feared. In fact, before they had fled to the Tree, he was sure they had taken out more of the Dairne-Reih than Morgui had taken out men. So the retreat came as a surprise, but not without merit, given the frenzied drive the demons displayed.

Perhaps the Dairneags knew they would lose?

Perhaps it was a final push to thwart defeat?

Or perhaps…

…perhaps there was another reason.

Fane led onward, Luik grateful for the respite.

"If it's all the same to you," Gorn said behind him, "I'd like to remain here. You need more rest than I."

Luik turned. "Very well," he replied. "But be wise."

Gorn nodded and signaled Fane to keep the King moving back.

Men on each side acknowledged Luik's presence and made the sign of blessing, thanking him for his valiant effort. Luik lowered his head and thanked many of them as he passed. Eventually Fane and Luik came under the leafy canopy of the Tree.

"May I leave you here?" Fane asked.

"Certainly," Luik answered.

"Your orders are to stay here until you are fit to fight again."

"Understood."

"And I mean it, Luik." Fane edged closer.

"I understand. I won't fight you on this one." Fane waited. "Away with you! I'm fine," Luik finally said. Satisfied, Fane smiled and headed toward the army.

"I almost forgot," he turned back.

"Aye?" Luik looked up.

Fane withdrew a tattered piece of folded parchment from within the fold of his robe. "Li-Saide asked me to give you this."

Luik reached out and took the strange gift. "What is it?"

"That's only for you to know. Something about the time you were last in the Library."

"In Ot?'

"He said you'd know what it was about. 'A secret,' he said."

The fires. Pursuit. Luik suddenly remembered waiting with Brax for Li-Saide to reappear in the Library during their escape. The flames were devouring the ancient texts and the Dairne-Reih were close behind. Something had delayed him. This? "A piece of parchment?" Luik looked up to Fane. "That's what he risked his life for?"

"You know as well as I that the dwarf only acts with good reason." Fane waited a moment, thinking. "Ah, I will leave you to your rest. And to your gift."

Luik surveyed the area and looked up into the Tree. Archers lined the branches overhead and loosed a barrage of arrows into the distant enemy ranks. While he was convinced this was not the Tree of Life, he was at least grateful for the tactical advantage it provided.

Luik placed his hands on his knees and caught his breath. Sweat poured from his head as he worked his helmet off. He wiped his forehead and looked at the carnage that came away on his forearm. He felt the cramping in his legs and back. While he was grateful for the chance to catch his breath, his body was becoming aware of its injuries. Torn muscles, bruises, cuts.

He looked for a place to sit and spied a rock newly upturned from the Tree's sudden appearance. He walked over and noticed he was limping, before collapsing on the rock. He situated himself so he could lean back against the hard surface and stretch his legs out. All around him people were scrambling, archers climbing up the Tree, men running for new swords or bundles of arrows; even those attending the wounded searched for skins of water, fresh cloth, and food. What few supplies could be found were in short order, a prized commodity. He closed his eyes, trying to relax.

The parchment.

His mind would not let him rest until it was read. He lifted up the item and gently unfolded it, trying not to mar it with the grime of battle on his fingers.

His eyes met the strokes of a great many words, each crafted with utmost care. The ink was old, the page cracked and dry. The first words seemed as if they were continued from a previous page, a sentence in mid-stride. But knowing for sure was futile, as the page was written in Ancient Dionian. Halfway down, however, the margin was filled with words he recognized, the translation of a sentence in the middle of the page, circled by fresh ink, not more than a few days old. Luik tilted the parchment sideway and read aloud.

"'In that day I will pour out my Spirit on all flesh.'"

Luik paused, considering. But nothing of significance came to him. Annoyed, he looked at the page again, searching for more. He flipped it over, but the back was blank.

"That's it?" He shook his head. *Perhaps he grabbed the wrong page?*

"My King," came a soft voice.

Luik was startled and glanced to his right. An attractive young woman offered him a skin of water.

"Are you thirsty?"

He nodded.

"Here," she said and knelt close to him, her dark eyes searching his face.

Grateful, he accepted the vessel and drank. "C'symia," he said, wiping his mouth.

"And some food for you." She held up a soft piece of apple flesh.

"C'symia," Luik said and reached for it. The fruit was moist and heavy in his hand. He felt the lump rise in his mouth. He was famished.

"There's more if you want it," she said, standing up, her full figure before him.

"O, aye. Please," he said and was about to eat when she turned and brought a larger piece of apple beside him. Luik paused. "Where did you get that?" suddenly looking at the piece in his hand.

"Why, from the Tree, of course."

"It fell? From this Tree?" Luik looked up. "And you've eaten it?"

"Aye! It's delicious! And so filling," said, rolling her eyes. Seeing Luik still hadn't eaten, she raised the larger piece to his face. "Here."

It looked so luscious. And this young woman was so beautiful. It was then he noticed her shapely body, and his eyes scanned her frame. He wanted the fruit. He wanted…

…her.

If this were the other Tree that Li-Saide had shown him, how could she still be so lovely, having eaten of the fruit herself? She was not *taken*.

She was *amazing*.

He dropped the small piece in his hand and opened his mouth for her to feed him.

• • •

Anorra had followed Luik from the re-formed battle line all the way back to the Tree. Watching him skirt two brushes with death in one battle was enough for her. Her heart leapt when she saw him emerge from the Dairne-Reih with Gorn, and only logic kept her from leaping out of the Tree.

She tried her best to get down to the lower limbs but the archers were too packed behind her. "Excuse me," she pardoned herself. "Excuse me!" But there was nowhere for them to go. They'd have to all move back down for her to get through. And there was no rope or vine to descend on. She was stuck and would have to wait to see him until the battle was over.

"Luik!" She resorted to shouting, hoping he'd look up. "Luik!" But her voice was lost amidst the *whoosh* of arrows and the din of war. At least he was all right. She blessed Fane for bringing him out of harm's way and watched them walk under the Tree.

As Fane left, she yelled to Luik again, but her voice was a bird's song lost in a gale. She was about to turn back and continue fighting when she noticed a young woman—one of her girls—appear next to Luik. She handed him a water skin and then…

"Nay!" Anorra burst out, nearly falling from the limb. Two of the archers caught her as she tipped forward.

"Princess, are you all right?"

"Let me go!" she struggled to get free. The girl was offering him the apple.

"But you'll fall!"

"I'll not fall! Unhand me!" She yanked her right arm free and reached for an arrow. Seeing the action, the man on her left released her and Anorra laid the shaft across the bow. A swift pull back—a release—and the arrow was away.

. . .

Luik was about to take his first bite when the apple dropped and the girl shrieked in terror. Luik jerked away as he saw an arrow shaft binding the apple and the girl's hand to the ground. The girl wailed, trying to pull the feathered end of the shaft out of her hand. But it was held fast.

All at once her face changed, and she lashed out at Luik. Her nails missed his face and nicked his collarbone. Luik rolled to his side and jumped to his feet, body stiff but responsive. The girl made to follow, but the arrow held her in place.

Luik glanced up, searching the canopy of leaves. His heart was racing. What was going on?

There. In a dark spot higher up, he could see a lock of blonde hair. *Anorra.*

Of course! He looked to the arrow; her mark was there. The girl continued to thrash about like a caged animal, seemingly possessed. The fruit was vile after all.

It was then Luik had a sickening thought. *How many knew about the fruit?*

He immediately looked around and saw any number of men carrying the apple pieces into the battle lines to distribute among the soldiers. Others were huddled in groups, consuming the apples like ravenous dogs. Why hadn't he seen them before?

Then it dawned on him.

Morgui was trying to purposely push them back. It was he who had summoned the Tree to the surface. And Hadrian who had watered it all these years.

Luik picked up his sword and raced back to the battle lines.
"Don't eat the fruit!" he hollered.

The first few men who heard him shout were incredulous. But when they turned and recognized who it was, they immediately fell silent. "Don't eat the fruit! Pass the word!"

Instantly the order was carried on, echoed forward through the ranks. Some of those closest to Luik did not speak, however, but kept staring at him. "What is it?" he asked one man. But the look in the man's eye said it all…

He had eaten.

This was maddening to Luik. By now he wondered just how many had tasted of the wicked fruit. If something were not done soon, his men would soon be fighting one another.

"Great God, I need Your help."

Luik looked down and saw a piece of apple lying between his feet. His mouth began to water, and it was then he came face to face with the darkest side of himself. There was nothing he could do to change his lusts.

He was utterly powerless.

He knew he shouldn't eat. He knew it was cursed. Yet he longed for it, even when he *didn't* want to long for it!

He looked up. Only those who had eaten were watching him now, the rest of the men were intent on the battle ahead. No one would notice. Just one bite. *Just one.*

He bent down and reached for the morsel.

Chapter Thirty-Six

PROMISED

Time slowed as Luik's fingers inched closer to the fruit. Then it stopped. Everything did. The battle. The arrows flying overhead. Even the sound of his heart as it beat in his head stopped. His hand was suspended just a finger's breadth above the white apple piece.

Luik felt the air move against his cheek. It was soft at first, like a gentle breeze. But then it turned wild, a rushing wind swirling about him, threatening to knock him off his feet. Yet still he remained motionless, aware of only the wind. The sound filled his ears, as loud as a waterfall.

His stomach suddenly grew hungry—not for physical food—for something deeper. Something grander. It was as if a secret need for *more* had been revealed in his life. More of what, he knew not. He felt naked and exposed, but he welcomed it. For somehow he knew that with it came freedom. With surrender came life.

He was tired of himself, of desires he could not satisfy, needs he could not control. Staring at the apple he suddenly realized how shallow a soul he was. Empty. Pitiful, even. Whatever nature he had been given, whatever drove him on the very inside of his being, he no longer wanted. Yet he was powerless to overcome it. He needed something else. *Someone* else.

Luik knew plenty, had learned plenty, and had lived plenty. But yet there was something more. Something he felt he had never touched… something none of them had ever touched. Dionia had known the presence of the Most High since her inception. There was not a day that the Great God was not among them, even in their darkest hour.

They knew Him, but only with a limited degree of knowledge.

They were close to Him, but not intimate.

They were aware of His presence on the outside, yet never knew what it was like to feel the Almighty breathing…on the inside.

"I want more," was all Luik could think to say. He wasn't even sure if his mouth moved, or if his ears heard. Whatever the Great God had for him, Luik wanted it. There were always two choices. Belief; unbelief. Dependency; indulgence. But now he knew what he wanted.

And he wanted it now. Not for greed's sake…

…nor for lust's sake…

…but because he could no longer live with himself.

As if a fiery torch had been set off in his stomach, Luik suddenly screamed. All at once the fire was replaced by the sensation of a river emanating from somewhere deep within his bowels. He jerked upright and raised his hands. His spirit was opened and in rushed the Mighty Counselor. The Promised One.

Luik felt as if pure light filled his entire being. He had believed the Most High, even felt His presence. This, however, was something altogether new. Strength such as he had never known! All his doubts were suddenly put to flight. No cares of the battle ahead. No worries for what would happen next. Luik seemed to have instantaneous and limitless trust in the Mighty Hand…

…everything was going to be all right.

For the first time in his life, Luik felt *alive*. Something had died. And something else had been awakened.

Then a voice spoke to his spirit. *Luik, my son. Today I take up residence in you. Not just a visitation, but a habitation. You will never be alone. I have sent the One I promised to imbue you with power. Nothing will be impossible for you now. I am with you always.*

Tears streamed from Luik's eyes as reality came rushing back to speed. He held his hands even higher and began to praise his Maker. Words of life and blessing flowed from his mouth. He began to prophesy life to his people, to Dionia herself: that she would live and not die; that the Almighty Father had created her with a purpose, with a destiny to fulfill. Then, as if his mind had run out of words to speak, his spirit took over. He loosed his tongue and spoke in other languages of praise, heavenly languages he had never heard. He knew not what he was saying, but he didn't need to. He was finally free of himself. Free of his old nature, and consumed with a new one. The nature of the Son. The mind of the White Lion.

Luik took a deep breath and lowered his hands. Limbs shaking, his entire body felt as free as if heavy burdens had been lifted. He wiped the tears from his face and glanced around.

Throughout the battlefield other men seemed to be experiencing exactly what he had. They looked a bit dazed, some almost as if they had drunk too much wine, but all had a wide grin on their faces, beaming with light.

A scant few stood as they were, looking irritated at the others. Perhaps these were the ones who had eaten of the other Tree? He wasn't sure.

What Luik did know, however, was that he was changed. Transformed. He felt brand new. He eyed the awaiting enemy that had somehow been held at bay during the whole experience. Whatever fear Luik and the others had been carrying before was gone. And for once Luik saw fear, true fear, in the eyes of the Dairne-Reih. Perhaps they had seen what Luik and the others had felt.

The rushing wind was not finished yet.

Luik heard a rustling in the Tree behind him. He turned to see leaves and limbs churn from a twisting gust of air. Shouting from above told Luik the archers would quickly vacate their perches. They scrambled to get down, each man descending the trunk and leaping the last short distance to the ground. The wind whipped at the limbs, dirt and rubble tossed through the branches. More men fled, and Luik saw Anorra drop down. She rolled in the soot and stood up.

"Over here!" Luik yelled, waving his arms.

Anorra spotted him and raced forward. Grasping her arm, they backed away from the Tree and watched.

Once every soul was clear, the wind picked up and swirled violently. The leaves strained to hold on, and the branches flailed as if they might be ripped from the trunk. The sound escalated as well, mounting to a deafening roar. Luik shielded his face, and Anorra buried her head in his chest when a massive gust blasted through the Tree and ripped most of the leaves away. They swirled into a funnel, a shimmering cone of green that raced through the air. Bark was torn from the hardwood, peeled back like layers of skin. The limbs waved around like stalks of wheat, until they broke away, only to shatter in midair.

Soon all that remained was the massive trunk column, naked and trembling. Luik peeked over his arm to see it shaking itself into a blur, the roots making the dirt dance on the ground. The wind grew stronger and stronger until the stress became too great, and the trunk exploded into oblivion. The pieces were swept away in a swirling cloud of debris and then hoisted skyward, leaving a gaping hole in the ground.

As quickly as the wind had come, it was gone, and everything was silent. Luik held Anorra close and took a deep breath.

"Is it over?" she asked, squinting at him.

"Aye," Luik replied, staring at the wide hole in the terrain ahead. Anorra pulled away and surveyed the scene. Then turning back toward the warband she said, "Luik, look!"

Over the entire army of Dionia were small flames of fire, as if the whole company was ablaze. The burning came without smoke and without smell. Just the presence of light.

"What's happening?" she inquired.

"It's time to take our land back," Luik said quietly. He let Anorra go and then raised his voice to summon all the warriors to him. "Men of Dionia! We no longer fight alone! But it is the Most High who fights within us!" His words were echoed back through the ranks so all could hear. Luik raised his sword and let out the deepest war cry he could muster. "For the King and His Kingdom!"

Luik felt invincible. He lowered his head and started forward. At first he jogged, the men starting to part ahead. But as the path opened, Luik took off into a full run. Those ahead saw him coming and turned on their enemies as well, running forward.

Luik let out another war cry. It was answered, not by the few, but by the many.

Soon the entire host of Dionia was charging forward, flames above them, swords in front of them, and their voices shaking the air. Blood would soak the ground this day.

• • •

The sight was so horrific that even Morgui took a step backward. He could sense the mounting fear in his generals, and even though his hordes acted as though they were hungry for the fight, he knew they were pretending.

That, or naive.

Dionia's warband looked like a wave of fire devouring the ruins of Grandath. Something otherworldly had transpired. And Morgui didn't like it at all.

The front line of men closed on the Dairne-Reih with frightening speed. The demons raised their arms and opened their toothy mouths, screaming in defiance as loud as they could. But they were drowned out by a more powerful force. An unstoppable force.

From where he stood, Morgui sensed everything go silent…

…a moment where time stopped…

…and the balance of power shifted…

…the land was no longer his to rule…

…the Children of the Almighty were now invincible if they wanted to be.

He knew then, it was finished.

• • •

The deafening collision shook Jerovah at its foundation. The warriors of Dionia blasted into the front lines, and through them, without so much as a contest. The bodies of their enemies blasted apart like eggs thrown against a stone wall. Row after row of Dairne-Reih was consumed, their enemies barely seen before it was too late.

The Dibor fought beside the rest of the Lion Vrie, and on either side the Immortals held the flanks. The demons had no chance at all; scarcely a man in Dionia later remembered if a single Dairneag ever landed one blow in defense. The vast army of the Most High swept forward and utterly destroyed every beast that had ever tormented the people of Dionia, stolen their fathers, and slaughtered their mothers and children. The men struck back for every village that had been razed to the ground, and for every hour that a daughter had gone without her mother, every day a son had failed to feel the embrace of his father.

The Dionian warband swept forward uncontested, plunging deep into the enemy's heart. They knew Morgui was dismayed, and while he feared them, they would think nothing of dispatching him from Dionia forever.

And Morgui knew it.

Whatever gift the Most High had sent, it had erased the power he had previously held over Creation. The army before him no longer feared him. And they would not hesitate in their recompense. His only escape to the Sif Gate in Grandath had been cut off, and all that was left was to retreat to the open plains of Jerovah.

The advance was getting closer by the moment, and Morgui's generals looked to him for some sign of direction. Some plan of attack. This was unlike their previous battles—storming Adriel, or moving against the well-protected fortress of Mt. Dakka—nay, this was altogether different. This is what it felt like to be bested.

When Morgui finally said it, his generals could not believe what they heard.

"Run."

Chapter Thirty-Seven

PURSUED

When the enemy finally turned and fled eastward, Luik heard the entire army of Dionia break into a terrifying bawl. Luik couldn't help but join them when he saw that even Morgui was fleeing.

The men ran down the enemy stride after stride, cutting them down one after the other. They laid waste to everything that moved, disemboweling, splitting spines, and breaking skulls. They spared nothing and gave no quarter. If the enemy ran, they ran faster. If the enemy screamed, they yelled louder.

Though the work was laborious, not a man among them thought of stopping, not until every demon was driven from Dionia forever. They surged forward, aggression consuming them and victory thick in their heads. For the first time in their lives, they had the enemy on the run.

They had won.

It was a glorious moment for them all. Their heads swirled with excitement as their swords and spears brought justice back into the land. The archers ran forward, sending wave after wave of stinging missiles into the throng ahead. Even the horses routed the enemy, driving into the demon hordes and trampling them under their hooves. Farther and farther east they went, driving the enemy relentlessly. There was nowhere to hide, and the men of Dionia were enthralled in the euphoria of triumph.

Many times Luik could see Morgui's generals shouting orders and trying to make a stand. But the army's momentum was too great, and any Dairneag that stopped to oppose was overrun and consumed in the maddening rush.

With every step they took, the Dionians reclaimed their heritage and took back what was rightfully theirs. Most of all their courage to live again. No longer would the hand of an oppressor torment them or dictate their lives. No longer would an invisible iron hand smash them when they least expected it. Tyranny had met its end on the tips of their swords and the shouts of their hearts.

It was too marvelous to comprehend. Everywhere they looked the enemy was stumbling, struggling to keep pace with those in front, some even clambering over the backs of others just to get away. Yet it was all futile. There was no outrunning the Dionians, there was no undoing what the Great God had done. The Mighty Counselor had come, just as promised, and baptized them with fire. They were invincible.

"Push them harder!" Jrio yelled out.

Luik looked over to his swordbrother and grinned. They had dreamed of this day for so long; they just had never planned on it taking this much time, or costing so many lives. Benigan and Boran pushed forward on the right, Cage, Daquin, and Quoin on the left. Gorn was there, as were Li-Saide and Fane. Rab whooped as he exacted payment from a faltering Hewgog, running up the creature's back and driving his sword into its thick neck, and then leaping off as the giant skidded in the grass. Anondo carried two spears, having sheathed his sword, and plunged them ruthlessly into the backs of demons too terrified to look back at him. Kinfen fought alongside his three brothers, Fallon, Neffe, and King Fyfler.

To Luik, they were all magnificent. They were his brothers.

• • •

The men of Dionia pursued the enemy until nightfall, the glory of the victory keeping them afoot and running. The sky was clear, so the moon and stars continued to illuminate the enemy throughout the night as if purposely assisting the warband in their course. Driven like a mad man, Luik ordered his men onward. Though thirsty, they did not drink. Though tired, they did not slow.

They left a swath of dead bodies in their wake, littering the plains with the corpses of Haides. The long grass of Jerovah was stained with blood, and the ground exulted in the honor. Creation had waited for this moment, for the Sons of Light to be revealed in their splendor. For their presence heralded the soon and coming redemption that Creation had been promised; not yet, but soon, would be the day of its redemption. A new Athera and a new Dionia.

When dawn came the next day, the enemy had been reduced to a fraction of its previous size, routed far to the east. The dead were strewn all the way back to Grandath and the men of Dionia showed no signs of letting up.

Morgui led the retreat and suddenly turned to the south.

"What's he up to?" Gorn yelled over to Luik and the others, dried blood caked on his face.

"I'm not sure," Luik replied. His mind raced. What would make Morgui change direction? What was south? "The shore," Luik said to himself. He glanced to Gorn, and then to the others. "There's a Sif Gate!"

"What?" Fane replied.

"Of course," Rab interjected. "The one used to access Kirstell, the southern shore of Jerovah...they even used it to gain the Somahguard Islands."

"Aye!" said Jrio. "We can't let them make it through!"

"Beat them down!" Luik hollered. "Beat them down and make them pay!"

With that the whole army turned south and followed the Dairne-Reih toward the Sea of Lens. The enemy picked up its pace, hope for escape being too great a prize to submit to their own mounting fatigue. But whatever speed they took was met with equal zeal from those following, and the slaughter continued. Luik actually wondered how many demons would be left to escape through the Sif Gate, if indeed they made it at all.

The sun was high in the sky by the time the sea appeared on the horizon. It wasn't long after that a slender archway stood out against the sky, two columns of standing stones spanned by a bridge of granite. And Morgui would be first through.

As the charging ranks of demons and men neared the Sif Gate, it sparked to life, and the strange transparent blue wall filled the center.

"He's going to escape!" Kinfen yelled, infuriated.

"Faster!" Fyfler screamed. "We must be faster!"

But Morgui was too far in the lead.

"Let him go," Li-Saide said, and then had to repeat himself to be heard.

The Dibor nearby simply looked at the dwarf.

"What do you mean?" Luik finally asked, slowing in step with the dwarf.

"Let him go. Kill those who wait in line, but let Morgui run."

Luik still didn't understand.

"Do you not remember in Adriel?" asked the dwarf. "The Dairne-Reih were slaughtered on the walls, only to reappear from the Sif Gate much later. It was unending."

"So you're saying we cannot kill Morgui?"

"Slaughter his body? Surely. But he would only reappear in a world where he does not need a body. He is spirit, as are his minions. We cannot kill them. Only the Creator has the ability to utterly destroy what He alone has fashioned."

Luik's mind went back to their previous conversation in Ot. "Then, if we can't kill them, what are we doing this for?"

"Teaching them a lesson," Gorn interrupted. "And showing them what they'll face if they ever try this again."

"Right," Luik smiled grimly. He thought for a moment. It was then he knew what must be done. He raised his voice so all could hear. "When they slow, circle around and destroy the Sif Gate ahead!"

The orders were passed down to the rest of the Lion Vrie and the Immortals, and they began to fan out in preparation.

Luik strained ahead and watched as Morgui neared the gate, ducked his head, and slipped through the shimmering blue wall. It was the last of that enemy Luik would see for a very long time, perhaps present for his final humiliation and eternal imprisonment one day in the future.

The Dairne-Reih, on the other hand, jostled for position, shoving each other out of the way. Soon a brawl started, and their retreat was completely stalled. The pursuing army collided with the slowing Dairneags, yet continued to dispense their bloody vengeance. With nowhere left to run, the Dairne-Reih attempted to fight back, but they were too weary, and too disheartened to give much of a fight.

"Varos! Now!" Luik ordered and waved his sword around.

The kings nodded in assent and gave orders to their Captains and on down to the soldiers. The right and left sides of the army flanked the Dairne-Reih and converged quickly on the Sif Gate ahead. The body of the enemy was too consumed with their survival to even notice the force about to close off their escape for good.

Luik watched as his men met on the opposite side of the enemy army and began their assault on the Sif Gate. At first the Dairne-Reih didn't know what to do: defending the gate meant giving up their place in line. They would start out against the men only to pause a moment later and go back to fending off the other demons from stealing their position. But when the warriors started pushing as one against the backside of the columns, the demons couldn't help but engage them. About two tens of men in all worked the stone columns while the rest kept the demons at bay, slashing wildly to keep them back.

The columns began to move ever so slightly as the men pushed against them in a steady rhythm. At least two men lost their lives in the ordeal, one falling off balance and tripping through the gate into Haides; another swinging his sword against an attacking Dairneag only to be flung into the blue wall, backhanded by the monster.

Eventually the men rocked the stone pillars off their bases, but a host of demons were on the other side, staying their means of retreat. It took more men charging in on the flanks to cut away those that resisted the inevitable destruction of the gate. Once clear, the arch fell forward and collapsed in a blaze of light. The stones exploded, and bits of molten rock shot up into the air.

Then all fell silent.

The demons stared at the ruins, their failed route of escape. Then reality set in: their defeat would be total.

A beat later the men set upon them with shouting, swords swinging and spears jabbing. From all sides men assaulted the remaining pack of demons and worked their way inward. Not a single Dairneag was spared in those final moments; the men would not rest until the only things that breathed in Dionia were beings intended to be there in the first place.

Luik stood back and watched as his warriors finished the war that had been started so long ago, bringing justice to the unfinished battles of his father and his father's father before him. All the way back to the very beginning, when those who had fought in the First Battle had thought they had expelled the enemy for good, Luik knew this was the end they had dreamed of. The end they had wished for their children. He wished Lair were here to see this. He missed him.

Luik lowered his sword and let the tip touch the ground. His hand was stuck around the handle, and gore oozed between his fingers. His arms and legs were trembling, and he realized his lungs were screaming for air. He hadn't stopped warring in over a day and had run the enemy of his people right out of the land.

As the men converged on the final demon—riddling it with arrows, spears, and swords—Luik felt a hand rest lightly on his shoulder. He turned.

Anorra.

"It's finished," she said.

The look in her eyes was captivating. She had never seemed so at peace, so whole. Strands of hair had worked their way from her braid and stuck to her sweaty face. Her skin was soiled, as were her clothes, and her armor tarnished. But she had never looked more beautiful to Luik in all her days. Despite his horrific appearance he threw his arms around her and picked her up. They twirled twice before he kissed her and set her back down. Then they both laughed deeply and held each other there.

It was over.

Suddenly a shout went up from over the last fallen demon and all the warriors started chanting. "Vic-tor-ry! Vic-tor-ry!"

Luik and Anorra linked arms and addressed the massive crowd. "Vic-tor-ry!" they cried. "Vic-tor-ry!"

Swords and spear shafts beat against shield rims, fists pounded the air.

"*Vic-tor-ry!*"

The air shook with the declaration. The blood of their fallen loved ones had been avenged at last.

"*VIC-TOR-RY!*"

From the plain of Jerovah to the shores of Ligeon, from the mountains of Tontha to the gleaming jewel of Adriel, the call would go out far and wide that Morgui had been defeated once and for all.

"*VIC-TOR-RY! VIC-TOR-RY!*"

EPILOGUE

Chapter Thirty-Eight

WRITING FROM THE END

It took seven days for the returning army to reach the northwestern shore of Jerovah, another three days to build rafts and use diji-hi to cross the channel, two days to gather the women and the wounded in Grandath, and four days after that to reach Mt. Dakka. Those of the *taken* who recanted their allegiance to Morgui were restored to their former states, while those who hadn't were bound and eventually imprisoned, wooed daily by those desperate to see them made whole.

The weather was fair for the ten-and-six day journey to Tontha, thanks to Morgui's control being shaken from the land. Messengers had run ahead, so by the time the army came into view of the mountain city, the entire holding was bursting with fanfare.

The banners fluttered in the swift morning air, and the warriors didn't know whether to weep or shout at first sight of them. The massive stone towers poked over the final mountain peak to the shouts of thousands of people gathered along the ramparts and outside the City Gate. Like a war cry, their voices lifted the hearts of the men and drew them in…

…this time there was no war.

Only peace.

Minstrels and musicians welcomed the victorious warriors into the city as baskets of flower petals were poured from above. Color and sound pervaded the senses, overcome only by the embrace of loved ones—wives, mothers, daughters, and sons—who bounded through the crowd with tears smeared across their cheeks.

Luik sat atop Fedowah, a euphoric sense overtaking him as he passed beneath the City Gate. "Gorn, I remember the celebration before, of the Kings' Coronations after we returned from Ot, but this…this is unlike anything I've ever seen."

"Aye, Luik, and so it should be. Think on this: The enemy is slain. History will be written to tell of these exploits. Your children, and your children's children, will learn of them and will take heart! The Most High God will gain renown for many an age. Your charge now is to be grateful for your role in these events, but to make clear to all that this victory belongs to the Most High."

In the short time since the inhabitants had received the news of the victory, they had prepared a feast unlike any that their people had ever seen. Luik had smelled the cooking fires even before he came into view of Mt. Dakka. And he, like the others, hadn't eaten in days; his body was weak from all that had been spent on the battle. The scent of fresh bread was enough to make the water rise in his mouth. The aromas of roasting meats—a meal they'd grown accustomed to, not just because other foods were rare—seasonings, and warm mead followed. He could picture mounds of fruit, and knew the vats of wine would not be far behind.

The welcoming of the victorious was only the first cause of celebration, however. Luik had been plotting a more glorious escapade since they first set out for Mt. Dakka, kept from the beautiful ear of the one it was intended for.

His bride-to-be.

On the third morning after their return north, Anorra's chamber was flooded with maidservants, washing, grooming, and primping her. All her suspicions were confirmed the moment Meera and Ciana brought in the dress—a gloriously white gown, shimmering with the embroidered swans of her seaside homeland, and adorned with diamonds. A string of translucent seashells wove around her neck, and pearls hung from her ears. The sides of her hair were pulled back with a cluster of roses, while the back lay curled down her neck. And atop her head was the crown of Legion, worn last by her long-departed mother, watching today from the realm beyond. This was to be Anorra's wedding day, and she had never seen a dress so magnificent; nor would her husband ever behold a woman her equal.

Luik had requested the King's Garden be flooded with white roses—countless lettings never witnessed before or since. Trellises full of them lined the garden; heavy-laden arbors arched before the walkways; pergolas drenched in white covered the sides; and roped nets stretched down from the castle walls and reached to the far side of the garden, each bounding with the pale pedaled beauties. The summer breeze passed through the floral array and washed the audience with the scent of Athera itself.

It was her brother Anondo who walked her down the aisle, escorting her to the songs of minstrels and the gasps of onlookers. And it was Luik who stood in wonder, confusing his dreams with reality; he sided with what his eyes beheld as his dreams had never been this radiant.

Fane conducted the ceremony, bathed in the palpable presence of the Most High now returned to the lands of men. Luik and Anorra sang their vows of dedication and faithfulness, *until we are called home to the Great Throne Room*, and meant it; they supped on bread and wine in remembrance of the Mighty Son who laid his life down for His Creation, an example of sacrifice they would always follow; and handed a rose to their closest friends as a symbol to help guard the beauty and purity of their union in the summers to come. Then they exchanged arm bands, rings, torcs, and crowns, pledging the seal of love upon their arms, hands, necks, and foreheads.

Luik squeezed Anorra's hand as Fane was beginning to sing the final pronouncement over them. "This is it," he whispered. "No going back now."

"Why would I do that after how far we've come?"

"One of the other Dibor may be more—"

"Courageous, passionate, and loving than you? I think not, my King. I stand in honor of you."

Luik meant to say something back, but Fane was inclining his head.

"What?" Luik whispered to him. "What am I supposed to do now?"

Fane dropped his head, laughing. The audience began shouting: "KISS HER!"

Luik looked back to Anorra. "O, right." And with that, he took her in his arms and summoned all his love into a single moment of adoration, willing his most passionate affection to conform to a single kiss that would be remembered forever by all those in attendance, and spoken of for generations by those who wished they had been.

Dionia has never seen such a reception banquet. Boards were set up all throughout the King's Gardens and heaped with more food than anyone had ever seen. It took days for them to finish it all. Even after the feasters were full, the kitchens continued to send out trenchers of beef and fish, stuffed chicken and roast duck. Wheels of cheeses were sliced and served with goblets of wine and fresh date cakes. Such a feast had never been imagined before, let alone consumed. And dine they did!

The afternoons were filled with games and the noise of cheering. Rokla matches were played wherever open ground could be found, even in the city streets. The Dibor joined in easily enough, and friendly rivalries were rekindled from summers past. The players paused long enough to quench their thirst before scrambling for the next gita to begin. Luik took every occasion to tackle the other Dibor but never quite managed to get a hand on Gorn, who continually eluded him. Anorra shouted from the sidelines, content to sit this battle out. And Ciana stood beside her, screaming her brother's praises.

Luik played the boyhood game with all his heart, letting his body feel the joys of play once more. He tackled Fane more than once, reminiscing about their childhood together; it was only then that his heart felt sorrow, as he wished Hadrian could be there to share in their revelry. Aye, he had betrayed. But who among them had not betrayed the Most High in some way? And who was to say the quality of one man's peshe was more grievous than another man's? All sin was detestable. And therefore they were all in need of mercy. Hadrian had betrayed, without question... but he had also ended well. And that was the most important decision of all: to repent and make right the wrongs. To Luik, Hadrian would always be a hero. A friend. A brother.

The nights were spent around hearth fires, faces illuminated by flickering orange flames. Children listened to the heroic stories of their fathers, and more than one bard could be heard singing tales to eager ears. The dwarves lost no time in weaving their ancient tales and using their song craft to paint pictures in the mind.

Luik sat against a tree under the clear night sky as Fane's song pulled him forward into the otherworldly realms found between waking and sleeping. Anorra snuggled beside him, comforting herself in his warmth. The fire painted their faces in soft yellows and took away the evening chill. Luik had lost track of time, his count of the days adrift somewhere between the trek home and the feasting. But what did it matter? Dionia would never be the same, and this was the occasion for losing oneself in the mood of victory and the wake of love. He had never celebrated like this, nor had any of them. Yet despite his merriment there remained a part of his heart that was misplaced. Something melancholy gnawed at the depths of his soul. And it bothered him. As Fane's song ebbed with the dying flames, the group in the King's Garden said their farewells and retired for a well-deserved rest.

When the sun beat warm upon Luik's face the next day, he kissed his wife, rose and took something to eat in the kitchen. Staying just long enough to greet the cook and thank her for the fare, he made his way to the northern part of the palace and then out into the morning air. He stretched and meandered through the streets, relishing being in Mt. Dakka once again. However, he still could not rid himself of the strange feeling that now sat like hard cheese in his gut.

His feet eventually took him to his favorite conversation spot. To the place where others didn't talk back.

The stables.

He walked in through the open threshold as the smell of horse sweat, mixed with grain and straw, filled his nostrils. It was so…

…comforting.

Few horses remained in Mt. Dakka, for most of their holdings had been whisked to the Final Battle, as it was being called, and then left in the plain of Jerovah from whence they came. Only those that had not seen war stayed. All, that is, save one.

Fedowah chewed a mouthful of hay and nodded as Luik approached his stall. The horse snorted and shook his mane as if to greet his friend. Luik drew near and blew softly into the animal's nose, Fedowah's mind flooding with countless memories in that instant.

"Feeding you well, are they?" Luik asked, patting his neck. Luik still remembered the day he had found Fedowah, or rather the day Fedowah had found him. They had ridden a long way together since then, had seen their share of loss. Their share of bloodshed. But no more. They would never ride into battle again.

There it was again.

His heart longed for…

…for *something*.

A season had ended. A journey had come to an end. Luik stroked the smooth part of Fedowah's neck and then scratched vigorously behind his ears. Fedowah had followed Luik all the way home to Tontha, even swimming across the channel when all the other horses had stayed behind in their homeland.

"We've seen some hard days together, eh boy?" He paused. "But we won. We won, my friend."

Fedowah bent to take another pull from the hay mounded in his stall.

"No small thanks to you," Luik continued. Images of charging into battle filled his head.

His spear strummed against Fedowah's flanks.

Dirt flew into the air.

Blood stained their skin.

Blood and water soaked their bodies.

Men screamed, demons shrieked.

Pain.

Defeat.

And then the Lion.

Victory.

It had come to such an abrupt end. One moment they were measuring the time until their final breaths, the next they were feasting in the Great Hall of the Mountain King.

"But no more," Luik concluded. "Now we will enjoy the life we were meant to have. Perhaps I…"

Luik didn't know how to finish the sentence. Fedowah swallowed and returned for another tuft of hay.

"Perhaps I am just so used to fighting…to having an enemy, that I don't know what to—"

A door swung open and slammed against a stall. Luik and Fedowah turned.

"O! I'm sorry," said a tall man, suddenly realizing whom he addressed. "Pardon me, my Lord." He carried two buckets; water sloshed out of one, the other was filled with grain. He made to turn. "I will come back."

"Nonsense," Luik raised his hand, gesturing the man forward. "If you are here for my valiant friend, then by all means, finish your task."

The man looked to Fedowah and then back to Luik.

"Your friend?" inquired the man, taking a few slow steps forward. Fedowah watched him carefully.

"Aye. Fedowah is my horse." He slapped the animal's neck again. "My *war* horse," he corrected with a grin.

"So it is true then," remarked the man and then looked at the horse. "You made it into the service of a King. And not just any King, I might add."

Luik watched Fedowah hold the man's gaze.

"You—you know my horse?"

"Indeed," the man replied, setting the buckets down in front of the stall. He took Fedowah's muzzle and blew into his large nostrils. He then nuzzled his face with the side of his head. "For I was once his."

Luik stared, trying to sort out this man's words.

"I guess you could say I started all this, well, at least what we've endured as of late."

"I don't understand," replied Luik.

The man addressed him and extended his arm. "Tadellis, son of Trinade. First of the *taken* in the Second Age. And now...now I'm..."

All at once Luik recognized him and remembered him from Haides. "Now you're a beloved friend of Dionia's High King." Luik pulled Tadellis to himself by the forearm and embraced him as a brother. It was then he recalled the conversation with Cage: *I think you'll know his horse,* Cage had said.

Of course!

Tadellis was overwhelmed with love, moved to tears. "C'symia," he said softly. It had been a long, hard road. Never had he thought he would be in the embrace of Dionia's King once again. Ragnar had appointed him to the Lion Vrie, and now Luik was welcoming him back into the land of the living.

Luik held the man back and said, "So, this is your stallion then?"

"Was my stallion, my Lord," he corrected.

Fedowah looked between them.

"Well, I don't plan on riding into battle anytime soon," Luik said winking at Fedowah. "So…"

Fedowah whinnied excitedly and stomped his foot in the straw.

"My Lord, whatever do you mean?"

"I mean that an animal this fine should only be used for war, or ridden by the man who has known him the longest." He looked at the horse. "Fedowah, will you have him back?"

Fedowah snorted and threw his head up.

"It's settled then," Luik concluded.

"My King?"

"He's yours once more," Luik replied, smiling widely.

"I don't know what to—"

"You can start by feeding him," Luik said, indicating the buckets.

"Aye," Tadellis replied. "C'symia."

"It is as it should be. Here now, I'll leave you two alone." Luik watched as the pair renewed their friendship over a bucket of grain and a fresh draft of water, and then left the stables and walked back out into the morning light. He stood for a moment, preparing to take the street to his left that curved away down the hill. But a voice called out his name, and he turned toward the palace.

"Luik!"

A small figure came bounding down the avenue from above. A blonde braid of hair swung back and forth behind her.

"Luik!" Ciana yelled. "You're needed in the Great Hall!"

She finally ran up beside him, and he knelt to embrace her. "What is it, my sister?"

"It is Ta na," she smiled. Just hearing her make reference to their father so freely felt wonderful. No more secrets. Just light. "He has asked for you to come."

"Has he now? Whatever for?"

"He said it was important. That is all."

She took his hand, and the two of them marched back up the hill toward the towering palace above. When they arrived, the halls were bustling with activity. Everywhere they looked someone was moving about, most carrying armloads of clothing, goods, or baskets full of empty sacks waiting to be filled.

Luik grabbed one man by the arm and stopped him. "Pray, tell me.

Where are you going in such a hurry?"

"My Lord, is it not your own command?"

Luik became uneasy. "Excuse me?"

"Why, I'm going home," said the man with a smile. "Everyone is going home."

"Home?" Luik's hand released, and the man strode away with a smile. "Home," Luik whispered again. His heart ached. Was that it?

"Come on." Ciana pulled his hand forward.

They passed more and more people, each on their own errands, crisscrossing the many hallways with a sense of urgency. At last the siblings came to the doors of the Great Hall. Luik paused, confused as to the man's response. *Home.* Luik had given no such order. Yet it was not without merit; going home to Bensotha was a thing he had coveted for so long a time, he nearly had forgotten the desire to return. Until now. But still, he had not given the order. Perhaps it was Ragnar? But he would never dream of usurping Luik's authority.

"Well?" Ciana wondered.

"Well, what?"

"Aren't you going to go in?" She turned and looked to the massive iron handles and the articulated latch. The Great Hall.

"Right," Luik nodded and pulled open the heavy door.

Once through the threshold, Luik looked across the empty chairs and tables to the dais. His heart skipped a beat. The White Lion stood tall beside Tontha's throne. Luik nearly missed a step as he fought to breathe. *What was He doing here?* He walked forward, and Ciana steadied him, gripping his hand with both of hers. Luik then realized they were not alone; the Dibor were gathered near, as were the Lion Vrie and the Immortals. Li-Saide and Gorn stood there, with Ragnar, Meera, and Anorra. Even Pia and Rourke were there, their faces glowing—and Sheffy, whose hand had been restored. The presence of so many friends—of his family—was a beautiful sight. He only wished more were there…those who had paid the ultimate sacrifice for this moment to be shared by all.

"You need not worry," the White Lion spoke as Luik arrived. "It was I who gave the order to return home."

"So we're all going home?" Luik wondered like a little boy.

"Aye," replied the Most High. "It is time Dionia received her people again."

Luik stopped just in front of his Maker and then looked to those gathered. They stared at him with expectancy in their eyes. The White Lion went on.

"It is time that the ruins be rebuilt. The city walls, the palace towers, the villages and their homes. All of it. Luik, I charge you this day with the restoration of Dionia. Bring her back; but may she be even more glorious than she was before, so that the enemy will know he cannot destroy My people."

"As you have spoken, so it will be done."

"Very good. Your people will march on your word."

"C'symia, my King." Luik paused for a moment. The White Lion didn't speak; neither did any one of Luik's men. A thought was nagging at Luik's mind, one he longed to ask. He feared he might be rebuked, but it must be posed for him to get any rest in the days ahead.

"My Lord," Luik said, "what about our enemy? What about Morgui and his army?"

"I have defeated Morgui and conquered peshe, even death. I have placed him under My feet and so, too, shall he be under yours. No longer will he threaten Dionia or your people. You are to destroy every Sif Gate that remains. In doing so you will cut off his ability to reenter this world. But even if he should find his way back here, know this: You are no longer the pursued, but the pursuer. He will always be hunted and never find rest. For my Father has sent the Great Spirit, and He will forever abide in you."

"The Gift you spoke of," Luik concluded.

"Indeed. He is the mighty Rushing Wind who baptized you in Fire."

Luik noticed that everyone nodded in acquiescence.

"Now where will You go, Most High?" Anorra spoke up.

The White Lion looked to her. "My Father calls for Me. I must heed His summons and return to Athera."

"Will you take us?"

"Nay, my child. It is not your turn to journey home yet. You are needed here to lead your people and," He paused, "to support your King— your husband."

Anorra looked to Luik and blushed with pride.

"Nay, you shall all live a prosperous life here," the Lion raised His voice. "The best is yet to come!"

"Hey'a!" the men cheered as one.

"There remains a few matters more," the White Lion added. The throng followed the Lion's stare to Gorn. The dark warrior returned the gaze and stepped forward. "It is time, Gorn."

Gorn bowed his head. "Aye. It is time indeed."

Li-Saide stepped beside him and took his hand. "It has been nothing but my life's honor to serve with you for this season."

"And I with you," Gorn replied.

Luik noticed that both of them had tears streaming down their cheeks. "I—I don't understand. What's happening?"

The White Lion looked to Gorn. The warrior pulled the Ring of Bensotha from his finger and moved in front of Luik. Handing him the ring he said, "The fruitful hills and thatched homes you saw on my crown did not look like anything in Bensotha …because they are not *from* Bensotha." He paused. "I am not from Bensotha, or any other realm in this paradise." He looked to the White Lion.

The Lion prodded him onward with a dip of his head.

"I am from the First World. I am from Earth."

There was an audible gasp from everyone that heard it.

"Earth?" Luik said.

"Aye, from a massive land with mountains and plains, deserts and forests. My people roamed throughout the great expanses hunting and foraging for food. But eventually we settled along a mighty river and built our cities on the edge of the sea where all matter of life sprung up around us. An oasis in the desert. I was born to a long line of warriors within my tribe, and I grew strong under the tutelage of my father, as he had done under his father. When I had grown to a man, I had become the greatest warrior in the land.

"It was long proclaimed that we would harbor a peculiar people, a people that would bring curses upon us. When that people finally came, they were weak and pitiful, and I was given charge over them. I ruled over them with an iron fist as I was the Chief of Warriors, pledged to my Pharaoh in blood. But when the Great God came to rescue His chosen people, I could not help but follow them, for I had never seen such a display of power in the midst of such weakness." Gorn's eyes drifted to a far-off place. "What I saw—what we all saw—were miracles. Surely their God was greater than any of ours. And the allegiance of my life changed. I made a new covenant; my life was no longer my own.

"It was not long after our escape into the desert land that the Most High had need of me elsewhere. That is when He brought me here, to Dionia, and gave me charge over a new people." He looked hard into Luik's eyes. "You, Luik. And the rest of the Dibor. You were my calling. And now that my orders have been fulfilled, it is time I, too, return home."

Luik tried desperately to wrap his mind around it all. "I—" He looked to Gorn. "I don't have any words."

"I don't expect you to understand, my King. I hardly do myself at times." He chuckled. "But I do want you to know this one thing: It has been the greatest honor of my life to teach you, to train you, and to see you become the man you are today. You will forever be my friend. My swordbrother."

With that he handed Luik the Ring of Bensotha. But Luik refused it, saying, "If it is true, these things that you say, then you are far more noble than any of us will ever be. To risk your life for your own people is one thing, but to give it for another, twice over, demands the utmost respect. Though Rourke may well rule in your place, you will forever be a King of Dionia." He took Gorn's weathered hand and folded his fingers back over the jewel.

Gorn fought back more tears and thanked Luik. The two embraced, after which the rest of the Dibor surrounded him and said their own farewells. It was a solemn moment as unplanned words were exchanged, tears smeared with the backs of hands. This man had taught them how to fight, taught them how to survive. But more than that, he had taught them how to be a team. How to give everything and endure anything. How to be victorious.

"Gorn," said the White Lion, "we must leave. And you, too, Li-Saide."

"What?" Luik blurted out.

"Now make no fuss about me," Li-Saide spoke up.

"But you are not from Earth!" Luik paused. "Are you?"

"True enough," the dwarf nodded. "True enough. But I have been called to the Great Throne Room in service of the Most High."

"This is not true." Luik turned to the White Lion. "Is this true?"

Li-Saide removed his billowy hat to reveal a bald, blotchy skinned head. "Luik, I have lived long ages, countless ages, and have recorded every spoken word, both of Man and of Creation. *Faithfulness* has been my call.

And I have served well, I trust. But I am tired, dear one. It has been a long road. And I fear I could not live well with the memories of so much loss continually in my mind. It is too great. Perhaps that is why He has called me onward. He has called me home."

"I understand," Luik conceded. "I will have enough trouble as it is living with those memories."

"Ah, yes, but you are Man, and your memory fades. You think this a curse, but it is a blessing, in fact. We dwarves never forget. Good memories bring hope, bad ones plague us. And I fear that I have more bad than good at this point."

"Then may your last memory of Dionia serve you well in eternity. If there be anything you wish—anything at all—it will be done for you, Li-Saide of Ot, Chief of the Tribes. Just name it."

Li-Saide looked in silence to Luik, fingering his patchwork hat. "There is one thing."

"You have only to speak it," Luik replied.

"You once made a promise when the tall trees of Grandath still stood in all their glory. Before the new kings were crowned, before you crossed the border of Ligeon, you spoke of a legacy that you wished to one day undo." Li-Saide paused. "Free the dwarves."

"Free the dwarves," Luik repeated. His mind raced back. From the foundation of her Creation, the Tribes of Ot had always served Dionia. Sworn to record and protect the written history of her existence and that of her inhabitants, theirs was an unending duty of loyalty. Never had they ceased, never had they missed a moment. Under their attentive care, not a single word had fallen to the ground. "In the name of the Most High God, be it known this day that you and all your kind are loosed from the bonds of your vow. You are free."

Li-Saide wept and walked into Luik's embrace. He shed tears for a life lived in service of others and never in pursuit for himself; he wept for long ages spent listening to the cares of the world, never once voicing his own; and he cried for the lives of his people, a people that he would see only from afar as they ventured out into the unknown, living their lives without any task in mind. To *live* simply for the sake of *living*.

"C'symia," Li-Saide quivered. "You are the greatest of all Kings that have ever lived."

"In truth, I am nothing," Luik confessed into the dwarf's little ear.

"I know. That is what makes you so great."

When Li-Saide finally pulled himself away, the same throng that had bid Gorn farewell greeted him. The Dibor showered him with affection and words of endearment. They owed him their lives.

At last Li-Saide stood before Fane.

"The mantle passes to you now, Fane of the Mosfar." Li-Saide took his hand and plopped his hat into it. "Something to remember me by."

"I will always remember you," Fane said.

"And I you," replied the Chief. "My people will need a leader now, and I trust no other as I trust you. You have learned the ways of the Mosfar, and the secrets of Dionia will live on in you and those who learn from you. Teach well; be quick to listen and slow to speak."

"Aye, as you have taught me."

"As I have taught you, aye."

"Li-Saide," the White Lion reminded him.

"I am ready," replied the dwarf, smoothing out his robe and turning to the Lion. He and Gorn walked to the Lion's feet and then looked back to the company around them.

"Grinddr, you and your men may come as well," said the White Lion. "Should you remain, you will forfeit the blessing on your life of longevity and be subject to the aging of your brothers until I see fit to call you home. But I give you the choice, something I offer no other."

Luik watched as the noble warrior turned to his men and said, "You may stay, each of you. Take wives and have children. Or you may proceed to the great beyond. It is as you wish."

The Immortals had been in protection of the people of Dionia since the First Battle, surpassed in age only by the dwarves. Grinddr looked back to the Lion and stepped forward a pace. "You have my sword in Athera, my King."

"And mine," said another man who stepped forward. The declaration of fidelity was echoed numerous times thereafter until more than half the Immortals stood before the Great Lion. Those that remained behind bid their brothers farewell. While the parting was bitter for those watching, the warriors knew that it was but a momentary parting, as their perception of time had shown how short the season of a man truly was. They would be reunited soon enough. While some of the men longed to have what they could not while in service to the Most High here on Dionia, Grinddr longed only for one thing: to see the vast and ever increasing frontiers of Athera. New worlds and expanding spaces unexplored by Creation, known only in the mind of the Creator Himself.

"There is much to see," Grinddr said to the Most High. "I am ready." He looked back over his shoulder. "And Luik, c'symia. It has been my honor to protect you." He made the sign of blessing and took his place with his men, leaving the remnant, and stood behind Gorn and Li-Saide.

Though Luik could not be more content, there was a part of his soul that was torn—he wanted to stay...but to go to Athera was an awfully grand adventure. He was jealous...of them all. Of Gorn, to actually walk the Earth where the Most High had sacrificed his own life; of Grinddr, who would finally rest from his duties and explore all that the Mighty Father had for him; of Li-Saide, who would quickly be in Athera, surrounded by the Magnificent—those who had already gone on to glory. Luik saw each of their faces in his mind's eyes: Thero and Thad; Brax, his dear friend; Gyinan; and Najrion; Lair would be there, as would Hadrian; the Kings killed in Adriel and Grandath would also be there: King Thorn, King Purgos, King Nenrick, and the Horse King of Jerovah. It had been so long since Luik had seen them.

Had he forgotten what they looked like? But all at once their faces didn't seem so foreign. In fact, they were as clear as day, shining radiantly before his eyes.

Luik snapped out of his daze and looked about. A majestic light filled the Great Hall, coming from somewhere far behind the White Lion, as if from another room that stood an eternity apart. Gorn, Li-Saide, and Grinddr with his men stood before the Lion as before, but to their right and left were a host of others, men and women that Luik instantly recognized. Not just them, but children also. Babies clutched in their mothers' arms, boys and girls smiling back at him from across time. The slaughtered were now whole.

Luik raised a hand and waved. Lair waved back first and laughed. Hadrian smiled, his dark complexion glowing as if in the presence of the sun. Anorra clutched Luik's arm and wept as she waved to her Ta na, his red hair and curly beard jouncing as he let out a deep guffaw. Gyinan stood beside him and raised a hand as well. And there was Brax, whole and handsome, his face as regal as they all remembered. The Sons of Jerovah wept with joy as they saw their father, King Daunt, as did the other Dibor who had lost the patriarchs of their family lines.

"We are waiting for you," King Thorn said loudly. "We're all waiting for you!"

"I love you, Ta na!" Anorra yelled, choking on her tears with one hand wrapped tightly around Luik's arm, the other waving frantically.

"And I love you, my princess," Thorn replied

"Don't go!" she screamed.

But the light around them was fading, as if retreating back into the far-off room. Those gathered searched for the faces of their loved ones, willing them not to dissipate. Anorra called again, but the scene before her soon disappeared.

All was still.

The White Lion was gone, as were some of the greatest warriors Dionia had ever seen. It felt like a dream, but was too powerful to be anything less than reality. No one moved for a long time after that. They stared at the far wall as if the strange apparition might suddenly reappear. But it never did.

A sense of awe still hung over them all as they slowly shifted on their feet and moved to face one another. Anorra turned in her husband's arms and held him. Others placed a hand on a shoulder or embraced in the moment. It was the end of an era. But the beginning of a new one.

Three days later Luik set out for Bensotha with his bride and his people, and after the long trek through Ligeon and over the Border Mountains, he settled in the land of his forefathers. There Anorra would bear him two sons and three daughters. Together with their people they would rebuild the walls of Adriel and bring glory back to the jewel of Dionia.

• • •

While Adriel Palace housed Luik and his family officially, they much preferred the small home he had grown up in to the east in Bensotha, spending most of their time in the restored cottage. Luik sat in his chair late into the evenings, writing in a massive *book*...an invention adopted from Earth, something Fane had told him of. The candlelight flickered atop his desk, a piece of furniture modeled after those he had once seen in the Scriptoriums in Ot.

He hesitated, holding his quill above the ink reservoir, wondering if he had spent too much time writing again tonight. Anorra would be cross with him, surely. There was just so much to record. And it was always his habit to lose track of time. He was sure the hour was late. She would probably give him only stale bread for dinner.

Just then he heard giggling from behind the wooden chest on the floor, the children hiding all too unsuccessfully in their evening ritual.

"Ta na's at it again!" the middle one whispered.

"I say we hide his quill!"

"And the book, too!"

Suddenly Luik stretched out his arms and then pretended to fall asleep on his work. At once the children leapt from their cover and piled on his back. Luik roared and turned on them, wrestling the lot to the ground. They laughed and wiggled, each tickled ruthlessly, gasping for air and begging him to stop.

Anorra poked her head in the door just then. "Always have your nose in that book of yours, I see."

"It seems the children have made sure I pull myself away."

"Aye. I do love you for it though, Luik. You always have so much to say."

"But isn't there? What a thing we have lived to see."

Anorra nodded. "So you say. And your children's children will bless you for recording it. Still," she turned back toward the hearth fire and called over her shoulder, "you'll have nothing but cold stew for dinner."

THE END

FROM THE AUTHOR

If you're reading this, it means a large chapter of my life has been successful. Not in the amount of money I made, the notoriety of my name, or the fame of three book titles. But successful in the fact that the story which the Most High placed in my heart to write is not only complete, but captured your imagination enough for you to finish it with me. Such an honor is one any author worth his ink space would willingly spend a lifetime achieving.

This final edition of the *Chronicles* has taken me five years to complete. I can't even begin to explain the heights and depths of life the manuscript you hold in your hands was written through. During it, two children were born, two restaurants launched, international travels made, three albums written and recorded, ministries expanded; our church relocated and grew to three services, and I transitioned from sixteen years as a Youth Pastor to the role of Associate Pastor.

All the while God was refining me. Testing me. Correcting me. As He does with any child He loves. He taught me through the story I was writing, too. I carried pieces of each character in my soul. And like Luik, I found God slaying the old man and breathing life into the new. A long absence from working on the book was like a cold *inussle*. We all suffered. Resuming work on it was like the arrival of spring. And every word I wrote was one moment closer to the inevitable. Completion.

If I could point to just one thing that kept prodding me to the finish line, it was the countless emails, phone calls, and personal words from readers saying, "I can't wait for book three! Where is it?" I never realized how powerful those simple words of encouragement were until I was on the homestretch and felt like giving up. To say I'm sorry for the length of time my readers had to wait for *Athera's Dawn* would be an epic understatement; I literally thought of this book every day for the last five years. It's been very close to my heart. Seeing it now in print or on the screen of an e-reader is truly a joy. But it was the voices of my readers that made this book what it is—I hope the best yet.

If it needs to be said again, I'm far more a spontaneous author than I am an outlined author. I tend to write *from the seat of my pants*. There are pros and cons to each of the polarized extremes, but it's the former that tends to excite me the most. For if I don't know where things are heading, I'm confident that my readers won't either. I ended *The Lion Vrie* on what's easily considered a far more tumultuous cliffhanger than *Rise of the Dibor*. The main reason for this is that I wanted to paint the characters into such perilous situations that not even I could foresee a way out. Literally, I wanted to be as clueless as the reader. And I was.

It took a few months, in fact, to finally figure out how I was going to save them—and for Thad and Thero, I never did find a way. Certainly writing this way requires more thoughtful note taking during the process, and more faithful rewrites after the manuscript is complete; minor changes at the end mean careful examination of the beginning. But the end product, I believe, is tremendously exciting and unpredictable right to the last moments.

The goal of the *Chronicles* was always to accentuate the intricate role that God plays in the history of humankind, inevitably pointing to the person of Jesus and His infallible redeeming work. Albert Camus said that "Fiction is the lie through which we tell the truth." And what a beautiful truth it is if done correctly. My aim was never to create an alternate theology—or defame our present theology—in creating a coexisting universe, but merely to illustrate even perfect man's ultimate need for a Savior, as Christ Jesus *is* our perfection.

The idea of the Two Trees, taken directly from the Biblical Garden of Eden, was inserting personifications to play with, truly characters in and of themselves. To me they emphasized man's unrelenting dependence on inferior means of sustenance when compared to relationship with God Himself. While a Tree of Life was indeed created to sustain man, it was only a harbinger of the Bread of Life that was to eternally sustain man. We must always remind ourselves that even reflections of God are never meant to replace the indwelling habitation of God. Many people *experience* the Holy Spirit, some vicariously through watching others; but it's those who *encounter* the Holy Spirit whose lives move from a *visitation* of God to a *habitation*. And there lies a stark difference between the two. O, how I long to know and be filled with Jesus to the greatest depths of my soul.

I have learned more about writing during the process of penning (or keystroking) the *Chronicles* than any class on literature I've taken. I attribute such growth to two main things. The first is reading. This "slow reader" is now a *read-a-holic*, and my books have been my teachers, both how to write, and how not to. I cannot stress enough to budding writers that reading good literature is the path to writing good prose. Likewise, the influence of poor writing will actually leak into your subconscious and greatly confuse that which you know you should write with that which you ought not to. When in the middle of writing the *Chronicles*, or any of my works for that matter, I've had to put many books down simply because of their poor quality. I do not boast in the excellence of my own work, mind you, only that I did my best at the time I wrote it. But it would have been far worse had I not been obedient to lay aside manuscripts that unwove whatever fibers of integrity I had gained. Keep sound books and authors close to you. Let them work on you, sift you, and teach you. Break them down, dissect them, and analyze them. Then write. Your audience will thank you. So may history.

The second avenue of growth is my relationship with some of the most amazing authors and friends I have ever met. Wayne Thomas Batson is not only an amazing writer but has grown to become a confidant. He's an endless source of inspiration and creativity. Yet he's very *real*, allowing his faults as a man to be exposed, and walking through the struggles of husbanding, parenting, and growing in God with tremendous humility. Christopher and Allan Miller have also been great encouragers, and have sown a great deal into my life and productivity at their own expense. Their zeal for marketing and reaching the next generation with stories that capture minds and hearts for the Kingdom is awe-inspiring.

All the authors of the Fantasy Fiction Tour challenged me not only in my walk with the Lord, but also in my craft: Bryan Davis, Sharon Hinck, Donita K. Paul, L.B. Graham, Eric Reinhold, and Jonathan Rogers. Thank you for the privilege to live a real-life adventure with you for the King, and affect our generation.

When there was no writing group in our city, a few of us decided to start one. Many thanks to the original Ink Blots: Chris Mooney, Jeff Domansky, and Nathan Clement. Your encouragement and banter are the stuff of legend. Here's to Sackets Harbor Brewing Company. And to my Proofies, those that have polished this manuscript until it shined: Nathan Reimer, William Kenney, Brian Fetzner, Esther Bovier, Elsi Dodge, Lou Rathbun, Leah Stockholm, Sarah Pennington, Glade, Noah Arsenault, Heather Ciferri, Emma McPhee, Laura Friemel, Daniela Arreola, Dannal Newman, and Ryan Paige Howard. And to Sue Kenney, my sister Hillary Hopper, and my dear friend Jason Clement for making these books standout. Your sacrifice of love astounds me. I can never repay you.

Many people have housed Jennifer and me while I was working on this novel, some never even aware I was writing in their homes. Phil Springthorpe in Argyle, Scotland, is responsible for providing some of the most amazing panoramas in the world; David, Helen, and Philip Meldrum in Edinburgh, Scotland, made us feel like royalty and reminded us of our divine inheritance; Pascal, Anne Marie, Juliette, and Sophie Sureau were friends who encouraged us when we were weary; and Papa and Mama Fernandez and family in our home away from home at Moncel in the north of France—you remind us to always live life and enjoy the details.

I would point out two special guest appearances, men whose personas added so much to this book: Abel Larkin, better known as *Bi-Bablar*, and my brother, Manu Fernandez, who inspired the noteworthy dwarf *Spid*.

Many thanks once again to my original publisher, Pam Schwagerl, who was never ever to finish publishing this series that she so believed in. While her imprint is absent from this final work, her name will always be printed in this first edition.

Lastly, I would like to thank Pastor Kirk and Carolyn Gilchrist for fighting with me through the darkest of battles; my parents, Peter and Nina Hopper and John and Joanne Nesbitt, for their unending support; my children for refining my character, making me laugh harder than I ever thought imaginable, and teaching me how to stay childlike; and my wife, Jennifer Lee, for reminding me that I'm a conqueror even when I feel defeated, and forever teaching me about the Secret Place in God. I so admire who you are. You are my best friend. Thank you for allowing me to pursue this dream to its completion.

It is done.

C'symia,

Christopher Hopper
Saturday, November 12th 2011
Driving NYS I-90

ABOUT THE AUTHOR

Christopher Hopper is a true modern-day renaissance man. A published author and co-author of numerous novels, he is also a recording artist, pastor, visual designer, and restaurateur. His prolific writings in both book and blog form have captured the imaginations of loyal readers around the world. He is a founding member of Spearhead Books, and lives with his wife, Jennifer, and their four children in the 1,000 Islands Region of northern New York.

CONNECT ONLINE

Christopher always enjoys hearing from his readers. You may contact him via e-mail at: ch@christopherhopper.com

Visit his website at: www.christopherhopper.com

On Facebook at: facebook.com/christopherhopper

And follow him on Twitter for daily musings: @find_ch

Every World Needs a few good mice

MECH MICE
Genesis Strike

In a post-apocalyptic world, a colony of remarkably advanced rodents harness the power of machines to defend their valley from natural enemies. But when a new threat of mutant insects bred to destroy are released on the Colony, its up to a squad of misfit soldiers to save the day.

THE MILLER BROTHERS

Award-Winning Authors of *Hunter Brown and the Secret of the Shadow*

united we write. SPEARHEAD BOOKS

Visit **SpearheadBooks.com** Today!

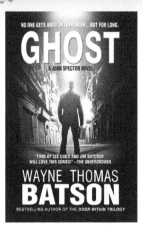

Made in the USA
Monee, IL
21 December 2020